T0131351

A CHAMPION FOR
TINKER CREEK

Visit us at www.boldstrokesbooks.com

A CHAMPION FOR TINKER CREEK

by

D.C. Robeline

2022

A CHAMPION FOR TINKER CREEK

© 2022 By D.C. Robeline. All Rights Reserved.

ISBN 13: 978-1-63679-213-2

This Trade Paperback Original Is Published By
Bold Strokes Books, Inc.
P.O. Box 249
Valley Falls, NY 12185

First Edition: July 2022

THIS IS A WORK OF FICTION. NAMES, CHARACTERS, PLACES, AND INCIDENTS ARE THE PRODUCT OF THE AUTHOR'S IMAGINATION OR ARE USED FICTITIOUSLY. ANY RESEMBLANCE TO ACTUAL PERSONS, LIVING OR DEAD, BUSINESS ESTABLISHMENTS, EVENTS, OR LOCALES IS ENTIRELY COINCIDENTAL.

THIS BOOK, OR PARTS THEREOF, MAY NOT BE REPRODUCED IN ANY FORM WITHOUT PERMISSION.

CREDITS
EDITORS: JERRY L. WHEELER AND STACIA SEAMAN
PRODUCTION DESIGN: STACIA SEAMAN
COVER DESIGN BY INKSPIRAL DESIGN

Acknowledgments

First, my most impactful teacher, Faye, for fanning a spark of interest in reading and writing into a bonfire that still fuels my creativity many years later.

Second, Bold Strokes Books, for reading a novel set in a mythical neighborhood in a fictional town and believing in it enough to publish it.

Third, thank you to my mom, stepdad, and sister, Catherine, for supporting the idea as soon as I told you about it. My sister especially for being the manuscript's most graceful and critical early reader.

Last, but not least, to my longtime partner and husband, for persistently overcoming my every objection to writing a novel and then making insightful suggestions along the way as I did. Without his dogged encouragement, I might never have written it, so, in front of God and everybody, thank you, Rich, for everything. I'm not sure I could have done it without you.

CHAPTER ONE

The Contract

I had turned on our lights and neon Open sign when a full-size, cherry red Ford F-150 truck swerved up to the door. I stepped outside as a stubby little man in a short-sleeved white shirt, lightweight dress pants, and cowboy boots thumped to the pavement from the cab and shut the vehicle door. The truck's electronic security system locked the vehicle with a loud click.

"May I help you?" I asked.

"You might," he said. "If your name is Lyle James."

"Then you're in luck."

His face lit up. "Mr. James, I hoped I might catch you before the day got too busy." His enthusiasm felt out of place for an auto repair shop at ten past seven in the morning.

"Well, you got me. How can I help you?"

He paused. "It's actually a little complicated. May we go into your office?"

"I don't see why not," I replied, ushering him in. "Take a seat," I said, pointing to the two client chairs opposite my desk. I stepped into the small kitchenette next to my office and started to fill the coffeepot. "I haven't had my second cup yet this morning," I said. "Would you like to join me?"

"No, thank you."

I poured the water into the machine and turned it on before returning and taking my seat behind my crowded desk.

"So, how can I help you," I asked for the third time.

He reached into his front shirt pocket, pulled out a business card, and handed it to me. It bore the civic seal of St. Michael's Harbor and identified him as Benoit Corde, Director of the city's Procurement Department.

The coffee maker bell rescued me from an immediate response. I stood up and went to the kitchenette, where I splashed some milk in my mug and followed it with a healthy dose of my weekday fuel while my mind whirled.

Three weeks ago my business, Bonne Chance Motors, bid on a contract from St. Michael's Harbor to service its utility and safety vehicles.

I knew the bidding would be competitive and ours would likely not be the lowest offer since I specified using a better, more expensive paint than others would have chosen. Further, this would be our first contract with the city.

Now, less than one month later, the procurement department director shows up looking to get work done? I walked back in my office and sat down, stirring a teaspoon of sugar into my coffee. He looked at me with anticipation.

"Mr. Corde, I'm delighted you would consider us for work. But as you probably know, we have an outstanding contract bid that your department will decide whether or not to grant. So, our taking any other personal work from you right now strikes me as really inappropriate."

I sipped my coffee as his face fell, then registered confusion and a bit of annoyance.

"No, no," he blurted. "Please, you misunderstand me. Of course that would be inappropriate. We don't work that way." He pulled a handkerchief from his pocket and wiped his forehead. "Please, let me explain."

I nodded.

"You might remember about two weeks ago, two of my colleagues came by for a site visit at your facility."

Actually, I had been out delivering an expensive car to one of our more finicky clients and had been gone during the visit. But I remembered it was on the schedule. I nodded.

"Well, I was supposed to be on that visit but missed it because my daughter fell ill. And since three of us are supposed to conduct these site visits, I thought…" His voice trailed off, and he raised his hands, palms up.

"You thought you would go ahead and make up your site visit right now?"

"Exactly. But only if it's not too much trouble. We know you're in business for your clients and not for us."

"In that case, thank you for coming," I said, draining my coffee mug and putting it down. "I'd be glad to give you the nickel tour."

I showed him around the shop and introduced him to my chief mechanic, Mr. Parker O'Brian, and his assistant, Vahn Dinh. We went through the mechanic and body shops, then out to the new paint shed, ending up in the parking lot, where I stood with Corde beside his truck.

"Thank you for the tour," Corde said. "It was very informative. I can tell you're proud of what you've built here."

"Thank you for being thorough and wanting to see it," I replied. "And thank you for your personal business. We look forward to being able to help you after the department awards the contract." I paused as Corde opened the door and climbed into the cab.

"Without breaking any rules or anything," I said, "I don't suppose you might be able to forecast when we might hear about a decision? I'm not trying to be inappropriate, but if we knew a timeframe we could know when or whether we might need additional resources."

Corde rolled down his window and extended his hand to shake mine.

"I might be able to help," he said with a trace of a smile across his lips. "Congratulations, Mr. James. Bonne Chance Motors will service St. Michael's Harbor utility and safety vehicles for the next five years."

"Wow. Oh my God! Thank you," I exclaimed as I pumped his hand. "You will not regret this decision, Mr. Corde. Thank you so much for the opportunity."

"Well, I need to get to the office," he said. "I'll call you with a formal notification later today, and then we'll have a series of meetings to set up a schedule, but welcome aboard. The City of St. Michael's Harbor looks forward to working with you."

❖

An endless line of cars stretched in front of me when I finally eased onto I-95, so I hit the outskirts of St. Michael's Harbor three hours later than I intended. The place had grown since my last visit, and not in a good way, I thought. But downtown had remained much the same. I smiled and beat a rhythm to the radio on my rental car steering wheel until I turned right into Tommy's new neighborhood of bungalows and fading Victorian manors.

I glided into one of the diagonal parking spaces in front of number

34. A solid-looking wall with a cracked adobe facade and two tall trees prevented me from seeing the house, but the ornate wrought iron gate said 34 above it in new, shiny black numbers. I must be at the right place, I thought.

Getting out of the car, I stretched, feeling like one of my mother's pleated origami animals, holding the memories of their previous creases after unfolding. A ring attached to a chain stuck out from the wall next to the gate. I grabbed it and gave it a solid pull. From somewhere in the depths of the property, I heard a series of deep gongs.

I waited, but no one came. I stepped up to peer through the wrought iron but saw a primordial tableau of trees, ferns, and bushes. When I thought I might pull the ring again, I caught sight of Tommy hurrying to the portal.

"Manny! Oh, it *is* Manny, isn't it?" he called out as he approached the gate. "I was afraid you might not make it here until tonight, and after I took off work to be here when you arrived."

"Not to worry. It's me. A bit worn from the trip, but otherwise fine."

The deadbolts fell with a series of clicks, and Tommy swung the gate open. He was wearing shorts, a tight white T-shirt, a tropically colored three-quarter robe, and sandals.

"I'm sorry, did I get you out of the shower?"

"Oh no," he said with a giggle. "I'm making bread. This is what I wear when I don't want to get flour or anything icky on my regular clothes. Is this all the luggage you have? You do travel light. Here, let me take the hanging bag."

The gate swung closed behind us with a metallic chunk.

Tommy is cute, but in a nerd meets twink way. Think button-down shirts and sweaters, bow ties, khaki pants in different shades of gray and brown, and loafers. The thing is, it works for him. Tommy is about the smartest person I know. He's two years younger, but he graduated with my high school class. He's dressed this way ever since I've known him, although I got him to ditch the shirts with front pockets.

He's about my best friend in the world and someone I thought I knew, which is why seeing him dressed so casually and in a kitchen had me floored.

"I never knew you baked bread."

"I don't. Or at least I didn't. This is my first time. I'm trying to make Danny's favorite bread from his late grandmother's recipe."

I flashed him a confused look.

"Hmm, you know Danny's grandmother died, right?"

Danny is, inexplicably, Tommy's boyfriend, currently two-thirds through a five-year Army tour of duty in Afghanistan. I replied I vaguely remembered seeing an email about her passing, following him as he set out walking down a narrow brick path, almost overgrown with different plants.

The path turned and opened up on a small, highly stylized Victorian whose once-vibrant colors had faded to a gentler pastel palette. With its wraparound porch, steeply pitched roof, and gingerbread trim, the building resembled less a house than a retired amusement park ride.

"Welcome to Shangri-la," Tommy said, waving with a flourish. "Which it isn't really, of course, but the foundation and roof are sound, and we're far enough from Washington Street that we don't hear traffic."

We walked up the short staircase to the porch, and Tommy gently opened the front door and we started down the hall. "First door on the left, living room or salon. First on the right, formal dining room. And now, we have the kitchen."

The hallway opened up to a large, sunny space, slightly dated but functional, with a double oven, two microwaves, and two refrigerators.

"This part of the building was redesigned in the 1960s," he said. "If I understood correctly, the quarters for the butler and cook were sacrificed for the larger kitchen footprint. Now, here are the back stairs. They are the only ones to your room. Let's go up carefully. Some of them really creak."

We moved up slowly, and I tried to place my feet on the risers where he had stepped to keep from making too much noise.

"This is the floor with your room," Tommy said. "There are three rooms up here. You can choose which one you want, though the one at the end is bigger and closer to the bathroom, and I cleaned it up yesterday."

We walked down the hall to the end chamber and paused at the open door.

As a room, it didn't supply a whole lot. The space included an iron bed frame with both a mattress and box spring, a dressing room mirror, a small desk with a plain lamp, and a smallish wardrobe about the size of an old-fashioned telephone booth.

"The bathroom is just down here," Tommy said, pointing eight feet to the door at the end of the hall.

I took a look at the bathroom and then came back down the hall to review the room again.

"It's fine," I said. "But fess up, these were the servants' quarters, weren't they?"

"Yes. But that's why you're getting it for only a hundred and fifty per month, basically half of what we pay—and without a lease. You pay month to month, so when you find a place of your own, you can move."

"Then I'll take it. Thank you." I reached in for a hug.

"It is really good to see you," he said, hugging me back. "Leave your bags up here and let me make you something to eat and you can tell me what's up."

Later, over a slice of his first cinnamon bread, we talked about his work at the *South Georgia Record* and what I hoped to do there.

"I'm glad to have you staying here, don't misunderstand me, but I don't know I would have chosen a former chauffeur's room if I knew I could have a place at Albemarle," Tommy said.

Albemarle Estate has been my parents' home since I left. It's a bit farther down the coast, forty-five acres with everything you would probably expect from an estate.

"But I don't really have a place there," I said. "Surely, you must see that. I'm already going to ask Dad for a job. I couldn't very well do that from a position of strength living under his roof as well."

"Okay," he said. "But even if I concede the point, which I am not sure I do, what do you think Dame Isabella is going to say about her baby boy living in the community but not under her roof?"

My mother's family belongs to one of those wealthier Cuban clans that fled Castro's revolution, then structured their entire lives around returning and reclaiming the past. That meant my childhood was athletics and academic achievement mixed with grievance, paranoia, and conspiracy. And while passing years had muted some of those motifs, they still made the thought of actually living in my parents' house less appealing.

"Has she ever backed off the marriage thing?"

"Nope."

Officially, I am out to both my parents, but their reactions have differed and fallen short of supportive. My father told me he didn't care how I lived my personal life, but he had no desire to hear about it. My mother, by contrast, simply slipped into denial.

"It's up to you," Tommy said. "You're welcome here, but I'm afraid life is not going to be as smooth as you seem to think. When do you meet with the Old Man?"

"Ten thirty tomorrow morning," I said. "That's really the meeting that makes or breaks this whole thing, so I should have conditionally accepted your housing offer. I will be glad to stay here conditional on my father hiring me for the *South Georgia Record.*"

❖

Tommy warned me that construction equipment had taken up all the guest parking spots at the paper, so I took a rideshare to the *South Georgia Record*'s imposing building north of town. As I headed down the long hall toward my father's office, my nervousness rose. Although we had spoken roughly every six months for a number of years, I hadn't actually seen him during that time. Outside the door to my dad's office suite, I paused and knocked.

"Come in," called Rosa, my father's longtime secretary and my onetime babysitter.

She had her head down, flipping through a pile of papers in front of her printer.

"Hello, Rosa."

She looked up as if mystified for a moment, then her eyes focused and widened.

"Manny? Is that *Manny*? Oh my God. Oh my God." She got up from her chair, ran around the desk, and gave me a deep hug.

Out of the corner of my eye, I saw my father's door open, and he leaned on the doorway with an amused expression. She was still embracing me as my father cleared his throat.

"Oh, tell me you can stay for lunch," Rosa said.

"Probably, but look." I pointed to my father in the doorway.

"Ahem," he said.

"Oh, Mr. Porter, look, Manny's home."

"I can see that, yes. Hello, son."

"Dad."

"Rosa, Manny's here for an interview, so please hold my calls until it's over. Can you stay for lunch, Manny?"

"Yeah, sure."

"Rosa, please call Alfredo's and make a reservation for three, if you can join us, of course."

"Yes, Mr. Porter."

Turning to me, he motioned to the inner office. "Shall we get started?" He walked behind his desk and directed me to one of the deep chairs facing it. I began to sit down when he held up his hand.

"Let me get a look at you," he said. "You've added a little bit to your height."

"I just learned to stand up straight."

"Put some muscle on too, I see."

"A little. Nothing extreme, but I like to stay fit."

"Well, I'm not going to jump around the room, but it's good to see you. Your mother will be ecstatic."

I shifted my stance slightly and sat down. "About that..." I started to say.

"Don't bother. I've already had a talk with her about your moving back in with us. You *don't* want to do that, do you?"

"God, no."

"Good. Any other personal details?"

"You're looking good," I said.

"Yeah, I'm okay, I guess. I stopped smoking except one cigar on Sundays. Cut my drinking back to weekends only. Doc says my cholesterol is not bad, my blood pressure is on the high side of normal, and my heart beats like a machine. Can't do much about my hair, though."

"I wouldn't sweat it, Dad. You actually rock the bald."

"Thanks. Your mother says she likes it too, so I guess it's a consensus. Now, are we done with the personal?"

"Yes."

"So, now I am officially putting on my publisher hat."

"Okay."

"You know how I feel about nepotism. If I didn't believe you had skills and talent independent of being my son, you wouldn't be sitting there."

"Yes, sir."

"Good, because I want to be clear about that. I know we haven't communicated a lot, but I have been following your work, and I don't mind telling you that I am eager to hire you. But I don't want either you or the paper to be open to the charge that you got the job because of your last name."

I nodded.

"Okay, I have a couple of things. You're going to start in business. Then if you can show through your stories that you belong on the beat in the first six weeks, we'll keep you there," Porter said. "How's that?"

"Sounds fine to me."

"The second thing is that we don't currently have a business editor."

"What happened to Ms. Owen?"

"Extended medical leave. We're holding her job for her and won't hire anyone else, but that means you start by reporting to me."

"Okay, I guess."

"What do you want to be paid?"

"What are you offering?"

"Our reporters in the first two years start at between twenty-seven and thirty thousand," he said. "But you're coming in with more experience, so how about thirty-six to start? Performance bonuses possible up to forty. When you pass eighteen months, we'll review."

He stood up and extended his hand. I rose from the chair and shook it.

"Welcome aboard, Mr. Porter. Someone from HR will contact you with the details. I look forward to working with you."

"Thank you, sir. I expect to contribute a great deal to this paper and to make you proud."

Five minutes later, I poked my head around the door frame into Tommy's office and saw he was on the phone.

"On hold," he said, taking the handset away from his mouth. "How'd it go?"

I gave him a thumbs-up, and he shot me a wide grin.

"See you back at the house," I said.

Later that day, after a light supper, we debated on how to celebrate. Tommy wanted to take in a French film debuting at an art house theater, but I craved going out to a club. The move, finding a place, and then the interview with my father had left me tense and wanting to cut loose. Once upon a time, Tommy would have been my partner on these evenings, but now I met resistance.

"You were always more of a club boy than I was." Tommy laughed. "Plus, Danny and I agreed that discos on our own are off-limits. But I can still help you pick one out and take you, if you want. You can rideshare back."

"The L&F was always my favorite. If it's open, of course."

"Oh, it's open all right," he said. "I'll drop you in front about nine."

CHAPTER TWO

Hooking Up

The St. Michael's contract news arrived like a jolt of adrenaline at Bonne Chance Motors.

"We should do something to mark the occasion, boss," Christine proposed. "This is our first public contract."

She was right. In all the years my dad ran the shop—and in the time I owned and ran it after he died—we had never received the vote of confidence a public bid represented. That deserved some recognition.

"Okay," I said. "On the day we deliver our first St. Michael's vehicle, we'll have a staff dinner. You all handle choosing the restaurant and making the reservation. Bonne Chance will handle the bill."

"Alllll right," Joe crowed. "Barbecue!"

I laughed. "You all will have to negotiate the cuisine, but I trust you can work it out."

The boost of enthusiasm Mr. Corde's decision brought into the business infected me too. By nature I am a loner. But when I feel like company, I most often call one of my oldest friends, Eva Almisra. I walked into my office and closed the door.

"Darllling Lyle," Eva said, answering my call. "Are your ears burning? I was just thinking it had been too long since we hunted together," she purred.

"Great minds. What are you up for, tonight or tomorrow night?"

"Definitely tonight, baby. I have a bridezilla rehearsal dinner tomorrow night, and she wants the whole ghastly thing shot, including the crumb crunchers. If I don't burn off some of this frustration beforehand, who knows what could happen."

"Nothing good. Where? I'm in the mood for Blitz or L&F."

"Hmm, the L&F, darling. I got a tip that the Edwards College crew team won one of those rowing things this week."

"A regatta?"

"That's it. It's so good to have literate friends. Anyway, whatever it is, they won it and they're holding their victory party there tonight, so I thought we would both stand a good chance of getting some action."

"I'll be by your place at eight," I promised, and I arrived right on time. She, however, came to the door in her bathrobe and parked me in a comfortable chair outside her walk-in closet while she dressed.

Until about five years ago, anyone who followed international news knew Eva's photographs, though they might not have known her name. She became known as one of the bravest—or most reckless— conflict photographers in the business, winning prizes along the way for her photos.

But she stopped chasing and dodging bullets after her mother died, dropping out of sight, moving here, and founding the Femme Formidable photo service, along with teaching classes in yoga and self-defense for women.

We met when she drove her beaten-up Mazda Miata into Bonne Chance after discovering stop signs in the U.S. really mean stop. We get along because she learned I didn't want to sleep with her, and I didn't mind competing with her. I discovered a serious and active woman whom I could befriend without feeling alienated and who could give me a good kick in the ass when we decided I needed one.

"But you really perturbed me when you told me you weren't just burning to take me to bed," she said as she rolled the black stocking up her leg.

"Really?"

"Of course, darling. I did everything short of throwing you my panties, but you remained aloof as an old stump. I thought I had lost my touch."

She adjusted the red vinyl skirt with a tug and brushed her hair in her dresser mirror.

"But surely you clued in that…"

"Of course I knew about gay men, love. We had those in Lebanon too. But the gay men I knew helped my mother choose curtains and sometimes wore more makeup than she did. None of them ever looked or acted like you. You were, are…unique. Now, which one?" She held up two red lipsticks, one slightly redder than the other.

"The darker one."

"Darker?"

"I don't know. I never get lipstick right. The less shiny of the two."

"Okay." She deftly applied the color and turned to me, pursing her lips.

"Are we ready, honey?"

I nodded.

"Then let's go."

We had played these evenings so often together, we could perform them seamlessly. We arrive as a couple a little older than the median age for whatever venue we choose, but not old enough to qualify for the sugar daddy or cougar category. We flirt, both with each other and with bystanders, leaving the impression we might be open to a threesome with the right young man. When Eva decides the hook is set, she signals me. I suddenly need some air. While I'm gone, she convinces the youth they don't want me, and they leave together, either to her place or his. Someplace private enough for him to learn, to his surprise, that Eva has taken firm control of the rest of his evening.

Later, when I return from catching a breeze, I act the disappointed partner and find a young man for my own bed. It's a strategy that has worked more times than it hasn't.

As our ride dropped us off in front of the Lost and Found, popularly known as L&F, I noticed the parking lot was two-thirds full. SUVs topped with boat racks confirmed the crew team was in the club, and from outside we heard the music's beat. The L&F is one of three gay-friendly venues in St. Michael's Harbor, all of them here in Tinker Creek.

We strolled up the walk past the line of people waiting to pay the cover charge, and Clem, the L&F's six-foot-two bouncer, waved us through. I don't think I've ever been asked for a cover charge with Eva. Inside, a banner stretched across the center of the dance floor reading "Congratulations Edwards Crew!"

And the club had done some work for the party. They changed the lighting, giving the entire room an underwater tinge. I found this charming at first, but then I observed the special effect turned us all an unhealthy, pale shade of green.

Not that anyone in the crowd appeared to notice. About a third of the dance floor had couples on it, same-sex and mixed, and the press of people in front of both bar rails was two deep. I spied an open two-top table on the edge of the dance floor with a bright red Reserved sign on it. I steered Eva that way, and as I expected, she sat right down. I followed.

A young man wearing board shorts, sandals, and nothing else but a muscular chest appeared in front of us as if by magic.

"Ms. Almisra, so nice to have you back," he said. "And Mr. James, you are looking fabulous as well. What can I bring you to start off your evening?"

"Something bubbly, love," Eva said. "It doesn't have to be champagne, but something in a flute would be nice."

He waited for me.

"An old-fashioned, but with rye whiskey instead of bourbon, and hold the cherry," I said. The waiter vanished as silently as he arrived.

It took me a minute to adjust to the eerie lighting, but I could tell our entrance had drawn attention. From three tables down, a young blond I'd left with before waved slightly. His date wouldn't notice, and I didn't let on that I saw him.

Another set of eyes followed us. One of the booths diagonal from our table had three of the Edwards crew members. They wore the team's maroon baseball caps, jeans, and polo shirts. Two of them were big men, tall brunettes with shoulders that could have supported London Bridge. But the third was smaller, slighter, and blond.

One of the auburn-haired guys locked his eyes on Eva, and I leaned toward her to speak softly.

"Turn in your seat to your right and then tilt into me. Yeah, like that," I said as she adjusted herself. "See the pair of brunettes at seven o'clock?"

"Mm-hmm."

"The one on the left hasn't stopped watching us since we sat down. What do you think?"

"He'll do nicely," she said with a quiet coil in her voice.

I gently pulled her close. "Let's give him a show," I said, sinking my face into her perfumed neck as she arched her back. With my lips still pressed to her rose-smelling skin, I traced the outline of her breast with the fingers of my right hand and circled the nipple as it stiffened while my left slid under the red vinyl skirt. I brushed over the cord of her thong and then played on the field of bare flesh.

She moaned softly. "Did I ever tell you how good you are at this?"

"Once or twice."

"I'm officially telling you again." She gasped as I found her little soldier standing at attention.

My own cock was a pillar of iron beneath layers of cloth. It didn't matter she was a woman. The delicious reality of what we were doing in public with an audience sent frissons of excitement flashing throughout my nervous system, including my crotch. I kissed my way up her neck to the edge of her bangs and paused there, exploring under her earlobe.

"Oh my gawd, Lyle," she whispered as she tried to force my hand more firmly against her slick skin.

"No, no, no," I replied, easing my hand free and sliding back up and out from under the shiny red material. "Our drinks are here."

We parted, and she pulled away slightly to acknowledge the waiter, standing to our side, blushing a faintly brown color under the lights. How long had he been there, I wondered. Enough time for a lengthy, thick ridge to appear in his board shorts.

Eva straightened in her seat and shook her head like she was trying to wake up before motioning the server to her side of the table. I cocked my ears to be able to hear.

"Do you see the farthest away of those three gentlemen seated at that booth? Excellent. Please find out what he is drinking and buy him another one. When he asks, tell him it's compliments of the lady."

The bare-chested youth nodded and disappeared as Eva rearranged herself in her seat. She was still close to me, but not as evidently in a clinch. From where the trio sat, all they could see was my right hand vanishing behind her. It rested on the small of her back, but it could as easily have been playing with her ass.

Now it was a matter of waiting. The dance floor had continued to fill, and I suspected no spaces remained in the parking lot. In about half an hour, the club would be at capacity, and they would restrict entrants.

"Have you seen any other prospects?" I murmured to Eva. "Over my shoulder, the blond at the bar looks like he might be fun."

But she shook her head. "I'm all in. That boy's getting an education tonight, and I'm going to be his teacher."

I took my first sip of my drink, pleased the bartender remembered to keep it from getting too sweet.

"How about you?" she asked. "This has gone fast tonight. Seen anybody you like?"

"Could be," I replied. "We might both entertain members of the Edwards crew team this evening."

At the other table, our waiter arrived with what looked like a mai tai, and I chuckled as I watched Eva's prize protest at first and then blush when he learned who sent it. Eva was observing too and shot him a provocative stare. The poor lad reddened more.

That was my cue to leave. I made a show of getting up, stretching, taking my drink, and heading out across the dance floor and out onto the deck. Connecting with rower boy, luring him home and into her bed was up to her now. I was free to hunt on my own.

I passed by one of the of moveable walls and checked out my reflection. I wasn't twenty-five anymore but looked closer to twenty-seven than thirty. I showed some gray, but my short side cut kept it from being noticeable. My body was beefy, but solid. Nothing moved when it wasn't supposed to, I didn't have to use a flyswatter, and I still ran a hundred meters in under thirty-four seconds, so I felt pretty confident.

Generally, when I'm out, I'm all about looking sharp, but Eva wanted to do *Beauty and the Beast* tonight, so I agreed to step it down. This evening I wore a plain white tee that had been washed so many times it revealed my nipples, a vintage black leather jacket, older jeans that showed off my ass and crotch, and a pair of boots. The overall look was construction worker drag, but classier and definitely hot if you like that type of man.

I reached the railing at the edge of the deck and stood for a bit, enjoying my drink and the play of the lights on the water. I tried to leave enough time for Eva and the boy toy of the evening to clear out before returning, and I headed back in after what I judged a suitable interval.

I weaved my way through the crowd to the second bar and ordered a Diet Coke. The management had rented the back room to the Edwards crew party, but the bartender said they were not being exclusive, so I made them my next stop.

They welcomed me with a distracted, boozy hospitality, taking me as an older brother, cousin, or alumnus. I sipped my cola, made myself amiable in a mysterious yet unalarming way, and carefully observed the group dynamic.

The prospects weren't promising. The Edwards crew team clearly had an active fan base, and many of its female members had come to the party. I strolled my way back to the main room and kept on circulating.

I wasn't having a lot of luck. A forest of twinks overran the south bar in skinny jeans and tight tees, some with made-up faces, but they all looked like teens. Though I knew Clem blocked the underage at the door, none of them appeared old enough to drink, much less take to bed.

I sauntered past the wide open deck bays to the north bar. The crowd was a little older here, but still no one caught my eye. I paused to say hello to Clem. Since the club was at maximum, the line of people waiting to show him their IDs had shrunk, so he had time to talk.

"Headed out early, boss?" he said.

"Yeah, can't find much that catches my eye tonight."

He ogled a dancer on the floor who had pulled off his shirt to reveal an accordion set of abs and whose shorts promised a tantalizing set of buns.

"Are you sure you're just not too picky?" he asked.

I laughed. "I might be."

"Let me have your hand," he ordered, stamping it with a red L&F. "That will let you back in if you decide you want to," he said.

I nodded my thanks and stepped out to find Clem's staff had the crowd in an orderly line down the side of the building. I started to head to where I could get a rideshare when I saw a slim Latino youth, a little shorter than I, dressed sharp and looking frustrated with the line. On impulse, I stepped up to him.

"You want in?"

"Sure," he said.

"Follow me." I started to move back toward the entrance, then I turned to watch him use those long legs to step easily over the yellow rope and come up to the door. I flashed my hand at the entrée check and said "headed to Clem" when he shot a look at my companion.

I stepped back up to Clem and jerked my thumb over my shoulder at my friend. "Clem, he's with me."

He looked at me, grinned, and nodded. "Welcome back to the club, boss," he said.

After we passed Clem's velvet gate, I headed for the less crowded north bar, pleased that my new protégé stuck with me. We arrived in time to claim stools two young women had vacated.

"Old-fashioned straight up," I said, "rye whiskey, lemon twist, no cherry. You?" I said.

"Cuba libre," he said, "on a separate tab." A moment passed before he spoke.

"I suppose I should say thank you. If it wasn't for you, I'd still be drinkless and shut out."

"You're welcome," I grunted.

"Do you do this often?"

"What?"

"Rescue random people waiting to get into the L&F."

"You weren't random," I said, "and no, this was the first time."

"Should I be flattered?"

"You could be. I don't care."

"Then why do it?"

"I hoped you would have a drink on the deck with me."

"Then I am flattered. What if I said no or had been meeting someone here?"

"Your loss. And no one tries to meet up inside, but at the front. If you were going to meet someone, they would have been with you already."

"Okay," he said.

"Okay what?"

"Okay, I'll have a drink with you on the deck."

"Cool," I said, downing the rest of the concoction and signaling the bartender. "Another round for both of us, and on my tab."

❖

After we picked up the drinks he'd ordered, we threaded through the crush to the deck's far rail without speaking. The music remained audible, but the crowd sound faded, and I became more aware of his physical presence.

He smelled of metal, soap, and a little bit of sweat, and I couldn't help but admire how well he filled out the plain white tee he wore.

"Aren't you a little underdressed for this place?" I said, glancing around.

He grinned.

"Construction drag," he replied, adding, "It's like a costume."

"The goon at the door didn't seem to mind how you were dressed."

He frowned. "Clem's not a goon," he said. "I've known the club owner for a while."

We turned to look out over the water for a moment. I could feel my cock start to chub and stretched to force it back to regular size.

"I'm Manny," I said, offering my hand and using the name my friends use.

"Lyle," he said. His calloused palm scraped mine as we tested each other's grip for a second before releasing.

"Pretty good handshake," he said, though I suspected his was a lot stronger than mine.

"Likewise." We turned to each other again.

"What brings you out tonight? I'm not a regular here, but I haven't seen you before."

"I'm from out of town," I said. "I grew up here but haven't been back in a while. I'm in the middle of transitioning back to living here."

"Well, welcome home," he declared, offering his glass for a light tap from mine.

"Thank you," I said, looking directly at him. "I'm feeling more welcome all the time." I paused to take another sip. "What about you? You said you knew the club owner, so you must have been here for a while."

"Depends on what you mean by here."

"Well, St. Michael's Harbor. I grew up a little to the north of town, but we still said St. Michael's before we would have said anywhere else, like Savannah."

"I meant here, the neighborhood, Tinker Creek."

"Oh, wow. Tinker Creek. You really meant like *here* here," I said. "I don't mean to offend, but when I was a little boy, Tinker Creek was someplace we were told to stay away from. I guess it's gotten better. Or has it?"

"Oh, it has," Lyle said. "I didn't grow up in TC, that's what we called it, but my dad had a business down here that I have now, and I've watched it grow and change. What's brought you back to St. Michael's?"

"Career, mostly. Family, a little bit," I said.

We paused and turned to watch the lights again. He moved closer.

"Sorry for the twenty questions," he said, "but you looked like you could put more than two words together, and I like that."

I laughed. "Thank you, I guess. Or was that a polite way of telling me I look nerdy?"

"Not at all. No nerd is going to have those shoulders, legs, and ass," he said as he ran his hand slowly up and down my butt.

"Heyyy. Did you just cop a feel of my ass?" My cock leaped again.

"Did you mind?"

I thought for a second. "Normally, yes...but right now not so much," I said.

He took my hand and pressed it to his firm chest. "For what's it worth, you can feel anything you want."

My mouth went dry with desire as my cock swelled fully hard.

Through the T-shirt, his chest felt warm, solid, and alive. It moved gently beneath my fingers with his every breath, and he shivered slightly as I brushed his nipple with my fingertips.

I tried to take my hand back, but Lyle held it easily, pressing it harder into his solid heat as he reached around me with the other to paw my ass, grabbing and holding it as he pulled me close.

"You never said what brought you out tonight," he whispered in whiskey-scented breath. "Was it this?" He pulled me into him harder.

"No!" I protested. "Well...maybe."

"Of course it was." And suddenly his mouth was on mine, growling into me, his tongue tickling my bottom lip, demanding entrance. I was determined to deny him, to keep my lips closed—until his fingers found my nipple, teasing and pinching it to a peak.

"Do you want to get out of here," he said low and aggressive in my ear.

"Yes."

"Where?"

My mind flashed to my little chauffeur room in Tommy's house with its wrought iron bed frame and skimpy mattress. "Yours."

"Follow me."

Trailing Lyle out the employee exit, I admired his back, legs, and ass. His shoulders were straight and strong, so the bubble on a level laid athwart them would not move and lines drawn from them to his butt would form a perfect V. We piled into the back seat of a rideshare. Lyle confirmed the destination with the driver, then scooted back.

"Come here," he said, pulling me closer and kissing me again. He was gentler but remained insistent. He held my head as I explored his chest and back with my hands. My mind spun in a mix of confusion and delight. *What am I doing?* Then I realized I didn't care. All I wanted to do was to kiss him and see him naked.

The smirking rideshare driver let us out on a commercial corner somewhere in Tinker Creek. I felt confused and a little alarmed. I thought we were going to Lyle's place.

"Where are we?" I said, looking warily around us.

"Home sweet home," Lyle replied, smirking. "Follow me," he said again, passing in front of a car repair shop and then up what looked like an alley.

I hung back. "Here?"

"C'mon," he said, jerking his arm. He was about halfway down the alley, where the streetlight didn't reach, facing a wall. The street was quiet. I thought of Tommy's emergency whistle in my pocket, then shrugged and joined him.

The wall he was facing was actually a metal door. He opened a little box to the right and pressed his thumb against a pad inside the box. Somewhere in the building, machinery clanked to life.

"I live upstairs," he said as metal crashed behind the panel and it slid up to reveal an industrial elevator cab. I followed him in, and he hit the Up button. The door closed, the cab began to rise, and we were together again, standing this time, his body large and hard against mine, pushing me into the wall and gulping my kisses the way a parched man takes water.

He broke off to start snuggling my neck and unbuttoning my shirt.

"Damn, you're so hot," he growled. "I'm gonna fuck you so good."

"But I don't get..." I started to object, but his mouth was back on mine, and I vanished into the kissing storm once more. He had become a force of nature, and all I could do was hold on.

By the time the elevator door opened again, he had unbuttoned my shirt entirely and found my nipples. He had to hold me up when he tweaked them and my knees buckled. We broke apart, panting, and stepped out of the cab. I stared after he turned on the lights.

"Chez moi," he said.

We stood at the edge of what felt like a vast space. It must have taken up the second floor of the whole shop downstairs. Large shade-covered windows along with various screens lined the walls, and pieces of modern sculpture dotted the room.

"You *live* here?" I said.

The smirk again. "I do. Nickel tour tomorrow, but all we need now is to the right."

We moved in that direction, and the lights behind us shut off while spaces we were headed to lit up. I followed Lyle through a gap between two shoji screens and stepped into his bedroom. A large, wooden platform bed with headboard stood on a prominent colorful carpet. The bed would have dominated an extremely good-sized traditional room, but in this space it appeared tiny, like an atoll in a sea of polished concrete.

He took me in his arms again, bits of my now-bare chest against his tee, sliding his hands down my back to grip my ass.

He moaned low in my ear. "Hmm, how you feeling, baby boy?"

"I don't know," I said. "Who the fuck are you?"

He stepped away from me, looked into my eyes, and began a deep, rolling chuckle that rose from somewhere around his knees. He stripped off his shirt and dropped it behind him.

"Tonight I am the Prince of Desire," he said. "And our first stop is a shower to wash off the smell of that funky club."

He picked up his shirt and tossed it easily into a basket against the wall, then removed his pants and socks to the container as well, padding back to me in a pair of black boxer briefs.

"You can leave your clothes at the end of the bed," he said.

In his underwear, his body was more magnificent than it had been clothed. Arms with biceps the size of baseballs dropped from softball-measured shoulders down to thick wrists. Pectoral muscles stood out from his frame like plates of armored flesh, each capped with a cute quarter-sized nipple and scattered with hair. A washboard of corded strength rolled down his abdomen to his waistband along with a healthy treasure trail that disappeared under the cloth, covering a substantial bulge.

I gazed at him, both enraptured and intimidated, torn between lust for his body and shame at my own skinny frame. I stopped removing any clothes. I had never seen a man as incredibly sexy, but rather than want to dive into his bed, I longed to jump out the nearest window. What was I doing here? How could he be anything but disappointed with what I had to offer?

But he looked at me, smiled, and gently slid my pale blue shirt off, laying it softly on the bed. He opened my belt next, letting my sand-colored khakis slide down my long legs. He knelt in front of me and patiently removed my trousers, kissing his way along my torso as he took my socks and placed them all next to the shirt on the bed.

We each stood before the other wearing our underwear, my boxers barely obscuring one of the largest and hardest erections of my life, and his tight briefs losing the fight with his thick bulge.

He draped his arms over my shoulders and looked at me intensely.

"Feel better?"

I nodded.

"Ready for the next step?"

I nodded again, but then grabbed his hands.

"One question," I said.

"Only one?"

"Why? Why me? Out of all those people waiting outside L&F, many better looking or more successful or sexier than I am, why did you focus on me?"

"Share my bed tonight," he said. "And I hope to show you."

Chapter Three

WTF

Manny had an early meeting this morning, so our time together ended more cursorily than I like after a successful hookup. Even so, I marveled at how much he changed from the night before. The boy who had almost jumped at every shadow when we came home and who I had to undress to overcome his embarrassment became a man who grabbed my head in the shower to pull my mouth onto his pole.

"Oh God, papi, take it. Take that cock," he yelled as his spunk splashed across my tongue and down my throat.

Now he sat close to me on the front seat of my truck, one hand resting on my thigh and the other playing with his cell phone.

"I regret we didn't get to share breakfast," I said. "I feel like you haven't been able to enjoy the full treatment."

"You mean there was more?"

"For you, yes. I haven't met a man as sweet, funny, or sexy in ages, and I felt you deserved a red carpet experience."

"Oh God, papi. Don't even front," he said, laughing. "I don't think I could have taken any more. I might never have left. You would have had me moving in and needed to call the sheriff to get me out."

"Don't call me that."

"What, papi?"

"Yeah."

"Why?"

"I'm not *father* older than you, more like *older brother* older."

"Lyle, age is only a small part of it. Trust me, last night you were papi and then some."

I surprised myself by blushing. "I might not have minded."

"Minded what?"

"Minded if you stayed longer than a day."

"No, you would have minded. What's that old saying about guests and fish starting to stink after three days?"

"Ha."

We fell silent.

"All kidding aside, I had a lot of fun, thank you," Manny said.

"Thank you, but I couldn't have done anything we did without you," I said, leering at him.

He laughed. "You know, if you had asked me before last night, I would have said I didn't bottom."

"And yet..." I said, grinning at him.

"Definitely and yet."

"I'm not surprised. Before last night, I would have bet I gave you your first blow job," I said.

"Was I really that bad?"

I glanced over at him.

"Okay, I was. But you weren't scared off. Thank you."

"Here's what I think. You've always liked guys but never felt comfortable about it. Your first blow job and full-on sex weren't until university and were probably a mixed bag, Blow jobs had been furtive and felt dirty, and the first sex was with someone who didn't know what he was doing, and it hurt like fuck. How am I doing?"

"Pretty close, but you left out the closeted paranoia and alcohol. The closet meant I reserved the blow jobs for glory holes in adult bookstores, and I was pretty far into the wind when my first frat boy fucked me to 'show the faggot what's up.' Both experiences kept me away from any boyfriends or even much positive experience...until last night, actually."

I turned off Breaker and soon stopped in front of the address he gave me.

"There's a house here?"

"Behind that wall. See the gate?"

"What's it like?"

"Old, creaky, Victorian. I sleep in the chauffeur's old quarters on the top floor."

"Sounds charming."

"My best friend is the lead tenant, so that makes up for a lot."

We fell silent again.

"So, where do we go from here?" he asked. "Or do 'we' go

anywhere from here? I'm total crap when it comes to this part of the hookup."

"Look, Manny, I had fun," I said, tapping my fingers on the steering wheel. "Fuck, I had more than fun. I wish I had a whole plan for what's next. But I can't really promise anything based on my history. And I'm not telling you this to be an asshole but because the last thing I want is for you to leave this truck looking for something that might never happen. In my opinion, that would really be the asshole thing to do."

He gazed at me and then shrugged. "Papi, I'm not looking for a whole plan or anything like that. I was just wondering if there was any chance I might see you again because, yeah, I will put it out there, I would like that. I would like it a lot."

"Pass me your phone." I typed my number into it. When my mobile rang, I answered the call, then hung up both and handed his back to him.

"There, we have each other's numbers. If something is going to happen or not, that's on both of us. Trust me, this is the furthest I have ever gone with a hookup before, and it's the best I can do for now."

Then he broke out in a smile that reminded me why he stopped me in my tracks from his place in line. "Can't ask for more than that, papi," he said, offering me his fist to bump. "Don't be a stranger 'cause you already know I'm not going to be one."

Later that morning, after returning home and grabbing some breakfast, I hit my compact gym.

Living above the business gave me the freedom to design and develop the space pretty much as I liked. If I wanted to take twenty feet of wall on the northwest corner of the apartment to install a rope ladder, I could. And if I desired that cord to connect to fifteen feet of monkey bars, I could do that too.

After the circuits, it was time for a quick splash off and then to the office. Among the circulars, bills, and offers for credit cards came a large white envelope from the Georgia Superior Court for the First District. It was a notice that Bonne Chance Motors had ninety days to show a judge why it should not be condemned, demolished, and its land titled to another company. I sat down in my office chair with a thump.

What the fuck, I thought. *What the fuck?* My mind whirled. *What the fuck?* Can they do this? Whoever they are? This must be a mistake. All the taxes have been paid, right? Of course they have. We haven't gotten any notices, and Terry would never let us file late. How can this be? They can't show up and say we're gonna take your stuff, right? *What the fuck?* My heart pounded in my throat as suddenly the room felt way too hot. I burst out in a sweat.

I tried to focus on what little yoga training I had, breathing in through my nose and out from my mouth and imagining Mt. Everest.

There she is. Everest. A mountain. Rock-solid. Can't be moved. Unchanging. Covered in snow. Stable. Unconquerable. Breathe in steadiness. Breathe out chaos. Breathe in stability. Breathe out anxiety. Breathe, one-two-three. Breathe, one-two-three. Breathe, one-two-three.

Gradually, my heartbeat slowed, my mind cleared, and the room returned to normal temperature. Whatever this was, I needed to better understand it before I made any decisions. I picked up the phone.

❖

The drive from St. Michael's Harbor to Savannah is normally one of my favorites. I avoid the overburdened and dangerous speedway that I-95 has become and instead stick to State Highway 17, a slower, more civilized route winding through the low, flat, marshy south Georgia coast.

But today my spirit's turmoil prevented me from enjoying the journey, though a small pod of pelicans kept me company off to the right for much of the trip. I was headed to an appointment with Father Joe Zandusky, my old history teacher and guidance counselor at the St. Martin Military Academy, where I had been a scholarship boy and football star. He would have some ideas about this letter, and I needed his focused words and perspective.

The St. Martin Military Academy sits atop a small rise that counts as a hill in the Georgia low country. A buzzer let me into the building, and I entered the office where a young, tall and angular man dressed in the all-black Benedictine habit busily fielded calls and attempted to type at the same time.

"St. Martin's, will you hold? Thank you. May I help you, sir?"

"I have an appointment with Father Zandusky."

"Of course, sir. Let me ring him…St. Martin's, will you hold? Thank you…Father Zandusky, Mr.…." He looked up at me expectantly.

"James, Lyle James."

"Mr. James is here to see you. Thanks. I'll tell him." He turned to me. "Father Zandusky is on his way down to meet you, sir, if you want to have a seat."

I chose to remain standing, and in a few moments Father Joe arrived. "Ah, my boy, so good to see you," he said, coming in for his usual hug.

He seemed smaller in my arms but appeared much the same, from his mostly bald head with its fringe of gray curls, down through his long face, eager to smile, and a wiry body that always felt coiled beneath his clerical uniform. He smelled the same too, that familiar mix of chalk dust and Old Spice cologne.

We started up the stairs, and I paused at the second landing since his office used to be on the second floor.

"No, no, my boy. One more. They have me on the third floor now. Seniority, they said, but I think they just want me farther out of the way."

"When I was here, the third floor is where you got sent if you really fucked up."

"Well, that's one difference," he said. "The third floor is rather benign now. Our assistant principal, Mr. Turnbull, has his office and his wayward cadets on the first floor."

We stepped into the spare but comfortable space I remembered. He retained the big oak desk that been his father's during World War II. Bookshelves still covered one wall, and a collection of large maps dominated another. The fourth was made up of windows, along with a small table and two comfortable-looking chairs.

"Please, have a seat," he said, pointing to one of the seats and taking the other for himself. "So what brings you here? As much as I enjoy seeing you, I doubt you've taken time from your workday to visit your old counselor."

I dug the envelope out of my pocket and passed it to him.

"This arrived in the mail this morning," I said. "I need to understand what it means so I can decide what to do about it."

Father Joe opened the envelope and read the notice slowly, pursing his lips and grunting several times. When he finished, he handed it back to me.

"What do you make of it, Father Joe?"

"First, I'm sorry. This sort of thing can really discourage whole communities, but I can't say I'm terribly surprised."

"Why not?"

He shot me a sharp look. "Do you remember nothing from my class about what we used to call 'the signs of the times'?"

"Maybe. I don't know. Something about being aware of social, political, and economic trends. It was more than a minute ago, Father."

"Exactly right. So what signs of our times might have led you to foresee the possibility that this could happen?"

"I don't know."

Father Joe sighed. "I presume you drove up here along Highway 17, am I right?"

"Of course."

"What do you remember about the trip? Did you notice anything different along the way?"

I shrugged my shoulders again. "I'm sorry, Father. I was pretty distracted on this trip."

"So, pay attention on the way back. Count the stoplights on the way out of town. How many do you expect? Two, maybe four? Now it's fourteen or fifteen or even seventeen. Savannah's growing, Lyle, and so is St. Michael's Harbor."

He got up and perused a pile of glossy magazines on one of the bookshelves, giving a small grunt of satisfaction when he found one named *Coastal Georgia* with a big photo of the St. Michael's light-house on the cover. He handed it to me on the way back to his chair. The publication's lead story was "Top Three Georgia Coast Communities for Quality of Life," and St. Michael's Harbor was at the top of the list.

I handed it back to him. "So we're growing. Of course we are. That's not news. But what does that have to do with this notice?"

"What happens when communities grow, Lyle? Property values rise, and when property becomes more valuable, people begin to want to do things with it that they might never have wanted or been able to do before."

I sat back in my chair as the meaning of Father's words washed over me. "So, you're saying because the land Bonne Chance Motors sits on has increased in value, someone out there might think they could make more money with it than I can?"

"Maybe. And remember, making more money for whoever they are means more tax revenue for the government, so they have an interest too."

"Damn. Can they do that?"

"Unfortunately, they can. When you get some time, google *Kelo v. City of New London*. That's a 5–4 decision from the U.S. Supreme

Court that said the general public benefits of increased tax revenue qualified as a legitimate public use for eminent domain under the U.S. Constitution. Many states have since passed laws that effectively limit the practice, but it remains legal."

"Where does this leave me and my business?"

"In my opinion, this could be one of two situations. The first and best case situation aims this at your business alone because of something you did or didn't do. Maybe you didn't pay a tax or fee? Maybe you're handling some of those dangerous chemicals incorrectly? Who knows?"

"Why would this be the best situation for me?"

"Because if it's just aimed at you for some singular fault, you can fix whatever that is and stop the process. Pay the fee. Pay the tax. Stop leaking chemicals. Do whatever to fix it, and the eminent domain goes away."

"And the second situation?"

"This is someone's effort to build a big enough parcel of land at a cheap enough price that they can redevelop to make a handsome profit. This is a worst case situation for you because it's not about you. You won't be able to just remedy some previous error and stop the eminent domain. In this situation, you don't have any easy options."

I sank back in my chair. This was worse than I expected.

"If they take your property, however, they have to pay you for it," Father Joe said. "They can't just take it for free. But their payment doesn't have to reflect a market value. They might pay you for the land the business owns, but not the business itself, much less the capital you would need to relocate and rebuild your customer base."

"Can't I fight this at all?"

"Of course you can. Americans can always petition their government for redress of wrongs," Father Joe said. "But the question is can you fight this and win. I think the record shows that while many do battle, few win."

I rose from my chair. "Thank you, Father. If it's as you say, I feel like I have to fight it."

"I understand, and I'm not surprised. But, Lyle, you need to be careful. If developers are really behind this, there is likely a lot of money involved, and they will have a lot of power. Keep me informed and know I will add your intentions to the Mass list, so the entire school will be praying for you."

As I drove back to the shop, the gloomy weather seemed to match my mood. A snapping west wind drove low, flat clouds the color of dirty sheets in from over the marshes as I tried to wrap my mind around Father Joe's opinion of the situation.

Hoping he might have overstated things, I counted the stoplights in the first fifteen miles out of Savannah, but discovered twenty, three more than his figure. Altogether, I numbered eight billboards for new developments; six for existing residential subdivisions with homes for sale "from the 300s," one for a new commercial mall, "Publix, open soon!" and two for mixed-use parcels that had yet to break ground, "Georgia Shores, Coming Soon."

I clung to the possibility that Bonne Chance might have been uniquely singled out for the eminent domain threat all the way back to the shop, where I found Parker seated behind my desk.

"Have I promoted you to administration and just forgotten?" I barked as I walked in, making him jump and stand up quickly, holding a fistful of telephone message slips.

"Someone had to stay in here to answer the phone, boss!" Parker protested. "It's been blowing up since you left. What the fuck is going on?"

He handed the small pile to me as my heart sank. There were calls from almost a dozen businesses, all of them clients and all of them in Tinker Creek.

"I'm calling an all-staff meeting in my office at five," I told Parker. "I'll have a clearer picture by then."

Parker headed back into the repair bay, and I sat down to start returning calls.

❖

My office had a much more serious vibe today than it had when the topic was how to celebrate the acquisition of the St. Michael's Harbor contract.

Christ, I thought. Was that only a couple of days ago?

One by one, the staff filed in.

"Thank you all for coming," I began. "As some of you might have become aware, Bonne Chance Motors received a significant communication this morning from the Georgia Superior Court for the First District in Brunswick. This came in the form of a notice informing me that in ninety days, the company will have to show the court why the state and city should not be permitted to seize the title to the land our business sits on, evict the business, and do whatever it likes with the property."

Shocked looks. Some wide eyes.

"In all likelihood that will mean the sale of the property to a developer for inclusion in some larger development project, the scope and details of which are currently unknown. As all of you know, my father founded this company but could not grow it successfully. You also know my uncle bought it from my father to keep it from going bankrupt. He sold it to me after my father died, and I've been able to grow it successfully with your help."

Heads nodded. One or two people quietly wiped the corners of their eyes.

"So, my roots in this company are very deep and very firm, and I am resolved to make the strongest possible case to the court as to why this company's property must not be turned over to the whim of another owner who likely has no roots in this community.

"Which brings me to all of you. I have absolutely no guarantee that we will win this fight and remain open at the end of the ninety days. But I must ask you for the favor, the consideration, of remaining in your job with us, with me, for at least the next ninety days.

"If you do, I am willing to increase your pay by twenty percent across that time. I would be willing to let those wage increases remain after we win the fight. But I will surely not be able to obtain victory in this struggle unless I know for certain that at the end we will still have a business worth the battle.

"I know this is a lot to think about, and I don't expect you to make up your minds now. But I will be in and out as normal to take your questions, and I will ask you to let me know your decisions by close of business Friday. Thank you. Are there any questions now?"

Parker raised his hand and stepped forward slightly. "Thank you, bos—er, I mean, Mr. James," he began. "When your uncle hired me to work here with your dad, I was to watch over the place and make sure, frankly, that he didn't kill himself or someone else or destroy everything. Later, when you bought it, your uncle asked me to stay on for a bit because he wasn't sure you could run it. Well, within two weeks I told your uncle he need not worry. I felt confident you would run Bonne Chance Motors fine and I told him I would be pleased to stay on here working with you if you would have me." His voice caught. He took a deep breath.

"I'm here to say that I still feel that way, sir. If you say you will beat off this threat and keep us open, then I expect that is what you will do. Nothing I have ever seen from you would lead me to think anything different." He stopped then and stepped back to his former spot.

At first no one moved. But then Vahn or Carlos or someone started to applaud and soon they were all clapping, and I daresay everyone reached for a tissue to dry their eyes.

CHAPTER FOUR

Getting Organized

In the week after the meeting, the shop's atmosphere took on a more serious, dedicated feel. Jobs that used to take two days to finish started being done in one, and Parker streamlined billing so the shop could work more efficiently. These changes allowed me to focus on the notice and what we could do to protect the business.

Drawing on the phone calls I got the first day, I identified twelve commercial and residential properties that also received the notice, all of them in a fifteen-square-block area of Tinker Creek. I suspected more than a dozen businesses have received one of the notices. But how to find out who they were and reach them?

One of the calls I hadn't been able to return had come from Lucinda Alverez, the founder and owner of Lucinda's Café and one of my favorite Tinker Creek personalities.

Lucinda had fled her native Nicaragua with her toddler grandson after the murder of her immediate family. Helped along the way by sympathetic churches and truckers, Lucinda mostly walked, carrying the boy across Honduras, Guatemala, and Mexico to the U.S. border. There, dehydrated and exhausted, she collapsed and requested asylum from the bed of a nonprofit clinic.

After recovering and being granted sanctuary, she moved in with a younger sister in St. Michael's Harbor, and with the help of family and community funders, she bought and renovated an abandoned space to open Lucinda's Café, a twenty-four-hour diner offering traditional American fare along with specialties from Nicaragua.

Since we hadn't connected by phone, I decided to go out for breakfast and headed down the couple of blocks on Third Avenue to Lucinda's.

Lucinda's throbbed with the controlled chaos every good diner should have. A sign ordered me to stop and wait for a table, and soon Esteban, Lucinda's small, dark-skinned grandson, approached and held up his index finger. I nodded, and he stepped up onto a pair of boxes to better survey the room.

"A two booth or a place at the counter," he shouted. "That's all I got." I bent over so he could hear me speak loudly rather than yell, and said I would take the table. He grabbed a large, laminated menu and beckoned me to follow him. Once seated, I motioned him close again.

"No school for you today?"

"Teacher training day, so nope. I'll tell abuela you're here. You want water?"

I nodded, and he headed off toward the back where Lucinda kept her small office. I divided my attention between the menu and my fellow diners until a tall blond in a bright red blouse and white apron set a glass of ice water in front of me and blocked my view.

"How you doing, handsome? Finally decided to come back and see me?"

I looked up in time to catch a wink. "Maxine, you're shameless," I said.

"Oh no, I'm not. I just like having a good-looking man in my section from time to time, ain't nothing wrong with that. What can I get you?"

"Coffee, cream, and sugar. Western omelet, hash browns, English muffin, well-toasted. Also, find out what Lucinda wants so she gets some breakfast too, will you, doll?"

She bent down a little and lowered her voice. "You here to talk to her about the notice thing?"

I nodded.

"Thank God. She'll never let on about how much it's getting under her skin, but I can tell it is. Do you think we can fight this thing off?"

"I'm not positive," I said, trying to sound cautious. "I am reasonably confident we can, but we need to get organized, so I guess that's why I'm here."

"I sure hope we can. I haven't had as good a job as this one in a while, and I would hate to lose it."

"So would I. It's not like good-looking servers just grow on trees, you know."

She surprised me by blushing. "Now who's acting shameless," she said as she headed for the kitchen.

Lucinda appeared almost immediately afterward.

"There you go, chasing my best server off the floor. How will I make any money?"

I got up to give her a hug and let her slide her short but ample frame into the booth. As usual she smelled of vinegar, soap, and sour milk and wore her everyday black skirt, white blouse, colorful vest, and a necklace of large, bright glass beads.

Maxine appeared with my coffee and a mug of spicy-smelling tea for Lucinda.

"That's smells good, what is it?"

"It's called corcha in mi lengua. It's a bush, and old people throw its dried leaves in with tea. It's supposed to help with sore muscles and joints."

I asked if it worked, and that earned me her trademark shrug. Our food arrived, my Western omelet, hash browns, and toasted muffin. House-made tortillas, scrambled eggs, black beans, and salsa verde for Lucinda.

I paused while Lucinda crossed herself and offered a silent prayer over her food.

"Don't worry, I covered your food too. For at least an hour you can stop living like a heathen." She glared at me but not in an unfriendly way. "Now can we talk about this notice?"

I related what Father Joe had shared with me and what I had identified since I returned, including my thought that the notices might be confined to a fifteen-block area on the eastern side of Tinker Creek.

"What does that mean?"

"I don't know yet. Since that's the beach side of the neighborhood, I'm thinking someone wants to build ocean condos, expensive shops, or maybe a new mall or entertainment district. But we really can't tell more until we figure out which people have gotten one of the notices."

"Well, no matter how many others we find," she said, "it's bigger than just those fifteen blocks."

"What do you mean?"

She picked up some up egg with a folded tortilla, dipped it in the salsa, and took a bite.

"Why do you think someone is doing this?"

"Money. Greed. Someone thinks they and the city can make more money from our property than we can."

"Yes, that is the *motive*," she said. "But why do they think they can do it, particularly why do they think they can do it here?"

Now it was my turn to shrug.

She finished the tortilla and picked up a fork. "Do you remember when I got this place? Do you remember what it was like? You were one of the ones who helped me make it happen."

Of course I remembered. The place had been a wreck. A settling foundation and termite damage gave the kitchen a twelve percent slope, north to south. "I recall, it was terrible."

"It was," she said. "But look at it now." She waved her fork. "And do you remember the neighborhood? Did you know the first time my sister drove me here to look at the property, she wouldn't get out of the car because she was afraid of rats?"

I smiled. I hadn't heard that, but I wasn't terribly astonished. Her sister Blanca never struck me as having any of her sibling's fearlessness. "I didn't know. But I'm not surprised."

"Tsk, Blanca," she said. "But she was right. Back then the neighborhood was terrible and there were rats. But the café's not what it was, and the neighborhood's not what it was. Nobody really understands that."

I stared at her blankly.

"Look, the whole reason I could even buy this place was because nobody believed in it or in Tinker Creek," she said, exasperated. "But even though we've progressed, too many people don't know that we have moved forward. It's like we're a secret, and that hurts us. You know it's true. City Hall acts like it's a great thing that our tourist numbers are higher, but that just means tourists come up Breaker Street to go the Breaker Street beaches and maybe the beach stores and restaurants on First. They don't come into the neighborhood. They don't really get to know Tinker Creek. We have to change that."

Lucinda said she and Oscar Torres, the manager of the Tinker Creek Community Credit Union, had been talking about starting an organization that would primarily publicize and promote the neighborhood as well as fight off the eminent domain.

"We are thinking of calling it the Tinker Creek Environmental Protection Agency," she said. "Tinker Creek EPA."

"But Lucinda, people will hear EPA and assume it's a nature group trying to preserve trees or water or, you know, the environment. Besides, even though I understand the tie-in between a poor reputation and eminent domain, how will this group help us to fight off this specific threat?"

"Our environment includes where we live and work, so EPA is

appropriate," she replied. She told me she and Oscar had convinced Father Silva at St. Benedict the Moor parish to let them use the church's hall for a meeting that night to build support and start to organize the EPA.

"We want you to be a part of our effort," Lucinda said. "Will you come to the meeting?"

I hesitated. Not that I disagreed with them, but I'm not a joiner.

"Just come to the meeting. See what we have in mind. If it's not for you, I understand, but we need you, Lyle. Please come."

Reluctantly, I replied I would.

❖

I arrived at St. Benedict the Moor's parish hall about thirty minutes early and found Lucinda, Esteban, Oscar Torres, and five or six college-aged people breaking down circles of chairs in the large room.

"How many people are you expecting?" I asked Lucinda, stacking some chairs to move them to the front.

"I have no idea," she said, with a worried look on her face. "We haven't been able to advertise much at all. I'm hoping for word of mouth."

After we rearranged the chairs into three rows in front, we moved up on the stage itself. The credit union had used the hall for tax preparation clinics, so Oscar knew how to turn the mic on and fiddled with the knobs, amplifying our voices without screeching.

In the end, she needn't have worried. By the time we started, all the chairs in the three rows were filled, and we had a diverse crowd of at least sixty there. The young people who had been helping with the chairs took seats in front of tables at each set of doors, and the meeting began. Lucinda got up with the microphone.

"Good evening and welcome," she said to the crowd. "Buenas tardes y bienvenidos. Thank you for coming. My name is Lucinda Alverez, and I am the owner and manager of Lucinda's Café." She paused for scattered applause. "Thank you. I recognize many of you from eating with us, thank you." More clapping.

"With me this evening are Señor Oscar Torres, the manager of our own Tinker Creek Community Credit Union, and Mr. Lyle James, the owner and manager of Bonne Chance Motors, where I know many of you get your cars serviced.

"This is a meeting to talk about how we can defend ourselves and our property against the government seizing it with something called eminent domain," Lucinda continued. "Some of us, including all of us on the stage here, have received notices about this possibility, and we have started to draw up plans to fight them, but we need to know how many other people have also received them. Can I see a show of hands of anyone who has received one of the notices for either a business or residence?"

Almost every person responded. Even some latecomers sitting in the back raised their hands.

"Okay. Wow, that's a lot," Lucinda said. "Thank you. You can put down your hands. Now, please raise your hand if you know of someone else, a family member, a neighbor, or a friend who also received one of these notices but who is *not* here tonight."

About half of the people in the front seats raised their hands.

"Okay, thank you," she said. "At the end of our program, please see one of the young people at the doors with clipboards, and they will take your contact information. Please also tell those other people who received notices about us. Now, I know many people here have questions about the notices and what they mean, so I am going to call on Mr. James to tell us what he has been able to discover about them. Mr. Lyle James."

Holy crap. I thought. Nobody mentioned my speaking, but now everybody was waiting for me to say something. What the fuck. I slowly stood up and took the mic from Lucinda's outstretched hand, shooting her a dagger look as I did so.

"Thank you, Ms. Alverez, for this…unexpected opportunity. My name is Lyle James and I own and run Bonne Chance Motors, at the corner of Jackson and Third Avenue. And like she said, we got one of the notices a few days ago."

I paused and took a deep breath, letting it out slowly.

"The first thing you need to know is that I am not a lawyer. Nothing I say here tonight should be considered legal advice. If you have legal questions about these notices, by all means consult a lawyer.

"Second, these official notices look final, but they start the fight, not end it. All they say is at the end of ninety days, we are going to have to come before a judge and show the court why our property should not be condemned and seized by the city and handed over to other people. We can still make our case effectively or appeal whatever the judge decides if it doesn't suit us.

"Third, the notices don't say anything about eminent domain, so I will do that now. Eminent domain is the power to seize private property if the government deems that property is needed for a greater public good. A frequent example is that of a new expressway. If a local, state, or federal authority determines the community requires a new or improved road that would run right through your holding, the government can use eminent domain to seize the house so the highway can go forward.

"The last thing to add is that the powers that be cannot just take your property without paying you for it. But the amount the government wants to pay is rarely enough to cover full costs," I said.

I looked over at Lucinda and handed her the mic.

"Thank you, Mr. James, for the information about the notices. With that, we would like to open the floor for questions. Please move to the microphone stand in the front and state who you are and what the name of your business, if you have one."

An older man and young girl got up from their seats in the second row. She pulled the mic down to her level and spoke.

"My name is Maria Aguera, and my grandfather, Tomas, owns the Royal Tailor shop on Madison Street. This question is for Señor Torres. My grandfather has an account at the credit union. If the credit union is also in danger of losing its space, what would happen to all the money in his account?"

Oscar gave a small jerk and stood up. He looked pale. "Thank you for that excellent question," he said, I thought a little too eagerly. "I'm glad for the chance to clarify. First, the credit union only received a notice for its branch office and little ATM kiosk on Second Avenue, not for the main office. Second, even if something did happen to the credit union, your grandfather's deposits are insured one hundred percent by an independent agency of the U.S. government, so the safest place for your grandfather's money is the credit union."

Maria and her grandad walked back to their seats while another middle-aged woman got up and approached the microphone.

Unlike most of the people in the conservatively dressed audience, this woman wore glittery high-heeled sandals, tight leopard-skin pants, a thin white blouse over a fiery red sports bra, and a light blue summer blazer. Surrounded by the cluster of browns, rusts, and beige, her appearance made me think of a tiger lily set among some cabbages. I bit back a chuckle.

"My name is Suzanne Johnson, and I am the owner and proprietor of the King's Kastle Health Salon on First Avenue between Jefferson and Madison," she said. "This question is for the whole panel. Aren't we jumping the gun a little bit by deciding to fight this right away? I mean, you said they are going to pay us something for our property. Why not wait and see how much they will offer us before we decide to fight it?"

I rose. "I'll take this one," I said.

"Ms. Johnson, thank you for the question," I replied. "If this were a normal state of affairs where we were trading our land on the open market, that would be logical. But this situation is different. There is only one buyer, and that buyer is only going to give us the price he wants to pay whether we like it or not. We will not have the option of just pulling our property from the market. The only logical thing to do is to fight having to sell it at all under these constraints."

Ms. Johnson sat down.

A burly man with a beard, checked shirt, and jeans strode up to the microphone from the back row of chairs.

"I'm Frank Taggert, of Taggert's Hardware, on Sixth and Madison. Didn't we just vote a new councilwoman in last year? Couldn't she help us out of this mess? Is she even here at this meeting?"

Oscar rose and took the stage mic. "Mr. Taggert, thanks for those questions. Yes, the voters chose Allison Sanders to take the empty council seat representing Tinker Creek, and we are in regular communication with her office. She wanted to attend this meeting, but given the short notice, she had a conflict and could not attend. However, she is interested in the outcome and said she will be at all future meetings."

"Well, that's good since I think we're all interested in the outcome of this meeting," Taggert said, I thought sarcastically. "I presume you three have some sort of plan, one that doesn't involve all of us having to hire our own lawyers at God only knows what cost to fight this?"

Lucinda took the microphone from Oscar. "Hi, Frank," she said.

"Hey, Lucinda," he replied in a quieter voice. "I'm sorry to get so heated, but all this is a big deal, you know?"

"Of course we know. And I want to assure you we are working on a plan. And I promise it won't involve all of us having to hire our own lawyers, okay?"

Taggert shrugged and headed back to his seat.

"It's getting late," Lucinda said, "and it's been a long week, so unless there are any other questions, I propose we adjourn this meeting for now. Please he sure to give your information to the young volunteers at the doors. Thank you."

The small crowd buzzed and began to move as people gathered their things. Next to me, Oscar heaved a sigh.

"Thank God that's over," he said. "This is why I worried about taking news of our notices public. The last thing we need is a run on the credit union!"

"I thought you answered the question fine, Oscar," Lucinda chimed in, taking care to turn off the stage microphone.

"And you," Lucinda exclaimed, turning on me. "You were fantástico. Really great."

"All that proved is when you threw me into the deep end, I could swim."

"I had faith in you," Lucinda said. "I have heard you talking to your staff. We needed you to more or less tell them what you told me over breakfast, and you did that very well."

The lights in the room blinked on and off several times, and we realized we were the only people left in the space other than the young volunteers gathered near one of the doors.

"I guess Father Silva wants to lock up," Lucinda said. "Vamos. I hope us three can meet in a couple of days. Oscar, are your lawyers on it?"

"They are, but again this is all they can do on this matter. At least right now."

"Lyle, can we count on you to meet with us in a couple of days?"

I hesitated.

"Don't even start with me," Lucinda said. "What's that saying in English? Some people have leadership put upon them? This is your time to stand up and be counted. I'll contact you and tell you where we're meeting."

I shrugged. "In for a penny, in for a pound," I said.

"What's that?"

"Another saying in English."

Later, as I got ready to turn in, my cell phone rang with a number I didn't recognize.

"Hello."

"Hello?" said a young, male voice. "Is this Lyle James from Bonne Chance Motors?"

"It could be, depending on who you are."

"My name's Mann—Jose Immanuel Porter, and I have some information you might want about the eminent domain notices."

Now I was all ears.

"What sort of information?"

"Well, not really information, but a source where you can find information you might need to help your court fight."

"Go on."

"The city clerk controls a database that has the names and addresses of all the property owners that got sent one of those notices. It's called the Property Standing Dataset, or PSD for short."

"And why should he give me that information?"

"Because you ask for it," the caller said. "It's all public information. They have to give it to you under the law."

"And what's your interest in this? Did you get a notice?"

"Me, oh no. I'm a renter in another part of town. I'm a reporter with the *South Georgia Record*. I was at the meeting tonight and thought if you didn't know about the PSD, I would tell you and maybe save you some time and effort."

Damn. A reporter. Of course. I fought to keep my voice calm.

"Thank you for the tip, Mr....Porter. But I don't like reporters and generally don't deal with them. This has *not* been an interview, and I don't want to see myself quoted anywhere in your paper, do you understand?"

The young male voice sounded flustered. "Of course this wasn't an interview, I didn't mean to imply—"

"Do you understand," I demanded more firmly.

"Yes sir, I understand," he finally said.

"Goodbye, Mr. Porter."

I hung up.

CHAPTER FIVE

Aunt Sammy

"Will you hurry the fuck up," I said, sticking my head into Tommy's bathroom to glare at him as he stood in front of the vanity mirror. "I swear you're slower than your mom."

"Oh, I am not," Tommy snapped back. "You're always exaggerating."

"We're going to be late," I said.

"To an event we don't even know is happening, much less exactly when."

"It's happening. Three sources told me it's on at St. Benedict the Moor at around six p.m."

"There," Tommy said, flashing a quick smile into the mirror. "I'm ready to be seen in public."

I rolled my eyes as we walked back into the hall and headed for the stairs.

"It's not like there are going to be any cruising opportunities at this thing," I pointed out. "Your smile is always great, and anyway, you have a boyfriend."

"First, it always pays to be on point when you're out in public," Tommy said. "Second, I had spinach quiche for lunch, and you never know when a bit of leaf is going to show up on a tooth, and third, who said having a boyfriend means I can't flirt? It's not like I get lots of offers, so flirting helps my self-confidence."

We descended the stairs to the front door.

"So," Tommy said.

"So, what?"

"So, spill. You came in this morning with that ridiculous smile on your face looking like you just got away with something, but won't say what it is. I would have said you got laid, but that would have violated the Manny Porter code for 'Narrowly Escaping a Good Time.'"

I shot him an annoyed look. "I seem to recall someone being far too stressed getting out the door yesterday morning to talk to me."

"Fair point. But you know I can't be late to the editorial meeting Friday morning."

We strode off the porch through the grounds to the garage. Tommy had finally found the right person to authorize proper gardening. The cars were parked along paths lined with blooming purple fountain grass, and we got in my rented cherry-red Mazda Miata. As usual, she started right up and I drove toward the gate.

I glanced over to find him gazing at me expectantly.

"Okay, since someone has decided to become Nosy Nancy, yes, yours truly got laid Thursday night."

"I knew it," Tommy said.

"And more than laid."

"More?"

"Laid times three. Would have been four but we ran out of time Friday morning."

"Really?"

The car gave a jolt as we pulled up short to allow the gate to open. I waited for traffic to ease for my right turn.

"Yes, really. And the reason I didn't come running into your office after HR on Friday was because I'm still processing what happened and didn't want to talk about it yet."

"But—" he said.

I gave him a hard look.

"Okay, no talking yet. Where are we going anyway?"

"First, Tinker Creek. A church on Third Avenue called St. Benedict the Moor. Do you know it?"

"Of course." He laughed. "It's the most famous church in town. It's been there since like 1870 and played a role in the civil rights struggle."

"Sorry. I don't have an encyclopedic knowledge of local churches. All I know is where we're going."

I took the left on Washington, soon getting closer to the beach.

"Remember, can't turn onto Third from Washington during rush hour," Tommy pointed out. "Better take Fourth instead."

"Right," I said, speeding up and hanging a fast left onto Fourth in front of a wall of oncoming traffic, leaving a cacophony of horns and curses in our wake.

"Every time I ride with you, I swear I never will again." Now it was Tommy's turn to grumble.

"And yet you do," I said as we pulled into the parking lot behind a large gray stone church at the corner of Madison and Third. There were few cars, and no lights in the windows.

"Are you still sure this is the place?"

"Yep. Meeting would be in the parish hall, not the sanctuary," I replied.

We both got out of the car and made our way toward the building, finding our way on the Madison Street side until we saw some stairs leading down to a lighted doorway.

❖

The meeting's program had started. Three lines of chairs were set up in front of the small stage, but they were all filled. I nodded to Tommy and pointed to two seats more toward the back of the room.

"Good turnout," I said. "I count somewhere between seventy-five and a hundred."

"Probably. It's hard to tell without all the lights on."

The well-lit platform held three seats, with their eventual occupants still in the shadows stage right. In a few moments they walked out to the chairs, an older woman who appeared to be from South America and two men, one who looked like he might be an accountant and the other who was the man from last night.

"Holy crap, holy crap, holy crap," I whispered to Tommy.

"What?"

"It's him," I squeaked. "The guy on stage, farthest right. He's the guy from last night."

"He is?" Tommy craned for a better view without leaving his seat. "Oh my God, you slept with Superman."

An older lady seated about fifteen feet away stiffened her back.

"Could you speak a bit more loudly, please? Someone in the front row might not have heard you," I whispered furiously.

"Oh my God, Manny. No wonder you were smiling. Did you get his number? Is there going to be a follow-up?"

"Shh. Can I remind you that at least *I'm* working. Pull yourself together. Aside from the one onstage that I happen to know, who are the other two?"

"The woman's named Lucinda Alverez, and she runs Lucinda's

Café over on Monroe. I don't know the other one. My God, he's beautiful."

I shot Tommy a glance. "Put your tongue back in, Tommy," I said, but I secretly agreed.

The program continued from the stage.

"Now, I know many people here have questions about the notices and what they mean, so I am going to call on Mr. James to tell us what he has been able to discover about them," Alverez was saying. "Mr. Lyle James."

Well, now I have his last name, I thought, studying him as he rose to take the microphone. I used this chance to get a clear, detailed look without him knowing I did it.

As I remembered, he stood at least six feet, but I found it no easier to guess his weight tonight. He kept fit, but he's a big man and all that muscle mass must weigh something. Under the stage lights and without any product, I thought his short haircut served him well and favored his frank, open face. Tonight he wore much the same as last night, a pair of dark jeans and a white dress shirt with what might have been a silk vest, and cowboy boots. The outfit worked for him. He was hot as fuck, which was how he looked all the time, I thought.

"I am not a lawyer. Nothing I say here tonight should be considered legal advice. If you have legal questions about these notices, by all means consult a lawyer," James said in a solid baritone.

"Too bad he's not a lawyer," Tommy said. "He's got a lawyer's voice."

"If he's not a lawyer, what does he do?"

"Weren't you paying attention? She introduced both of them."

"I missed it," I said.

"Well, didn't you ask last night?"

"We didn't get around to discussing careers."

Tommy rolled his eyes. "For the sake of the record and to save you from sorry reporting, he's a mechanic," he whispered.

"What?!"

"He runs Bonne Chance Motors, over on Jackson."

He lives above his own shop, I thought. Interesting.

"The last thing to add is that the government cannot just take your property without paying you for it," James was saying. "But the the amount the government wants to pay is rarely enough to cover full costs."

"What do you know about eminent domain," I asked Tommy.

"I'm trying to remember from political science. He's mostly got it all, I think."

The program moved on to questions and ended in a few minutes. People began talking and gathering their things.

"So, what do you think," Tommy asked. "Is there enough to write?"

"Not right now, but I want to know more, and I'm definitely going to follow the story," I said. "I'll ask Aunt Sammy about it over dinner."

"What time is it?" Tommy asked.

"A little bit before seven thirty."

"Oh damn. When's the reservation at Au Pied?"

"Not to worry," I said. "We're eating at Aunt Sammy's table, and she's somewhere here."

"She is? What does she look like?"

"Short. Probably wearing something extraordinary. Likely has two-toned hair."

❖

Then Aunt Sammy let loose one of her trademark staccato laughs from somewhere on the other side of the room. We headed over as she started to pull on her coat.

Of all my unique relations, my Aunt Samantha Calabria is my favorite, packing more joie de vivre, wisdom, humor, and backbone into her five-five frame than the rest of the family combined.

Tonight she had dressed in a black silk business suit, white blouse, dark low-rise pumps, and her trademark two-toned, bowl-cut hair—the top third white and the bottom two-thirds black. A pair of dark jade earrings and brooch of the tragedy and comedy masks finished the ensemble.

"Manny!" she called out to us as soon as she saw me. "We found each other at last. Now come give me a hug."

I dutifully obeyed, and after recovering my breath from her bearlike embrace, I turned to Tommy.

"Aunt Sammy, may I present my best friend and social reporter for the *South Georgia Record*, Mr. Tomas Kingsbury. Tommy, may I present the noted Broadway actress, director, producer, and current restaurateur, my aunt, Ms. Samantha Calabria."

"I hate it when people call me that. The only Samanthas in the world are on old TV shows."

But Tommy, remarkably unperturbed, bowed slightly, took her hand, and in a voice a good deal deeper than I had ever hear him use, said, "Enchanté, madame."

"Oh," Sammy gushed. "I could swoon, but that would leave all of us particularly hungry. Let's go, I have a rideshare waiting."

"It's only four blocks," I protested.

"You try walking four blocks in shoes that cut off circulation to the toes," Aunt Sammy said, herding us out to the parking lot where a Jeep with all its windows removed awaited.

"Ooh, a Jeep," Sammy said. "I love Jeeps. I call shotgun."

She quickly moved around the vehicle to hop in the front passenger seat while Tommy and I climbed in the back through the almost vestigial side doors. It had been years since I'd ridden in a Jeep, and I had forgotten how *industrial* the vehicle felt.

"Can you take us down Breaker?" Sammy asked the driver. "I like to smell the ocean."

"Of course. It's your ride, ma'am."

As the vehicle pulled out onto Madison, I leaned forward. "Aunt Sammy, I don't think I've ever seen you dressed in black before. You could have been at a bank board of directors meeting."

She smiled. "It was a serious meeting, so I felt I needed to dress in a serious way," she said. "After all, it's not every day your city wants to put a wrecking ball through the heart of your livelihood."

The driver got the green arrow and turned left from Madison onto Breaker, and we immediately heard the rhythmic roll of the waves against the beach. Sammy breathed it in deeply.

"God, boys, sometimes I feel like I could live on sea air and nothing more," she said, and we rode the rest of the way to the restaurant in silence, enjoying the evening.

Sammy's restaurant, Au Pied de Cochon, occupied the bottom two floors of Mansfield House, a rambling Victorian structure a prominent banker had built in 1880 as a beach home. The building's former ground floor, back, and side porches had been converted into the restaurant's bar and lunchroom, while the house's main living spaces and balconies on the lowest levels had been turned into dining rooms, another bar, and server stations.

Sammy lived in a renovated apartment on the third floor and used the building's widow's watch, the high tower overlooking Breaker Street and the sea, as her office.

We stood in the restaurant's front garden, enjoying the rose-scented space before we went in.

"Do either of you need a drink before dinner?" Sammy said. "I have a bottle of champagne at the table, but we can order something from the bar before we go up if you like."

Tommy and I looked at each other and shook our heads. Neither one of us were big drinkers, and the prospect of a full bottle of champagne split three ways was enough of a treat.

"I think we're fine, Aunt Sammy," I replied as Henri, her maître d', appeared at the front door.

"Your table is ready Ms. Calabria."

"Then we'll go in."

Entering Au Pied de Cochon was to travel in time back to the Belle Époque in Paris with all the art nouveau colors, textures, and design that characterized the era. Standing in the small entryway in front of the maître d's carved cedar podium left me awed, and a quick glance at Tommy suggested it had a similar impact on him.

"We're eating on one of the second-floor balconies," Sammy said as we followed Henri up the restaurant's spiraling central stairs to the second floor. Finally, we stood on the threshold of the spacious, enclosed balcony Aunt Sammy had set aside for our meal.

"Aunt Sammy, you didn't have to provide great champagne *and* close the space," I said, observing the distinctively orange-labeled Veuve Clicquot bottle in the wine chiller next to the table. "My original reservation would have been fine."

"But it wouldn't have been fine for *me*."

Suitably lambasted, I followed her and Tommy to the table.

"Should I open the champagne now, madame?" Henri asked.

"Of course, and let me offer a toast."

Henri deftly removed the cork cage and released the bottle with an audible but reserved pop, pouring the bubbling liquid into each of our flutes before retreating. We followed Aunt Sammy's move and raised our glasses.

"Gentlemen," she said, "to the birth and presence among us of Mr. Tomas Kingsbury and to new and existing friendships, I offer this lovely wine. Salud!"

"Salud!"

For many years after, the meal that followed Sammy's generous toast became the standard Tommy and I would use to judge every celebratory dining event to come. From the Caesar salad made tableside, to the onion soup steaming through its floating raft of cheese, to the steak, melting in each bite, and the chocolate mousse like a cocoa cloud, we were seduced and subdued.

At the end of the repast, I recalled her comment earlier from the evening. "I was a little surprised you were at tonight's meeting, Aunt Sammy. Do you really consider this eminent domain effort much of a threat?"

"Yes and no," she replied, taking a long sip of her cognac. "Yes, because if we were not to do something, all this could go away," she said, waving her snifter of cognac. "No, because I know the people leading the fight and believe they will win the battle for us."

"How do you know the leaders?"

"I've known Lucinda since she opened the café. Remarkable woman. She's had a tragic life but continues going in her indefatigable way. Oscar Torres helped me find the funds to renovate and repair this place so we could keep going when no one else would."

"I never knew that."

"Well, you weren't around then."

"And the last man, the one on the far right?" Superman, I thought, but I didn't say so. "What do you know about him?"

"Not a lot. He keeps my cars and delivery van running and in good shape. He keeps himself to himself. Lucinda trusts him implicitly. Why all the questions, darling?"

"I'm a reporter." I gave my standard answer. "Questions are part of the territory."

"Ahem," Tommy coughed.

I glared at him, and Aunt Sammy caught the look. "What?"

"As my Granny Woodrow used to say, it's always better to tell the truth and shame the devil. Isn't it, Manny?"

I could have cheerfully strangled him.

"What are we talking about?" Sammy asked.

"Oh nothing," Tommy said. "Just that Manny here has already met Mr. James and would probably give you his weight in gold coins to learn everything you knew about him."

"Why, Manny. Is this true? Where did you meet Mr. James?" Sammy sounded genuinely intrigued. I decided to throw in the towel.

"In a club last night," I said. "My interest in Mr. James goes a bit beyond the purely professional."

Sammy arched her eyebrows. "Well, I'm delighted to hear it," she said. "You should have had someone in your life for years now. Is there reason to think he shares your interest?"

I nodded.

"Excellent," she said. "I shall be glad to help. What would you like to know?"

"At this point, almost anything, Aunt Sammy. I've only met him the once, and we really didn't have time to discuss very much."

She settled back in her seat, and her eyes lost a little bit of their focus. "He owns Bonne Chance Motors, which he got after his dad passed away I want to say about a decade ago, but I'm not positive. The shop was never very much under his father, but he has pretty much turned it around and made it the best auto repair in St. Michael's Harbor. He competes on quality, not price. And that's about all I know, dear. Sorry."

"Actually, I expect if you went back to his place, you know more than your aunt and I," Tommy said. "After all, we've never been in there, but you have. Where does he live?"

"Above the shop."

I told them about the lights that turned off as you left and switched on as you entered, along with the multiheaded shower, the works of art and sculpture scattered around the place, including paintings attached to ceiling and floor by thin wires. They appeared to float in space.

"And I didn't see anything like all of it," I said. "We were supposed to take a little tour this morning before I left but we, um, got distracted."

"Uh-huh, I bet," Tommy said, sending a rush of heat to my face.

"Well, you should have plenty of opportunity to see him as you report the eminent domain story," Aunt Sammy said.

"Maybe. But I haven't even figured if that's going to turn out to be a story or not. I did some research before the meeting. A lot of these fights turn out to be mostly in the courts, and I'm not a legal reporter."

"Don't listen to him," Tommy chimed in. "He's drooling for this story. He'll jump on almost anything that's not about schools or parks and rec."

I shot him a look but conceded the point.

"On the other hand, It would be good to bring Dad a big story right away," I replied quietly.

"Then cover it," Sammy said. "Sunlight is the best disinfectant, and Lucinda thinks there is plenty here that needs disinfecting. Here, I'll help you," she said, fishing her mobile out of her jacket. After she tapped on it a few moments, I felt my phone vibrate in my pocket.

"There, now you have the cell numbers for Lucinda, Oscar, and Mr. James. And of course you already have mine. Go to it," she added before turning to Tommy.

"Now, for you, young man," she said, "what is it going to take to get you to review this fine establishment?"

I excused myself and left the balcony to find the bathroom and to make a call. I passed one of the restaurant's deep chairs in a hall alcove and sank into it before reaching for my *South Georgia Record* phone. It was late, but my blood sang in my veins. The pulse of a big scoop, I told myself, but I knew the story wasn't the sole source of my excitement. I was about to call him for the first time. If I didn't reach him, I could leave a message and lay the groundwork for a follow-up tomorrow. I typed in his number from my personal phone and pressed dial.

"Hello," said a deep voice I recognized from earlier that evening. A shiver flashed up my spine.

"Hello? Is this Lyle James from Bonne Chance Motors?"

"It could be, depending on who you are." Suspicious. But that makes sense these days, I thought. After all, I could be anybody.

"My name's Mann—Jose Immanuel Porter, and I have some information you might want about the eminent domain notices," I said. Damn, I thought. Try not to sound like you're twelve years old.

"What sort of information?"

"Well, not really information, but a source where you can find information you might need to help your court fight," I said. Okay, breathe. A phone call is normalizing, I thought.

"Go on."

"The city clerk controls a database that has the names and addresses of all the property owners that got sent one of those notices. It's called the Property Standing Dataset, or PSD for short."

"And why should he give me that information?" Okay, I hadn't seen that question coming.

"Because you ask for it," I said. "It's all public information. They have to give it to you under the law."

"And what's your interest in this? Did you get a notice?" Great. Time to reassure him I'm not a shady character, I thought.

"Me, oh no. I'm a renter in another part of town. I'm a reporter with the *South Georgia Record*. I was at the meeting tonight and thought if you didn't know about the PSD, I would tell you and maybe save you some time and effort."

Silence. One beat, two, three. *Is he still there?* I was about to say hello again when his voice was back. Audibly tense this time.

"Thank you for the tip, Mr. Porter. But I don't like reporters and generally don't deal with them. This has *not* been an interview, and I don't want to see myself quoted anywhere in your paper, do you understand?"

I think I stuttered briefly. I hadn't been looking for this response at all.

"Of course this wasn't an interview, I didn't mean to imply—"

"Do you understand?" he said more firmly.

"Yes sir, I understand," I finally said. Where the fuck had that come from? The sirs in my world were my dad and my editor.

"Goodbye, Mr. Porter."

He hung up on me. Motherfucker, what a jerk.

CHAPTER SIX

Back Off!

Despite the tip having come from a reporter, the news that the city clerk had data that could help our organizing effort was intriguing. I put a visit to the office on the calendar for Monday morning.

I had almost finished the first half of my Saturday workout when my phone rang, so I carefully racked the weights and scooped up the handset.

"This is Lyle James," I said. "Who is this, please?"

"This is Oscar, Oscar Torres, from last night's meeting. I sincerely regret calling so early, but I need your help."

"How may I help you, Mr. Torres?"

I heard him draw a deep breath and then sigh before he continued. "Mr. James, sometime between nine thirty last night and six this morning," he said, lowering his voice, "someone has vandalized my vehicle."

"Excuse me, what?"

"Vandalized. Someone has intentionally damaged my property."

"How?"

"All four of my tires were flattened," he said. "The car is sitting on the rims. And there's a message painted in red across the windshield."

"Have you called the police?"

"No! I can't involve the police. At least not yet. Please. Lucinda told me you would help. It's imperative we get the car away from here and fixed as soon as possible. Can you do that?"

"Yes. Probably. I don't know. I don't even have anyone in here for an hour. Technically, we aren't even open yet."

"Please."

"Okay, is this a good number to call you back?"

"Yes."

"I'll call my staff, see what we can do, and call you back." My next call was to Parker.

"It's a great BCM day, Parker speaking."

"Tell me that's not how you answer your cell phone all the time."

"It is when I see it's the boss calling," Parker said, chuckling. "You're working early, what's happened?"

"Who's opening today?"

"Me and Carlos."

"Okay, call Carlos and tell him he's opening by himself this morning. I need you to meet me at a residence. Also, call Joe or Christine and confirm that at least one of them is working today and let me know if they aren't. Okay?"

"You got it, boss, but I need to know where I'm going."

"I'll text you the address." I hung up and called Torres back.

"Oscar Torres."

"Good news, Mr. Torres. We're on our way to get your car. I need an address for you and some idea of where the car is."

"The address is in Tinker Creek, eleven ninety-eight Madison. I'll be out front to guide you."

"Okay, I'll be in a flatbed rollback truck, blue cab with Bonne Chance painted on both doors."

"How long do you think you'll be?"

"You're all the way across town, but it's early. Twenty minutes, something like that," I said, then I hung up and texted Parker.

12th and Mad Don't no abt parking txt me whn u arrive

As I drove to meet Oscar, I wondered who had wanted to damage his car. As I approached Twelfth and Madison, Oscar flagged me down and climbed into the passenger side.

"The car's right at the corner coming up," he said. "Look for the sand-colored tarp."

"You covered it?"

"Yes, I didn't know how long this would take, and I didn't want anyone hanging around gawking or taking pictures."

He told me to stop the truck, and we both got out to survey the situation. From my perspective, it could have been worse. The car stood close to the corner on Twelfth Avenue, and most importantly, it didn't have any cars behind it. Parker pulled up on his moto.

"You made good time," I said.

"Empty streets make all the difference." He pointed to the tarpaulin-covered car. "This the patient?"

"Yep."

While Parker unbolted the dollies and got them into position behind the front wheels, I knelt beside each of the back tires, lifted off the tarp, and looked at them closely.

"Oscar, how long have you had these?"

"Probably too long," Oscar replied. "Why?"

"Because whoever did this didn't want it to look like they did it," I said. "Their stealth may mean it'll be harder to get your insurance company to pick up the cost of new tires."

"But what about the fact that they all flattened at the same time? Not to mention the rest of the damage."

"Who knows how insurance adjusters will think?" I said. "We'll take good photos at the shop."

"Ready to start, boss," Parker called from the cab of the truck.

The news from the shop was mostly negative. I would do my best to get a fair price on replacement tires, but it was doubtful Torres could get four new ones for less than six hundred dollars.

But things got interesting when we took the tarp off.

"Boss, you want to come here?" Parker's voice squawked in the intercom. I walked to the second bay to find someone had painted "BACK OFF" across the windshield of Torres's Honda Accord.

"What the fuck," I said.

"Yeah," Joe said. "And it's not just paint, either. This is mixed with something else, maybe glue. I haven't started trying to take it off yet, but it might mean a new windshield."

"I'll give Torres a call."

When I reached him an hour later, I found him much less concerned about the money than I thought he would be.

"I understand," he replied. "But as long as the repair and replacement costs come in lower than two thousand dollars, I'll cover it," Torres said. "There won't be an insurance claim, so I don't need a police report."

"Are you sure? This seems really malicious, particularly the painted message."

"Call Lucinda," he said. "She can fill you in on the reasons better than I can. I have to go anyway, got to meet with a member."

Saturday morning rush had Lucinda tied up when I called, but she got back to me later in the day.

"Ah, Lyle. Mijo, what do you need?"

"Did you tell Oscar not to call the police about the damage to his car?"

"Yes."

"But why?"

"You've seen how many people facing these notices are immigrants like me," Lucinda said. "Whoever damaged Oscar's car knows that if they scare enough people, our effort to save our homes and businesses won't have a chance."

"But the attack on Oscar's car showed real malice," I said. "Shouldn't we let the police know about the attack even if Oscar doesn't file a report?"

"I don't know." Lucinda sounded skeptical. "I don't have a lot of confidence in the policía."

"I don't either," I said. "But I feel like we ought to let someone know what might be going on in case it gets any worse."

In the end she agreed to share what happened informally with the police, so long as nothing appeared on the police blotter to draw media attention.

But I discovered getting law enforcement to respond to the attack on Oscar's car was easier intended than accomplished. After a solid ninety minutes of trying, I was on the edge of giving up when I remembered a policeman I had met in passing. Officer Seamus Cork sounded surprised to hear from me but intrigued when I told him I had something to show him. He dropped by about an hour later.

"Damn, someone did a job here," Cork said, running his fingers along the painted lettering. "You're never getting that off. That's gonna require a new shield."

"We're already ordering one."

"And you said the tires were slashed?"

"Not slashed, but flattened. Punctured." I handed him a thumb drive. "All our pictures are on here, along with the owner's information."

"Any tags?" he asked, meaning the symbols gang members use to identify graffiti.

"Not a one," I said. "But we haven't had significant gang activity here in like five years."

"And why doesn't the owner want to make a complaint?"

"Because the owner believes filing a complaint and having it published in the media, particularly with photos, will only amplify the attacker's impact."

"I can see that. Does he know who did it?"

I shook my head.

"Do you?"

"Not yet. But I'm working on it," I said.

He looked at me in an appraising way. "You already know I can't do anything official without a complaint," he said. "Unofficially, if you can get me some scrapings from the paint on the windshield, I can get a buddy in the Georgia Bureau of Investigation to run some tests and find out what we can from it."

"Anything you could do would be a help. We just wanted to let someone know this had happened in case something similar or worse was to take place later."

"I know you don't know who did it. But who you do *think* did it?"

"I'm not sure, but I think I know why it might have been done."

I filled him in on the eminent domain actions and our suspicions, including the notion of someone wanting to cash in on rising value real estate without spending a whole lot of money.

At the end of my explanation, he let out a low whistle. "Damn, if that's true, it represents a whole pot of mess and definitely something the GBI would be interested in knowing about," he said.

"What would it take to bring them in?"

"Well, that's easier said than done. In this case, you'd need an elected official from the community or the chief of police to request the Bureau's help. But if your suspicion of a conspiracy is correct, this is the sort of case the GBI tends to investigate."

We thanked him for his time, and he left with a small envelope of scrapings Christine had gotten from working on the windshield before she threw in the scraper and gave up.

The rest of the day I spent on paperwork and preparing the shop for an upcoming bout of significantly bad weather. I checked the finished lot and made sure it was secure, along with our signage, and then went up to an early supper and bed.

CHAPTER SEVEN

A Rattle in the Dark

What would eventually come to feel like the longest Sunday of my life began with my rising at an early hour, getting a strong workout in along with coffee, toast, and yogurt before I went down to the shop.

I remember the shop's silence. Parker wouldn't arrive to open the doors for another ninety minutes, and the steady thrum of rain on the roof masked any of our machinery's beeps and buzzes. The elevator's chime echoed through my office as I stepped off into my space. The door shut behind me, and I had gone about two paces before I recognized the medium-pitched, whispering rush of a diamondback rattler shaking its warning. I froze in my steps.

I hadn't heard a rattler since I was a freshman high school football player, when one surprised us in our dugout before practice. We cleared that dugout fast, and even though we never saw the snake again, we always checked to make sure it was empty.

The sound came from the floor in front of me but to the left. I could see my desk about three feet away. I needed to put the table between me and the snake by getting behind it, or better yet, on it. I gathered myself for the move. On the count of three.

Things became confused after I said three, but I suspect the snake attempted to strike on the same count as my leap to the desk, missing me and crashing into furniture. I pulled myself on top of the table and yanked up my legs, grateful I hadn't sat on my laptop. The buzzing sound resumed from somewhere in front of the desk.

My heartbeat roared in my ears, and I realized I had been holding my breath. I released it slowly and reached for my phone to find the nearest Humane Society. They provided animal control under contract for St. Michael's Harbor.

"Humane Society answering service. How can I help you?" asked a young, female voice.

"My name is Lyle James. I am at Bonne Chance Motors, 301 Jackson Street. I need an officer who can remove a poisonous snake from my office."

"I beg your pardon?"

"I know it sounds like I might be pranking you, but I swear I'm not. I arrived at my office early this morning to find a rattlesnake inside. I don't know how it got in here. It's already tried to strike me once and missed. It may be injured but, here, you can hear the rattle," I said, holding my phone in the general direction of the sound.

"Um. I don't mean to put you off but we're only the message service. Usually we only take messages when they're closed."

"I understand. Please ask them to call me as soon as they can."

She hung up. I muted the sound on my phone to avoid agitating the snake any more since it continued to rattle without a letup.

After five minutes, my phone blinked and I found Humane Society Director Alvin Draper on the line, not happy about being called away from his breakfast.

"Al Draper here," he barked. "What's this about a snake?"

The viper began vibrating the rattle at a particularly good clip so I turned the mobile to face the noise. "Hear for yourself," I said.

"All right, all right. But just so you know, the St. Michael's Harbor Humane Society and Animal Rescue does not make a habit of recapturing escaped snakes, so if this one turns out to be yours, we're gonna bill you for this visit."

"Of *course* it's not mine."

"How'd it get in there, then?"

"I don't know yet, but I *will* find out. How long before you get here?"

"Fifteen minutes. Where is the snake now?"

"I don't know exactly. In this room, but the lights are off so I can't see the floor very well. I hope to have the lights on before you get here."

"Are you safe?"

"I'm up on top of my desk, so I think so."

"Well, don't move. We'll have this resolved soon." He rang off.

I dialed Parker. He answered on the first ring.

"On my way in, boss."

"Thanks, but we have a little bit of an odd situation here. I need to change up the procedure a bit."

"I'm listening."

"First, when you get here, unlock the front door but do not throw it open. Open it just enough to put your hand in and slide it up the wall to the light switch and turn on the lights. Then hang around outside, please."

"What's going on, boss?"

"Somehow a rattlesnake got in here last night."

"What!?"

"I don't know how it got in, but it tried to bite me earlier, and animal control is on the way. I need you to wait outside to meet them."

"Will do. How are you?"

"Okay, a little shaken up and major pissed off. Once this is resolved, I want you to check the CCTVs. Maybe we can see this thing getting in."

A few minutes later, Parker's car pulled up in front. His keys clicked loudly in the lock. The rattling paused and I heard the snake move, but as Parker cracked open the door and slid his hand up the wall to the switch, it picked up again.

With the lights on, I glanced down at the floor and, though I was safe on the desk, drew back involuntarily. The snake appeared definitely full-grown, a tangled rope of muscle that appeared as thick as my arm. Its triangle head looked half as big as my palm, and its eyes remained as unblinking as in any fairy tale.

"Can you see him, boss?"

The snake's head twitched at the sound of his voice but returned immediately to watching me.

"Yep. He looks big."

Another vehicle pulled up and soon two other shadows joined Parker behind the blinded windows. My phone blinked.

"Mr. James, Al Draper. We're here outside your shop with Mr. Parker. He said you believe the snake is of an unusually large size?"

"Yes, but I'm no expert. It just looks really big to me."

"Can you do me a favor? If your phone has a camera, could you text a photo of the animal to this number? We want to see what we're up against."

I took the picture and sent it. The phone blinked again.

"This is Draper. We have called for another officer and some other equipment. We are on this. The snake is large. Here is what we're going to do. When the backups arrive, we are going to simultaneously come through each of your office doors. We will keep the snake's attention divided as we get him under control, all right?"

"What can I do?"

"Stay put. Make some noise, not shouts but something to draw its attention as well."

And that's what they did. I heard another car pull up, and Humane Society officers appeared at the same time at both doors. I started regularly beating my hand against my desk and watched as the snake tried to keep all of us in view.

While we all stayed well away from the reptile, the two at the doors slowly maneuvered long capture sticks, with their hooks and loops of cord, toward and around it. Gradually, the group at the front door eased the biggest circle under the snake's head and, on a count of three, drew it tight.

The snake bucked and hissed as the door team hoisted it up into the air while the other trio maneuvered a large bag underneath the writhing creature. The door group lowered the snake into the bag, letting the bag team pull on cords that drew the top shut. The bag jumped and quivered for a few seconds, then became still.

"Snake secured," a young woman from the bag team announced, and the room's tension palpably eased. I slid off my desk and stood up as a short, bald man in a yellow rain slicker approached and extended his hand.

"Mr. James, I'm Alfred Draper."

"Mr. Draper, thank you for coming."

"Don't mention it. That was one of the biggest domestic snakes we have ever taken, so I'm glad we were able to help."

"Excuse me, domestic snakes? I already told you I didn't own that animal."

"No, sir, don't misunderstand. By domestic, I meant snakes native to the U.S. and here in Georgia. We have taken a fair number of bigger ones, but they've been snakes like pythons and boa constrictors. Invasive species, you know."

I nodded, though I didn't think I would recognize a python from a boa.

"I felt sure that snake wasn't yours as soon as I saw your photo of it," he said.

"Why not?"

"Because if you owned it, you would have never let it get away," he said. "There's not a legal outlet for poisonous reptiles, but one that size would probably bring thousands of dollars on the black market," Draper said.

"What's going to happen to it now?" I asked as I watched the slight, blond-haired woman pick up the snake bag off the floor. It hissed and quivered a bit, then remained still.

"We'll take it back to our facility. We have a herpetologist who volunteers with us. If it's injured, we'll try to help it recover. If it's not injured, we'll probably release it—unless the Atlanta Zoo wants it. They don't have a large collection, and a rattler of this size would be a find."

I caught sight of Parker signaling me from the door and excused myself.

"You need to see this, boss," he said, walking down the hall to his office, which housed the video drives from the closed circuit cameras.

He flipped on the monitor. The black screen's image flickered and jumped briefly but then clearly showed the shop's front under the bright security lights.

"The lights and cameras come on as someone approaches the door," Parker said. "The camera's housing has a skirt over the lens to keep it clear, but you can still see it's raining pretty hard. Now watch this."

A short figure in a dark green or black poncho with the hood pulled low approached the portal from the right, looking carefully over their shoulder. At the door they took out a tool or stick and did something to the mail slot. Then they pulled a pale gray sack from under the poncho.

"That's like the snake bag," I said.

The figure opened the bag enough so its mouth covered the mail slot, then tipped up its end, and whatever was inside slid forward to the slot. There was a brief, furious struggle where it appeared the individual barely kept control of the bag. The hooded figure drew the bag away from the slot, then pulled a plastic bag from the poncho. He withdrew what looked like an envelope from the bag, slipped it into the mail opening, pulled the tool from the slot, and quickly disappeared off the screen.

"Well, I guess we know how the snake got in," I said.

"What was in the envelope?" Parker asked.

"I don't know. I never got a chance to pick up any mail."

We returned to the office as the last of the animal control vehicles pulled away from the driveway. The quiet room looked normal. It was hard to believe what had happened over the last ninety minutes. The mail basket had vanished from its usual place under the slot, but Parker spotted it a few feet away. It was empty. But I saw a business-sized gray envelope behind a trash can, so I grabbed it.

It had no stamp, return, or regular address and might have been unused if it hadn't been sealed. I brought it to my desk and carefully slit it open to find one folded white page. The note on it, in keeping with years of extortionist tradition, consisted of words whose letters had been cut from newspapers and other publications. It read:

BAcK oFF FAggOT!

I passed it to Parker.

"I'm sensing a pattern here, boss," he said.

I nodded. I called Officer Cork and left a message asking him to drop by on his rounds, and he met me at about three that afternoon.

"Twice in two days. I don't know whether I should be alarmed or flattered," he said as he sat down across my desk from me.

"Neither," I said. "But you might feel needed." I passed the letter over to him with the envelope wrapped in a paper towel. He took the hint and opened it, careful not to touch it.

"When did this arrive?"

"Overnight. It came with the gift of a full-grown rattlesnake through the mail slot."

"You're joking."

"I wish," I said. "I spent ninety minutes this morning sitting on the top of my desk while two teams of Animal Control folks worked to get the damn thing under control."

He cocked an eyebrow at me. "I take it you weren't bit."

"If I was, I don't think I would be here. Snake struck, though. Just hit the desk instead of me."

"Almost the same message as on the windscreen, except for the sexual slur," he said.

"That's why I called. In case the two are connected."

"Do you think they are?"

"Probably," I said. "If that's an indirect way of asking whether I am gay, I am. But I've been gay with this shop in this community for years, so why send me a snake now if it's not related to the car and the eminent domain effort?"

He was silent for a moment.

"You don't look like one."

"What?"

"You know," he shifted and looked embarrassed, "you don't look gay."

I felt myself flash back to about a dozen different coming out conversations I have had in my life to this point.

"We don't all the look the same. And I don't think my sexuality was what brought on the snake. I don't broadcast it around, but I haven't been in the closet for years."

He stood up. "Can I take this? I want to run it for fingerprints and add to the file."

"Sure. Mine will be there, of course, but there might be others. I have a photo of the page."

"Keep me advised about anything else and maybe move to a different mail delivery system."

I spent the rest of the afternoon helping Joe and Christine finish up the work on Oscar's car so he could come pick it up tomorrow morning. After a bite to eat, I got cleaned up and headed over to Badda-Bean for the meeting.

CHAPTER EIGHT

IED

Badda-Bean Coffee Emporium is the oldest coffee house in St. Michael's Harbor and the most controversial in the region. Either you like and enjoy an organized crime–themed coffee venue with photos of famous mobsters, lawmen, and collections of criminal justice memorabilia, or you don't.

Folks who disliked the shop usually took issue with some of the memorabilia. The collection boasted a battered, shot-up cigarette case allegedly owned by Clyde Barrow, a chemically preserved finger purportedly from the hand of a mob underling, and a bandolier of bullets supposedly owned by Ma Barker.

I carefully remained neutral on the decor but appreciated Badda-Bean for its coffee and admired the perseverance of its owners, the brothers Jason and Jerome Keenan. Their father, a transplant from Chicago, founded the shop, and they'd done an admirable job keeping it competitive in fast-changing market.

When I walked into Badda-Bean promptly at eight p.m., Anna, the evening barista, nodded and pointed me to one of the private rooms where Lucinda and Oscar had arrived.

They both rose and gave me deep and sincere hugs when I walked in.

"Thank God, Lyle," Oscar said. "Was there really a rattlesnake in your office?"

"Absolutely, a great big one."

"Dios mío," Lucinda said.

We sat down at the table underneath a photo of Bonnie and Clyde taken early in their notorious career standing in front of a cliff face. Unlike many images, where the larcenous lovers focused on each other, in this one they stared directly into the camera, looking solemn and tragically young.

"I have never understood this place," Lucinda said in a whisper. "Everything they serve is good, but it's like they celebrate *criminals*." She glanced up at the photo over the table like she expected its subjects to come to life.

"I don't think they celebrate criminals as much as they remember that time in history," I said. "I mean, they have photos of famous lawmen and their memorabilia too."

"Still, it gives me…you know, the nerves."

"Nervous," Oscar said.

"Yes, nervous, exactly."

A young woman wearing an apron and carrying a tablet device arrived at our table.

"Café con leche?" Lucinda asked us.

We nodded.

"A café con leche service for the table, thank you," Lucinda said. "And please shut the door."

The young woman left, quietly pulling it closed behind her.

"So, my friends, where are we?"

"I have spoken to my board of directors, and they agreed to open our emergency loan program to any homeowners or business owners under eminent domain threat due to curable problems, such as a tax lien or physical repair," Oscar said.

"Do we know how many properties that is?" Lucinda asked. "Forty home and business owners gave us their information after the meeting the other night, but so far none of their notices have listed specific violations."

"Not yet," I said, "but I got a tip that the city clerk's office has a database we can access to find out how many property owners were sent notices, which ones they were, and why."

"Excellent," Oscar said. "Who tipped you?"

"A reporter for the *South Georgia Record*."

"Great, we need to get that info," Lucinda said. "How long before we can get access to that database?"

"I'm going to the clerk's office tomorrow. I had some other things to do today, but the snake got in the way."

"My God, I would have been terrified," Lucinda said. "I don't mind most snakes, but a big rattler?"

"It got my attention."

"Which lets us talk about these attacks," Oscar said. "Do we agree they are tied to the eminent domain notices?"

"Yes," I said. "There was a note with the snake that contained the same language that was painted on your windshield. Second, it's simply too great a coincidence. By the way, you can pick up your car tomorrow morning."

Someone quietly tapped at the portal.

"Come in," I said, getting up and reaching over to open the door. The young woman arrived, pushing a cart with a coffeepot, pitcher, three mugs, and a half loaf of something baked. It smelled delicious.

She set about making the café con leche at the cart, pouring coffee from the pot and milk from the pitcher simultaneously into each mug and then placing a hot and frothy mixture in front of us.

"Anna said the boss sent this with our compliments, so please help yourselves," the young woman announced.

"Thank you," Oscar said as she left. "So, what do we want to do about the attacks?" he asked. "I understand our position on calling the police on my car, but does that make sense now? And what do we do if they escalate?"

"I feel different things about the attacks," Lucinda said. "Obviously they are damaging and dangerous. Lyle, I would much rather have you here and at the city clerk's office than in a hospital bed recovering from a snakebite. But I also think these attacks signal weakness, not strength. Whoever has done this knows their position is legally weak. Their only hope to win is to keep us from fighting back, to scare us off. If we remain courageous and persist, we can beat them."

"Yes, but at what price?" Oscar said. "I had a cousin who died after a rattler bite. He was a child at the time, so it was not the same, but still."

"I agree with both of you," I said. "I think Lucinda's correct about the attacks signaling weakness, not strength. But I must confess meeting the rattler this morning shook me up. The only thing we can do, I think, is protect ourselves as much as we can. For instance, the café needs safety lights in that back parking lot, at least, if not CCTV cameras. And Oscar, it may not be a good idea for you to keep parking your car on the street."

"How did they get the rattler into your office?" Oscar asked.

"Through the mail slot. So I already decided to get that sealed. Postal delivery in the future will have to be through opening the door to come in."

"I don't know if the café has the capital for safety lights," Lucinda said, "much less cameras."

"I'm confident I can get a very good price from the suppliers," I said. "And if we have to, I think we can get volunteer labor to install the hardware. Where are we with the PR campaign for TC?"

"I haven't done anything with the campaign yet," Lucinda said. "But the café is sponsoring a 'We Love Tinker Creek' day at MLK Park on September twenty-seventh that I hope will kick off our efforts."

"Bonne Chance will also sponsor that," I stated.

"So will the credit union," Oscar said.

"Thank you both, but you have other things that also need sponsoring. I am hoping to draw some new money as well as using ours," Lucinda said.

"Okay," Oscar said, draining his mug. "Maria's asked me to come home as soon as possible tonight. Anything else?"

"I think we've covered everything that we have facts for," said Lucinda. "Shall we meet again next week?"

"That sounds good," I replied.

We got up and started for the door. "I'll walk you to your car," I offered Lucinda. "I don't think it's a great idea to have you walk that far at night on your own."

"Thank you."

We parted with Oscar at the front door. He went right, in the direction of the Badda-Bean parking lot, and we headed left, toward Monroe. The night carried that soft gentleness early autumn evenings sometimes have here, still warm but not nearly as humid. We stepped carefully around the caution cones and disturbed pavement left by recent construction teams.

"You're very, very...simpático...I don't know the right word in English...to walk an old lady to her car like this," Lucinda said.

"Old lady?" I feigned astonishment. "There's an old lady here? Where?"

She gave a low chuckle. "And you're silly too," she blurted. "Es verdad, I really wanted to get you involved in our effort," she said. "So, I am especially glad you are."

"Why would you want me involved?"

"Because you've been part of this place a long time, and its roots are all tangled in your soul now. That is the sort of champion we need. One for whom there is no place to go if he is defeated. Like us," she said, "your back is, how you say in English, against the wall."

I remained silent, unsure what to reply.

"And because you are what they call here a 'dark horse,' Señor James," she continued. "You have secrets you don't want to share and power you don't want to tap. I think both of those help make you a leader when you decide to recognize them."

I gave a short bark of a laugh. "Señora Alverez, you are exceedingly kind, but I am no leader. I make a very good follower—for example as your assistant—but I don't lead."

"That's not what Padre Joe told me."

"How do you know Father Joe?" I said, surprised.

"Researching schools for Esteban, of course. We hit it off right away. Such a solid priest. And he told me all about how you took over that team and won the All State Championship that year."

"Señora, that was high school football a long time ago."

"Yes, but the seeds of leadership don't die. They remain dormant, waiting for the right conditions to spring out again." She pointed. "I'm in the older SUV down the block."

"You haven't brought this car in yet?"

"It hasn't needed it," she replied. "I think she will need an oil change next week, so I expect to see you or Parker."

We walked past the Second Avenue bungalows and hedges in silence toward what I recognized as an older model Jeep Cherokee. We stopped about twenty-five yards from the vehicle, and she reached into her purse to pull out the electronic key.

"Thank you, Lyle. You can head back to your car. I'll check in with you tomorrow afternoon to see how the clerk's office went," she said. "Thanks again for everything."

Then she pressed the button to unlock the doors. Out of the corner of my eye, I registered a flash of orange and a burst of energy as a blast wave sent me flying through the air into the dark.

CHAPTER NINE

In St. Clair's

Dark. I come to in the dark. I reach my hands up and tentatively feel my face. Eyebrows. Eyes. Nose. Ears. Lips. Cheeks. Chin. Everything's there. Am I blind? Why is it so black? My ears ring.

"One, two, three, four, five," I say.

I heard that. I can hear. But did I hear it? Or did I think I did because I should have? I touch my arms, each hand down an opposing arm. I feel across my chest. No pains. No gashes. No mysterious warm fluids. Am I naked? Nope. Shorts. Gym shorts? Socks and shoes.

Should I sit up? Sure. Give it a shot. Hands palm down on the grass? Both? I push, and I am sitting up.

Light starts to show, and I see I am on the fifty yard line of a football field, the same gridiron from my high school.

I look at my feet, my legs, my whole body. Nothing wounded, missing, bleeding. What the hell has happened to me?

Want to stand up? Sure, why not? Sitting up worked okay. Feet underneath me. Legs. Up I go. Oh wow, dizzy. World spinning. Back down. One knee now. Much better.

Light getting brighter above the field. I see benches on the other side. Do I want to try to stand up again? Okay, but more slowly this time. One knee, now two knees. Now straighten up, gently, like a plant. As they taught you in first grade a million years ago. Success.

Take deep breaths. In, one-two-three. Out, one-two-three. I feel better, but can I get some food? Damn, I'm hungry. Light keeps brightening but nothing in the sky appears to be a sun. Or a moon. It's more like someone is slowly dialing up the brightness on a lamp.

The field is creepily quiet. I've known it full of shouts and tackles, pads against pads. Now nothing.

Someone else comes out of the opposing dugout, somebody who looks like a man, walking in my direction. I don't know what to do. Is he a friend? An enemy? Should I hide? In the distance, he doesn't look dressed but may not be naked either.

As he draws nearer, I think that we've met. I recognize his walk, his sort of jaunt. His size is familiar too. And the color of his skin. He's cute too, and I feel the blood start to move down into my crotch. Damn it, not now.

Oh my God, it's the guy from the other night. Manny! How could he be here? He walks straight up to me and we kiss, just like the last time. God, it feels so good. I can't get enough, but he pulls away. What? Why? He smiles shyly and thrusts an envelope into my hands. I look down at it and when I glance up again, he's gone.

I tear it open and find a single sheet, typed, but in a language I cannot read. I am still staring at it when I hear Father Joe call my name from the highest tier of bleachers, just underneath the scoreboard. He commands me to join him. I start to climb but his shouts get more urgent. He motions to come on, come on. I break into a run. Up the tiers. Heart pounds, breathing labors. I begin to hear a beeping sound as I push most strongly for the highest step, and just as I reach it the sky breaks around me, and I am lying in a bed looking up at Father Joe.

"What the fuck?" I said.

I felt fine a second ago, but now everything hurt. My right arm and shoulder felt like they were on fire.

"How do you feel?" Father Joe asked.

"Like I've been hit by a truck. Where am I?"

But Father Joe had turned away to talk to someone else in the room. "He's awake. Tell the nurse's station they should call the doctor."

He turned back to me. "You're in St. Claire's. You were brought in unconscious last night and only just now woke up."

I groaned. "God, I feel awful. What happened? Why are you here?"

"Lucinda's SUV exploded. You were apparently far enough away that you weren't killed, but not far enough away to avoid being hurt. I'm here because you had a note about our last meeting with my phone number in your wallet."

"Oh my God, Lucinda!"

"She's in a room down the hall. She wasn't killed either. You were both very lucky."

The door opened to admit a Black woman in a lab coat, carrying a computer tablet.

"Oh good, you're here," Father said. "Lyle, this is Dr. Lundi. She came in last night to look after your care."

"Pleased to meet you, Mr. James," she said in a low, gently accented voice. "You are in remarkable shape, but you still gave us a bit of a scare last night."

"What happened?"

"We hoped you would be able to tell us," she said. "Ms. Alverez remains in a therapeutic coma for now. What can you recall?"

"A coma. My God." I paused to collect my thoughts. "I remember the meeting ending. Oscar and I parked in the Badda-Bean lot but Lucinda parked on Second. Oscar went to his car, and I walked Lucinda to hers. We talked on the way. We said good night, but that's it. The next thing I remember is being here and being in pain."

"Of course," Dr. Lundi said. "When you were unconscious, we used minimal pain medication, but now that you're awake, I'll order something to help make you feel more comfortable."

"What are my injuries?"

"Both of you came out remarkably well, but not unscathed. You both received significant brain injuries that we will want to assess over time, and I think you each may experience some PTSD. Do you know what that is?"

"My father saw combat in Afghanistan, so yeah, I'm familiar."

"But what many misunderstand is that anyone who goes through a traumatic incident can experience PTSD, and you and Ms. Alverez have both survived the equivalent of an improvised explosive device attack. Your youth and good physical fitness helped you, and you landed in a patch of very thick ivy. We found no broken bones, but we also found significant muscular trauma, contusions, and deep bruising. Your left arm and shoulder, in particular, may take some weeks to regain full movement. Ms. Alverez, by comparison, suffered more severe injuries."

"How long will I have to stay here?"

"You can check yourself out at any time, but I wouldn't suggest it before tonight at the earliest, and I would like you to remain until tomorrow night or the next morning for observation."

"This was an attack," I said. "I'll stay until tomorrow morning, but probably not longer than that."

"Let's see how you feel. I'll keep you up to date about Ms. Alverez's condition."

"She is guardian of her grandson, a boy named Esteban. Where is he and is he all right?"

"I believe he's staying with a friend of hers. He's in her room now."

"Please let him know I'm awake."

"Will do." She smiled. "Now I think there are some folks who would like to see you," she said. She walked to the door and opened it. "You can come in now."

Parker appeared by my bed. "Aww, man," he said. "You look like five miles of rough road."

"Yeah, well, they haven't brought me drugs yet, so I feel like about a hundred miles of it."

"What happened, boss?"

"I don't remember exactly, but the doc just told me I was standing too close to a car that exploded."

"Is *that* what happened?" Parker sounded surprised. "It's all over the media this morning that a gas line blew."

"I remember pretty clearly it was a blast near a car or under a car, and I don't remember smelling gas. How are things at the shop?"

"Everything's fine," Parker reported.

Someone knocked on the door and then it cracked open to reveal Esteban, Lucinda's grandson, followed by a young female nurse.

"Come in, little man, good to see you!" I said.

He ran to my bedside. "Oh, Mr. James!" he cried, hugging me around the neck and sobbing. "My abuelita is dying."

"Whoa, whoa, whoa," I said, moving him away from my neck so I could look him in the eye. "Hold on. Who told you that?"

"Nobody, but she's in the hospital, and she can't wake up, and I know she's hurt." His eyes shone with tears.

"Now, listen up," I said. "Remember what I taught you about breathing? Deep breaths. Okay? Breathe in. One-two-three. Breathe out. One-two-three. In. One-two-three. Out. One-two-three."

He did what I said, and presently his little body shuddered and his regular breath returned.

"Your abuelita and I were hurt. That's why I'm in here too. But she is not going to die, okay? She and I have a very good doctor named Dr. Lundi, and Dr. Lundi has made sure she can stay in a deep sleep for a while so she can heal. Do you understand?"

He nodded.

"Have you met Dr. Lundi yet?"

He shook his head.

"But you know Parker, right? From baseball last summer?"

He nodded again.

"Well, Parker and my friend Father Joe will be able to introduce you to Dr. Lundi, and she will answer your questions. Is that all right? Look, buddy, your abuelita is my friend, and we both know she's a strong lady, don't we? When you meet Dr. Lundi, ask her how you can help her, and I bet she has an answer for you, okay?"

"Okay. Thank you, Mr. James."

The nurse approached from the other side.

"I need to add some painkillers to your IV," she said, taking out a syringe.

"That will help, thank you," I said.

After they left, I settled back into my pillows and waited for the painkiller to kick in. My body throbbed, and I wondered how much it was going to hurt when I got out of this bed.

I heard a knock at the door and Officer Cork came in with a younger man dressed in a suit. He took off his dark glasses when he entered the room.

"Officer Cork," I said. "We have to stop meeting like this."

"Believe me, I would've been fine not seeing you again so soon either, but that's what happens when you're at the site of a car bomb. The police come to call."

"So, is it definite that's what it was?" I asked. "Parker told me some of the media outlets were speculating on a gas explosion."

"No. It was a car bomb," the younger man said. "The nearest gas line was more than fifty yards away and wasn't big enough to trigger that much of an explosion."

"Lyle James, meet Agent Anthony Blake with the Georgia Bureau of Investigation," Cork said. "Agent Blake, Lyle James."

I smiled at Agent Blake and motioned to the tubes in my arms. "Please excuse my not shaking your hand," I said.

He didn't smile back.

"Officer Cork will need to take your statement today, and you need to sign it when you can," Agent Blake said. "And we need you to stay in town, please."

I nodded. He brought up a small tablet I hadn't noticed in his other hand.

"We need to ask you about these," he said, tapping the device several times and holding it where I could see it. On the screen was one of the walls of the shop where we had painted over some gang tags years ago.

"That's one of the walls at Bonne Chance Motors," I said. "What of it?"

"I was referring to the gang tags," Agent Blake replied. "Is your business cooperating in any way with an organized street gang that uses these tags?"

I started to laugh but choked it back when I saw his face darken.

"Agent Blake, many years ago, when my father ran the business and I wasn't even regularly on the scene, a street gang in Tinker Creek tried to extort him. The tags in those photos date from that period. We have painted over them about five times, but as your sensitive camera picked up, you can still see them, however faintly. I assure you those are not active tags. To the best of my knowledge, Tinker Creek has not had an active gang presence for at least five years and probably more like eight."

"Thank you for your information. Of course we will look into what you say," Agent Blake said. "Officer Cork, you may proceed." He closed the tablet with a snap, turned on his heel, and left the room.

I looked at Officer Cork. "What's with him?"

"I'm not sure. I'm only the liaison from the local department on this investigation. My guess is that he's new and wants to go by the book."

"You said you thought it was unlikely GBI would get involved here."

"That was before a car exploded on a public street," Cork said. "Remember when I said one way for the GBI to get involved would be if the governor asked them? A vehicle exploding on a public street is the sort of thing that gets a governor's attention."

He sat down beside the bed and turned on a pocket tape recorder.

"Aren't you supposed to use a notebook?"

"Haven't used one in years," he replied. "I will ask you to speak clearly so the voice-to-type software on my laptop can recognize what you say."

I recounted the meeting ending at Badda-Bean, Oscar having to head home, deciding to walk Lucinda to her car instead of worrying over her getting mugged, about her saying good night and then the vehicle exploding and my waking up in the hospital. At the end, he turned off the tape recorder.

"And in your mind this is also linked to the eminent domain thing," he asked.

"Yes, isn't it in yours? Take off your patrol hat and put on a detective badge. There were three of us on the stage at the organizing event the other night. Someone has attacked all three of us since that meeting, and the attacks have escalated. The first merely damaged property, but the second and third involved our persons."

"There wasn't a back-off message in the last one," he pointed out.

"That we know of. If there was a note, it could have gone up with the vehicle."

"So, who's behind the eminent domain effort and these attacks?"

I shrugged. "I don't know yet, but as soon as I can catch my breath, I am damn sure going to find out," I said.

"I suppose you've guessed that the only conspiracy GBI wants to hear about for now is a gang war in Tinker Creek," Cork said.

I sank back onto my pillows. "They're twenty years behind the times," I said.

"I can see why you would conclude that, but the good news is that they won't remain so far off forever. What's your next step?"

"I told the good doctor I would stay in here until tomorrow morning, and I'm going to honor that pledge. Then I'll head to the city clerk's office to follow up on a research tip I got a couple of days ago."

"Keep me posted," Cork said before he left.

The painkillers kicked in, and as I felt my body relax I slipped into light sleep until I heard the door and Oscar came in.

"Dios mío," he muttered as he turned to leave.

"Come in, Oscar," I said. My voice sounded blurry, like I was underwater.

"Oh, excuse me. I didn't mean to wake you."

"You didn't. I've had some painkillers, so I'm a little…relaxed."

"I just came from Lucinda's room," he said. "I can't believe it. What are we going to do?"

"What do you mean?"

"Mr. James, there were only three of us leading the fight," he said. "I don't think I can do this by myself."

"You're not going to have to do this by yourself. I promised the doctor I'd stay here until tomorrow morning, but after that I'm checking out, and I'm still committed. Nothing has changed. I think we outlined a good medium-term plan of action with Lucinda last night, and we should pursue that."

Oscar looked down at his feet. "I'm scared, Mr. James. Not so much for myself but for my family. I told my wife the car got sideswiped while parked. She never saw the graffiti or knew about the tires. I never told her about the snake. But I won't be able to hide this from her. It's all over the news. And she knows Lucinda. We participated in the café's Christmas toy drive last year. What should I do?"

"I think you have to tell your wife the truth."

"After the explosion? She'll be terrified."

I paused to consider. It wouldn't be perfect, and it wouldn't do as a medium solution, but I could find them a place to stay in Savannah for a short time if Maria thought it too risky to remain in St. Michael's Harbor.

"I understand what you may be up against," I said, "but she deserves to know how committed we all are to this important task. If it will help at all, I am confident we can provide her and your boy a safe, comfortable place to stay in Savannah if she doesn't feel safe staying here for now."

"I understand," he said. Then he sighed.

"What?"

"Years ago, in my grandfather's generation, our family and others were driven off our properties during a conflict over water. I always said I would never let my family be treated like my grandparents were," he added sharply. "So I am fighting, come what may."

"You're a good friend, Oscar." I yawned as the wave of sleep overcame me.

CHAPTER TEN

City Clerk

"Sweet Jesus," I groaned as I slowly sat up in my hospital bed.

"I really wish you would reconsider checking yourself out," Dr. Lundi said. "After all, just because you can do something doesn't mean you should."

"I hear you, Doc, I really do, but I have too much to do to lie around in a hospital bed. Especially with Lucinda also laid up."

"Well, at least promise me you won't drive yourself anywhere for another two or three days," she said. "There's only a small chance of your losing consciousness again, but it's not impossible."

"All right. Someone on the staff can temporarily chauffeur me around."

I moved my body to the edge of the bed, and she stepped up to one side while an orderly approached the other.

"I want to do this myself, so hands off, please, unless you think I'm falling."

They nodded.

I moved my butt to the edge of the mattress.

"On three," I said. "One. Two. Three."

I stood up and instantly regretted it, but kept my balance through the pain and stayed on my feet.

"Congratulations," Dr. Lundi said to me, looking a little impressed. "I know that took something."

"Thanks," I said, smiling weakly.

"Okay?" She looked closely into my face.

"Okay," I lied.

"Here are your pain medications."

"Sure thing, Doc."

"Now, last thing. What's the rule I taught you about life outside the hospital for the first week?"

I closed my eyes and tried not to feel like a schoolboy surprised by a pop quiz.

"Any loss of memory, call you," I recited. "Any change in vision, especially blurred vision, call you. When in doubt about anything else, call you."

"Exactly right," she said.

Later, after they wheeled me outside, Parker pulled up in the shop van to pick me up.

"Jeez, boss. Are you sure you should be checking out today?" he asked as he came over and started to push me closer to the van.

It wasn't just the wheelchair. I also wore a brace that ran from my left shoulder to my right hip to restrict my arm for at least a week.

"It looks worse than it is," I muttered, but I felt his eyes on me as I gingerly eased myself into the van's passenger seat and he shut the door. He got in the driver's side and started the engine. "Where to, boss?"

"City hall. I want to visit the city clerk's office before I take any more pain medication. I still have three and a half hours left on my last dose."

"City hall it is. Am I hanging around until you're done, or are you going to call me?" he asked as he eased the van onto Lighthouse Parkway headed to the business district.

"Wait for me, would you? You can grab a coffee and something to eat at the downtown Starbucks."

"What are you hoping to get from the clerk's office?"

"I got a tip from a reporter that they should give me a list of all TC property owners who got one of those eminent domain notices."

Parker took the Harbor Plaza exit and two stop signs later pulled into the parking lot opposite the municipal compound front gate. I opened the door and gingerly stepped down to the pavement.

"I'll text you if I beat you back to the van," I said. He nodded as I turned and headed for the gate.

The walled two-square-block St. Michael's Harbor Municipal Center contains four buildings: city hall; the courthouse; Hawley House, the mayor's official residence; and the old Turnby jail, now a museum.

I don't hold the other buildings in much regard, but I admire city hall, both for its architecture and its symbolism.

First, it's large. The three-story structure takes up a third of the total space in the compound. Second, it's a circular building with a lovely garden in the center. Third, it's divided along a line running east-west, so that the northern portion, housing the city council and its staff, is cut off but connected by two pedestrian bridges to the southern half-circle, which houses the mayor's administrative offices. Its structure embodies the separate but unified nature of our government. I love it.

I went through the compound to the administrative side's main door, signed in at the security desk, and showed some identification. The office I wanted was on the second floor, so I took the stairs.

Eventually I stood in front of 212, office of City Clerk James O'Hara, which had a white sheet of paper taped up on it that read "Please knock." I dutifully rapped and then opened it after a loud buzz.

Inside, I faced a thirty-foot slate-gray counter opposite a line of modest wooden chairs against the opposing wall. It looked like a bank interior, with a ledge and three teller stations at intervals along it. Two of the posts were unoccupied, but behind the one immediately facing the door stood a thin, pale man of medium height, with a pencil mustache and large, wire-rimmed glasses. I could have assumed he was an intern, but underneath his station, a removable sign identified him as Pierre Chamell, Assistant City Clerk.

"May I help you?"

"I hope so," I replied. "My name is Lyle James, and I'm looking for some information from one of the city databases."

"Not a problem," he said. "Would that be the Contractor Database or the Permit Database?"

"Neither," I replied. I got my slip of paper out of my pocket. "The one I need information from is called the Property Standing Dataset," I said. "It might be called the PSD."

Chamell peered at me through his round lenses as I realized a hint of red had begun to color his neck.

"I beg your pardon," he said. "I took you for a contractor."

"Not to worry." I tried to smile in a reassuring way. "Can I get information from that database from this office today, or do I need to go somewhere else?"

"No, no, this is the right place," Chamell said, nervously. "It's just we don't get many—hardly any actually—requests for that one. Will you please excuse me a moment?" He disappeared behind a wooden door.

I braced myself against the counter while I waited. Two hours remained until my next round of painkillers, and my body began to share its desire for the pharmaceuticals.

When the wooden door opened again, it wasn't Chamell who returned, but another man wearing expensive shoes, suit pants, and a white dress shirt with sleeves rolled up on a pair of meaty forearms. My mind flashed momentarily to what Clem, the bouncer at the L&F, might look like if he ever put on a business suit. The man spoke.

"I'm City Clerk James O'Hara," he said in an accent I couldn't place. "And you are?"

I guessed from his face and hair he had to be past fifty but with a body much closer to forty, powerful and fit, with shoulders so muscle-corded they gave him a slightly simian posture. The weight and heft of his tattooed forearms, combined with their out-of-season tan, enhanced that impression. His knotty face was capped with a friendly if insincere smile. Nothing in his smirk matched his eyes' cool appraisal.

"Name's Lyle James," I said, extending my hand. "I came in today to see someone about some data."

He moved quickly, catching my hand with an audible slap then watching my expression as he applied much more pressure than demanded by the standard grip. I kept my face empty, but took care not to clench back too hard. I didn't want him able to size me up too accurately just yet.

"That's what Pierre said." He jerked his head at the ghost assistant, who had quietly come back through the door. "Said you wanted information from the PSD?"

"That's right."

"Thing is, we don't usually have too much call from the general public for that one. Usually just from lawyers or big-name companies. Who did you say you worked for again?"

"I didn't. But I'm a small St. Michael's business owner, and I'm doing some research. That's okay, right?"

"Oh yeah, certainly," he said. "Of course, you're going to have to fill out a GORA request for the data, but we're fine with giving it to you."

"What's a GORA request?"

He gave a sharp, barking, laugh. "Gora. G-O-R-A. Stands for the Georgia Open Records Act. Says we have to give you the government data you want, unless it's exempt, of course. Provided you follow our procedures getting it." His eyes now looked more amused than anything else.

"What are the procedures?"

"Fill out a request form here and pay us a fee when you pick up the data or when we send it to you."

"What's the fee?"

"At least fifty dollars, but it could be more if gathering your information takes a lot of extra time or work. Chamell," he shouted.

"Yessir," Chamell said as he got up from a desk behind O'Hara.

"What was our highest fee ever?"

"The highest fee GORA lets us assess is five hundred dollars. We assessed that fee twice in the last fiscal year."

"And that's the only way to get the data."

"From the PSD, yes." His eyes had narrowed.

"Then I guess I better fill out the form."

"That would definitely be your best option," he said. "Chamell, help him fill out the form, since he's one handed."

"Yessir."

"Now, if you will excuse me, Mr. James, I have a meeting," O'Hara said.

Turning on his heel, he left Chamell facing me, looking sympathetic. "H-h-how did you hurt your arm?" he asked me as he turned on a computer terminal next to him.

"Work accident. What's involved in filling out the form?"

"Not much. I'll ask you questions and type your answers right into the online form and then you can sign electronically."

"Okay."

The form's basic name and contact information only took a few moments, but the process slowed significantly when it came to describing the data desired.

"We can go as detailed as you want," Chamell said, "but the search will take longer and be more expensive. You'd be better off running a search of the whole city over a tight timeline, say a month or two months."

In the end, I agreed that would be the best approach. If it worked, the database would give me the names and property address of all the estate owners in St. Michael's Harbor who had been sent eminent domain notices over a three-month period this year.

"How long will this take to run?"

"Oh, not too long, I shouldn't think," Chamell said. "I'll have an estimated completion date in a just a second." He tapped the keyboard a few more times, then frowned.

"Problem?"

"It keeps giving me a date that's like eight weeks out, but this search shouldn't take that long. Let me see if I can resolve it. I'll return momentarily," he said, vanishing behind the wooden door again. A few minutes later, I heard raised voices. Chamell's, I thought, and another I couldn't identify. After ten moments he reappeared, looking flushed.

"I apologize, sir, but we seem to have be having a technical problem I could not resolve on my own. I'll keep working on it, but as of now I'm afraid it's slated for release in December."

I started to protest, but without the next round of drugs, my body throbbed painfully. "Okay, if that's the best you can do. But we really do need that data more quickly."

"I understand. I'll keep working on it, but I can't guarantee anything. If we can get it more quickly, I will let you know."

"Anything left to do?"

Chamell brought out a small black box with a pocket-sized pen-like item.

"Just sign this screen," he said, handing me the pen substitute.

"I can't believe this is going to look much like my signature."

"It doesn't have to be perfect, but I can't have a blank signature line or the data request won't be valid, and we won't be able to work on it."

I used the pen as best I could to sign my name. Chamell watched his screen.

"Okay, got it," he said.

"Thank you for your help. I hope I didn't get you in trouble with your boss."

His face darkened. "He shouldn't be the boss," he said in a lower voice. "But it will be okay. We'll get you what you need."

"Thank you," I said again as I left. Every step reminded me I hadn't used any more painkillers yet, and I decided to take the elevator instead of the stairs. That meant going a bit out of my way to get back to the main door, and I was fully half an hour late when I made it to the van.

"I was about to come looking for you," Parker said.

I eased into the van. "Turned out to be more complicated than I expected."

"Back to the shop?"

"Absolutely," I replied.

"Hurt a lot?"

"More than I would care to admit."

Parker stopped at the light for the Lighthouse Parkway Uptown exit.

I thought I needed to call Lucinda to let her know how the clerk's office visit went, but then remembered that I couldn't, and I had to turn my face to the window so Parker wouldn't catch sight of any tears.

But any temptation to self-pity disappeared when we pulled into the shop drive to see the multicolored WELCOME BACK! banner that hung across the front of the building. I groaned in mock complaint and turned to Parker. "Is this your doing?"

"Don't look at me, boss. I knew nothing about this," he said with a grin.

I eased my way out of the van. Damn, everything hurt. And I felt so tired. I passed my collection of paperwork and my wallet over to him. "Here are the paper copies of my prescriptions, along with my billfold. Would you pick them up for me?"

"Sure thing, boss."

I walked slowly up the drive to the front door when I heard Carlos shout.

"He's back!"

Then the whole staff came out on the drive, surrounding me, smiling and wanting to both give me hugs but not to hurt me. Christine, my painter, couldn't help from crying a little bit, and I noticed Carlos and Vahn dabbing their eyes. We moved into my office, where a box about the size of a case of booze sat on my desk. I looked around.

"A guy brought it for you earlier today," Carlos said. "He said he'd be back later today, and you were supposed to put the contents in your refrigerator."

"Can you bring it upstairs?"

"Sure."

He picked up the box, which didn't appear heavy, and we walked over to the elevator. I stopped in front before I hit the button and addressed the room.

"Thank you, everyone, for the wonderful welcome," I said. "I sincerely regret whatever anxiety or worry you might have felt in the past forty-eight hours. I'm in better health than I appear and mostly just need time to rest and heal."

The small gathering applauded, and I hit the elevator button, stepping in with Carlos as soon as the elevator opened. I put my thumb on the biometric key, and we started to rumble upward. "Do you know what's in the box?"

"I'm pretty sure it's food," Carlos said, looking embarrassed. "It's from that fancy French place up on Breaker."

"Thanks, Carlos. Put the box in the kitchen, would you?"

We exited the elevator, and I sighed, putting on the lights and turning on the heat. It felt good to be home.

"Should I put everything in the refrigerator?"

"Yes, please," I said, gently settling into my couch as he packed away the food.

"Who was the guy who brought it? Delivery man?"

"No," Carlos said, sounding a little uncertain. "He said his name, but I don't remember it."

"What did he look like?"

"Latinx, young. About my height. Short hair, Fit. Dressed sharp. Christine was like 'ooh la la.'" He laughed. "Anything else?"

"No, that's good."

"Then I'm headed back down, boss."

"Thanks, Carlos, man. When Parker gets back, ask him to just head on up. Thanks."

"Will do, boss. See ya later." And he was back down the elevator.

Damn, I'm glad I bought this couch, it's comfortable, I thought. I must have dozed off because the next thing I knew Parker was shaking me awake.

"Hey, boss, I've got your prescriptions."

"Oh yeah, thanks," I said, slowly getting up.

"Where you want them?"

"Put them on the kitchen counter. I'm heading in there anyway."

"Okay. You're on the schedule to open tomorrow. I assume you're probably good with me taking that instead."

"Oh, yeah. In fact, clear me on the schedule for the rest of the week. By the way, what time is it?"

"Coming up on five o'clock."

"Man, it feels much later," I said.

"You probably pushed it today, boss. You don't want Dr. Lundi coming down on you," he said with a grin.

"I hear that."

Parker said good-bye and headed down on the elevator while I took a look at the food. Carlos was right, it was from Au Pied du

Cochon. I opted for the soup and some of the bread. The doorbell rang. I hit the intercom button.

"Hello?"

"Hey, Lyle, it's Manny. Can I come up?"

I hit the button to summon the lift and went to the elevator as it began its clanking ascent. The door opened with the familiar chime. He stepped out uncertainly.

"Hello?" he said.

Damn, he looked good. He must have come from work, wherever that was. He wore a thick, black overcoat over a pale blue shirt and what appeared to be expensive pants and dress shoes. A small dark duffel bag hung from one shoulder.

"Hey," I replied. We looked at each other.

"Oh my God," he said softly. "What the fuck? Are you okay?"

We started to exchange hugs but the arm brace and my pain got in the way.

"I'd take your coat but…" I looked down at my arm with chagrin. "You can hang it and drop your bag on the rack just over there to the right."

"Right," he said, putting his bag on the top shelf as he took off his coat and hung it up. I watched his muscles flex beneath his shirt and admired how well he fit in those pants. I felt some blood start to head into my crotch. I chided myself. You can barely stand and you still can't keep sex off your mind? Dirty bastard.

"I was just getting something to eat," I said, going back to the kitchen. He followed me.

"Is this from you?" I asked, indicating the soup and brioche on the counter.

"Yes," he said, after a moment's hesitation. "I hope I didn't overstep. I heard about what happened, and I remembered what I didn't see in your refrigerator. I thought how I would feel if I came back from the hospital to find nothing to eat…"

"You didn't overstep, and it was very thoughtful. But it did make me wonder if you might be a little sweet on me."

"I don't know that I'd go *that* far," he said with a grin. "But you have been on my mind."

"Ah, I guess that's good to know. Will you join me?"

"No, thank you. I attended an event before I came by, and they fed us." He watched me preparing to warm the soup in the microwave.

"In fact," he said, moving around the counter into my space. He gently pushed on the small of my back. "Why don't we switch places so you can sit on the other side and I can warm your food?"

"Nonsense. I can prepare my own food."

"Yes," Manny said. "I agree. The one-armed man can spend thirty minutes getting into the container of soup so he can heat and eat it, or he can let his two-armed friend do it in thirty seconds and then move on." He opened the plastic container and poured the sweet, nutty-smelling brown liquid into a glass bowl. He covered it with plastic wrap, poked some holes in it, and slid the whole thing into the microwave before hitting the power button for two minutes.

"Point taken," I said. "What did I get in the box?"

"You're about to have what is almost surely the best soup you have ever tasted," he said, "combined with a rich, fortified bread that will make you forget any other bread you have ever eaten. Other food in the box includes a quiche Lorraine, which is a cheesy pie with bacon, and a roast chicken so tender it will melt in your mouth, leaving behind only the delicious crunchy skin. It all came from Au Pied du Cochon because I ate there recently, and I thought it was the best food I had ever eaten."

"You sound like a chef." We both chuckled.

"Not so much," he said, "but I'll take that as a compliment. Mostly, I just like to eat. I don't cook so well myself."

The microwave dinged, and when he opened the door, the room suddenly smelled wonderful.

"Oh my God, that smells good," I said.

"See? And it tastes every bit as good as it smells. Bowl for the soup?"

He opened the empty stand-alone cabinets that would hold dishes and silverware if I had any and looked over at me with a baffled expression.

"In the dishwasher," I said.

He opened the machine and pulled out one of the four bowls I owned. I had bought them at Walmart a few years ago, and each of them had a picture of a piece of fruit on the bottom. I know they weren't elegant, but they were inexpensive and functional.

"Are these all your bowls?"

"That's probably all my dishes and silverware in there," I said.

"Okay. Well, sit down, sir. It's dinnertime."

I sat down on one of the counter stools as he poured the thick liquid into the bowl and sliced the brioche on a cutting board and set out a little butter. I lifted the spoon to my mouth and let the lovely flavor envelop me. He was right, this was the best soup I'd ever had.

"Good, huh?"

"Everything you said."

He smiled again, that quick flash of white across his handsome face.

"No, for real. This is that good."

"I'm glad," he said.

I paused to take bread, spread on some butter, and use it to chase a spoonful of soup. "You have a lovely smile," I said. "I wish I saw it more often."

He laughed. "I don't know why I don't smile a lot. I think I'm a happy person most of the time. But I guess I show my serious side more."

I continued eating until the soup was a thin layer against the bottom of the bowl. "I'm going to be rude," I said, "so don't judge." I tore the remaining bread into pieces and used them to wipe up the thin layer of soup before I ate them. He laughed, watching me.

"I'm hardly one to judge," he said with a smile. "I do the same thing but without the warning."

"Now, for dessert, pass me that blue pill bottle over there."

"Hmm," he said, reading the label. "An opiate, so that's a serious pill."

"That's why there are only eight of them for over three days. The ones in the yellow bottles are basically over-the-counter meds at a higher dosage."

"Water?"

"No thanks, I got it," I said, gathering some saliva in my mouth and then swallowing the pill.

"Wow. That's something I could never do," he said. "If I have to take a vitamin, I'm like pour me a tall glass of water, tea, cola, something."

I stood up and started to collect the dishes, but he stopped me.

"I can handle that. Another one-armed thing that will go faster with two. How long do we have before you're legless?"

"From the drug? Probably thirty minutes or so."

"So, let's get you stripped and in bed," he said. "I have a hunch your doctor would have put you to bed hours ago if she let you out at all."

"Ha! I knew you had an agenda," I said, half-joking, but he didn't laugh.

"No question. If you were one hundred percent, I would absolutely want you naked. You're a beautiful man clothed and an even more beautiful man unclothed. But given your condition, my only agenda is to see you asleep. No fooling around."

To tell the truth, I wouldn't have minded some fun. But my vision had started going fuzzy at the edges. I let him steer me from the kitchen to the bedroom space as he followed behind.

"Let's see about this thing first," he said, indicating the layers of webbing that made up my arm brace and kept my arm from going more than an inch. Once freed, I tentatively moved my arm and shoulder, encountering an ache but no sharp pain. I didn't press the arm too far.

"Turn and sit," Manny said.

"Enjoy ordering me around now. It won't be as easy when I can stand up straight."

"I look forward to it," he said as he unlaced my boots and eased them off my feet, followed by my socks.

I began to relax. My body didn't ache at all anymore, and I could almost see sleep rushing up at me. The last thing I felt was Manny's hands at my belt buckle, and that was all.

I woke up in the dark with a sudden flinch. The clock by my bed read 2:35, and I badly needed the bathroom. My eyes gradually accustomed themselves to the shadows and I gently sat up, then stood. Aches, yes, but nothing sharp.

Naked and alone in the room, I went into the lavatory and quickly eased the pressure on my bladder. My body still hurt, but not as much. I decided to tour the apartment before I went back to bed.

I turned on the kitchen spots. Everything appeared extremely clean. The washing machine had been run. Was Manny still here? The guest bedroom was empty, but I thought I heard faint snoring from my living room. He was sprawled on the thick, leather couch, partially covered with one of my grandparents' quilts and using a couple of folded bath towels as a pillow.

Damn, he's cute, I thought. Not everybody looks hot asleep, but he did. Lithe and strong, his body at repose still looked poised to act. Tribal Aztec or Incan tattoos circled both his biceps, and I loved the way his fine hair darkened and thickened as it moved down his body until it finally disappeared as a lovely treasure trail beneath the waistband of his underwear. Everything about Manny screamed grace, strength, and masculinity. All I wanted to do was make him mine.

I gave my cock a quick snap to the head. Down, boy, I thought. I softly pulled the quilt up farther on his body, but not carefully enough. His eyes snapped open.

"What's wrong?" His voice tense, eyes alert.

"Nothing. Relax. I had to piss and decided to see if you were still here," I said. "Why are you sleeping on the couch?"

Manny moved up onto his elbow so he could rearrange his towel-pillow and yawned. "We didn't talk about it before you fell asleep, and I didn't want to disturb you. I thought about staying in the other bedroom, but that seemed like it was for guests and I didn't feel like that, either. It was getting late, and I thought this couch looked big enough to sleep on, so here I am."

"Well, come on back to bed with me," I said. "If I knew you were going to be here, I would have been fine with your sharing my bed."

"Are you sure?"

"Absolutely. In fact, I won't be able to sleep thinking of you sleeping out here."

He stood up and pulled the quilt around his shoulders like a cape, and we walked back to my bedroom. "How are you feeling?" he asked.

"Truthfully? Still a little bit achy. But better than yesterday. But I still have some time on the painkiller, so ask me again in like four hours."

The bedside clock read three o'clock when we both got into my bed and pulled up the blankets.

"Lyle." A stiff voice.

"Yes?"

"Just because I'm in your bed, I don't think fooling around is a good idea yet."

"Agreed."

"Really?"

"The lust quivers, but the body aches. Sleep tight, Manny."

"You too, Lyle."

CHAPTER ELEVEN

Getting to Know You

I woke up from a dreamless sleep, one of Lyle's massive arms draped around me as he spooned into my back. God, this is nice, I thought, feeling the steady stream of his breath on the nape of my neck and his cock firmly nestled against me. His regular exhalation signaled a deep sleep after our early-morning encounter. I hated to wake him, but I needed to get to my phone to check voice mail and call in to work, not to mention use the restroom. Gently, I tried to untangle our bodies, but I couldn't without disturbing him.

"Mm-mmm," he groaned. "Where you going?"

"Um, bathroom, then phone."

"Come back after." He let go of me and slipped under again.

I found the quilt I'd wrapped around me last night on the floor beside the bed and put it back on. The room's slight chill brought on a burst of goose pimples across my arms and back.

I used the facilities and took a quick shower. The multiple heads and steam chased away the goose bumps, and I stepped out feeling refreshed. Dried and wrapped in the quilt again, I found my phone in the living room. No voice mail but three texts. One was from Tommy.

Didn't come home so guess food was a good idea?? Hit me back so I no ur not dead–T

Food went over great. Remind me re: card for Aunt S. Patient recovering nicely, I typed before going back to the bedroom.

Inside I found Lyle sitting up, propped against the pillows, naked with his lovely thick cock pulsing softly.

"Damn, look at you," I said.

He gave me a wry grin. "Thank fuck you're finally back," he said. "I thought I was going to have to come hunt you down."

"You know. Phone and texts and stuff," I said, feeling stupid.

I tried not to stare, but seeing Lyle in the altogether, that orchestra of muscle, tattoos, and attitude still mesmerized me.

"You look like you want to eat me up," he said with a chuckle.

"I know. You're just so…damn."

He slid his hand slowly down his torso, took hold of his cock, and shook it at me. "Well, if you want your favorite toy, come and get it!"

I dropped the quilt and sat back down on the bed with what I hoped was a stern expression. "How are you feeling?"

"About one thousand percent," he said. "In fact, I'm going to try not to take any of the opioids today. If I have to take painkillers, I'll take some of the glorified aspirin."

"So, good enough for sex," I asked, smiling and crawling up between his spread legs.

"Yes." he said slowly. "Probably nothing too acrobatic, but a basic sixty-nine would just about hit the spot." He paused. "What's wrong?"

"Nothing."

"Don't lie, I saw something come across your face just now."

I felt my previous blush deepen further. "I can't do sixty-nine."

"What? You don't know how?" He looked at me, surprised. "Trust me, it's dead simple."

"No, I mean I can't. I love sucking cock, and you know I do that great."

"Absolutely!"

"But if someone else is on mine at the same time…I just can't. It's like I can't focus on sucking if I'm getting it. It's too distracting."

I was looking at the blankets when I felt the bed move as he came down to lie beside me and speak softly in my ear. "Don't worry. We can do something else."

I detected the relaxed smile in his voice and grinned back. "Thanks," I said. "Not everyone has been so patient."

"I hope I'm smarter than whoever else you've been with!" He moved back into position against the pillows and leered at me. "Now how about you get busy!"

Afterward, we showered together again, not because I needed another, but I wanted to be there with him. I could tell from his face he wasn't as far along the healing road as he wanted me to believe.

"Damn, that feels good," Lyle groaned as he stepped into the warm shower flow I got started for him.

"I thought you were being a little optimistic about your progress earlier," I said.

"Yeah? Well, whose fault is that being so damned cute," he shot back, but with humor in his voice.

I smiled at him and turned around slowly. "What can I say? Not everyone can control themselves in the face of all this," and I moved my hands down my body in my best impression of a stripper.

"Ha!" He started to soap up.

I noticed he favored his left hand, so I came up on that side with some soap. "Let me," I said, and I began lathering where his injured arm would not let him reach. He started to object but then gave in as I soon had him clean and rinsed.

"Ready to get out?" I said.

"What about you?"

"I've already showered, remember? This was just so I didn't go through the day smelling like sex."

Outside I toweled him off, then let him hold on to my shoulder to pull on a pair of shorts and helped him maneuver into a loose shirt. I thought getting him showered and at least partially dressed had gone well, but I could read the frustration and pain on his face.

"Can't wait for this to be over," he muttered as we went back into the bedroom.

"Ready for some painkillers?" I asked. "Earlier you talked about not taking the opioids. Are you sticking to that position?"

"I think so," he said. "But let's hold off on that decision until after breakfast."

In the kitchen, we faced the next challenge. What did he have to eat?

"One of those push-down coffeepots is in the center cabinet," he said, "along with a bag of coffee. Creamer is on the fridge door. Sugar is in the side cabinet. Bagels in the freezer. The wide mouth toaster on the counter will make them nice and brown. Peanut butter in the cabinet top right or soft cream cheese in the fridge."

After he caught my glance, he bristled slightly. "What? It's usually only me, and I don't have time to cook breakfast. I got things to do and places to go."

"Okay, chill," I said. "Sit down, and today I'll make you some breakfast."

He sat at the counter while I busied myself with heating water for coffee and dropping three frozen bagels into the toaster. The peanut butter and cream cheese were just where he said they would be.

Coffee made and poured, bagels toasted on a plate, small bowls with cream cheese, peanut butter, and honey waiting with spoons or spreaders, I looked over the counter with some pride.

He grunted. "This is nice. I don't usually go to this trouble for just me."

He sipped his coffee, smiled again, and spread some peanut butter on a bagel. I grabbed one as well but went for the cream cheese. He took a bite of his and then put it down.

"Manny, this is nice and all, but we need to talk, and now is probably the best bad time to do it," he said.

I put down my bagel. "This sounds bad," I said.

"It's just...man, what are you doing here?"

I didn't have any words then.

"I mean this was—is—very nice and all. And the dinner was great. And it's been great having help to do stuff I can't do, and of course you're sexy as fuck, but the last time we saw each other we were gonna leave things on hold until—maybe—maybe a couple of phone calls and *maybe* go on from there."

I felt a red tide of embarrassment creeping up from my neck to engulf my face but still lacked any words. He got off the stool, refilled his coffee cup, and started pacing back and forth on his side of the counter.

"Now you're here like Florence Goddamn Nightingale, and you're in my bed, and you're making sure I'm fed and I take my meds and I get dried off after I shower. And please don't get me wrong, I'm thankful as hell for what you've done, but man, what the fuck? Why are you here? What's your angle?"

"Maybe I don't have an angle?" I ventured softly.

"Bullshit. Everybody has an angle. What's yours?"

"Okay," I said, thinking aloud. "One, you're the sexiest man I have ever been with in my life, so I'm naturally drawn to you. Two, you made me feel things in bed the other night that I've never felt before, and I don't want that to stop. Three, you're the most mysterious man I know, and I can't stop thinking about you."

"Nonsense. There's nothing mysterious about me."

I laughed. "And you're the least self-aware man I know," I said.

"What do you mean?"

I was also standing by this point, leaning back against the refrigerator and holding up my hand to count down my assertions.

"You live in a space that looks like it came right out of *Architectural Digest*," I said, "but you eat off dishes you bought at Walmart. Your staff appears to adore you, but you don't number a single friend among them as far as I can tell. You're out to your inner circle, such as it is, but are okay letting the broader world assume you're straight. You work at making yourself unapproachable, but you're actually one of the kindest men I have ever met."

"What's your point?"

"Nothing, except that all these things intrigue me and make me want to learn more."

He sat back down on his stool, appearing frustrated. "Look, I appreciate all you have done for me—I genuinely do. And I can even buy that you might find me interesting. But there's a reason I don't have a lover or boyfriend or partner or whatever we're using as the term of the month." He pushed the coffee mug toward me. "Can I get a refill?"

"I'll make another pot."

We munched on our bagels while we waited for the water to boil. After letting the liquid brew, I poured us both another mug and slid his back over to him.

"So, why don't you have a boyfriend?" I asked.

"I don't want one," he said immediately, almost like pulling down a shield. "Or, to be more specific, I don't want to do what it would take to have one."

"And what would that be?"

He almost visibly squirmed in front of me.

"You know, all that 'relationship' stuff," he said, using his voice to add the scare quotes. "All the honesty and trust and compromise and consideration and all of that."

"You don't think you would be good at those things?" I asked, a little bit surprised because I believed he had them.

"No, I think I would be fine offering those things. I just don't believe anybody else would be."

I guess I looked perplexed.

"Look, I don't have a lot of close personal history with other people," he said. "My mom died in a pedestrian hit-and-run when I was ten. She'd been struggling with the booze for a while, so I was the adult in the relationship. It wasn't great, but it was stable. My dad was deployed with the Army up until then, and I thought he might get out and come be my dad after we buried her, but he decided to stay in. I had to go live with his older brother, my Uncle Donovan.

"That was okay, but I really didn't fit in. Plus there weren't any other kids around. But he knew this priest chaplain from his old Army days who left the Army to teach history at the Benedictine military school in Savannah. He got in contact with Father Joe, and then both of them contacted my dad, and they talked him into sending me there."

"Wow. Did they ask you about it? How did you feel about that?"

"Naw, they didn't ask me about it. I was twelve. I don't really remember feeling much of anything at all about being sent to the school, to tell the truth. By the time Uncle Donovan told me I was going there, I had pretty much ridden that emotional roller coaster as much as I could ride. Mostly I remember hoping the school would be a place I could stay a while."

"And could you?"

"Yep. Boarding schools can be lonely places, but I was already lonely, so that wasn't a big change. Plus its rules, norms, and traditions gave me structure and identity nothing else could give me. On school holidays, I would go join Uncle Donovan at his place or sometimes someplace else. But even when I was away from school, I kept my school identity. Like, if we were someplace else, I would store my clothes in the hotel room just like I folded and stored them in my dorm room at school."

"When did your dad come back into your life?"

"The year after I graduated. Father Joe worked it so I could live in one of the caretaker's houses on school grounds and work part-time as a handyman and assistant football coach as well as take classes at Savannah Tech. Dad came out of the military later that year."

"What was that like?" I asked, but he smirked and slid his mug back over.

"I'm not the only one who's gonna spill his guts today. Let's kill the pot, and it's your turn to answer questions."

"Okay," I said, pouring the last of the coffee. "What do you want to know?"

"Let's start with basics. Like what do you do for a living?"

"Okay, but you're not going to like the answer."

"Try me."

"I'm a reporter for the *South Georgia Record*," I said softly.

I predicted correctly, he didn't like it. A grimace flew across his face, and while it lasted a moment, it left a shadow in his eyes.

"Is that really so bad?" I asked.

His mouth made a crooked smile as he took another sip of coffee. "Yes," he said, pulling his hand over his face. "Or no. Maybe. How'd you know I wouldn't like your job?"

"Because I called you the other night to give you a tip about the information you could get from the city clerk's office. You weren't thrilled to hear from me."

"That was you?" He looked bewildered.

"I was working, so I called from my work mobile. Then I was waiting, trying to figure out what to do, when the explosion happened. And now I'm here."

"So, how'd you really find out about me being hurt?"

"I haven't lied to you. For real, my friend and housemate Tommy had to go to the courthouse for a permit or something, and he overheard someone talk about it there. My aunt owns the restaurant and I had just eaten there, so that's where the box of food idea came from."

He started taking utensils and cups to the sink.

"Let me," I said, but he kept on until he cleared the counter.

"So, are we good?" I asked quietly.

"My dad hadn't planned on getting out of the service when he did," Lyle said. "He had eighteen months left and had a promotion pending to master sergeant. He was going to come out with a good pension and well situated for civilian life. But then a reporter wrote a story about a unit that my dad had belonged to years before, when he was just a private first class, almost the lowest rank in the Army. Turned out a bunch of guys from that unit had been involved in some shit involving smuggling and civilian murders—"

"The Al-Fawad scandal!"

"Yeah, that was one name for it. All the reporter had was allegations, but he was off to the races, and then they all were. Like a pack of fucking dogs."

"But the Al-Fawad allegations were true," I said. "There was evidence and court-martials and everything."

He turned on me, eyes blazing. "Yeah, there were! Four. Four guys got terms in Leavenworth, and then kicked out of the Army for that shit. You want to know how many guys had served with that unit while in country? Almost five hundred. You want to guess how many guys got fingered as guilty with no trial, no evidence, no chance to clear their name, because of the media firestorm? Almost five hundred. My dad had belonged to that unit for thirteen weeks. He never knew the guys who had been involved in that shit, and they never knew him. But nonetheless they put his pending promotion into administrative review and then, three months later, informed him that they wanted him to go ahead and take retirement. His commander told him, privately, that it was all he could do to make sure his discharge would remain honorable."

I looked down to find his knuckles white from holding on to the counter.

"He never recovered from that shame. That and the PTSD he already had tipped him into the bottle, and he never could get out of it. He died only a few years later."

"I'm sorry," I said, overwhelmed by everything I had heard.

"Yeah, well, one of the things I have discovered is that sorry is a pile of shit," he growled, before turning and stalking out of the kitchen.

I numbly rinsed the dishes and added them to the dishwasher. Afterward, I found him in the corner of his apartment he had set up as a gym, sitting on a weight bench looking up on the monkey bars. He stood up as I approached.

"I owe you an apology," he stated stiffly. "You didn't deserve that."

"Thank you, but I understand," I replied.

He grimaced again. "I appreciate everything you've done, but I think you should leave now," he said.

"Um—"

"Please."

I nodded.

"I also think you should know your tip about the city clerk's office was only half right," he said. "They have the information, but they made me file a request for it that'll take weeks to fulfill."

I nodded again. That was weird and, I thought, possibly against the law, but I wasn't about to argue with Lyle now.

"The elevator will lock itself after you get off," he said, before he turned back to the exercise equipment he couldn't use.

Back on the pavement outside the shop, I texted Tommy.

Headed to office. Things ended rougher than they started. Lunch??

Sorry 2 hear. Absolutely. Meet me at front door at 12:30?

Good to go

CHAPTER TWELVE

A Leak in the Dam

As the sound of the elevator died away, I paced beneath my now-useless monkey bar gym and finally smacked my palm into one of the poles.

"Dammit," I said out loud.

I built the gym for days like these. Working out calmed and quieted me, offering a package of natural rhythms I used to regain my sense of control. Each heartbeat coupled with every inhalation, each breath tied into every movement, all of them working together to remind me that I remained master of my life.

But now injury locked me off from working out, and all that lovely source of peace stood like a distant mountain across an ocean of pain.

I walked back to the kitchen and grabbed my mobile to call Parker. Voice mail. Dammit again, I thought. I tried the office line. Success this time. Carlos picked up.

"Morning, Carlos, where's Parker?"

"Out front giving an estimate," Carlos said. "You can probably see him from your front windows. You need to speak to him, boss?"

"Naw, it's okay. Just tell him I've decided not to come down today. Gonna try to rest and heal up a bit more quickly."

We hung up, which gave me the time to wonder if I'd made a correct decision not going in. At least I'd be busy in the shop. Up here, I wouldn't have anything to do but think about Manny, dammit.

It wasn't that I hadn't ever had a crush on somebody or hadn't had a fling or ten before. I had done that. But those had been facile, easy to control. Because they were all shallow, on the surface, sex but nothing close to the heart. Manny wasn't any of those things. Or he was all of them, but not them alone. I could hang out with Manny and talk, I realized. It didn't boil down to sex by itself. We could have lazy weekends, spending time together and doing shit or nothing at all—until I had to put up with his character assassinations on people in that damn paper, I thought.

Argh. Fuck, I was a mess. It had been too hard to tell Manny to leave, and thank God he had been a gentleman and left. If he had objected, I might not have been able to kick him out.

My phone rang with the royal trumpet ringtone I had assigned to Eva's personal mobile a few years ago.

"Yes, my queen," I answered.

"Oh my God, Lyle. I just got back into town last night and heard you were in the hospital? Are you all right? What happened? Was there really a bomb?"

She spoke in a higher range than I had ever heard her use before and breathed like she had climbed four flights of stairs. I deliberately lowered my voice and slowed my speech in response.

"Calm down. I'm ninety-seven percent fine. Yes, there was an explosion, and it involved a vehicle, but I don't believe the authorities have declared it a car bomb," I said. "The blast blew me off my feet, and my left shoulder and arm got hurt, but I've seen a doctor and I'm mending."

"Oh, thank God," she said in a more normal voice and cadence. "Is this a good time to talk? Can you tell me what happened?"

I told her about everything, beginning with the snake encounter, which made her scream, up through the explosion and Lucinda remaining in the hospital in an induced coma. When I finished, she accused me of being in denial.

"Of course it was a car bomb," she snapped. "The police may not say so because they don't want to panic people, especially tourists. But I grew up in Beirut, and I know that cars, especially SUVs, do not just blow up in the street by themselves. Trust me on this. The only remaining questions are who planted it and who was the intended target."

I agreed with her, but I tried to downplay the attack when talking about it to damp down fear.

"So, were you the target?"

"I don't think I was the direct target. I think I was the snake's target, but the bomb was focused on Lucinda. However, I also think that neither one of us was supposed to die."

"Why not?"

"Because the snake was never a very accurate weapon. It could have bitten me, but I might not have died. Or it could have bitten someone else entirely. If they really wanted to kill me, they could have waited outside until I came downstairs and shot me. And I think someone set the bomb off from a distance, while they were watching the car."

"Why do you think that?"

"If you think about it, a car bomb is a pretty expensive weapon. It draws a lot of attention. The Georgia Bureau of Investigation is involved now. It gets you on the national news. For that kind of cost, you're going to want more control."

"I suppose," she said. "But I have to tell you, this really shook me up, Lyle. I mean really."

"Really? But you're a veteran war correspondent. You're used to this sort of thing."

"Lyle." She sounded exasperated. "Don't you know the phrase 'context is everything'? When I was in a war zone or where there was an insurgency, of course I was used to such things. But this is home, and you are my friend."

"I understand. Of course you're right. I was trying to make light of the incident."

"Well, enough of that for now. How is the rest of your life? I guess we're not going out for two months while you heal up?"

"I'm not sure we'll be going out for a while—at least not hunting."

"Why not? What did the doctor say?"

"It's not the doctor," I said.

Then I told her about Manny and all that had happened since I met him the last time we had gone out. She listened quietly until I paused, and then I heard her chuckle.

"I thought it might happen someday," she said.

"What?"

"Someone managed to get past the barbed wire and steel facade into the fortress you call a life. That it's a reporter who managed to pull this off is even more extraordinary."

"Very funny. You're not helpful."

"Okay. How can I be helpful?"

"I don't know what to do. My common sense says cut him off. No more communication. What's done is done and all that."

"You know, I've never been a big fan of this American common sense," she said. "Often people bring it out to justify doing stupid things. What does your *gut* say?"

"Get to know him better. Keep spending time with him. Hell, when I was kicking him out this morning, a part of me felt about a matchstick away from proposing, for Christ's sake. Which would have been crazy."

"I agree, that would probably have been crazy. But kicking him out of your life would be just as crazy, in my opinion," she said firmly.

"Why?"

"Because like John Donne wrote, 'No man is an island.' Lyle, you have always been the most magnificently lonely man I have ever known. Your ability to incorporate it into yourself as a strength amazed me, but now you finally have a chance to move away from it. Take it."

"What happened to my friend Eva the Cynic?"

"Eva the Cynic is still right here, but don't forget she is much more cynical about words than she is about actions," she said. "If he brought you food, stayed to help you with your dressings and your pain, and did not invite himself into your bed, your wallet, or your liquor cabinet, the man is worth considering as a possible saint. Or at least a mensch, from the Jewish side of my extended family tree."

"What's a mensch?"

"A doer of good deeds."

I considered her thoughts. For admittedly the short amount of time I had known him, Manny definitely seemed to fit into the category of doers of good deeds. But talking about all this had worn me out. "Well, actually he may be that," I said.

"So, here's my advice. Don't make any decisions about him now. Your voice sounds a little tired. I already know you're not in the shop because I haven't heard a pneumatic tool even once. Chill out. Get some sleep. Get better. Just remember that later I am going to want to meet this paragon."

"Ha! I'll take your advice, and thanks for listening."

"Of course," she said. "Just remember, my advice is only worth what you pay for it." And she rung off.

❖

After Tommy and I walked back from the restaurant, I settled in to start pulling my beat together. I had just begun the job when my office phone rang. "Manny Porter," I answered.

Silence.

"Hello?" I heard a sound of traffic and then the voice resumed.

"Mr. Porter, my name is Pierre Chamell. We used to go to Bethesda Academy at the same time. You probably don't remember me. I was two years behind you."

My mind flashed back to a skinny, blond middle-school kid. "Pierre! Of course I remember you! It's been a long time," I said, trying to sound friendly.

"It has been," he said. "I heard from Tommy Kingsbury that you were back home and working for the *Record*."

"Yes, that's right."

"I don't have much time," he said. "I wondered if you..." The sounds of a city bus drowned out his voice.

"Pierre, I'm sorry. I lost the end of the last sentence. Where are you anyway?"

"At one of the Tourist Aid phone booths on Washington Street. I couldn't call you from my office."

"That's okay," I said.

"I wondered if I could meet you later today. Maybe after work?"

"I don't know about tonight, but—"

"Please! It has to be tonight! I have something very important to give you about the Tinker Creek thing."

"Okay, where?"

"Do you know the Memorial Fountain in MLK Park?"

"No, but I can find it."

"I'll be there at six thirty. I'll wear an Atlanta Braves hat and sit at one of the back-to-back benches. Sit on the bench behind me so we can talk and not look like we're talking."

"Okay."

"Please! It's very important not to tell anyone about this. Not even Tommy."

"I won't."

"See you then," he said and hung up.

At precisely 6:27, I stepped left off Washington Street, past the gigantic stone lions guarding the park gate, and down the short path to the memorial fountain. Shadows had begun to creep across the space, mostly empty now except for a few people cutting through the park on their way home from work.

I spotted him in his Braves hat and sat behind him on the bench. I noted he positioned himself so he sat facing outward, presumably to watch for anything suspicious, whereas I sat toward the fountain.

"Thank you for coming." he said. "And for being on time."

"You're welcome. What did you want to talk about?"

"Yesterday an injured man came into my office wanting help using a database."

"What office is that?"

"I'm the assistant city clerk," he said.

A slight thrill ran through me. It must have been Lyle, I thought.

"He wanted to query one of the public datasets we have. The one called the PSD. I needed some forms for the query, so I went to get some. My boss asked me what the man wanted, and when I told him, my boss told me he would do it."

"And did he?"

"No. He lied to the man and told him he had to fill out a GORA request to get what he wanted when he really didn't. Do you know what that is?"

"I am familiar with the law," I said.

"He wanted to know all the property owners in the city who received a notice of condemnation in the last ninety days. I helped the man fill out the request, and I took a screen shot of the application before submitting it."

"Why?"

"I had a hunch," he said. "And I was right. My boss put a hold on the request."

"How do you know he did that?"

"I can see the GORA request queue. The man's request doesn't move. Only my boss has the authority to do that."

"Okay."

"If you look to the right of where you sit, you will see a crack in the wood that starts small but gets wide," he said. "If you run your finger along this crack where it gets wide, you will find something."

I looked to my right, and sure enough, a crack that started as a hairline under where I sat grew in width. Running my finger down the crack, I found the usual bits of trash and leaves but also something significantly larger. It took me a moment to lever it out and to discover a sleek black flash drive.

"Is this from you?" I asked.

"Yes. Nobody else knows I made it."

"What's on it?"

"It's everything the injured man requested. Plus some extra."

"What's the extra?"

"I took the data from his request and put it against census tract data so you can see which owners in Tinker Creek are being targeted."

I carefully slipped the drive into my jacket pocket and zipped it shut. This could be explosive, but I wasn't sure yet if I would, or could, use it.

"Why did you do this?"

"Two reasons," he said. "My boss, Mr. O'Hara, lied to that man. He should have walked out of our office on that day with what he wanted."

"And the second reason?"

"Mr. O'Hara is a bad man. He's taking money from people. Bribery!"

"You're very brave to do this. What would happen if you were caught?"

"They'd fire me."

"Then why do it?"

"Because I know you. And because we went to BA. I love BA, and I remember the motto."

"One more question. I'll never tell anyone it was you who gave me this, but if I write a story about this, won't they realize it was you who did it?"

"Not at all," he said scornfully. "I used a terminal that they don't even know is on the system. They think their networks are secure, but I hacked them years ago. I own their system, pretty much."

He looked around. The shadows had grown, and they closed the park at dark.

"We should go," he said, standing up.

I stood up too. "Can you get home okay from here?"

"I live close. Good night, Manny."

"Good night, Pierre," I said as he set out across the park to the Freedom Street gate. I returned up the short path to the Washington Street gate. My heart went to my throat for a second when I saw it was shut, but it opened easily when pushed from the inside and then locked securely behind me.

I hailed an eastbound cab on Washington and pondered the impact our experiences in high school can have on us. I appreciated the education I got at Bethesda Academy, but I can't say I loved it then or treasure it now. But it clearly had a deeper impact on Pierre. I remembered the cadence of the school's motto, but not the words, so I looked it up on my phone.

It was from former Irish statesman and British parliamentarian Edmund Burke. "The only thing necessary for the triumph of evil is for enough good men to do nothing." That, I reflected, may be the most concise statement of Pierre Chamell's motivation as I would find anywhere.

The next morning, I dropped by Bernie Sluice's office at the *Record*. Bernie is the company's IT guru and computer guardian. By order of my father, Bernie had to check every piece of hardware that came into the building before it connected to any of our existing terminals, drives, peripherals, or network.

My father's confidence in Bernie stemmed from their relationship of more than two decades. But my idea of an IT guru and computer wonk ran a lot closer to Pierre Chamell.

Whatever misgivings I had about Bernie, if I wanted to see what was on Pierre's flash drive, I had to get Bernie to approve it first. At 8:15 a.m., I made sure to stand exactly in the middle of the large X Bernie had installed in red tape on the corridor floor in front of his office door. I reached out and pushed the large gray button on the wall.

"Well, well, well." Bernie's voice came out sounding tinny from the poorly mounted speaker. "The prodigal finally deigns to descend to Hades. Whose account do you suppose we must thank for this unexpected visit?"

"Good morning, Bernie," I said, trying to sound as perky as possible. "May I come in, please?"

There was a blare of trumpets, and a heavy door clicked and cracked ajar. I pulled it open and stepped inside before it could close on me. Bernie came forward toward me, yawning.

"Late night?" I asked, trying to avoid stepping on anything or knocking over a waist-high pile of keyboards.

"*Warrior World III*." He yawned again. "Against some fiends in Japan. The gaming is awesome, but the hours are hell. What's going on?"

I dug into my pocket, pulled out the drive, and handed it to him.

"Hmm," he said. "Very sophisticated. A Four-Box, double V. I've actually not seen very many of these. They are much more popular in Europe than they are over here. Where did you get it?"

"A source."

"Confidence?"

"Pretty high, but not perfect. That's why I brought it to you. That and the rule, of course."

"Of course. Well, let's see what we've got."

He stepped to a terminal on the far side of the small room and slid the drive into a USB port. The machine whirred, and a screen came up with two separate blank icons on it. Bernie frowned, bent down and hit some buttons, and the device hummed again, but the images didn't change.

"So, the good news is that there are no recognized viruses or malware on this drive," he said.

"That means there's bad news."

"Not really bad, but curious. I can't read these files."

"What do you mean?"

"I can see two files. I can tell, generally, that they are large. But that's it. What are they?"

"Data files. As far as I know, Excel files or some other database system."

"Well, they might be that," he said. "But fucked if I can tell."

He tried to shift them onto the computer's hard drive. The machine whirred and the screen blinked, but the files did not move.

"Do me a favor, would you?" he said as he dismounted the drive and removed it from the computer. "Log in for me on that machine over there." He pointed to another terminal on the other side of the room.

I sat down and logged in. He handed me the drive. I inserted it into the USB port. The computer whirred and a box appeared like before, but on this screen both files clearly bore the image of Excel.

"See that?" he said in an excited voice. "Now, where do you want them?"

"On my desktop, I guess."

"Go ahead and move them." I selected both files and moved them. The machine whirred while a box appeared that tracked the record being copied. Then it was finished.

"Dismount it," he ordered. I did so. Excitement and a kind of manic look flushed his face.

"I don't understand," I said.

"I am not sure I do either," he said. "But somehow the drive was programmed to only open for you, no one else."

Bernie begged me to bring him back the drive when I was done with it, but all I would do was promise to talk to Pierre about it. It occurred to me Pierre must know what he had in the drive, particularly if he had hacked and manipulated this one to personalize it to me. But since I was still knee-deep in another story, the drive matter would have to wait.

When I got back to my post, I phoned my dad's and got Rosa.

"Arthur Porter's office."

"Rosa, it's Manny. Is my dad around?"

"He is, but he's on the phone now."

"Ask him to give me a call when he gets off. I need to run a story by him. Oh, and what's his schedule like today?"

"Pretty tight."

"Do me a favor and try to find five to seven minutes I could see him face-to-face, please?"

"I'll do my best," she said, and she rang off.

I locked the door to my office and settled down in front of the computer. There were actually three files, not two. The largest was a database of all the property owners who had been sent condemnation notices in St. Michael's Harbor during a ninety-day period this year. While a few places received announcements in other parts of town, particularly where there had been a fire or some kind of damage, the overwhelming majority were in the part of Tinker Creek that was within three or four blocks of the beach.

Further, the second database took those addresses from the first and put them against the most recent census tract information tracking race, ethnicity, and income. This data set made it starkly clear that if you received a notice the city was moving against your property, you were almost certainly a person of color or an immigrant and without a lot of wealth.

Rosa rang back.

"I carved out a few minutes for you before he leaves for a lunch meeting," she said. "Be up here at twenty after twelve."

But when I walked in at the appointed time, I found Dad relaxed on the big leather sofa in his office.

"Whoa. I thought I was going to have to brief you on your way to your car," I said.

"And if you were anybody else, that's what I would have done. But for my son and my newest business reporter, I can find some time. What have you got for us?"

So I sat down with him and laid out what I had. The meeting at the church, the condemnations in the near-beach Tinker Creek, the tie-in between resistance organizers and the car bomb, and the most recent, the city's own data showing that it had aimed its efforts almost overwhelmingly at non-white property owners. He listened, taking notes, then started the questions.

"Why hasn't Smalls reported the bomb link?" he asked first thing. Smalls had covered the police and justice beat for the paper for almost a two decades.

"You would have to ask him, but I imagine they have played down any link and asked him to do the same. Also, that line has been easier to hold since one of the victims remains in a medically induced coma and the other is media shy."

"Have you interviewed any of the property owners yet?"

"Not yet. I wanted to get a feel for how big this story might be before I went more granular with it."

"Well, don't put that off any longer. I think perspectives from homeowners should lead at least one of the reaction stories we carry. Where and how did we get the city data?"

"A confidential source in city administration leaked it to me."

"Who?"

"You're asking as my editor?"

"Of course."

"You might remember him from when I attended BA. Blond kid named Pierre Chamell."

"I don't, but it's been a few years. Where does he work? Do you trust him?"

"The city clerk's office," I said, and I went on to tell him Pierre's story about the inquiry that shouldn't have required a GORA application except for O'Hara's intervention and Pierre's claims against his having the job. When I finished, I looked up to find Dad leaning back on the couch and gazing intently at a space over my head.

"Going forward, double-check anything Chamell tells you about O'Hara. It looks like he's got an axe to grind. But at the same time, don't discount it either."

I nodded.

"Now if I understood you correctly, anyone with a city-connected computer terminal could have gotten us this data, is that right?"

"Yes."

"Good. We won't necessarily burn Chamell when we run it. But he put that info up against public data from the census too, correct?"

"Right."

"Try to find someone in bookkeeping or one of our number crunching sources to go over that analysis, just to make sure we're interpreting it correctly."

As we stood up, he extended his hand. "Good job, Manny. This is the sort of story I hoped for when I hired you."

"Thank you, sir."

Later that afternoon I called Lyle, both pleased and surprised when I heard his baritone in my ear.

"Hey, Lyle. It's Manny."

"Not on your cell."

"Nope, I'm calling from my office at the *Record*, so I guess I'm on the Jose phone."

"So, what's up?"

I paused. Suddenly it didn't seem like such a good idea to have this conversation over the phone, but he had made it clear anything in person was out for a while. I plunged ahead.

"Look, I know you're not very keen on seeing me, and I get your trust issue. But I wanted to let you know what I discovered about your experience with the city clerk. I would rather not speak about it on the phone. May I come see you?"

He paused a long time while I almost felt myself burning and twitching in his gaze before he spoke.

"I suppose it might be for the best," he said. "I'm meeting with some people for an update on Lucinda's condition tomorrow morning, so I could meet you afterward. Do you know Badda-Bean?"

"No, but I can find it."

CHAPTER THIRTEEN

A Proposal, Sort Of

I arrived at the hospital fifteen minutes early, then sat in my car in the parking lot.

With about five minutes left, I entered the facility on my way up to Lucinda's room. They had moved her to the fourth floor, and the check-in desk gave me a little black disc to make the elevator stop on four. More security.

Agent Blake from the Georgia Bureau and Officer Cork were inside with Father Joe, Oscar Torres, and Dr. Lundi.

"Sorry I'm late," I said as I entered.

"You're not late," said Father Joe. "You're the last to arrive early, so you're the most on time."

Dr. Lundi cleared her throat.

"Gentlemen, I asked you to this meeting so I could more easily brief you on Ms. Alverez's condition and share my recommendations for treatment going forward. We have made the decision to keep you informed because her nearest relative we can find is a minor and because we have been unable to locate any other members of her family. The hospital administration has made a request to the State Department and the Embassy of Nicaragua for assistance, but these channels have not yet yielded any results. In the meantime, I have a patient to care for. You three appeared to be the people who know her best and care for her most."

Each of us nodded.

"Ms. Alverez's condition has improved steadily over the last few days. We're seeing better numbers across all her vital indicators, and the fever disappeared three days ago. Given this, I am going to begin bringing her out of the induced coma tomorrow morning."

Dr. Lundi's beeper went off, so she had to leave. The rest of us sat around the small table in the room to hear from the two law enforcement officers.

"Officially, we've categorized the car bombing as drug related by person or persons unknown. That keeps the case open while we keep looking into it," Agent Blake said. "Unofficially, Officer Cork here has convinced me it's likely tied into this whole real estate thing." He turned to me. "I believe I owe you an apology," he said. "Your account of those tags on the shop walls checked out, and even more important, I hadn't heard the account about the snake in your office."

"Thank you," I replied. "Since Dr. Lundi was able to give us a little briefing on Lucinda's condition, can you share anything from the investigation?"

"Right now, it feels like a real jigsaw," Blake said, "and we're at the stage where we're still grouping like pieces before we start putting any together. Officer Cork can fill you in on the necessary details."

"If I had to characterize this bombing in just one word, it would be sophisticated," Cork said. "We've had a good deal of success finding the timing and triggering mechanisms as well as traces of the explosive, but we haven't had any luck actually identifying these materials or their origin."

"In fact, we hit so many blank walls on the explosives in this country," Blake said, "we put the explosive's material profile on a couple of the global police information channels. And we got a hit."

"What was it?" I asked.

"It looks like the explosives that blew up Lucinda's car were stolen from a shipment of munitions the Irish Republican Army was delivering to be destroyed as part of their commitment to the Good Friday Agreement of the year 2000."

"Needless to say, gentlemen, all this is highly confidential and should not leave this room. But we wanted to let you know where things stood, and that we're still actively working the case."

"Thank you," I said.

"We'll let you know if we find out anything more." Agent Blake and Officer Cork shook our hands and then departed, leaving a quiet vacuum in their wake.

The current city clerk had an Irish name, I thought. But then I might be wrong about that too.

"How are we going to find someone who would be willing to look after Lucinda at home?" I said, worried. "And how can we help pay for that? For that matter, how do we help her pay for this extended hospital stay?"

"We might have the hospital stay covered. She has adequate insurance, not the best but still pretty good," Oscar said. "And I have links to the hospital's board of governors. I'm pretty sure they'll be open to writing off whatever part of her bill she cannot pay as charity care. I don't know about this skilled nurse's aide, though."

"I think I may have that in hand," Father Joe said. "We have a Franciscan nun serving as our school nurse and, frankly, not finding the job very challenging. She is definitely skilled in long-term care, and I've seen her in action, so I know her bedside manner is wonderful."

"I think that is definitely a good idea to run by Lucinda," Oscar said.

Once we discussed a lot of the practicalities, we each spent a moment saying goodbye to Lucinda and then left. I texted Manny and told him I was headed for Badda-Bean. He replied after a couple of minutes that he would be on his way in shortly.

I took my customary table in the far corner of the room, close to the windows, and spotted Manny getting out of a car.

I smiled to myself for having chosen a seat that let me observe him walking up to the coffee house door. He wore pale gray khakis that hinted nicely at his cute ass and a light blue shirt that fit snugly to his brown torso. A small, forest-green backpack completed the outfit, and as I imagined his body moving beneath his clothes, my mind flashed back to the previous weekend.

"Down, boy," I muttered as Jerome led him to my table. I got up to shake hands with him, and we sat again as a young woman dressed in black approached and asked for our orders. He set his bag on the floor beside him.

"Do you do café con leche?" Manny asked.

"Of course."

"I'll have one of those."

"Make that two," I said, "and an order of alfajores."

"I believe I might have been twelve the last time I ate alfajores," Manny said, eying me. "Those are pretty high calorie for a man who's not able to work out for a while."

"They come three to an order, and I expect you to eat two. One isn't going to kill me," I replied, smiling.

"You're like my Uncle Andres," Manny said, "sweetening bad news with a dessert."

"So, you're expecting bad news?"

"Let's admit that we have had a relationship of extremes so far. We can be very hot or very cold," he said. "I guess I'm hoping for the former but preparing for the latter, just in case."

I eyed him, then sat back a bit in my chair. "So, this is your first time here. What do you think of the place?"

"I'm down with it." Manny chuckled. "Tommy told me about it beforehand, so I was a little prepared. He calls the decor 'hipster ghastly.'"

"Okay, all cards on the table," I said. "You've already figured out I haven't done boyfriends in the past, and you know something about why. But what you might also want to know is that I have never met another man like you. If I was to start trying to have a boyfriend, it would be you."

Manny sat still. "I'm flattered," he finally said. "Really. More than flattered. Because you are easily the most extraordinary person I have ever met, and the thought you might be attracted to me seems silly. Too amazing to be true. The ultimate where's-the-catch moment."

"But you know there's no catch."

"How do I know that? 'If I was to start trying to have a boyfriend'?" He used his fingers to make air quotes. "Could you be any more tentative? That sounds like the start to a long-range business proposal. But we're talking about my heart—our hearts—here."

I sighed. "I said it wrong. That's not what I meant."

"But it *is* what you meant," Manny said. "You see this is as something to ease into, and a lot of it is going to be like that. The details. But the fundamental decision can't be like that. Look at me," he demanded, taking my hand. "Lyle James, if you ask me to be your boyfriend, you will have me one thousand percent. I will be yours until you die or push me away. We'll work out the details over time, but the bedrock of our commitment to each other will remain unchanged. Is that what you want? Is that what you want right now?"

I looked into the eyes of the wonderful man I was coming to love and I realized what I had to say. "I don't know. Manny, I want to say yes, but you deserve nothing less than honesty, and I can't say that yet."

Manny sat back. "I know."

"How do you know?"

"Because," he said, smiling wistfully. "If you had been certain, we wouldn't even be having this conversation right now."

"So, where does that leave us?"

"Where we were before. Getting to know each other. Getting to know ourselves too. Keeping on until we each finally figure out if the other is what we want. And in the meantime, we have to keep your business from being demolished."

The server coughed quietly, standing by with two large mugs of café con leche and a small plate of chocolate-glazed alfajores. She set down the coffees in front of us and the pastry between us.

"Anything else, gentlemen?"

We declined, and she thanked us and headed to the next table down from ours.

"Wow. They're bigger than I remember," Manny said, taking one.

"I wouldn't know because I've only had them here. But Lucinda says they're larger too."

I bit through the crisp cookie and into the cream center and then followed the bite with a mouthful of coffee. Splendid. "So, what do you have that I should know about?" I asked.

"Well," Manny said, "I felt really curious after you told me about the response at the city clerk's office since, in my experience, that was not supposed to have been the outcome."

Then he related having done some digging and discovering both the list of names of property owners facing condemnation but also the socioeconomic data about those people.

"That's fantastic," I said. "But how did you get that information so fast? The city clerk's office hasn't even called me back yet."

Manny's face clouded briefly. "This is a part you may not like as much," he said. "A source gave me the data."

"A source? What source?"

"A source in city administration who believes in open government. They were the ones who crunched the numbers for both the list and the socioeconomic reporting."

"Who was it?" I asked.

"I can't tell you."

"Of course you can't. Reporters always have their own agendas."

"No, I can't for a reason that ought to make you smile a little. I can't tell you because I promised him I wouldn't reveal his identity, and I keep my promises," he said. "And," he added, "there's something else."

"What?"

"I'm writing a story about the data and the socioeconomic analysis."

"What?"

"Lyle, think about it," he said. "I *had* to. A municipality as big as St. Michael's Harbor condemns minority- and immigrant-owned property for redevelopment? That's news. That's not a little dispute about a property owner fighting city hall over zoning. This is a bigger deal."

I sat back and let his words sink in. He was right. It was news. When we didn't know the full size of it, we hadn't understood what it meant. But now I could see it.

"How long do we have before it runs?"

"I'm about three-quarters finished, but then it will need to be fact-checked and there will be graphics that go with it, so probably later this week." He slid a card over to me with a web address on it.

"What's this?"

"That's a public-facing website that has the data and the report on it," Manny said. "You can use my name as the password. I wanted you to have a chance to look into it before the story runs, and you and Lucinda might have to start fielding questions whenever she's healthy."

"Oh, I forgot. The doc's starting to bring Lucinda out of her coma today."

"Really? That's good news. When do they think she'll be awake?"

"They're bringing her out slowly, so maybe two or three days."

"What do you think that'll mean?"

"Huh?"

"I mean she was bombed for her part in this fight over the condemnations. Do you think she'll still want to continue?"

"I don't know," I said. "I know her, but I can't say I know her that well."

I recalled the briefing from Agent Blake and Officer Cork. "So, you think the bomb was connected to the condemnations?" I said.

"Absolutely," he snapped back. "I know the police aren't linking them, but I think they are."

"Is that what the *Record* thinks?"

"Officially, no. As long as law enforcement keeps them separate, the paper will. But privately, yeah, we think they're linked." He narrowed his eyes. "You know something about the investigation," he said.

"Yes, but nothing I'm at liberty to say, particularly not to a reporter."

Manny laughed. "Fair enough. Now it's my turn to trust." He drained his coffee cup and eyed the last alfajor. "Split it?"

"Nah, they're sweet enough that one is good enough for me."

Manny ate the last one while I drained my coffee. "We good for now?" he said.

I looked at him and realized what I wanted most was to bring him back home to bed with me. "Yeah, for now. You wanna come over for dinner tomorrow night? I can fire up the grill."

"Hmm. Tommy's boyfriend is back, and I'm supposed to have dinner with them. Would you object to hosting three and not just one for dinner?"

I laughed. "Sure. The more, the merrier. Tell them it's barbecue, so I'll supply the food. You all need to bring the beer, wine, or whatever booze."

"Deal," he said and stood up.

I rose too and offered my hand.

CHAPTER FOURTEEN

Deutsch Onstage

Back at the office, I braced myself, picked up the phone, and prepared to call Angela Beaufort, the director of press services for the Perkins administration and the principal gatekeeper for any interviews with city officials. When I told Lyle the story was three-quarters done, I didn't tell him I still needed to finish the hardest twenty-five percent.

To my surprise, Beaufort picked up on the third ring. I'd expected voice mail.

"Good afternoon, Ms. Beaufort. My name is Jose Porter, and I'm the new business and economics reporter at the *Record*."

"Oh yes, Mr. Porter. Are your ears burning? I was just looking over your credential application. I wish we had your photographers here. How can I help you?" Her voice sounded as round and sweet as a jelly doughnut, I thought.

"Normally, I would have invited you to lunch to introduce myself before making a business request," I said, "but I'm afraid I need to break protocol and seek an interview right away."

"Oh, that's quite all right. We can always catch lunch later. Who did you want to interview, dear?"

"Well, that's just it. I'm not sure since the interview topic appears to cut across a number of areas," I said.

"Oh?"

"Yes, ma'am. We have St. Michael's Harbor records from this year indicating the city has moved to condemn the property of hundreds of its residents, almost all of whom are minority members, immigrants, or otherwise low income. So, I guess I need to interview someone who knows about these condemnation notices as well as someone in charge of tourism and economic development."

"I see," she said in a voice that remained round but had dropped most of its saccharine quality. "Can you hold, please?"

"Of course."

I listened to a string quartet playing something sprightly for about five minutes until she returned to the phone in a voice even more businesslike and less honeyed than before.

"Did you say that you have city records?"

"Yes, ma'am."

"Well, might I ask which GORA request contained them? I have an account of every GORA request fulfilled since the beginning of the year, and none of them would have held records such as you describe."

"They didn't come from a GORA request, ma'am," I said. "They were leaked to me."

Silence for ten, twenty, thirty seconds. "Oh. I see. You understand, I hope, that the administration doesn't generally comment on information that has been stolen, but I will see what I can do."

"Thank you," I said. "I've just sent a summary of what we have to your email so you can more easily discuss the topic with any possible interviewees," I said. Then I rang off.

About an hour later, my own phone rang. It was Beaufort calling back.

"Mr. Porter?"

"Yes."

"I can arrange an interview for you, but first I must strenuously object to the publication of stolen information."

"I understand," I said. "I even empathize. I prefer other approaches myself. But sometimes circumstance must dictate our actions."

"Hmph," she snorted into the phone. "I can get you twenty minutes with Alex Deutsch, an economic development consultant who is knowledgeable about the topic, any of the next three mornings this week between four and six a.m.," she said.

"My God, why so early?" I asked, picturing pulling myself out of a warm bed in time to take the call.

"He's traveling, and there are time differences."

"And there isn't a city official who can speak to this topic?"

"Yes, but none as passionate or knowledgeable about it," she said.

"Okay, tomorrow at five thirty."

"Excellent. Will this be the number, or is there another he should call?"

I gave her my mobile number.

"Very good, Mr. Porter. He will look forward to speaking to you then. And Mr. Porter?"

"Yes?"

"The interview will be recorded on our end."

"Then rest assured, Ms. Beaufort, it will also be recorded on mine," I replied and rang off.

My phone rang at 5:34 a.m. As Bernie instructed, I let it ring once then hit the button on the recording app and answered it on the third. At first I heard the buzz of a long connection, but then suddenly a voice came on the line.

"This is Alex Deutsch calling for Jose Porter. Is this Mr. Porter?"

"Yes," I said. "Yes, this is he."

Deutsch had an accent I had trouble pinning down. Most of my British friends would categorize it as continental or northern European, but I didn't feel confident I could place it. It definitely wasn't the German accent I halfway anticipated from his name.

"Thank you for taking time to call me," I said.

"Hrumph," he growled. "Look, I have a brief statement to read, then I can take questions, how's that?"

"As long as we understand my questions may range beyond that statement."

"Well, the thrust of my statement will request that the *Record* not publish this story," Deutsch said.

"I'm sorry, but that's not a conversation I can have. I don't control what the *Record* does or does not publish. You will need to talk to the publisher."

"Then absolutely I will."

"In the meantime, would you mind explaining why you think it's so important the *Record* not publish this story?"

"Because St. Michael's Harbor is about to launch a powerful public and private partnership that will bring additional thousands of tourists each year and add over fifteen hundred well-paying jobs and millions of dollars in tax revenue. Publication now will slow the process and make it more expensive."

"What will this partnership do?"

"Well, I'm not at liberty to discuss the details, but our research identified the least commercially successful land in St. Michael's Harbor are some areas generally one or two blocks set back from the beach," he said. "It's what in English you call a no-brainer. It's as though land rich enough to feed a city of five million people was being allowed to lie fallow, to go to waste. Or allowed to be used by a few squatters or subsistence farmers who can barely feed themselves when it could be used efficiently to feed millions."

"I take it you mean the part of St. Michael's Harbor known as Tinker Creek?"

"As I said, I am not at liberty to discuss any details."

"But unlike your farming analogy, what if this land you're talking about already has owners and people living and working on it? What will happen to them as a result of this partnership?"

"Well, that's the genius of the Fifth Amendment to your Constitution, isn't it? The partnership, not the city, will pay all these little land and business owners for their inefficiently used, undercapitalized property at fair market value."

"But that fair market value will be calculated based on the existing, historic incomes, correct? Not the values likely proceeding from the development?"

"Of course. Trying to calculate value based only on future income streams would just be speculative."

"How much has the partnership budgeted for property purchase?"

"No comment."

"And what if that area the partnership wants to develop is of historic importance?"

"History is about the past, what's happened before. Not what's happening now or in the future. For example, I believe the Carmichael Commission's report identified five specific infrastructure improvements St. Michael's Harbor should undertake to help mitigate the impact of climate change. Those are going to take money, and coming up with those funds is a future challenge that keeping an area historic can't offer anything to solve."

He rang off then, claiming to have to return to whatever meeting was about to start wherever he was. To his credit, I could hear the sorts of chimes in the background that often call attendees back into session, so I decided to believe him.

I googled him afterward and came up with precious little. Alex Deutsch Associates was apparently a going concern with an office on Fifth Avenue in New York and other locations in Brussels, Berlin, Istanbul, and Hong Kong, but without much description of what the firm actually did.

The Carmichael Commission, I discovered from the archive

later that morning, had been a 2018 effort formally led by noted conservationist Alfred Carmichael to research the impact of climate change on the Georgia coast and specifically on the stretch by St. Michael's Harbor. As Deutsch accurately pointed out, the commission's recommendations were definitely going to cost. I had to include that in the story.

Now with comment from the administration's consultant, I needed a statement from an opponent of the project. Lucinda Alverez would be the obvious choice, but she was still in a coma. The next logical spokesman would be Oscar Torres, but he firmly declined to be quoted. That left the man who appeared to hate all newspapers, Lyle James. I called him.

"Hey there," he answered in a cheerful voice. I heard seagulls in the background.

"You sound happy."

"I am. Parker hurt his hand, so I had to deliver Mr. Dupree's Alfa Romeo myself."

"Lucky man. Where are you?"

"At his place about twenty miles north of town. His driver will bring me back in a few minutes. What's up?"

"One minor thing and one bigger thing."

"What's the minor thing?"

"Tommy and Danny said they would be pleased to join us for dinner at your place tonight. They'll be there at seven."

"Excellent! What's the bigger thing?"

"I need one more interview from someone opposed so I can finish up this story on the data and the analysis we talked about earlier."

"Call Oscar at the credit union."

"He declined."

Silence.

"You know I hate even the idea of doing this, right?"

"Yes," I said emphatically. "And if I had anyone else to ask in my hip pocket, I wouldn't have even called you. Further, I'm not calling you as Manny now, I'm calling you as Jose, the reporter. If you turn me down, it will not matter at all to our friendship."

"Of course it will."

"No," I said, standing up straighter and trying to sound as mature as possible. "It won't."

"Did you interview anyone from the city?"

I told him about my interview with Deutsch and how he framed the issue as one of development versus non-development, raising the Carmichael Commission report.

"Let me think on it, and I'll will give you an answer tonight," he said.

I left a hole in the story for his possible quote and sent the rest up to my dad for his review and editing for the Sunday deadline. Then I headed back to the house to clean up for dinner and relax a little.

CHAPTER FIFTEEN

The Party

Felix Dupree's chauffeur, Yoshi, came up to my shoulder, weighed a hundred pounds soaking wet, and was the most flamboyant young gay man I knew. He had the cutest bubble butt to ever slide down a stripper pole, and he made a point of wiggling it at me whenever we were together. I found him a lot of fun, in between parrying his advances.

He appeared now at the edge of the driveway, pulling a substantial-looking cart carrying a large Styrofoam cooler.

"Ooooooh! I hoped it would be you," he said, dropping the cart handle and clapping his hands. "You're so much more fun than boring old Parker."

I chuckled, looking forward to sharing this assessment with my chief employee. "Parker's not old. Particularly not when compared to me."

"Well, he acts old. Not that you've been acting all that young lately either."

"Just because I won't get naked whenever you shake that cute little booty at me doesn't mean I'm old."

"What does it mean then?"

"You work for one of my best clients, so it means I get to keep making money and you get to keep your job."

"Well, same difference to me. No fun."

"What's in the cooler?"

"Compliments of Mr. Dupree," Yoshi said, pointing at the ice chest like Vanna White presenting a prize. "Twelve pounds of fresh snapper, dressed, from this morning on the *Blue Pearl*. He said to thank you for making the Alfa pretty again."

"Tell him it would stay prettier if he didn't drive it into so many guardrails." I gave the cooler a second glance. "Must have been a pretty good haul."

Yoshi snickered. "Lots of fish, not much sport," he said. "He complained they were almost jumping into the boat. He doesn't like it when they're too easy to catch." He grabbed the cart handle again and started pulling the wagon down the line of cars.

"Which one we taking?"

"The Acura. Unless you want to take the limo? Plenty of space in the back for two people to party."

I laughed. "You're shameless!"

"And you're hot. How many times in a month do you think I get to drive a hot daddy like you around?"

"No."

"Your loss," he said, turning his back to me and smacking his right butt cheek. He stopped at the Acura and opened the trunk, put the cooler inside, then unlocked the doors and climbed in. I got in the back.

"Buckle up," he said. "House rules, especially for the boring." He stuck his tongue out at me, then turned to the front and looked at me in the mirror. "Where to? Back to Bonne Chance?"

I nodded as he started the car and moved out, getting on the access road to the highway.

"You know, I grew up right around there," he said.

"Where?"

"In the TC. My granddad owned a greasy spoon on Fifth Avenue, just off Jackson. We lived over the restaurant."

"Over by Taggart Hardware?"

He grimaced. "Yeah, racist old man Taggart. You know, he used to let the white kids rent push mowers cheap so they could mow lawns to make money for school, but he charged us Black and mixed-race kids double for the same mowers."

I shook my head. "I didn't know that. But I don't know old man Taggart much. Before my time here. Mostly I deal with his son now."

"What's he like?"

"Seems a straight-up man. He doesn't overcharge for his tools, and I have no beef with him. But then, I'm not Black. Your granddad still live over the store?"

"Yeah. He and my Aunt Tattie."

"How old are you, anyway?"

"How old do I look?"

"You look sixteen trying to look eighteen."

"Ha! Naw, dog. I'm twenty-five, twenty-six in January. Why?"

"I don't know. I'm trying to get a line on folks who lived in Tinker Creek a long time. Like where's your folks other than your grandpa?"

Yoshi got quiet.

"Don't worry about it. I withdraw the question. None of my business."

"Naw, man, it's cool. I just wasn't expecting it. My dad died from an overdose in jail when I was like fourteen. My mom was a nurse from the Philippines who went back there after I was born."

"So, no brothers or sisters?"

"Nope. But cousins. I got six first cousins and, God, like I don't even know how many second cousins." He eased the car into the exit for Washington Street, and in a few minutes, we were getting ready to turn on Third Avenue.

"Tell you what, can you go up and onto Breaker and then down Jackson? It's such a nice afternoon."

"Sure thing."

Once on Breaker Street, I hit the button and the window slid down silently to let in the sounds of seagulls and waves. Yoshi rolled down the one on the left side too, so the salty air moved through the car.

"I love to do that," he said. "Drive up and down Breaker with the windows open on a nice day."

"I know."

I left my window down when we turned on Jackson Street while Yoshi rolled up the one on the driver's side. We passed the line of dollar stores, T-shirt shops, and souvenir stands quickly and soon moved past older row houses, little bodegas, and garden-style apartment buildings. Yoshi pulled up across from Bonne Chance. He unlocked the doors but didn't get out.

"You ever have any openings at Bonne Chance?"

"Funny you should ask. We got a contract that's probably gonna make us hire a new hand or two. You looking?"

"No. Not actively looking. But driving for Mr. Dupree is not really a growth position, you know. Even though he pays me good. I gotta stay open to new possibilities."

"You any good under the hood?"

"You tell me," he shot back. "I'm the one that keeps Mr. Dupree's cars all running so nice. I could do the body work too except he don't have the right tools or space."

"It would mean working under boring Parker," I pointed out.

He grinned. "Naw, man, Parker's okay. He's just like the straightest straight man on straight man planet. He blushes so easy. All I have to do is bend over in front of him, and he's looking like Mr. Tomato Head."

"Well, if you're serious, I'll keep you in mind. But if you come to me, we'll have to find some way to finesse it with Dupree. I don't want to lose a good client by hiring away his driver."

I got out. Yoshi opened the trunk and I collected my cooler of snapper, then headed for the elevator up to my place. I had about three hours before Manny and my other guests arrived.

❖

Tommy and Daniel offered me a ride to Bonne Chance for the party, but I decided to head over a little bit early. I pushed the doorbell below the intercom. Silence. I counted to ten three times and tapped it again.

"Lyle James." He sounded stressed.

"It's Manny. Can I come up?"

"You're early," he grumbled, but the call button lit up, and I heard the clanking that heralded the descent. He stood at the elevator door when it opened, and although I prepared myself to see him again, I still trembled so much he had to catch the bag of groceries.

"Whoa," he said, taking the bag from me as it headed toward the floor. "You should have used the cart. It's right in there," he said, nodding to the back of the elevator.

Sure enough, there was a wagon with wide wheels, a big handle, and short sides to keep things from sliding off. I blushed red. "Of course. I didn't see it," I said.

"No worries," he said. I followed him back to the kitchen. He wore boat shoes and rust-red shorts that came to above his knees and showed off his legs, a rope belt, and a semi-sheer top. The shirt showed off his muscles as he hefted the bag, and I started thinking about rotten onions again to keep myself from going to full hard.

"What's in here, anyway?"

"Just some stuff I thought you might need. Some tequila, some wine, a small bag of charcoal, a medium-sized bag of ice, two jars of salsa, one jar of queso, two bags of chips, and some ice cream."

He looked back over his shoulder incredulously. "You know you're a guest tonight, right?"

"I know," I said, trying not to whine. "But you're hosting my friends, and I didn't know what you had or didn't have."

"Well, despite your lack of faith, I'm well stocked in everything you brought. Except maybe chips. Can't ever have too many of those."

He put my bag down in the kitchen, the counter already crowded with a large bowl of salsa, several tomatoes waiting to be chopped, fish fillets, two pineapples, and dishes of limes and lemons.

"Wow," I said.

"Sorry, I'm running a bit late," he said. "Some damn reporter was demanding a statement from me for some story or other."

"Very funny," I said. "But you didn't have to answer if you didn't want."

"Well, it so happens I did want," he said. "You'll find your statement all typed and everything on my desk. You can use my office if you need to send it in."

Large screens decorated with scenes of skyscrapers demarcated his business space across the living area from the kitchen. I walked over right away. Behind the partitions on the desk a sheet of white printer paper waited for me. I read:

> *The issue is not whether to develop or not. The issues are what sort of development we will have and who gets to decide. The people who have lived in Tinker Creek and endured hardships over many years deserve a seat at the table when discussing what will happen to their neighborhood. They do not deserve to be driven from their homes and businesses by their own government.*

Lyle had signed it underneath, identifying himself as Owner of Bonne Chance Motors, St. Michael's Harbor's Leading International Auto Repair Facility.

I carried the paper back to the kitchen. "Good job," I said. "It's about the right length too. What changed your mind?"

"I had a conversation with a long-term Tinker Creek resident after we spoke this afternoon," Lyle said. "When I got back, that was waiting on the tip of my tongue."

I sat down, typed the statement into my text app, and sent it to the copy editor. "They're not going to put in this bit about Bonne Chance being the leading international motor repair facility, you know," I said. "I think my publisher will say something like, 'if they want a plug, let them buy an ad.'"

"I understand. But I had to try. That just goes with owning your own business." He paused as a bell sounded overhead. "That will be the other guests. Why not go down on the elevator to let them in?"

I rode down the lift and enjoyed seeing Tommy and Daniel's faces when the door slid up.

"Oh thank God," Tommy blurted. "I thought we were at the wrong place."

"Why?" I asked while giving him a quick hug and reaching out to shake Daniel's hand. "I told you he lived over the garage."

"I know, but this place looks really closed when it's closed, and Daniel kept wondering if we got the address or the name of the business wrong." He shot Daniel a dirty look.

"You have to admit it's a really different setup," Daniel said defensively. "I've never heard of anyone living over a semi-industrial space before—particularly not one still in business."

"Well, just wait, guys," I said as the lift started to rise. "You haven't seen anything yet."

Lyle had the place completely lit when we stepped off the elevator so they were able to take in the full living space surrounded by the screens that portioned off the various rooms. Even I had never seen it with all the lights on, and the effect took our breath away.

"Someone lives here?" Tommy murmured as he stepped off while Danny just looked around, wide-eyed and, I thought, delighted.

"Welcome and thanks for coming," Lyle said, approaching out of the kitchen and crossing the living space toward us. He had changed into pretty formal pants and shoes but had kept the almost sheer shirt, albeit with more of the buttons fastened.

He extended his hand to Tommy first and then to Daniel. "Lyle James."

"Tomas Kingsbury," Tommy said.

"Do you go by Tomas or Tommy?" Lyle asked. "Manny refers to you as Tommy, but I don't want to assume I could."

"Tomas is fine, thank you for your consideration," Tommy said, glancing at me and Danny. "These two are the only ones who call me Tommy."

"Daniel York," Danny said, taking his hand. "And I go by either Danny or Daniel."

"First, let me thank you for being willing to serve in the armed forces," Lyle said.

"Thank you."

"Can I just say you live in an amazing place," Tommy said. "Manny told me about it, but he really didn't do it justice."

Lyle chuckled. "Well, in his defense, I don't usually turn on all the lights like this, so I doubt he has really seen all of it until now."

"Exactly right," I replied.

"I've never seen someone living above an actively working garage," Danny chimed in. "I'm surprised there weren't chemical and possible contamination issues."

"There were," Lyle said. "Mostly ventilation and sealing the space between the two floors. Both the repair bays ventilate directly to the outside and not to the upper floors, and I deployed a special layer of latex tiles to make sure none of the fumes get into where I live. Now, how should we divide the labor? Who wants to grill snapper and who wants to cut veggies?"

"I'll take the grill detail, unless Tommy or Manny objects. I used to do that at home and I've missed doing it since I left," Danny said.

"I guess that's settled, then," Tommy said with a laugh. "Manny and I will stay here and show off our knife skills."

We split up, with Lyle and Danny heading off to the grill on the outside deck while Tommy and I confronted the small pile of different vegetables that awaited chopping.

"What you think?" he asked. "A great big garden extravaganza salad?"

"Let's go for it."

We had the vegetables chopped and in the bowl when they returned from the desk with a platter of snapper fillets striped and steaming from the grill.

"Oh my God, those smell so good," Tommy said, and my own stomach rumbled in agreement.

Lyle shot me a glance. "I'm glad one of us is really hungry," he said.

Danny spoke up. "Um, more than one of us."

"Yeah," Lyle said. "Danny was telling me they don't get any fresh seafood on deployment, so I suspect he's pretty hungry too."

Once we were served, the conversation revolved around introductory questions before it turned to the bombing and the eminent domain threat.

"I guess what surprised me was that they could try to take someone's property merely to give it to another private party who *might* do better with it. I thought if they were going to take your property, it had to be for a public purpose that benefitted everybody, like a new highway or right of access for a new water line or something."

"So, what's the next step in the fight against the eminent domain?" Danny asked.

"Well, we'll see what impact Jose's story has," Lyle said, pointing to me and using my professional name. "And now that we know exactly who is under threat of eminent domain, we can more easily sign them up for the lawsuit against it."

The party wound down as the meal ended. After we ate all the fish and almost all the salad, Tommy and Danny shyly let on they were going to head back to Tommy's place.

"Danny's only been home a week," Tommy said. "We're still trying to cram as much time together as possible into our schedules."

We both walked them to the elevator.

"Thanks so much for the invitation," gushed Tommy. "It was delicious and a treat to eat home-cooked food I didn't have to cook."

Danny shook Lyle's hand and indicated the many different works of art around the living room. "I hope we get to look at some of those more closely next time," he said.

"Count on it."

As soon as the elevator door closed, Lyle pulled me into a tight embrace. I felt his strong hands slide down my back to cup and massage my ass while he left a trail of small pecks from the inside of my neck up to my cheek before claiming my mouth in a hard kiss.

"Whoa, someone's a little eager," I said.

"I've been wanting to do that all night," he growled in a low voice. "Looking at the curve of your neck from that open shirt...such a sexy man."

A shiver ran through me, and goose bumps burst onto the back of my neck. He was hard against my crotch as we kissed. Suddenly, he broke free.

"Bedroom," he said.

"Oh yes please."

Later, while we lay sprawled across his bed like two soaking wet rag dolls, he checked for a message from a call we had ignored. A grin split his face.

"Oscar called. The doctor says Lucinda is coming out of the coma even faster than she expected. She suggested we come by her room about one tomorrow."

"Oh, that's *fantastic*."

I checked for messages and found an unusual one. I couldn't remember the last time my father had called me, and certainly not on my personal cell phone. When I hit Play, his gravelly voice burst into my ear.

"Jose, I wanted to let you know I just ordered a second layout for your story. We had it for page one of the business section, but now I'm putting it on page one of the Sunday edition. That asshole Deutsch called here a few minutes ago and thought he could force us not to print. Well, this paper will not be bullied. See you Monday, and come prepared with some ideas for follow-ups." He rang off.

"News?" Lyle asked.

"The eminent domain story is going to be the *Record*'s front page tomorrow," I said. "If someone gave Deutsch the idea Alfred Porter would back down to threats, he needs better advisors."

"Your first *Record* story, and you pull the front page. Congratulations," he said. "What will this mean for the story?"

"A lot more attention."

CHAPTER SIXTEEN

The Story Breaks

If I knew how good a boyfriend could make me feel, I might have tried harder to have one a while ago, I thought, before I remembered Manny still hadn't signed on in that role just yet.

He lay beside me, asleep. I usually like a little bit of morning sex to get the day off right, but since we had been hard at it last night, I decided to let him sleep in a bit. I carefully eased out of bed, visited the bathroom, pulled on sweats, a thick jacket, some boat shoes, and then went out.

The crisp September air that hit me as soon as I stepped off the elevator made me feel glad for my jacket and regret my choice in shoes. I walked up Jackson quickly, crossing a deserted Third Avenue and then continuing up the empty street.

On any other day but Sunday, I would have stopped in at Marilyn's little newsstand and bought a *Record* there, but I knew she would be getting ready for Mass now and wouldn't open until noon. My next best option was the X-Chex, a little bodega on Jackson between First and Second Avenue. I felt pleased Henry, the bodega's longtime owner, stood at his post when the bells signaled my arrival.

"Good morning, Henry," I sang out as I walked in. "How's the Chevy running?"

"Why, Mr. James, this is a pleasant surprise. Chevy's still running well, but she's got a scratch on the driver's door I keep meaning to bring her in about."

"Remind me, you don't garage that car, right?"

"No sir. A carport keeps the rain and sun off, but it doesn't have any walls."

"Well, don't let that scratch go too long. If the undercoat is damaged, it's gonna take more work and money to set right."

"Tell Parker I'll see about bringing it in Tuesday," he said. "Now, what can I help you with this morning?"

"Two of your good glazed donuts, please, Henry, and three copies of the *Record*."

Henry put the donuts in a brown paper bag and thumped three thick Sunday *Record*s on the counter. Across the front the headline read "City Moves Against Minority Property Owners" with the step-down heading "Almost 200 Sent Notices of Eminent Domain Proceedings."

Henry thumped the papers on the headline. "Terrible story about what they're trying to do," he said. "Have you read it yet? I saw you were quoted."

"Nope, that's why I'm here buying these copies. I'm looking forward to seeing what it says."

Henry lowered his voice. "You know, we got one of those notices they wrote about in this story," he said.

"Did you?"

"Yessir."

"What did you do?"

"We haven't done anything yet. Pearl, that's my niece in college, says we need to get ourselves a lawyer, but how am I gonna be able to afford legal help?"

"Well, my friend, as you read in the paper, you aren't alone. A bunch of us are getting together to fight this thing off," I said. "We don't know how much it's gonna cost just yet, but you know I'm in it, and so are Lucinda Alverez from Lucinda's Café and Oscar Torres from the credit union, and we're damn sure it's gonna cost less for us to fight as a group than to fight on our own."

"Well, please count us in it too," Henry said. "They can't just roll over people like this. Sure, we don't have a really fat bank account, but we pay our taxes, and I employ Emily and my grandson Terrance."

"Don't let it worry you," I said. "I'll keep you posted on what you need to do." I picked up the donut bag and the three papers and headed out.

Back home I left the stack of newsprint and donuts in the kitchen and found Manny propped in bed.

"Well."

"Well what?" I said, pulling off my shirt and hanging it on a hook.

"You've been out."

"I might have been."

"I know you were. I heard the elevator."

"Okay, so I've been out."

"Did you buy a newspaper? Is the story on the front page? Is it above the fold?"

I opened a drawer in my dresser, pulled out a favorite tee, and put it on. "Yes, yes, and yes," I said, grinning. "Yes, I bought a paper—three in fact. Yes, the story is on the front page and yes, if you mean is it on the upper half of the page, it is."

Manny whooped.

"Now, pull on the clean robe you'll find in the spare room's closet and meet me in the kitchen. I'll make some coffee, and we can read this monumental story."

I sauntered back to the galley, catching a glimpse of an adorable brown butt in a shiny cabinet door as I did. Manny was at my side in what felt like thirty seconds. He seized the top one of the papers and stared at it for at least a minute.

"Wow," he said.

"This can't be that big a deal. You've been doing the journalism thing for how long now?"

"Sorry. But this is only my second time on the front page. And Dad—my publisher—hates banner headlines. He thinks they're overly dramatic and a holdover from yellow journalism. I don't know what it took for him to approve this one."

"You get to reading," I said. "I'll make some coffee."

For the next ten minutes while I ground beans, heated water, and pressed java, Manny sat at the kitchen counter reading, humming, exclaiming, pointing, and thumping.

By the time I poured us each a cup and wanted to have the story myself, I could tell I was going to need the second copy.

"You act like you're reading this for the first time," I said. "But you wrote it, so how can that be?"

"I wrote the first draft. But I wasn't there when they edited it, and I never saw that version. Nor the laid-out version as it was going to appear on the pages."

"So, what do you think?"

"You read it first and tell me what you think." He stood up. "And this is important. I don't want you to read it as Lyle. I want you to read it as Mr. James and tell me what you really think."

"All right, I'll do my best," I said. And I meant it too, though I had resolved to find a way to keep anything bad from coming across as too terribly bad.

Fortunately, nothing in it stank. Though it could have used a few more graphs when reporting the stats, it still wasn't incomprehensible.

"The story's fair," I said. "Obviously I don't agree with this guy Deutsch, but I don't think it paints him in a worse light than his own quote. And you quoted me exactly and spelled my name right."

"Thanks. That's kind of the minimum bar, but I'll take it."

"One thing is clear, though," I said.

"What?"

"Well, the facts are the facts, but what makes this story is the analysis. That's spot-on. Is that yours or someone else at the *Record*?"

"No, it's not mine," he said. "But the official line is that one of our number-crunching staff did that for us."

"Why?"

"Because we worried that revealing it could help identify our source," he said, "and we don't want to do anything to compromise the source any more than absolutely necessary."

"Well, God bless them, whoever they are. That data and analysis might have given us what we need to win this fight."

Then I told him about the conversation with Henry, and his resolve to join in. I had a feeling this was going to be common across the neighborhood. By the time I finished my read and we discussed methods for turning the names and addresses into communications, we needed to set out for the hospital. I grabbed my final copy of the paper to bring with me.

"My gut says that if she's been awake for any length of time, she's already going to have read this," I said. "But in case she hasn't or just wants an additional copy, I'll bring it along."

The approaches to St. Clair's were as empty and quiet as you'd expect from an early Sunday afternoon, but not entirely. A large laundry delivery van parked in the staff lot close to the front, and I was relieved the GBI decided to send some officers. We approached the welcome desk.

"Lyle James and Jose Porter to visit Lucinda Alverez on the fourth floor," I said to the young guard behind the desk.

He consulted a clipboard. "Certainly, sir. I'll need driver's licenses from each of you." He collected them, then put them on a small glass window and covered it. There was a flash, and then he handed them back to us along with two ID cards.

"Wear these on the upper torso as long as you're in the hospital," he said. "Place the cards in front of the reader on any locked door, and it will open if you're authorized. Elevators are behind you. Have a good visit, gentlemen." We pinned the cards to our collars and went to the lifts.

Oscar, Esteban, and Dr. Lundi were already inside Lucinda's room. If Oscar and Dr. Lundi looked upbeat, Esteban looked almost transformed. His wide smile lit up his entire face and never seemed to leave.

"Thanks for coming," Oscar said in a low voice while shaking my hand. "I know she wants to see and talk to you."

"Of course."

"And who is this?" Oscar asked.

"Oscar Torres, may I introduce Jose Porter? Jose is the reporter who wrote that front-page story we woke up to this morning," I said. "Jose, this is Oscar Torres, manager of the Tinker Creek Community Credit Union."

Oscar took Manny's hand and pumped it enthusiastically. "Thank you so much for all your hard work writing such a comprehensive story. I think we really have a chance of fighting this off now."

I leaned into Oscar to keep my voice low. "Is she still not awake?"

"Oh no, she came out of the coma at about eleven last night, but she just dropped off to regular sleep about five minutes before you arrived," Oscar said.

Dr. Lundi, who had drifted closer, chimed in. "Irregular sleeping and waking times are a normal part of the recovery process," she said. "I expect she will be awake again in about another ten or fifteen minutes."

"Dr. Lundi, this is Jose Porter, a reporter for the *South Georgia Record* and a friend of mine," I said. "Jose, Dr. Lundi." They shook hands. "I should add that Dr. Lundi looked after me very well when I got too close to that exploding bomb."

"A privilege," she said. "By the way, how are the shoulder and arm?"

"Almost one hundred percent, Doc. Just for fun, I tried a couple of pull-ups the other night and didn't even get a twinge."

"Well, don't push it too hard. I still want to see you for final X-rays and scans next week."

"Shh! She's waking up again," Esteban said in a fierce whisper from beside her bed.

We all drew close to the bed so Lucinda could see us without raising her head.

"Ah, mis amigos," she said, smiling. "I'm so glad to see you. Lyle. You are okay? The last thing I remember is seeing you fly through the air like a doll."

"I'm fine, Lucinda. I'm just glad you're back with us again. I was afraid we'd lost you."

"Pah!" she spat. "It takes more than an explosion to kill this old crow. But I am glad to be back too. Esteban told me I was gone for five days?"

"Actually, almost six," Dr. Lundi said.

"And in the time there has been a newspaper story? Esteban read it to me this morning, but I am still not certain if I dreamed it or not."

"You didn't dream it, Lucinda. In fact, I have the reporter who wrote that story right here," I said, pulling Manny from slightly behind me to the edge of the bed where she could see him. "Lucinda Alverez, this is Jose Porter of the *South Georgia Record*."

"Ah, señor! Muchas gracias," she said, beaming. "You have done everyone in this neighborhood a very great service." Then studied him more closely. "How old are you, señor? You look so young. Tan joven."

I watched a sudden blush flame up Manny's face. "I'm twenty-seven, ma'am. Tengo veinte y siete años."

"Ah, a baby," she said, laughing a little. "Why don't you all go to the guest suite down the hall and get us some sodas while Lyle and I talk a bit. Esteban, you can stay, and Doctor, you too."

Dr. Lundi laughed. "Thanks, but I was already planning on it."

She waited until the last person left the room before she spoke again. "Lyle, Dr. Lundi says I can go home soon but not back to work—the restaurant, our efforts, nothing—for like a month."

I glanced up at Dr. Lundi and received her quiet nod.

"The café doesn't bother me. I trained a good staff and I trust them. But we can't spend a month doing nothing about our properties. This article gives us a chance to craft a strategy más pronto, understand?"

I nodded.

"Oscar will email you the contact information for an old friend of mine," Lucinda continued. "Her name is April Hewitt. H-e-w-i-t-t. She is local. I want you to go to talk to her. She will give us advice for our next steps. After you talk to her, we can decide how to move forward."

"How will I meet her? Why will she want to talk to me since she's never met me?"

"Tell her you are a friend of mine, and we are working on this thing together. I will be extremely surprised if she doesn't already know all about it. But in case she wants proof we are friends, tell her I know she made that deposit."

"What deposit?"

"That's all you need to say. Find out all you can from April and then come tell me. We can plan what to do then. Now, I can hear them coming back."

Sure enough, the door opened and the others returned.

"We bought you a ginger ale," Oscar said.

"My favorite." She smiled. "Esteban, can you put a little in a cup with some broken ice in it, please?"

"Yes, abuela."

A nurse entered the room with a tray of paper cups on it.

"Ah, and I am going to exercise my doctor's prerogative and kick you all out," Dr. Lundi said. "Here's the latest round of meds, and she won't be awake that much longer anyway. You can all come back tomorrow."

Esteban looked upset and cast sorrowful eyes up at her. She shook her head at first but nodded.

"Okay, everybody but Oscar and Esteban. You can have thirty minutes more, but then she has to be able to get some rest," Dr. Lundi said as Esteban settled back into what had clearly become his seat beside her.

We all put on our outerwear and left by ones and twos. We turned our badges in at the guard station and headed out in silence. Halfway back to the car, Manny said, "Did she say she was still heading up this group or whatever it is?"

"Yes. Well, no, not explicitly. She gave me instructions she expects me to follow, so she still considers herself in charge."

"What were the instructions?"

"I'm supposed to look up an old local friend of hers."

"Did the friend have a name?"

"April Hewitt."

"April Hewitt, with two T's?"

I nodded. "Why, you know her?"

"I might, but I thought she was dead," Manny said excitedly.

"And if it's the woman I'm thinking of, you know her too. You've just forgotten."

"So, who is she?"

"You might know about her husband, Gus Hewitt, because he was a real political character while he was alive. One of the first Black federal representatives elected after the implementation of the Voting Rights Act. He cofounded the Congressional Black Caucus."

"Drawing a blank here, sorry."

"He always wore a tux whenever he was on the House floor and was known for his speeches."

"Yeah, it's coming back a little. Didn't he do like a follow-up to a Frederick Douglass speech about the meaning of July Fourth?"

"Yes! That's probably his most famous. Well, he died in office as a relatively young man in 1979 and his widow, April, took over his seat. She held it for three more terms until the Republican legislature gerrymandered her out of a seat in the mid-1980s."

"What happened to her?"

"I don't know. I did a paper on prominent Georgia political families but don't remember too much from it."

"Maybe she fetched up here," I said.

"Well, he was a Georgia politician, so anything is possible, but it would be remarkable."

CHAPTER SEVENTEEN

At Sea Oates

Oscar sent April Hewitt's number from his mobile phone. I thanked him, then turned to Manny. "I have the number. Do I call now?"

"Why not?"

"It's Sunday afternoon. She doesn't know me from Adam."

"That's true," Manny said. "But Lucinda called her an old friend. People are happy to hear from old friends anytime. It's not like you're trying to sell her something."

Lucinda had described her as an old and *local* friend, and sure enough the number had the first three digits for the Tinker Creek exchange. The phone rang four times before someone answered.

"Hewitt residence," said a low, dry voice I couldn't identify as male or female.

"Good afternoon. My name is Lyle James. Mrs. Hewitt and I share a mutual friend, Ms. Lucinda Alverez. Ms. Alverez suggested I should call Mrs. Hewitt and request an appointment."

"Hold the line, please," the voice said, letting me listen to Duke Ellington's "Sophisticated Lady" for two minutes.

"Ms. Hewitt asks if you will come for coffee at Sea Oates tomorrow at ten a.m. You may bring one associate if you wish."

"Thank you."

"Thank you," the voice said. "She will expect you then."

"Oscar and I are going to Sea Oates," I told Manny.

"What's Sea Oates?"

"You know that big house at the end of Breaker Street you can only see the roof line from the street?"

"Yeah."

"That's Sea Oates. It's an estate a railway executive built back in the 1920s, and I thought a foundation owned now. I didn't know anyone actually still lived there."

"Is that where she lives?"

"I guess. It's where Oscar and I are going for coffee at ten a.m. on Monday."

Only Oscar couldn't make it. When I called him later to let him know, he begged out because his board of directors meeting took place at the same time.

"We got people flying in for this thing," he said. "And I am kind of the emcee and the main attraction, so I have to be there."

In his absence, I offered to bring Manny along.

He jumped at the chance. "Of course. She's a political legend. Meeting her will be an honor."

He went home Sunday night, back to the butler's quarters at Tommy's place. He needed to get some different clothes for Monday morning, and we both agreed slowing down a little might make sense. Though my comfortable bed had always brought me sleep quickly, it didn't do the job as well without him in it. I had to admit I missed him even after this small amount of time.

I picked him up outside the gate at Tommy's place at 9:40 and turned onto Breaker Street off Jefferson.

"Have you ever been to this place?" Manny asked.

"What? Sea Oates? Nope. I think a grade school class might have had a field trip there once, but I missed that day. It was one of those days Mom was too blitzed to get me to school, so I just heard about it next day."

Past the Dead End sign that let drivers know Breaker doesn't go on forever, we started gliding by the estate's walls with their cracked and faded yellow stucco. A placard read "SEA OATES Keep Right" as we entered a traffic circle. That brought us before a large wrought iron gate complete with a gargoyle overhead. I rolled my window and checked my watch. It read 9:55. I punched the button beside a loosely mounted wall speaker.

"May a help you?" A definite male voice this time. Younger and crisper. More military.

"Lyle James and associate for a ten o'clock meeting," I said.

"Hold please." There was a hum, and the huge gates began to open. "Proceed the length of the driveway, and you will find available parking on the left side of the front door," the voice said.

I eased the car forward as the gate opened.

"Lyle James and associate?" Manny shot me a look.

"I used the word they used when I set it up."

I knew from my city maps Sea Oates covered a fair amount of area, but it felt like it took us twenty minutes to drive past numerous flower beds, hedgerows, fruit trees, and ponds to finally reach the front. I pulled into the first spot on the left. We got out and approached the massive wood door with a dangling rope beside it.

"I think we're supposed to pull the cord," I said, so Manny stepped up and gave it a firm tug. Somewhere in the distance, we heard what sounded like a gong or a deep bell. We waited. I was ready to pull it again when the door opened to reveal a slight, formally dressed Asian man.

"May I help you?" he asked, and right away I recognized the voice I heard when calling yesterday.

"Lyle James and Jose Porter to see Ms. April Hewitt," I said.

"Do you have cards?" he asked. I reached into my pants pocket and fortunately found one of mine lurking there.

Manny whispered to me, "My cards haven't arrived yet."

The Asian man looked at him.

"I'm Jose Porter. I don't have any cards yet."

The man took mine and motioned us into a richly furnished entryway. "Please wait here," he said, disappearing behind the door ahead of us. We studied the space.

To our right a large portrait of a severe Black woman wearing mourning black with a single strand of bright white pearls looked down on us from her post above a large, inlaid entry hall table. Her expression managed to convey both surprise and disdain as though to demand we explain how we got inside. Up ahead, a diminutive suit of armor flanked a doorway set into the right wall. The antique looked entire, but about two-thirds the size of others I had seen.

"It's not enormous, but it's intimidating," Manny said, meaning the space. He pointed at the painting. "Who do you suppose she is?"

Before I could respond, the Asian man reappeared and motioned us to join him in front of the door beside the suit of armor. He moved forward, swung it open, and announced, "Mr. Lyle James and Mr. Jose Porter." Then he stepped aside, bowed slightly from the waist, and motioned us to enter.

Inside, sunlight streaming in through three large bay windows made it clear the room looked out to the building's southern side, and the built-in bookshelves on two walls argued for its purpose as a library.

In front of us stood a round, glass-topped games table with four ornate wrought iron legs shaped like stylized dragons. The platform had comfortable-looking medium-sized leather chairs on three sides and one antique wicker one facing us on the fourth. In that chair sat a thin, older Black woman wearing a bright yellow blouse and a single strand of pearls. Whether because of the luminance of the room or of her top, her skin could have been carved of ironwood or ebony, though I doubted any artist could have completely captured the network of fine wrinkles on her hands and face.

"Please come in, gentlemen," she said in a low, melodious voice. "Pardon my not getting up to greet you, but I have only just gotten myself comfortable in this spot and, like one of my cats, I am loath to move once I have settled myself."

We stepped forward.

"That's quite all right," I said. "I'm Lyle James, Ms. Hewitt, and this is my associate, Jose Porter. Thank you inviting us."

"Not at all, not at all," she said. "Thank you for coming. The pleasure is mine. Please take a seat, gentlemen."

We each sat in one of the leather chairs, which turned out to be as comfortable as they looked, just as the Asian man reappeared.

"Ten minutes, Duc," she said. "Then a full coffee service with maybe some of those biscuits that Alicia brought."

"Yes, ma'am," he said, disappearing again.

She smiled. "How may I help you gentlemen?"

I cleared my throat and leaned a bit forward in my seat. "As I described to Mr. Duc when I called seeking a meeting," I began, "our mutual friend, Lucinda Alverez, advised us to consult you about an ongoing situation of ours but didn't give us anything other than her assurance that you would know what it is we need."

"I see. Well, may I ask if this topic has anything to do with the eminent domain controversy I read about in the *Record* yesterday morning?"

I think Manny and I both sighed with relief.

"Yes ma'am," I said. "In fact, the reporter who wrote that story is here with us now," I said, indicating Manny.

"Really? I thought I recognized the name but wasn't sure." She sat up a little straighter and gazed at Manny intently. "Young man?"

"Yes, ma'am?"

"First, that was a very well-researched and presented piece. Thank you for applying the time and attention to the topic," she said. "Second, in order for you to continue in this meeting, I must have your assurance everything discussed and reviewed here is off the record and will not be used by you or another *Record* reporter. If you can agree to this, we may continue. But if you cannot, I will have to ask that you depart. Duc can call you a cab if you need one."

"May I circle back to seek other interviews to follow up on a topic or piece of information I might learn about in this meeting?" he asked.

She eyed him and smiled slightly. "You may, but I will not guarantee such an interview will be forthcoming or will be conducted on your terms. If you're thinking this is lopsided and I hold all the cards, you are correct. But take it or leave it, gentlemen."

She said this last bit looking at both of us. Manny gazed intently at the middle of the table. "Fine," he said, looking up at her and then over at me. "This was his meeting, not mine. I'm not crazy about your conditions, but it's literally your house, so your rules."

"Then we can proceed," she said. "Duc, you can bring the coffee tray?"

Duc approached pushing a cart laden with three large mugs, a stack of small plates and napkins, two steaming pots, and several platters of baked goods.

She turned to us. "Do you both take cream and sugar?" she asked.

When we each replied we took one of each, she smiled and clapped her hands.

"Excellent, café au lait all around," she said to Duc.

Coffee poured, Duc distributed mugs to each of us, starting with Ms. Hewitt. He also presented the dessert plate with a napkin and flourish for each of us before discreetly retiring again.

"Ma'am, what do you think Ms. Alverez meant for you to tell us or give us? Do you know more about this situation than we do?" I asked.

Ms. Hewitt took another sip of her coffee and set down her mug. "Well, from what I know of Lucinda, I expect she thought I would be able to help you construct a legal strategy to fight the eminent domain motions in court," she said.

"And can you?"

"Construct a legal strategy? Yes. You will have to do the work, but I have some suggestions and some of the means to help you. Although I never sat for the bar, I nonetheless have a law degree and enough experience to find half a dozen arguments you might use to stop that eminent domain move in its tracks."

She looked hard at Manny.

"Young man, you may draw on this part of the conversation on background for future stories, subject to Mr. James's limitations."

"Thank you," Manny said, pulling out his notebook and pen.

She turned to me. "I presume you have access to the list of property owners as well as the analysis of their socioeconomic status."

"Yes."

"The first thing you need to do is to establish how many of those property owners actually have problems with their properties which could make them vulnerable to an eminent domain filing," she said. "That means a letter to each of them, but you'll probably have to do site visits to each of them as well."

"Why?" I said. There was no way we had either the time or the personnel to make that many visits. Not to mention knowing what we needed to find.

"Because you'll need to get as many of these property owners as possible to sign on as part of a class of litigants," she said. "That may not be very hard for most of them, but ideally you need them all to participate, and face-to-face visits will help. Second, a key element of all your arguments will be that none of these properties would otherwise be candidates for eminent domain if not for this redevelopment effort. That means you have to make sure all participating property owners have any problems resolved, whether that be code violations or tax problems."

"But that may be a huge effort. Ms. Hewitt, meaning no disrespect but, including myself, I have a staff of six and a business that keeps us all busy. I lack the people and the resources to be able to do this."

"I am aware of the size and scope of your business, Mr. James," she said. "I know you probably were not on the scene at the time, but your father was my go-to mechanic for my beloved BMW Z3 until I sold it. So I became familiar with your business before it became yours."

I sat back in my seat. "You're right, I didn't know." I sensed the grin on Manny's face.

She tapped a small button she wore like a watch on her wrist and Duc appeared in the doorway.

"Please ask Amos Whitlin to join us," she said to him.

"Yes ma'am."

"Fear not, we have been thinking about this problem," she said as he left.

I cast my mind back over my time with my dad in the shop. Surely I would have remembered a client as classy as April Hewitt, with a BMW Z3 as well. She looked at me and smiled.

"It would have been around the year 2000," she said.

"Was Parker working then?"

"Oh yes, I remember Parker quite well. I think he loved my car as much as I did," she laughed again. "Ah, here's Amos."

A tall Black man who looked to be in his mid-twenties entered the room, wearing a well-tailored suit and carrying a file folder. Manny and I stood up.

"Amos Whitlin," he said in a mellifluous voice as he shook both of our hands, then took the remaining chair at the table. We sat again.

"Amos is the executive director of the American Spirit Foundation," Hewitt said. "I invited him to join us because the foundation will provide some of the assets you will need to accomplish these goals. Mr. James, I believe you were concerned about the number of people these visits would require and perhaps their cost," she said. "Amos?"

"We've taken a good look at the list Mr. Torres forwarded to us and believe a team of five people should be sufficient to conduct these visits over the span of a week to ten days, or possibly two weeks, if some of the owners are hard to track down," Whitlin said. "The team would consist of one professional researcher who is already on the foundation staff and four senior level undergraduate or graduate college students the foundation would hire. The foundation already has a relationship with over a dozen students of this type, so we don't anticipate problems in locating necessary people."

"What about training?" I asked.

"Training?"

"Training in what to look for, how to relate to these property owners, that sort of thing."

"The students we choose will already have experience interacting with the public as census takers, pollsters, and educational surveyors. We believe they will handle this fine. As for what to look for, we don't expect they will need to inspect these properties to find any problems."

"Most problems severe enough to draw an eminent domain filing are quite noticeable to the naked eye," Hewitt said. "If a building has boarded-up windows or smells of gas or has a back or front yard you can't get through without a machete, those are the ones we want to know about."

"And what happens when they find a place with boarded windows or the back porch falling off the house? Who pays to fix all that?"

"That's where Oscar and the credit union come in," Hewitt said. "Or, in cases where the credit union cannot provide financing, the foundation may step in."

"While we can't know for certain what problems we may find in these properties," Whitlin said, "we know from our research most of the problems can be solved for very little money. A similar redevelopment effort in a majority Black neighborhood of San Francisco, for example, condemned properties that needed, on average, just over fifteen hundred dollars' worth of work and none of them needed more than five thousand."

"What about property owners who owe back taxes," I asked. "Those aren't going to show up in site visits."

"But they will show up in city records," Whitlin said with a smile. "The students are the ones who will perform the site visits, but our researcher will conduct a review of city records to see who, if anyone, has overdue tax bills or liens."

"But I doubt the credit union is going to want to finance those types of problems."

"True," April Hewitt spoke up. "So in that situation, the foundation is prepared to act. But just as with the amounts for repairs, research has shown the property owners of color lose their property for sometimes the smallest amounts of money. If the late fees are stripped away, which they often can be, sometimes for less than two thousand dollars."

"May I ask a question?" Manny piped up.

"Of course," Ms. Hewitt said. "Amos, Mr. Porter is the reporter who broke the story in yesterday's *Record*."

"You're assuming all the property owners will go along with this effort and join the litigant class, but isn't it possible that some won't? I mean, one of the things about eminent domain is that they have to pay you for your property. Maybe some property owners would welcome a guaranteed purchaser for what might have been a hard property to sell. What about them?"

"Certainly, that's true," Hewitt replied. "And in those cases, they don't have to join. Maybe for them a condemnation and subsequent payout minus back taxes, if any, might be the best course. But we can't know that in advance," she said. "All we can do is try."

Amos caught Ms. Hewitt's eye. She nodded. "First, I reaffirm what she said. We will cast participating in this case as an opportunity for those who didn't want to leave their homes, not as a burden for those who do. But I also want to express my admiration to Mr. Porter here for arranging to get the ever-so-slippery Alex Deutsch on the record as part of his story. I know a fair number of people who tried and failed to do that."

Manny blushed but spoke up quickly. "I wish I could take credit for having done some magic, but all I did was call the mayor's office for a spokesman on the issue, and they gave me Deutsch as a consultant. I didn't even know enough to ask for him."

"Really?" Amos said. "That suggests more disorganization on their part than we expected."

"If you two will be able to stay for lunch, we would like to share some information we have about Mr. Deutsch with you," Ms. Hewitt said.

I shot Manny a glance and he shrugged. "As long as we can call our offices to check in, I imagine that would be fine," I said.

She tapped the button on her wristband again, and Duc reappeared at the door.

"There will be four for lunch, Duc."

"Yes ma'am."

She turned back to us. "Once we have a list of property owners who have agreed to join the suit, we can proceed with finding a legal firm to take the case. I have some possibilities in mind, but nothing concrete yet. With that said, I am going to suggest we take a break to make necessary phone calls and take some fresh air. Mr. Duc will call us with the dinner bell when lunch is ready."

She tapped the button on her wrist and Duc appeared at the door.

"I'm going to my suite, Duc. I would like to unwind a bit before lunch."

"Yes ma'am."

I heard Manny from the hall checking voice mail and returning calls while I examined the set of French doors between the bay windows. They were locked but opened easily when I found the switch. I stepped out onto a small veranda in front of Ms. Hewitt's garden, and I decided to explore.

After a brief stroll, I came upon a clearing where a bench stood underneath a lovely pair of trees. I sat and checked voice mail to find nothing urgently demanding my attention. I thought about calling Parker but decided to sit and enjoy the fall sunshine instead.

I had almost decided I needed to get back to the house when Amos crunched up the path to where I sat.

"Oh, hey," he said.

"Hey," I replied, then decided to take the plunge. "Thanks for all your help in there and going forward. Believe me, prior to today, I really had no strategy."

"We didn't have one either until Ms. Hewitt found that article in the paper yesterday. She followed the eminent domain situation through Ms. Alverez until the explosion but she lost contact after Ms. Alverez's injury. If you hadn't called us, I expect we would have invited you to come to lunch," he said with a grin.

We had turned to head back to the house when a deep gong resonated across the grounds. "We'll be right on time," he said.

Duc met Manny, Amos, and me on the veranda and led us through the previous space into a bright dining room in the rear of the structure. A medium-sized square table had been set with a tablecloth, blue and white plates, light glasses, and a vase of yellow roses whose aroma perfumed the room.

We each stood waiting for Ms. Hewitt to arrive, and when she appeared, she did so on her own, unassisted but for a cane.

"Gentlemen, please sit down. I shan't start feeling rushed by the concern that people stand about waiting for me."

Amos pulled her chair away from the table as he was the closest to her chair, and she sank down with a happy sigh, breathing in the scent of the centerpiece. The rest of us took our seats as Amos slid hers into the table.

"Roses are lovely any time of year," she said, "but they're especially beautiful in the late summer when it feels like they are holding the stage for their encore."

Duc appeared again with a lunch cart upon which sat a medium tureen and four small salads. He set each down to the sides of our larger plates, then began filling the bowls with a creamy soup that smelled faintly of dill.

"Gentlemen, vichyssoise and Caesar salad," Ms. Hewitt declared. "Bon appétit."

I hesitantly dipped into my soup as I do not generally favor any food served at room temperature, but found this one tastier than I expected. Ms. Hewitt cleared her throat and addressed Amos.

"I believe we promised our guests a discussion of Mr. Deutsch and his likely role in all this."

"We did," Amos said. "Under different conditions, I would usually present this information in a more formal way, but since we hadn't anticipated discussing Mr. Deutsch, I will proceed less formally."

"Mr. Porter, likewise, this is on background from the foundation's point of view, though how Mr. James prefers you treat the information will depend on him," Ms. Hewitt said.

"I understand," Manny said.

"Alex Deutsch is the chairman and CEO of FairWinds Holdings, LLC, a multinational company chartered in the Netherlands but headquartered in the Cayman Islands," Amos said. "Since the company is privately held and does not issue stock, we have only a general understanding of its structure and no real knowledge at all of its governance or decision-making. So we know, for example, that it is divided broadly into three divisions, but we know little to nothing about how each of these divisions functions.

"FairWinds Development handles the company's real estate, most often in underdeveloped markets in Asia and Africa, where regulation and operational controls are found less frequently. FairWinds Logistics runs the company's network of cargo tankers and warehouses. FairWinds Finance provides financial consultations and investments to well-heeled international clients looking for a return on investment without too many questions from tax authorities."

"And all these are illegal?" I asked.

"No," Amos replied. "Like organized crime everywhere, Fair-Winds LLC represents a mixture of the unsavory with the aboveboard."

"As in how," I asked.

"Well, provided you comply with existing regulations, real estate development is a perfectly legal business," Amos declared. "But structuring your real estate development project so investors can use it to launder funds is not. Providing financial advice and investment tips is perfectly legal almost all the time. But advising clients to use your projects or any others to launder their gains is not."

"So why is Deutsch involved here in Tinker Creek?" Manny asked. "Since you said FairWinds Development works primarily in the developing world?"

"Obviously, we don't know. But there is a long history, stretching back into at least the 1940s, of public officials explicitly using 'economic redevelopment' to disrupt Black communities sitting on high-value natural resources. In the past few years, awareness has built about this issue and it has increasingly fallen out of favor with legitimate developers."

"What do we know about Deutsch himself?" Manny asked.

"Again, the basics, but not as much as we want," Amos said. "He was born in then-Rhodesia and holds passports from South Africa, the United Kingdom, and the Netherlands. His net worth is a black box since, officially, he doesn't own anything and tends to use FairWinds assets as his own."

"Do we know anything about what Americans he might be working with?" I said. Then I described my encounter with James O'Hara, the town clerk, and Manny mentioned he hadn't been in the job for long.

"That would be interesting to know." Amos flipped open a notebook and started taking notes.

"You know, O'Hara used to be police chief here until he moved on, right before we announced a lawsuit against him and the city for three blatant incidents of police abuse and civil rights violations," Hewitt said. "We never went to court because the city offered settlement terms favorable to our client, but I was always interested in one of the city's supposed lines of defense had we gone to court."

"Which was?" Manny asked.

"The rumor was the general counsel was going to argue that since O'Hara had previously served as a police executive for many years overseas, he was not yet accustomed to the different rules around officer conduct and training in the U.S."

"That's interesting," Manny said. "Where had he been a police executive before here?"

"Belfast, Northern Ireland," Hewitt replied.

Duc returned, gathered our empty bowls and plates, and replaced them with lemon poached salmon, a collection of thin baby leeks draped in hollandaise sauce, and another little pile of marble-sized yellow potatoes, shining from a pat of butter. Topping off these delicious-looking plates, Duc placed a bread tray on the table with a cluster of Parker House rolls, still steaming from the oven.

In the face of this delectable meal, conversation moved to more appealing subjects. Ms. Hewitt described, with a mixture of poignancy and humor, the barriers she confronted taking over her husband's seat in the House. And Amos had us all laughing with his description of the brotherly rivalry that dominated his youth.

"I think it helps he lives in New York and I live here," Amos said.

"I'm just not sure any state short of California or Texas is big enough to hold two Whitlows."

Manny and I kept mostly silent. Duc came to collect the plates, and Ms. Hewitt offered coffee and dessert, but to my relief Manny declined and said he had to get back to the office. When we left Ms. Hewitt in the dining room, she kissed me and Manny on our cheeks, called us chéri, and urged me to pick up the phone and summon her if I needed anything in the weeks ahead. Amos showed us out, walking us all the way back to our car.

"Thank you again for coming," he said to each of us as he shook our hands. "It's always a treat to meet some of the people involved in much the same work we are."

"When do you anticipate getting started with the visits?" I said.

"We're working on letters now, so they should drop tomorrow. We'll start the visits the day after."

We remained mostly quiet on the drive on Breaker Street. Manny accepted my offer of a lift back to the paper, so I kept going past my usual turn. While waiting for a knot of post-season tourists to cross at Jefferson I asked him what "background" meant.

"If you tell me something on background, that signifies I can't quote you or really anyone specific as having told me, but I can paraphrase what you told me and use it in a story. Background information usually provides context or history for a given set of facts. So, for instance, as this story continues, I will have the information about FairWinds LLC to add to the next article. However, and this is important, background information is still subject to the multiple source rule, so I wouldn't feel comfortable using it unless I got two other independent sources to confirm what they told us about FairWinds."

"So practically, there isn't any way you can use it," I said. "Where are you going to find even one more source who knows about this stuff but who doesn't know Hewitt or the foundation?"

The light finally turned, and we proceeded past the line of usual beach shops, some of which had their seasonal closeout sale signs in windows.

"There are some sources I can try," he said. "For example, Interpol. They're not likely to let me quote them, but their public affairs staff is pretty good about letting a reporter know if he or she is on the right trail or not. Plus, they can also point me to any cases in other courts where FairWinds was charged and maybe even convicted. Those court case transcripts could provide another source to confirm what Hewitt told us."

"So you would just call up Interpol, just like that?"

"Well, I would start with their public affairs office and go from there," he said. "The worst they can say is no."

We came to the end of Breaker, and I turned right on Washington, heading for the freeway entrance.

CHAPTER EIGHTEEN

217 Breaker Street

As soon as Lyle dropped me off at the *Record*, I swung by Tommy's office. "Hey," I said. "What time is it in Lyon, France?"

"Good afternoon to you too. What am I, Google? Get your own answers."

"You're sitting right there, and it's already open."

"Ten o'clock at night."

"Are you sure?"

"Of course I'm sure. Continental Europe is six hours in front of us. Why?"

"It's too late to do it today, but I need to confirm some things with a source who I hope is still there."

We resumed the conversation the next morning over coffee in the kitchen while Danny made breakfast.

"Let me borrow your cell phone," I said, spotting the telltale square shape in the pocket of his robe.

"Why?" he asked, yawning. "God, cloudy mornings make me sleepy."

"Because I know your plan probably lets you call Europe for free, whereas mine charges me more if I call Atlanta. And you wouldn't be so sleepy in the morning if you and Commander Dan over there weren't up doing the nasty until all hours."

Dan turned away from the stove briefly, eyebrow cocked, and blew me a kiss.

"And I wish he would wear a shirt more often. It's distracting."

"Meow," Tommy said, pushing his phone to me. "Don't be jealous. It's not like you don't have plenty of beef in your fridge over at Bonne Chance."

"Yeah, well."

"Make the call in the living room. The reception's better there, and I would hate it if Dan made you lose your train of thought."

I retreated to the living room. Consulting my own mobile, I tried the first French number I had. The phone rang twice, then bleated the familiar tone for disconnected lines. Undaunted, I moved on to the next.

Two rings. A pickup.

"Interpol, bonjour."

"Veuillez me connecter au bureau de Bruno Carlisle," I said, straining to make my lips slide along the unctuous syllables with as much authority as possible.

"Oui, monsieur. Un instant s'il vous plaît."

The two rings. Another pickup.

"Bureau de l'inspecteur Carlisle, bonjour."

"Inspector Carlisle, please."

"Who may I say is calling?"

"Jose Porter."

"Will he know who you are?"

"Oui, mademoiselle."

"Please hold."

Three heartbeats and a familiar growl of a long-term Highland whiskey drinker filled my ear.

"Carlisle."

"Inspector Carlisle? This is Jose Porter. You might remember me from the FinCin anti-money laundering conference last year? I wrote about your presentation in the *Financial Times*."

Silence.

"I wrote about your insights into the money laundering process."

"Oh, yes. I'm sorry I am not as clear on your name, but I remember the story. I thought you did a fine job. I meant to drop you a note but never got around to it. How have you been?"

"Very good, sir. I've moved on from the *FT* to work for a paper stateside, and I have a few questions I wondered if you could help me answer."

"I dunno, laddie. I'm not authorized to talk to reporters these days. Have you called down to the public affairs office?"

"I haven't, but I'm not looking for quotes or to put your name in the paper. I've just been given some information by another source I was hoping you could confirm or deny for me. None of it directly ties to Interpol."

"Well, how long do you need?"

"No more than five, sir. Seven at the very most."

"Go ahead and shoot. No promises, though, and I'm taking your word the blessed name of Carlisle doesn't appear in print anywhere, got it?"

"Absolutely."

I went on to recount what Amos said concerning the three divisions of FairWinds and its Alex Deutsch.

He gave a deep sigh. "First, laddie, I don't know what you're asking about them for, but you should know they aren't a good bunch. Not at all. Second, I have good news and bad news. The good news is that your source gave you a pretty accurate picture of how law enforcement worldwide *thinks* FairWinds is structured. The key word there is *thinks*. Everything they told you is our best *supposition*, and there are no more court-tested facts in what you told me than there are teetotalers in Glasgow."

He paused and I heard him take a sip of something.

"Further, they're a litigious bunch. If you publish as fact any of what your source told you or that I am confirming, your paper will be facing a lawsuit so fast they won't know what hit them."

My heart sank. But I had one remaining card in my deck. "Well, can you maybe point me in the direction of any court cases? Any briefs I could read? Those are always on the record and sworn."

"Nae. One of the things that makes these folk so damn dangerous is that they're damn good at keeping out of the courtroom. Her Majesty's Revenue and Customs brought the only case against them to make it to trial in the past decade, and that was a civil matter for tax evasion. The company won on the major allegations, and to rub salt in the wound, the judge sealed the transcript for twenty years."

"So I got a pile of information I can't use," I said.

"At least not right now. But there was one verifiable fact in your account."

"Which was?"

"They're headquartered in the Caymans," he said. "That was one of the only tangible outcomes from the tax evasion case. Apparently, the fact Revenue and Customs brought the case at all put a scare into Mr. Deutsch, and he moved the company from its previous UK base."

"Where were they headquartered before?"

"Northern Ireland," he said. "Belfast."

Inspector Carlisle had to get to a meeting, so I thanked him for his help and time and rang off. The Belfast headquarters was a little intriguing, given that the town clerk and former police chief hailed from the same place. I noticed a call from Aunt Sammy had gone to voice mail while I was with the inspector. *I'll return that after I've showered and cleaned up*, I thought, and headed to the kitchen to give Tommy back his phone.

❖

I called Lucinda at the hospital and briefly explained what we had learned from our time with Ms. Hewitt and proposed following the legal strategy she had laid out.

"Of course," she said. "I knew we would need her ideas with me still in here."

She said she and Oscar had been in contact with the concessionaires and the city and decided to keep going with the rally and fair in Dr. Martin Luther King Park in a few days.

"We've had a lot of feedback, and this is starting to move," she said. "Already this morning two people have called to say those nice young people from the foundation have visited them and they want to join the case. So, it's happening. We have to have an event to consolidate and build support."

I hung up, promising to call her later to report on the day, then I started to get back to work. I had signed off on a fantastic paint job when Parker's voice came over the overhead.

"Boss, call on line one. Line one for you, boss."

"You really did a great job," I said to the painters before I grabbed the wall phone.

"This is Lyle."

"Mr. James, this is Amos."

"Oh hey, Amos, what's happening? I already heard your visitors are making an impact. That's fantastic."

"That's why Ms. Hewitt told me to call you. Our visitors have been out, and we're going to keep them out," he said, "but she wanted you to know they're being followed."

"What do you mean followed?"

"I mean followed. I started our visitors heading down Second Ave. at Jackson. Well, it was all good for like an hour and a half. But they just crossed Quincy when they noticed a car with two men on it hanging around on the street outside whenever they came out of the properties they were visiting."

"Describe the car."

"Older Mercedes. Sedan. A bit battered. Ugly color green. Tags too dirty and beat-up to be easily legible."

"And the men?"

"White. Mid-forties maybe. Both bearded. One in a cap. Both look like thugs."

"What do you want to do?"

"Ms. Hewitt said to keep our people out, and I concur. But instead of three, I'm adding an additional three to make it six. We originally thought one person on the doorstep would be less threatening than two, but I think two people are more prudent in the current circumstance."

"Should we call the police?"

"We don't think so yet. After all, whoever those men are, they haven't done anything, so what do we want the police to do?"

"Keep me informed."

"Will do," he said.

❖

It wasn't until after I got into the office that I remembered Aunt Sammy's message, so I called her back before I started my computer.

"Good morning, Aunt Sammy!"

"My darling boy who slept too late to take his aunt's call this morning?"

"Not at all. I'll have you know that not only had I had my coffee before you called, but I was also working. I was on the phone with a source in Lyon, France, so I couldn't take your call."

"Well, no matter. I especially wanted to call you because of that man."

"What man?"

"That man trying to justify the eminent domain. That Alexander someone."

"Alex Deutsch," I said.

"Yes, him. I thought you might want to know he has been here."

"Where?"

"Here at Au Pied. Multiple times."

"Are you sure? We didn't run a photo with the story."

"Well, unless it's the most extraordinary coincidence, it was the same man."

"Can you describe him?"

"Medium height. Five-ten, five-eleven maybe. Very fit. Gray hair but cut very short. Glasses. Modest dresser, but expensive. I'm sure everything bespoke. Navy blue blazer, white shirt, French cuff with silver cufflinks, no tie, gray pants, polished black shoes."

"Did he dine alone?"

"Usually, but the last time he had a woman with him. Young enough to be his daughter, blond, hair up, dressed nicely but not as expensively as he was. Off the rack."

"How long ago was this?"

"About five weeks ago. He's in on a Friday, the following Tuesday, Thursday, and then Saturday. Reservation made himself."

"Did he leave a cell phone number with the reservation?"

"Yes, of course."

I read her the number he had called from for the story.

"Yes, that's it."

"So, it's the same man," I said. "How did he pay?"

"Three of the four times in cash. Servers like him because he tips well. The last time he paid by card. That's what made me remember him. The card he used was on a foreign bank. It took us ten full days for the payment to settle."

"Where was the bank? Europe?"

"Hold on. I have the paperwork here. Merchants Trust Bank, Grand Cayman."

"Sammy, you're splendid," I told her.

"Nonsense. Just observant."

"One more question."

"Of course."

"Did he have a car? Did your valet team have to park anything for him?"

"Nope," she said. "Ubers. But the nice ones. Town cars or Escalades."

"Thanks so much, Sammy, you've made my day."

"My work here is done," she said.

❖

On a hunch I called Tommy. "Hello, Answer Man." I said.

He sighed. "I'm going to start charging one of these days, just you wait."

"If someone in St. Michael's Harbor arrives in an Uber," I said, "are they more likely to come from a hotel or from private residence or office?"

"Private residence or office," he said.

"That's what I think too, but I can't come up with a reason for why I think that. Why do you think it?"

"Because the hotels have taxi stands or relationships with existing taxi companies," he said. "When someone wants transportation, the doorman either signals the stand or the concierge calls the company. Sometimes the hotel gets a cut of the fare. Why?"

"I'm confirming a hunch," I said. "Talk to you later."

I reached for my phone and opened my Lyft app, then grabbed my jacket and headed out to wait for the ride.

I walked through the municipal center gates without being challenged but faced a stern older lady dressed in a security uniform once I stepped into the courthouse foyer. Everything passed but my mobile.

"Cell phones aren't allowed inside the court," she said, offering me a piece of red plastic with the number fifteen written on it.

"But I'm just going to the clerk's office. I'm not here for any case or trial."

"Mobile phones aren't allowed inside the courthouse," she said again, in the patient sort of voice a parent might use on an inattentive child.

"Oh, okay." I gave in, taking the piece of plastic.

"Don't lose it," she said. "You'll need it to get your phone back. Civil clerk or criminal?"

"Civil."

"First floor, room 129. Take the hall to the right," she said.

My footsteps echoed down the long, marble corridor, and I marveled at the quiet. Then I checked my watch and noted it was almost lunchtime. Any trials would be in recess and any staff at lunch.

Room 129 had a double pair of frosted glass doors but a small space once I stepped inside. A podium of the sort that speakers use stood to one side of the space, with a red-jacketed book and a counter bell. "Please Sign In and Ring For Service," the jacket read.

I signed in as Jose Porter, along with my phone number and personal email address.

"Just a moment," came a female voice from an adjoining room whose door I hadn't seen before. After a few, a young woman in a blue skirt and white blouse entered. She walked to the podium, looked at the book, and stuck out her hand.

"Mr. Porter, I'm Abigail Smalls, assistant court clerk. How may I help you?"

I took her hand, shook it briefly, and tried to look reassuring. "I'm doing some research in whether a certain person or company owns any property in St. Michael's Harbor. I wondered if you might be able to help me find a record."

"Certainly sir, we can give it a shot. Please step this way."

We walked over to the closest wooden desk, and she took a seat, motioning me to sit in the chair facing the table.

"What are we looking for first? Personal name or company name?"

"Let's try personal first," I said. "Alexander Deutsch—D-e-u-t-s-c-h. And maybe Alex Deutsch. Or A period Deutsch."

Her fingers tapped on the keys rapidly before she finally addressed me. "Sorry, I'm striking out on all Deutsches."

"No worries. That's still an answer. How about if we tried some company names?"

"Shoot."

"FairWinds, all one word," I said. "Or FairWinds Development, two words. Will the database give us any hits that contain parts of the words?"

"Yes," she said, typing quickly again. "But…we struck out. No hits."

My face must have registered my disappointment.

"Let me try something else. I've been looking at the property deeds database," she said. "Let me try a general search instead. That might be helpful." More rapid typing, but this time the computer gave a couple of small beeps at the end. I felt a thrill run up my spine.

"Ah, we might have a winner," she said. "Hold on." She moved the mouse around and typed a bit more before looking up at me with a smile. "The general search comes through," she said in a satisfied voice, motioning me to stand behind her where I could see her screen.

"So, according to this, this past April an executive named Hannah Mayo with FairWinds Development purchased a piece of property in

St. Michael's Harbor. However, in error, the purchase was titled in the name of the company when it should have been titled in her name. What we found was the amended title reflecting that change, moving the property out of the name of FairWinds Development and into the name of Hannah Mayo."

"Interesting. May I get a printout of that?"

"Of course, but I will have to charge you five dollars."

"Done," I replied. "Just out of curiosity, does Hannah Mayo own any other property in St. Michael's?"

"Hold on," she replied. More typing. "Nope," she said. "She was granted a license to run a boardinghouse from the property. But I can see that as data entry. If you actually want a copy of that, you need to go to the city clerk's office."

"That's fine," I said. "Thank you so much for your help."

After stopping at the sentry station to pick up my jailed mobile phone, I went to the lovely municipal compound grounds and sat on a bench beneath an old olive tree.

According to the document, Hannah Mayo was the true owner of 217 Breaker Street, a piece of property titled two days prior as belonging to FairWinds Development. The certificate didn't disclose how much Hannah paid for it on FairWind's behalf, nor any of the holding details, but it did state that because this filing was merely to correct the record, she didn't owe any taxes.

I carefully placed the document back in the envelope and called Lyle, loving that familiar "Lyle James" that rolled out of the device right into my crotch.

"Hey, sexy," I said. "Whatcha doing?"

"Making money, what are you up to?"

"I've been following up on a tip, to great success."

"Oh yeah?"

"Can you pick me up after work, like around six?"

"Sure, at work?"

"No. Come by Tommy's," I said.

❖

One thing about owning and running your own business: stepping away from it for a little bit doesn't mean the work stops. There were more than enough things demanding my attention to make me almost forget about picking up Manny. Parker and I watched the last customer's taillights vanish into the gathering dusk when he stretched and yawned.

"Damn, boss. I could use a beer. Want to join me at Fred's for a round?"

"Man, I'd love to, but I can't. I promised Manny I'd pick him up after work. He said he tracked down something else in the eminent domain thing."

"Damn, man. That's turned into a full-time job."

"Don't I know it. But the way I look at it, it's time and money I'm spending now to defend all the time, money, sweat and effort that everybody, you me, all the others, have sunk into this place over the years. When I look at it from that perspective, it's easier to take."

"I hear that," he said. "You sure that's all it is?"

"What do you mean?"

"I mean I seen the way that kid looks at you—and, hell, the way you look at him. Couple of times I've wanted to tell you two to get a room," he said with a laugh.

I felt myself blushing. "Nah, man, it's not like that so much."

"The hell it's not. Man, don't take this the wrong way. I'm not judging. I think it's great. I wondered how long it was gonna take for you to leave this bachelor life. I bet you're headed for your last single rodeo."

"No, man. Nobody is talking getting married," I said.

"But…"

"But he's still pretty special," I said sheepishly.

Parker smiled. "Glad to hear it. I'm happy for you. Go on, lover boy, go pick him up. I'll handle closing."

"Thanks, Parker."

As I pulled up to the gates at Tommy's, Manny stepped from the shadows and got into the car. He had dressed in dark jeans, a black T-shirt, and trainers, and carried a small purple backpack.

"Why are you dressed like a first grader's idea of goth?"

"Ha ha," he said. "I knew your clothes would suit. I wanted to make sure mine did as well. Let's go."

"Where?"

"Two seventeen Breaker," he said. "I'll explain on the way."

As I drove he told me about his frustrating conversation with Interpol, but his much more fruitful discussion with his aunt, along with the trip to the courthouse.

"So, you think Deutsch has been here?"

"We know he's been here. My aunt's seen him, and he paid for a dinner with a FairWinds credit card we know is authentic because it's issued by an overseas bank."

"You aunt could have been mistaken. And the FairWinds card doesn't prove it was him. Another executive could have been here."

"Who?"

"How about the mysterious Ms. Mayo?"

"If she was his dinner date the last time, we know she didn't pay for the meal," he said. "But I will concede your point that it might be another FairWinds executive, maybe someone sent to facilitate this property purchase."

As we approached Breaker, I turned left on First Avenue, drove one block, and then made a right onto Adams. We traveled slowly down the street until I coasted to a stop in front of a storage warehouse off Breaker.

"Do you have like a super flashlight in the back?" he asked.

"Yes, why?"

"Bring it. We might need it," he said, getting out of the car. I popped the trunk and got out. I hadn't been on lower Breaker for a long time, but the air still smelled of engine oil and ocean. I got my Maglite Industrial out of the trunk.

"Wow," Manny said. "That's some light."

"When you have to hunt the wet ground for a valve stem cap in the rain, the last thing you want is a feeble light. Let's go find this place."

There weren't any crosswalks in the first three blocks of Breaker, so we timed our dash across the street with care, reaching the other side as cars turned the corner from Washington.

Lower Breaker Street is a mix of poor-quality auto shops, warehouses, adult book stores, and strip clubs, all clustered in the shadow of the old three-story Empire Cinema. The Empire shut down about a decade ago and has remained the prize in several ongoing legal battles ever since.

We located 201 and went steadily up the block, sticking mainly to the shadows and surprising one or two homeless people on the way. Number 217 hung on a chest-high gate that blocked an alley between the two buildings. This gate also had two other signs on it, one reading No Trespass and another Beware of Dog. Between the two hung a chain and a bright, shiny, new padlock.

"So, this is a bust," I said.

"I guess," Manny said. "Or we could go over the gate and get a closer view."

"Except for these," I said, pointing to the two signs.

"So?"

"So if we ignore them, we break the law and maybe get bit," I said.

"Jeez," Manny said. "Were you ever a kid? We won't go in the house, but we need to get a better idea of the place. Plus, I have this feeling about the dog."

He reached in his pocket, and out came a black carabiner attached to a metal cylinder the size of a short cigar. He brought one end up to his lips and blew hard into it. I didn't hear anything but his breath, but to our right about a block away, we overheard a dog start barking enthusiastically, while from somewhere across Breaker Street behind us another dog howled.

"Dog whistle," Manny said, a little proudly. "I always thought they were a hoax, but they really do work. And since we heard dogs to our right and behind us but not in front, we can reasonably assume any canine attached to this property is either locked up inside where it can't hear or has moved on for now."

He took off the purple rucksack and dropped it carefully over the fence before climbing up and over, lowering himself as stealthily as a cat onto the pavement. I sighed and followed him, thinking this was almost certainly the worst idea I had acted on in a while. Once over, we quickly and quietly disappeared into the alley's gloom, moving forward twenty yards, then peering around the back corner of number 215.

A feeble streetlight showed 217 to be a sizeable bungalow built on pilings about fifteen yards away across a graveled parking area. There was a rectangular shape entirely covered by a tarpaulin parked in the lot. We couldn't see the entirety of the building, but there were no lights visible on this side.

"Nobody home?" I whispered.

"It looks that way."

"Do we go up to the door or not?"

The porch had been built from the same weathered lumber as the rest of the building, but the steps leading up to the deck appeared to be new. They were lighter in color, and I smelled the faint scent of newly treated lumber.

"I'll go," Manny said. "I'm lighter and I have sneakers on," pointing to his feet while I still had on my work boots.

"But only on the porch," I whispered. He nodded and was

off, moving catlike across the graveled space and up the stairs. I contemplated following him, but decided I could never take those steps as quietly as he did. But I could do something else.

Dropping to a low crouch and moving as softly as I could, I got to the covered car. The tarp had only been draped on the vehicle, so I could lift the corner of it easily. I almost let out a shout when the first glimpse of ugly green came into view. If nothing else, this was the car that had been following Amos's team. I went to the back of the car and lifted the tarp again. The license plate truly was a mess, covered with a mixture of mud and what looked like concrete. Nonetheless, I was able to determine it was a Florida plate and get a reasonably good idea of the possible letters and numbers, which I typed into the notes app on my phone.

About then, Manny returned, dropping down suddenly beside me. I almost jumped two feet.

"WTF, you scared me."

"Sorry," he whispered. "The porch wraps around two-thirds of the building. Basically, this side is living room, kitchen, dining room, and bathroom. The back of the house appears to be bedrooms but no lights anywhere. What did you find?"

"This is the car," I whispered excitedly.

"What car?"

I realized I hadn't told him about Amos's team being followed yet.

"I'll tell you later," I said. "C'mon, I want to check something else."

I moved quickly across the graveled space with Manny trailing, but went around the stairs and in among the pilings under the house. Here it smelled of stale beach and creosote, and we had to use the flashlights to see.

"Where are we going?" Manny whispered as I kept moving.

"To the end. I want to see how far back it goes."

We kept forward until we came to the end of the pilings and the end of the structure. If Manny was right, the building's bedrooms were above us, and I realized they would be over the waves at high tides.

"This way," I said, going to the right side of the bungalow. We came to the end of the pilings again and switched off our lights.

"Look at that," I said, pointing up at the bulk of the Empire Cinema building looming over us.

"What?"

"Anyone at any of those third-story windows would have an almost perfect view of everything that happened down here," I said.

"Yeah, they would," he agreed.

"Let's go," I said, turning my flashlight on and backtracking toward the front. We had almost arrived back at the parking area when a flash of color froze me in my tracks and made me switch off the light. "Stop. Kill the light."

Manny turned it off. Hidden by the pilings, we watched as two men strode into the parking area from the alleyway. They wore work boots, jeans, and flannel shirts, along with beards and one a cap. They looked about in their mid to late thirties, and they staggered a little. They'd been drinking.

They headed up the stairs with the help of the railing and gave me and Manny an excellent chance to overhear everything they were saying through the cracks in the boards.

"Key," the capless one demanded.

"I can open the door," the other responded.

"No you cain't," his partner said. "You cain't when you're sober and you are definitely not that now," he said, burping.

"Like you are?"

"I'm sober enough to gentle a lock," Capless said. "Locks and women need a gentle touch, and I can open up any one of them."

"Yeah, right," the other sneered. "So which one of us tonight almost got a beer thrown in his face, huh? Gentle touch, my arse."

"That only happened because that one bird's dyke friend poisoned her mind against me, but my wingman, aka you, was supposed to tie her up and keep her out of the way. There," he said, "the door's open."

The screen door slammed as Capless went inside.

"Ah, now don't go blaming me. That woman had a face that could chase the devil back to hell. Plus how much could a normal man be expected to know about rugby anyway," he said as he followed his companion inside.

"Sounds like Tweedledum and Tweedledee struck out," Manny whispered with a grin.

"Sounds like. Let's get out of here before they finish the argument."

As quickly and quietly as possible, we blended in with the alley shadows. The whole time I moved expecting to hear "Hey you, stop," followed by pounding feet, but none came. We paused to look back around the corner.

The living room lights and television were on. The capped one had removed his hat, so now they were both capless.

"Let's go," Manny said, and we hurried back to the gate which, to our surprise, was still shut and locked.

"Do they only open it up when they take out the car?" I wondered.

"Maybe. That lock looks like it's in the same position as it was when we came through." In a few moments, we were back in the car and headed over to Badda-Bean for a glass of wine from their small but quality inventory. I told Manny about Amos's phone call and how his teams had been followed by men whose descriptions matched the two residents of 217 Breaker.

"So what do we do now, call the cops?"

"And that does what?" I replied. "It tells them that we are on to them, that we know where they hang out, and that they need to change their tactics. It doesn't arrest them or stop them from doing these things, and it might make them more difficult to stop when it comes time to do that."

"All right. We have an advantage, how do we exploit it?"

"I have an idea."

I signaled Beryl from a nearby table, and she came over. "Gentlemen, your glasses look full, so what can I get you?"

"Who's managing tonight?"

"Jerome, of course."

"Great, would you ask him if we could borrow one of your private rooms for a few minutes? He can kick us out if paying customers come, but we need to make a phone call without letting the whole place know."

"I'll check, but I'm pretty sure it's not a problem."

She disappeared through a narrow door behind the bar, and a few minutes later Jerome stuck his head out. Catching my eye, he gave me a thumbs-up, and we went to the nearby room and shut the door.

I motioned Manny to one of the comfortable seats and rang Eva's cell phone, putting it on speaker. In a few moments, her husky, provocative voice filled the room.

"Lyle, darling, soooo good to hear you."

"Good to hear you too, Eva," I said immediately, shooting a look at Manny, whose eyebrows had risen a bit. "Actually, I'm here right now with the man I met the last time we went out. Eva, meet Manny Porter. Manny, meet Eva Almisra, the best photographer in the U.S."

"Ha!" Her laugh exploded over the phone. "Thank you, Lyle. That was true once, maybe not so true now, but that's okay," she said. "Mr.

Porter, I have been so anxious to meet you, ever since I heard you captured the heart of my tiger friend Lyle James."

I looked up to find Manny blushing. "I don't know about that," he said. "But we are very fond of each other. It's a pleasure to meet you, Ms. Almisra."

"Eva, please!" she burst out. "Ms. Almisra is the photographer you've hired to immortalize your daughter's trash wedding and who you have yet to pay. For Lyle and anyone Lyle loves, I am Eva. So, to what do I owe the pleasure of this phone call? Are you perhaps at long last coming up to Savannah so I can take you to dinner for once?"

"Sadly not," Lyle said. "However, we would like to discuss hiring you."

"Hiring me? My God, don't tell me you two are getting married."

"N-no, no." I caught myself stammering again, partly because I realized a portion of me thought that might be a great idea. "Not a wedding, another project."

"Let's talk about it," she said.

"Do you remember that time a few years ago when we went to New York and got snowed in?"

"Of course," she said. "That was the weekend when you told me that you weren't just playing hard to get but were gay and not attracted to me. Broke my heart."

"Well, after that. We got a little drunk and shared our life stories, and you mentioned you had done some work for the U.S. government."

"Yes. Under contract. But I told you I cannot talk about that then, and I still can't."

"I understand. I wanted to know if you might be interested in a similar sort of project."

"How similar?"

"Audio and photographic surveillance at a distance of between eighty and one hundred yards," I said.

"What? Are you going into the private detective business? Who do you want me to watch?"

"I can't tell you right now because it's a long story, but it's all tied into the people who tried to blow me up. I just want to know if you are interested."

"My God, Lyle, of course I'm interested."

"Great, can you meet me at Bonne Chance tomorrow morning? Anytime that fits your schedule, and we can talk about what this could look like."

"I will certainly be there and text you when I leave," she said. "And Mr. Porter?"

"Yes?" Manny replied.

"Please try to be there too so we can finally meet. Maybe we all three can go to lunch?"

"I will make every effort," Manny said.

After Eva hung up, Manny shot me a look. "I think I need to have some one-on-one time with Ms. Almisra."

"What for?"

"To find out more about her 'tiger friend' Lyle James, of course. What a character."

"She is unique. And what's funny, she's been that way ever since I met her. But a more loyal and talented friend you would be hard-pressed to find. She used to be in your line of work, you know."

"A reporter?"

"No, but a news photographer. Google her name when you get back to the office, you'll be surprised."

We left Badda-Bean and headed back to my car. Once inside, I turned to him. "Tommy's or Bonne Chance?"

"Is that an invitation?"

"If you think you still need an invitation, I haven't been very clear in my communications."

"I would love to come back to Bonne Chance with you..." he said.

"I hear a 'but' coming."

"But you're spoiling me."

"How so?"

"This. You. A wonderfully large bed to sleep in with a beautiful man who knows how to turn me inside out with pleasure. Waking up with you. Sharing coffee. Watching you show off for me on that silly monkey bar gym."

"Hey there!"

"I feel seventeen years old again. It feels like I'm living a dream."

"Should I be looking for a downside in there somewhere?"

"That *is* the downside. Dreams aren't real. We wake up from them. And I'm afraid when I wake up from this one, it's going to hurt. A lot. I've been there and done that, and I don't want to do it again."

I looked at him in the reflected light from the street, his dark hair cutting a line down his forehead, his eyes sparkling but worried. I wanted more than anything to kiss him then, a deep embrace that would reflect all my heart's passion. But instead I pulled him into a strong hug and held him there as minutes passed, letting him feel safe and loved. I hoped.

"I'm not a dream," I finally murmured in his ear. "And this isn't a dream. I would delight in you coming back with me to Bonne Chance, to my home and my bed. But that's something only you can decide to do, understand? I'm not going anywhere." I let him go then, and his eyes were wet.

"Hey now," I said. "It looks like someone needs a tissue." I pulled one from the package I kept in my door and passed it to him.

"Thank you," he said.

"So, Tommy's?"

He nodded. "For tonight, at least."

"Tommy's it is, then."

And I pulled the car out from the curb and into traffic. On the way there he turned to me again.

"I think I understand what you're contemplating, but just in case can I run it by you?"

"Of course."

"You want Eva to surveil 217 Breaker from...where exactly? The only place I can think of is the Empire Cinema."

"That's right. Only the middle part of the building is the actual movie theater. The rest is office space. I'm thinking we ask Eva to surveil with photos and audio equipment from one of those offices."

"Why would the theater let us do that?"

"Because I'm friends with one of the co-owners," I said.

Tommy had opened the driveway gate, so I dropped Manny off at the Victorian's front door.

"Thanks for the wonderful time," he said with a cheeky grin.

"This wasn't a date."

"But it could have been," he said.

"Right. Please join me for an evening of trespass, risking guard dogs, and eavesdropping on drunk thugs."

"Yeah, but I did it all with you, so from my perspective, it was a date," he said. Then he leaned over and kissed me good night, a surprisingly deep one that rolled down my body from my mouth through my crotch and to my toes. "Thanks for understanding."

"Of course," I said, though at that moment I don't think I understood anything at all.

❖

I made myself walk across the porch to the front door without looking back as I heard Lyle put the car in gear and drive away. Nothing could calm my surging emotions as hope and desire, lust and regret all went to war in my heart. Part of me longed to be with him again tonight, to feel myself bloom under his body until we both passed out, spent and lifeless as empty balloons.

But I felt proud not to have gone back to Bonne Chance, to have protected that corner of my heart he had not yet conquered, the part that would become my life raft whenever this thing with Lyle went south, as it surely would.

My key turned easily in the lock, so Tommy and Danny were home. I found them in the kitchen finishing up a spaghetti supper.

"Here's a surprise," Tommy said, looking at me. "When you told me you were going someplace with Lyle after work, I thought sure you would wind up at his place. I would have saved you some food."

"It's fine," I said. "I had a late lunch. I will have a glass of wine, if that's okay."

Danny got up and went to the sideboard, pulled down a glass, and gave me a large pour.

"Hey, you looking to get me drunk?"

"I was judging by body language," he said, shrugging. "Yours said you needed more wine."

"So," Tommy said, "why aren't you and Tarzan of the Oil Can getting all sweaty back at his place tonight? Did something happen?"

"No. Nothing happened. Well, maybe it did. Arrgh, I am so confused and pissed off at myself sometimes."

"Chill," Tommy ordered in his deliberately patient voice. "Drink a little wine and tell us what went on tonight."

I did. I drained half my glass and motioned for a refill, which Danny provided, then started talking, right down to the point where Lyle asked me if I wanted to come to his place, and I turned him down.

"So are you upset you felt conflicted about going back with him tonight or you feel conflicted about him altogether?" Danny asked. "I guess I'm a little confused."

"That makes both of us. I guess I felt conflicted about going home with him tonight because I feel unsure about a future with him."

"Okay," Tommy said. "That's at least a little clearer. Has he done anything to undermine your confidence in him?"

"Not really, no. But tonight we had a little awkward moment.

We were talking with an old female friend of his who wants to meet me, and she thought we were getting married. Of course, he said we weren't, which I was okay with one hundred percent. But at that moment I couldn't read his face. Was he thinking, 'oh my God, marry this fucker, what a disaster' or was he thinking 'that's at least an idea'?"

"Do you want to be married?" Danny asked.

"Honestly, I haven't ever thought about it. I want a long-term relationship, but I haven't ever put the marriage label on it."

"It sounds like you took his poker face to mean he feels ambivalent about any kind of long-term relationship with you," Tommy said.

"Maybe."

"But he hasn't given you any reason for thinking he's not interested in something long-term," Danny said.

"I know he hasn't, but I look at his life now, at least what I know of it, and I wonder where any space for me is. Or any long-term relationship, for that matter. He's one of the most self-contained people that I've ever met."

"But didn't you tell me a few days ago he's also the loneliest person you've met," Tommy said. "Maybe your role in his life is as simple as helping him not be lonely anymore."

"Is that enough?"

"I don't know. That's something for you two to talk about and decide. But I think there are lots of long-term relationships based on just that," Danny noted. "My parents, for one."

"I don't know what's gotten into me, then," I said. "I wish I had a way to know if he's the one I should be with."

"Manny!" Tommy blurted. "Nobody can know with one hundred percent certainty whether this or that person is the one they should be with. The best we can do is keep getting to know that person both now and as we change."

"I agree with Tommy," Danny said. "It's impossible to know if Lyle is the right guy for your future, but the chances that he is go down a whole lot if he's not the right guy for today."

"So, I shouldn't feel uncertain?"

"Did you hear either one of us say that?" Tommy said. "You're always going to feel at least a little uncertain, because love doesn't come with guarantees. But it's the uncertainty that proves its importance. No one feels uncertain about paper clips or confetti." He came around the kitchen island and wrapped me in a hug that soon drew Danny in too.

"You're my oldest friend, and I think Lyle really is good for you," Tommy said to me softly. "I can't know if he will be the long-term relationship you want, but I wouldn't bet against him."

"Nor would I," Danny said.

"Thanks, guys. I'm glad you're my friends."

"Now, how about you go put on some different clothes and come back. I'm pretty sure we have enough spaghetti and sauce here for another plate," Tommy said.

❖

Eva walked in on me fifteen minutes early, while I was in the middle of restocking tubes in the paint locker.

"Anyone in here?" she said as she stuck her head around the corner of the open door.

"Only if you want some paint," I replied, holding up a tube of red 429. "I imagine this might make for an engaging lipstick color."

"What is it?" she asked, taking the tube from me.

"One of the five colors St. Michael's Harbor paints its official vehicles," I said. "Since we got that contract, we have to keep their colors and their permitted undercoat compound on hand. Parker and Carlos are working on a difficult brake job, so I'm doing one of the chores."

"Can I help?"

"Sure. The shelves are already labeled, so just put the tube on the matching shelf, thanks."

The job moved quickly with two sets of hands. It wasn't ten minutes before we were done, and I escorted her upstairs. She stepped out into the living space and marveled again.

"I've lost track of the number of times I have been here, but every time I come, I feel amazed all over again."

"Thank you. Since I know you're someone who knows her way around design, I appreciate your approval even more. Please sit down. I can offer you more than coffee this time. Iced tea or mango juice."

"Mango juice," she said, arching an eyebrow.

"It's Manny's. He's here often enough that I keep it on hand. And yes, he showed me how to make the iced tea so it tastes good and not like one of my old socks."

"So, I take it that it's going well?"

"I'm not sure exactly what 'well' looks like, but I guess so."

"'Well' is that you're not at each other's throats, and you have things to do together outside the bedroom," Eva said.

"By that definition, we are doing well."

"Is the iced tea sweet?"

"Nope."

"So, a tall iced tea, please, and just a teaspoon of sugar."

I went to the kitchen and brought back two beverages.

She narrowed her eyes at me. "He is coming today, right?"

"Yes, he'll be here in about forty-five minutes. I decided we'd have lunch here, so I ordered pork and chicken barbecue from Lucinda's, with all her fixings, and that will be here about twelve thirty."

She sat back in her chair and sipped her iced tea.

"So, tell me who it is you want me to spy on."

I related our meeting with April Hewitt and Amos Whitlin, what they told us concerning FairWinds, and what our legal plans were. I shared what Manny had discovered about Deutsch having possibly been here and the location where we believed he might stay when he was.

"You're thinking a few things, then," she asked. "First, these two lunks at this house on Breaker Street are the same two who have been tracking your enrollment teams around the neighborhood. Second, that this Deutsch is controlling them somehow and stays there if he comes to town. Third, that the company really owns the property and uses it as some sort of safe house."

"That's about right."

"What about the woman? This mysterious Hanna Mayo? It seems like she could answer these questions more efficiently than I might."

"If she exists, which we presume, we can't find any trace of her around here. She can't be local, and we don't have the resources to look more broadly."

"You haven't called the cops?"

"And tell them what? That we think these two men might be taking orders to try to intimidate us in a civil court case? Besides, we don't entirely trust the local gendarmes."

"How come?"

I told her about my encounter with the former police chief, now town clerk, and that I believed the local cops tried to mislead the GBI about the bombing. "Do you not want to do it after all?"

"I didn't say that," she said. "But I have learned to seek the best understanding possible of a situation before I step into it. Especially one where it doesn't look like I will have any babysitters and the local authority might be hostile."

"Well, Manny or I, or I believe his friends Tommy or Danny, will be there with you most of the time."

"Which reminds me, where is this surveillance nest going to be, anyway?"

"In one of the west-facing third-floor offices of the Empire Cinema building."

"Access?"

"One door on the west side of the building front. We have one of four passkeys that also operate the elevator. There are emergency stairs, but they can only be opened from the individual floors and not from the lobby."

"And the amenities?"

"Such as?"

"Bathrooms. A fridge where I can put cold drinks. A Wi-Fi connection."

"You want a surveillance palace."

"I prefer to think of it as a well-feathered nest," she retorted. "Why do you think I retired from this kind of work? You get to a certain age and peeing into a milk carton loses its romance."

"There are bathrooms down the hall. Along with a Pepsi-branded cold drink machine that we can rig to give you free drinks. If you still want a small refrigerator, we can do that as well."

"You know this is like mining, right?"

"How so?"

"We could strike it rich in the first one, two, or three nights," she said, "or we could sift through the detritus of lunkhead life for weeks before we get something useful. How will you feel about that?"

"We'll let it go a week," I said. "If we don't get a glimmer of something by the end of the week, we'll pack it in. Now, how much am I paying you?"

"Nothing. Consider it payback for all your help over the last fifteen years."

"Not a chance. I know September isn't your prime month, but I don't want you canceling gigs."

"Who's canceling gigs? This is an afternoon or evening job, right? My two gigs this coming week are both morning shoots," she said. "So, let's compromise. My average weekly take in September going back four years is twelve hundred dollars. You pay me six hundred, and we can call it even, deal?"

"Deal. Thanks, Eva."

"Thank you. I groused about it, but I always kind of liked the limited spying I did. Doing it again will be fun."

The lift bell rang, and Manny's voice came over the mic.

"It's me."

"C'mon up," I said, pressing my thumb into the scanner. The machine kicked to life.

As the elevator rose, I felt my heart beat faster and tried to slow down my breathing. Nothing Eva or Lyle had said made me nervous about meeting her, but I still was. Lyle had met Tommy and emerged with flying colors, if not a medal, and I wanted to do at least as well when meeting his oldest friends.

The elevator doors slid aside, and Lyle stood next to a diminutive, dark-haired woman wearing a white cutaway blouse with small wine-red buttons and a long skirt over open-toed shoes. Silver earrings in the shape of fans dropped from her lobes, but not too far, and a red heart pendant made from what might have been a ruby occupied the space between her neck and her small bosom.

"Welcome," Lyle said, pulling me into a hug, which reminded me to close my mouth.

"Manny," he said, releasing me to indicate his companion, "may I present a longtime dear friend, Ms. Eva Almisra. Eva, this is Manny."

"Charmed, I'm sure," she said in a direct manner that seemed to flow straight from her gaze to her voice. She extended her hand.

I extricated myself from Lyle's embrace to take it. "Encantado, señora," I said, surprising myself. Until today, my mother alone could have involuntarily dragged Spanish out of me. She gave a delighted chuckle and a surprisingly firm handshake.

"Now it's my turn to be enchanted. Thank you, my dear. You couldn't have known my other language was French, but I received and accept your Spanish sentiment."

"I've been filling Eva in on what you and I have been working on lately," Lyle said, "and she's agreed to help us watch the house on Breaker a bit to see if we can't learn some more."

"Thank you," I said. "I think you could help us a great deal."

"Well, never let it be said that I wouldn't help the little guy," she said, "not that Lyle is at all a little guy." She smirked so hard I found myself blushing to the roots of my hair.

"Eva, be good!" Lyle said. "You've gone and embarrassed him."

"I'm sorry," she said, smiling at me. "But Lyle and I have known each other a long time, and we began speaking frankly a while back."

"It's quite all right," I said, determined to give as good as I got. "I can agree with every inch of that statement, from personal experience."

Lyle groaned. "See, Eva? Spreading bad habits."

"Nonsense. I knew he could take it if he's going to survive with you."

"Shall we go sit down until lunch arrives?"

"What are we having?" I asked. "I don't mind saying I haven't eaten since Tommy's oatmeal this morning, and I could eat a horse without salt about now."

"Lucinda's barbecue," Lyle said. "Pulled chicken and brisket with baked beans, potato salad, and collard greens."

"Yum."

"My God, a feast," Eva said.

Lyle's mobile phone rang. "Pardon me." He walked to the other side of the living room and came back after a minute. "One of those phone calls was from Lucinda's," he said. "I believe our food is on the way up. Would you please meet me in the kitchen?"

The rising elevator did contain our meal, which we shared family style. Most of the conversation centered less on their adventures together and more on her own escapades as a conflict photographer and occasional intelligence asset under contract.

"My family actually comes from a long line of lawyers and Christians," she said. "But by the time I was born in 1984, the entire country had endured almost a decade of civil war, so it was almost inevitable that whatever career I chose would have something to do with conflict."

We ended the meal by agreeing Lyle and I would meet her at the Empire Cinema the following evening.

"This job is going to be a nice change of pace," she said.

Chapter Nineteen

We Hire a Lawyer

After Eva left for home, Amos Whitlin called. Lyle motioned me in and switched the phone to speaker.

"Hey, Amos, can you hear me? This is Lyle, and I have Jose from the *South Georgia Record* here with me."

"Hello, gentlemen. Ms. Hewitt is here too, but she has a bit of laryngitis today, so I'm going to be doing most of the talking."

"Hay fever," Ms. Hewitt rasped out.

"We wanted to let you know we have had great success with our teams of property visitors. After we get off the phone, I'll be sending over a report about the status of all the properties we've reached so far."

"How many have you gotten?"

"As of this morning, one hundred and fifty-six."

"That's excellent!"

"And wait until you hear this. Our percentage of homeowners willing to join the suit so far is almost one hundred. The only holdouts are a couple of situations where the property ownership is in dispute, so it's unclear who could sign."

"Have the properties been mostly clean, or not?"

"Clean?"

"Free of issues that might need repair, back taxes, and the like."

"That picture is not quite as rosy, but not so bad. Twenty-two of the properties are in need of some sort of repair or restoration that impacts directly on their suitability as living spaces. Most of those can be addressed for under ten thousand dollars, and those folks will get a contact from the credit union to see what can be done about financing that repair. Only a couple are going to take more than that, and the foundation is going to help out with a grant as well as the credit union loan."

"How about the back taxes?"

"Six properties so far, but none of the tax bills is over five thousand dollars. The foundation is going to help out with those as well."

"It sounds like you all have it almost sewed up," I said. "When do you anticipate finishing?"

"Another couple of days, and that was part of why we called you. We think it's probably time for you guys to choose a law firm to carry the complaint into court."

"Okay, but I don't know much about how to do that."

"Not to worry. We have a candidate we think might be perfect, but of course you would need to make the final decision."

"Who is that?"

"Her name is Carolyn Mondial, and she's the in-house counsel for Romero House, a nonprofit organization that helps undocumented people in South Georgia."

"I think I know them. Don't they run a soup kitchen here?"

"Yes, down on Liberty Avenue, across from MLK Park."

"Why her?"

"Ms. Mondial has an interest in immigrant issues and worked as a real estate attorney before moving to Romero House. In addition, we have a good working relationship with the organization, so she'll be able to do the work pro bono."

"Well, you can't beat free."

"Oh yes, you can," Ms. Hewitt said. "Remember, there's all kinds of ways of paying for thing. Something can be free monetarily but cost a lot in some other way. That's why you need to meet with her."

"Text me her number, and I'll call her as soon as we hang up," I said. "What about our friends in the green car?"

"Still there. Still suspicious. But they haven't tried anything to keep our teams from visiting property owners, and they don't seem to have had an impact on the numbers signing on," Amos said.

I glanced up at Manny, and he nodded back to me.

"We have some news about those two and the car," I said.

"What?"

"I'll let Jose tell you since most of it was his work."

So Manny described how his aunt reported having served meals to a man who we believed was Alex Deutsch and how he linked him to a house on Breaker Street, and that we had found both the men and the green car.

"That's wonderful," Ms. Hewitt said. "I didn't know Sammy Fabrizio is your aunt! She is a dear friend and her food, ooh la la." She trailed off in a bout of coughing.

"Hold on," Amos said, and we heard different sounds in the background before he returned. "I had to get her some water. All of that is good news, but since we aren't going to do anything about them, I'm not sure it will mean a lot."

"Well, it will do us good to at least learn more about them," I said, deciding to refrain from letting them know about Eva and the surveillance.

Amos rang off afterward and texted me the number for Romero House. I dialed it right away and got a young, Hispanic-sounding man who transferred me to Carolyn Mondial's office where she answered her phone with a brisk, energetic voice.

"Ms. Mondial, my name is Lyle James. I believe we have a mutual acquaintance, Ms. Hewitt, who suggested I call you for an appointment."

"Yes. Mr. James. Thank you for your punctuality. She told me you would probably call. I have an opening tomorrow morning at nine. How would that do?"

"That would be fine."

"Until tomorrow then," she said, and we hung up.

"Did you want to come with me tomorrow?" I asked Manny.

"Yes, but I can't. There are other stories on my beat, and I have to get those covered as well."

"I get it. Thank God for Parker. Without him, I could never afford to have been away from Bonne Chance as much as I have been."

"What about tonight? I'd like to come over after work. Maybe grill some steaks?"

"Tonight probably won't work," I said. "We have the first of the city cars coming in, and I want to be on hand to help make sure those go as close to perfect as possible. Besides, I realized I've been monopolizing your time these last couple of weeks."

"Oh yeah. About the cars, of course it makes perfect sense," Manny said. "It'll be good to get some work in tonight too."

"Great, so it's settled," I said.

He retreated to another part of the flat to make some phone calls, and I settled in to review the spreadsheet Amos had sent me detailing each of the property owners they had contacted.

Next morning, I arrived at Romero House, a solid, two-story brick structure set back from Liberty Avenue a few doors past the intersection with Jefferson Street. It still looked like the St. Michael's Harbor Elementary School that it had been until the city built a newer, more up-to-date school in the late 1990s.

I got there a few minutes before nine, by coincidence at the same time a young-looking woman in a business skirt, blazer, and low-rise heels arrived. Since I got to the door first, and she carried a briefcase, I held it open for her.

"Thank you," she said in a familiar voice.

"You're welcome, Ms. Mondial."

She laughed. "I thought it might be you," she said. "It is Mr. James, correct?"

"I was when I woke up. But how could you tell? I didn't wear my coveralls, and I'm pretty sure all the grease is off my hands."

"My father is in the same line of work, so I recognized the white shirt and that brand of khaki trousers. And we don't get many Anglo men coming here. Plus, Ms. Hewitt said you were fit. Shall we go to my office?" she said, and I nodded.

After a brief tour along the way, we arrived at her office door. She unlocked her room, and we stepped into a nicely decorated salon with two windows.

"Very nice. Neither of my two offices has two windows."

"I lucked out," she said. "My office used to be the teachers' lounge." She crossed behind her desk and invited me to sit across from her. "Ms. Hewitt gave me an outline of what this is about, but do you mind if I ask you some questions to make sure I understand it correctly?"

"Not at all."

"You received a notice from the city of St. Michael's Harbor informing you that the municipality was preparing to condemn your property, is that correct?"

"No. I received a notice from Georgia's Superior Court for the First Circuit that a condemnation action was being brought against my business, and I had ninety days before I would have to show cause why the condemnation should not happen."

"All right," she said. "And you later discovered the other property owners in a defined area received the same or similar notices."

"That's right."

"I'll need a copy of that notice, and the notices of any of the other properties that are part of this action."

"Okay."

"Did the notice say anywhere on it who was bringing the action or why it was being brought?"

"No."

"I see." She took more notes.

"Do you think we have a winnable case?"

"I wouldn't want to say without doing more research," she said, "but I'm interested enough to start doing the work."

"What would we have to do?"

"Overall, there are two approaches to fighting eminent domain actions. We can attack them outright, and we can attack them on process."

"What's the difference?"

"Attacking the motion outright means we assert that whoever brought this motion lacks the authority to bring it. Usually, that's a more difficult path, but Georgia passed a law in the mid-2000s that stated explicitly that the 'public use' definition for eminent domain cannot include simply growing the municipality's tax base."

"But doesn't that prevent what they're trying to do?"

"You might think so," she said. "But based on what their consultant told the *South Georgia Record*, I wonder if they might argue they seek the funds to make the Carmichael Commission's recommended improvements. That might be their attempt to get around that restriction."

"What's the process approach?"

"The process approach means we say they have not followed the right steps in this kind of action, so it should be stopped. For example, I already suspect they made a misstep by not first notifying you they were thinking of filing this in court before they did so. But first we need to convince the court to certify these cases as a class," she said. "And that may be hard to do. I expect the other side will try very hard to prevent it."

"Why?"

"Because far more property owners lose eminent domain cases than governments win them. The cases tend to be expensive, and many property owners lack the resources to fight them, particularly when the government is going to offer them some sort of compensation for their property. Even if they don't think it's enough, they give up and settle. But by grouping together as a class, these property owners will have reduced the cost to a manageable level, which is why I think the other side will try very hard to keep them from doing that."

"What will you need from us?"

"I'm going to need your signature on a form that says you hire me. Your name is going to be on the title case. Then we'll need the signatures of as many of the one hundred and eighty property owners as are going to join us on similar forms, saying they join their case to ours. Then I'm going to need documents as well as a list of property owners who are willing to be deposed for this case."

"Deposed?"

"Essentially act as witnesses," she said. "We will want to do whatever we can to personalize the case and illustrate that real people, neighbors, and friends are at risk of losing their homes because of this."

"I get it."

She got up from her desk and left the room as I heard a printer begin printing nearby. She returned with a two-page document.

"This is the agreement that will make me your lawyer," she said. "Just initial the bottom of the first page and sign and date the second page. Please use the name that appears on your driver's license or other identification."

The agreement was a contract that bound Romero House generally and her specifically to act in my interest before the court and made me promise not to take legal action going forward in this case without consulting with her first. It set a flat rate of one thousand dollars for her services.

"Will all the other property owners face the same fee?" I asked, thinking that would be steep for some of the people on the list.

"No. Since you're the first and title case, the entire fee is there. The other participants don't face any direct fee at all, but I suggest you split the one thousand dollars among the total number of participating property owners so everyone feels they have played a role in helping the case," she said.

"So if we get one hundred and eighty participants..." I started doing the math in my head.

"Each participant would pay a nominal amount," she said. "Roughly five dollars and fifty cents."

"When would the money be due?"

"I think we would be fine collecting our fee after the case settled."

I initialed the bottom of the first page, then signed and dated the second with a small flourish. She stood up and extended her hand.

"Congratulations, Mr. James. You just hired yourself a lawyer."

I shook her hand. "I hope this is the start of a fruitful relationship," I replied.

❖

I felt a mix of emotions as I took the elevator down from Lyle's apartment, disappointment mixed with resolution.

On the one hand I had been spoiled lately. But I had to admit it had been nice to be pampered. Spending nights in Lyle's bed, regularly enjoying the dreamless sleep of the sexually satiated had been a revelation. Never before had I dated anyone as consistently exciting, frustrating, and demanding. As the elevator lurched to a stop at the street level and I stepped out into the drizzling afternoon, I felt the loss of not being upstairs.

But I felt a positive sense of resolution as well. I did have work to do. Now wasn't the best time in my life for a strong relationship. I had let hanging out with Lyle monopolize my schedule, and I couldn't blame him for that. I should have felt good that I put a stop to it. But then I remembered how he looked at me the last time I watched him peel off his shirt before he removed mine, and I almost stepped back in the elevator.

But I did have work to do. Abner Smalls, the *Record*'s police and crime reporter, had taken his first vacation in almost a decade, and the newsroom divided up covering his beat while he was away. Today and tomorrow were my turns.

An item from the police blotter caught my eye—an attempted armed robbery at Coastal Jewels and Watches, a small downtown jewelry store. No one had been hurt, but the brief write-up said the responding officer had been attacked with a knife and deployed his Taser. I dropped by the store first to verify the account.

Marie Trang, the shop's middle-aged owner, welcomed me into her establishment and locked the door behind me so we would not be disturbed. Two of her display cases were still smashed, and she had been sweeping up the last of the broken glass.

She had been alone in the store and about to close early when a fit young man wearing jeans, a hoodie, and a stocking mask burst in.

"He was in and on me so fast," she said. "He grabbed me, slapped me, and demanded I open my cases. But he hit me hard, and my glasses flew off, and my eyes started to tear up. I felt scared and I dropped my keys, and I couldn't see them on the floor."

She described how he cursed her and told her to get on her knees and find them, but when she couldn't right away, he swore again and smashed the first of the display cases. She stuck her head above the counter and saw him dropping trays of diamond engagement rings into a plastic bag from the neighborhood supermarket.

"Then he smashed up the second case with his elbow, but I think something went wrong because he yelled. I think he cut himself," she said.

While he looked at his arm in pain, Marie realized she was right in front of one of the under-counter alarm buttons that summoned police, and she described how she quietly and carefully pressed it three times, hoping someone would come fast.

"I think his hurt arm slowed him down. Plus his bag was getting full, and the trays weren't going in easily. He even dropped one tray and was starting to pick up the scattered rings when Detective Walker came through the door."

"You know his name then?"

"Yes. Detective Scott Walker. He introduced himself later. He said he had been driving a couple of blocks away when he heard the call."

"What happened next?"

"He came in and had his badge out because he didn't have a uniform on. The robber pulled a knife right away, and then things happened really fast."

She said the events had moved so quickly she could not see them all but that somehow the officer had gotten the intruder to drop his weapon and had tased him.

"The Taser was terrible," she said. "It made an awful sound and, you know, afterward the store smelled like burned hair."

As soon as the robber hit the floor, Walker had handcuffed him and waited for other officers to come collect him.

"He was very nice," she said, "and handsome."

After I left, I called the press desk at police headquarters. The officer on duty told me off the record that Walker had sustained a mild injury in the incident and stayed home today. They suggested I try him there and gave me his address, 464 ½ Second Avenue, down from Quincy, in the heart of Tinker Creek. I drove over but had trouble finding it until one of the neighboring business directed me down a side alley to a gate to its front yard.

Nothing prepared me for the half-naked man sprawled on a lounge chair facing the sun. He wore sunglasses, an NYPD baseball cap, and a pair of scruffy gym shorts while holding a reflecting screen in his hands at about mid-chest level. A white bandage marred the left side of his heavily muscled and tanned torso. Further, unless I hallucinated, a sizeable bulge in the shorts argued for a sexy daydream.

I quietly stepped inside, approaching close enough to view his washboard abdomen and to determine the reality of the boner. I was about to clear my throat and speak when he said, "You know it's at best rude and at worst illegal to spy on people on their day off work." His voice was a throaty growl that sent a shiver down my spine to lodge in my crotch.

He set aside the screen and swung around to face me, pushing down his glasses to fix me in place with hard, appraising eyes.

I blushed. "I didn't mean to creep, sir. I just didn't want to disturb you if you weren't the right person. I'm Abner Smalls," I said, immediately realizing my mistake. "I mean, I'm one of Abner Smalls's replacements. He's trout fishing in Vermont. I'm looking for Detective Walker."

At least he looked amused. "You've found him. And he feels relieved you aren't the competent but exceedingly homely Mr. Smalls. He spells our names correctly, but you're much easier on the eyes," he said, looking me up and down in a vaguely predatory way. "How can I help you, Mr....?"

"Porter, Jose Porter. I'm with the *South Georgia Record*."

"As we've established, since you're doing Mr. Smalls's job while he's off harassing innocent fish. I presume this is about the incident at the jewelry store yesterday?"

I nodded. "The police blotter didn't mention you had been injured."

"That's because I didn't tell the reporting sergeant," he said. "And I would appreciate if you didn't play it up either."

"Why?"

"Because I'm highly trained for physical confrontations. If it gets out widely that an untrained punk had managed to touch me with his blade, even for only a three-stitch scrape, I will have to endure a week of ill-informed joking."

"That's a pretty big bandage for only three stitches."

"What can I say? Nurse Ratched was enthusiastic. I didn't think I needed any stitches at all, but they don't consider an afternoon complete unless they stitch someone."

He stood up, which made the bulge in his shorts look larger, then he stooped to retrieve a longneck bottle from the other side of the chair.

"Now, as we seem to have lost the sun, I'm going inside for another beer and to cool off a little. If you have any more questions, you are welcome to join me or not, at your discretion."

He went toward a door in the building I hadn't noticed before. I briefly considered not following him. With Mrs. Trang's account, I had enough for a rough story. But the way his back and arms flexed and moved as he walked pulled me the way a magnet draws a paper clip, and I found myself hurrying after him.

He held the door for me, which I took as courtesy until I felt his hand slide slowly over the cheeks of my butt. I dropped my hands down to my waist as some defense.

"You first," I said.

"Suit yourself," he replied.

We proceeded through a small foyer with a rack of takeout menus on one side and a Dutch door with a glassed-in upper half on the other. The darkened space inside looked like an office.

"The redoubt of the formidable Ms. Basta, my landlady," he said as we passed the door. "Bitter as hemlock with a face that could stop a truck, but she holds the rent down and lets me keep to myself."

We climbed the stairs to the second floor and walked down a hall to the end. He unlocked the door on the left with 2A on it.

"Home sweet home," he said as we entered.

The room was larger than I expected, more of an efficiency flat. There was a queen-sized bed, a comfortable-looking easy chair, a television, a wooden card table that might be for eating on, a small refrigerator, and a two-burner hot plate. A door in the opposite wall led, I presumed, to the bathroom and a large armoire in the far corner provided storage. The room felt remarkably cool.

He opened the fridge and grabbed another longneck bottle from what looked like a dozen or more.

"Make yourself comfortable," he said, pointing to one of the chairs at the table. "I am," and he disappeared into the bathroom and shut the door.

I sat down and waited as water ran, until he finally reappeared wearing a towel around his well-muscled waist. He looked magnificent, like he could have modeled for a Michelangelo or Bernini sculpture but for the grotesque scar that ran in a jagged course from below his left nipple to above his waist on the right side. I forced myself to shut my mouth as he sat down in the chair opposite mine in a way that made clear his cock was about twenty-four inches from me.

"So, what other questions do you have?" he asked.

"Could you maybe pull on a T-shirt and a pair of shorts?"

"Nope," he said with a smirk. "I'm in my own home, and I feel comfortable. Are you uncomfortable, Mr. Porter?"

Whatever, I thought. Fuck it. "You're a detective," I said, "not a patrolman. What made you respond to that call?"

"The call came across as a likely robbery in progress," he said. "At the time I was only three blocks away. All officers would respond to that sort of call."

"Do you carry a sidearm, Detective?"

"I do."

"Why didn't you deploy it right away when you entered the store?"

"I started my law enforcement career in the Marine Corps," he said. "I learned there that firearms are the last resort. I still believe that."

"You received a small wound in the altercation with the alleged robber. How did that happen?"

"The gentleman lunged at me with the knife. I successfully parried his thrust and knocked the blade from his hand. However, the weapon had enough forward momentum remaining that it still scratched me slightly."

"I understand it was enough to send you the emergency room?"

He shot me a fierce look. "No comment."

"Last question, would you tell me how you got that dreadful scar across your chest and abdomen?"

"No."

"Thank you, Sergeant. That wraps all my questions."

"So, I can ask you questions now?"

"That's not usually the way it works."

"Fuck usually," he said. "Let's be different."

"What do you want to know?"

"Do you like what you see?" That smirk again.

"No."

He laughed. "Liar. Never play poker, you'll lose your house."

"Okay, so you're very fit. Fit people are usually attractive. You're not the first man I've seen wrapped in a towel."

"Why don't you stick around for a while? We could have some fun. I can tell you want to play." He looked hard at my traitorous crotch and traced his fingertip slowly up his abs.

"Naw, man, I can't," I said, resigned. "Any part of me that wants to play is not the part that has to meet deadline and get paid."

"I'll never understand what's happened to this younger generation."

"For this member of the younger generation, it's called making a living," I replied and got up.

"Hold on." he said, getting up. He walked to the chest, opened the top drawer, and took out a card. He flipped it over and wrote something on the back. Then he returned and handed me the document. "This is my personal mobile number. If you feel like some company on a day when you don't have a deadline, give me a call."

"Maybe I will."

He grabbed my hand with a steely grip and pulled it to his chest. Beneath my fingers, I felt the warm skin and the muscles moving gently with his breath and his heartbeat.

"There's a lot more like that," he said, "only better. Call me."

I closed my notebook, made sure I had my phone, and went back downstairs, my head spinning. I had never considered myself bad looking, but to have not one but two completely hunky men come on to me left me a little disoriented. I made sure to add his number to my contacts on my mobile.

I had finished writing up the jewelry store robbery story when my desk phone rang. It was Rosa, from my dad's office.

"Manny, your father's asked you to join a meeting, can you come?"

"Hold on a second," I said, hitting the Send button at the bottom of my story, then waiting for the Accepted button to light up. When it dinged, I said, "Yes. Tell him I'm on my way." I got on the elevator and passed my ID card over the reader on the wall. I got off on the fifth floor and walked quickly down the hall. Rosa waved me right in.

"Buena suerte," she whispered as I walked by.

I opened the door and stepped in, only to feel my jaw drop. Lyle was standing in front of my dad's desk and both were looking at me.

"Good, here he is. Manny, I believe you know Mr. James?"

"Of course."

"Mr. James is here on the advice of Ms. Hewitt, who I believe you have also met," Dad said.

"Yes, I have."

"I believe you're following up on the news that this coalition of property owners fighting eminent domain has gotten itself an attorney?"

"Yes, I just filed a story on Smalls's beat and was about to call the attorney for an interview," I said.

"Good. You don't have to now. She's going to be on the phone with us in a few moments."

"All right," I said, bringing out my notebook and pen.

"No sooner did she file to represent Mr. James here than Romero House was told that its primary operations grant was being severely cut—almost to zero," my father said. "Essentially, they were told to drop the James case or go out of business. She naturally contacted her client, who notified Ms. Hewitt. She sent him to me, and Mr. James suggested you join us."

I shot Lyle a glance that I hoped said thank you. We heard Rosa's phone ring, and then Dad's intercom beeped.

"Carolyn Mondial from Romero House is on the line, sir. I'm sending her to the speakerphone in your office."

"Thank you, Rosa."

"Hello? This is Carolyn Mondial calling for Mr. Porter."

"Welcome, Ms. Mondial," my father said. "This is Arthur Porter, publisher and editor-in-chief of the *South Georgia Record*. You're on speakerphone. With me are your client, Mr. James, and Mr. Jose Porter, who covers business news for us. Would you please tell us what you told Mr. James and then Ms. Hewitt earlier today?"

"Gladly," she replied. "It's been quite the morning."

After Lyle left her office, she'd accessed his case on the electronic system the court used to allow remote filing of briefs and decisions.

"That's where I found Lyle's case and entered myself on the record as his counsel. About three hours later, I received a call from Helen Barclay, the executive director. She said she had received a call from the Georgia Department of Human Services. The Georgia DHS official told Helen, I mean Ms. Barclay, that the agency would cut off our funding if I continued to represent Mr. James."

"How bizarre," Lyle said.

"Did she give any reason why?" my father said.

"No. When Ms. Barclay asked, all she was told was that we would receive a notice in the mail."

"I presume you're familiar with the laws and regulations under which Romero House operates," Dad said. "To your knowledge, is there anything in statute or regulation that would allow them to do this?"

"Yes, but we haven't done any of them."

"Thank you, Ms. Mondial," my father said. "Don't resign as Mr. James's counsel just yet, and hold tight. We're working on correcting the situation."

"Thank you," she said.

She hung up, and Dad hit the intercom button. "Rosa, please place a call to April Hewitt for me," he said, then he turned to me and Lyle.

"Mr. James, I want you to know that for at least this eminent domain fight, you have this newspaper's complete editorial support. Jose, if you need some extra help, just ask and I'll be glad to rearrange some beats to get you any help you need, understood?"

I nodded when Rosa's disembodied voice floated in from the intercom. "April Hewitt for you, sir."

"On speaker, please, Rosa. Thank you."

"Good morning again, April."

"Good morning, Arthur. I must say this feels a bit like old times."

"Doesn't it, though? I was just thinking that myself. I'm here with Mr. Lyle James and Mr. Jose Porter, both of whom I think you know. So, what do we have?"

"The foundation staff and I think George Canon is probably our path of least resistance," she said. "He faces a strong primary challenge and is going to need the Black vote. He's also the vice chairman of the Senate Health, Education, and Labor Committee, so he is in a position to make things difficult for that agency."

"What's our best approach?"

She hesitated. "Before we discuss that, I think we should go off speaker," she said. "Mr. James and Mr. Porter, I think we will serve you best if we keep our discussions with the senator off the record."

"And I agree," Dad said immediately.

"But…" I started to protest.

"Jose, you have to trust me," Dad said looking straight at me. "Nothing will be illegal, but we may have a very strong lever to pull if we can promise to keep some potentially embarrassing information private. On the other hand, we potentially lose that lever if you and Mr. James are in the room."

"But that's not the—"

"We understand, sir," Lyle said. "Thank you and Ms. Hewitt for everything you're doing to help with this issue. C'mon, Manny, let's go."

He clapped me on the shoulder, spun me around, and before I could object or say anything intelligent, we were halfway to the door. I tried to slow down on the wooden floor, but Lyle grabbed hold of my belt, and in a few moments we were in the hall, where he finally released me, and I turned on him in fury.

"What the fuck!" I howled at him. "Who the fuck do you think you are? How dare you treat me like a little kid in front of my own father."

Then, in an act of what I regarded later as temporary insanity, I balled up my fist, gathered all my energy, and swung at him. Of course, he parried easily, grabbed my wrist, and in less than a second, I stood in front of him on my toes with my arm held at a painful angle.

"I think we need some water, don't you?" he said quietly in my ear as he maneuvered us past a woman who edited the opinion page and into the fifth-floor men's room, where he released me.

"What the fuck, what the fuck?" I muttered as I paced the small space in front of him. "Of all the arrogant, ridiculous, pigheaded men I have ever known, you might just take the cake. How dare you try to speak for me. 'We understand, sir...' We *don't* understand! Or at least *I* don't understand! Arghhhh." My voice echoed in the empty, marbled space.

"Are you done shouting now?"

"For now. But I'm still furious with you."

"Why?"

"Why?" I shouted, glaring at him.

"What would you rather have?" he said in a low voice. "A little political story about what might be a long-dead scandal, or a prime seat on one of the biggest business and political stories of the year?"

"Both. I want *both*."

"Well, you probably wouldn't have gotten both if you'd stood in that office protesting and stamping your feet like a little kid. You might not have gotten anything at all."

I resumed pacing. "What do you know about it?"

"Manny, put down your pride for just a second and listen, okay?" he pleaded. "Tinker Creek is getting close to winning this thing. Really winning. Every day that goes by gets us a little closer, and the other side knows that. That's why they're pulling out all the stops and digging into the bag of tricks to stop us. What would you have gotten by demanding to sit on that call? Nothing. They either wouldn't have called at all, or they would have done it when you weren't here, which still shuts you out. But they might also have concluded that you're a hothead and kept you out of the real story too."

"Dad would never have shut out the paper," I countered.

"Maybe not, but he could choose another reporter. Nothing says the paper's reporter has to be you."

I stopped pacing. I didn't want to admit it, but that had a ring of truth. My father would not let blood ties keep him from making a decision for the good of the paper.

"Besides, your dad said it was nothing illegal, and I take him at his word. Don't you?"

"Of course," I said. "But you had no right to speak for me like I can't speak for myself. You aren't even my boyfriend! You're just a grease monkey hunk who knows how to use his dick, and that's not that unusual a skill," I said, stalking past him and out the door. Once in the hallway, I stepped into the waiting elevator and rode down to my office level. If Lyle James was cocksure of everything, he didn't need my help.

Manny was supposed to meet me at Bonne Chance after work and then go with me and Eva to get together at the Empire Cinema, but when he didn't show or answer his phone, I went on my own.

I spotted her car about a block away on Washington and pulled in behind her. Then I got out and went to join her in her car. The sun had begun to dip under the horizon, and the shadows lengthened.

"If I'm not supposed to be in the building, I didn't think it was a good idea to park right in front," she said.

I agreed, but I wasn't thrilled about her walking back to her car each night. At least one of us would be with her most evenings.

"Where's Manny?"

"I don't know, and he's not taking my calls, so I can't find out," I said.

"What happened?"

I told her about the other side's full-court press to prevent us from bringing this case and how Manny had been winding himself up to make a scene in front of his father that he couldn't possibly have won. "What do you think? What should I have done?"

"Maybe let him speak and then be ready to clean up the pieces," she said. "But it sounds a little bit like there was more going on." She looked at me. "Did you really frog-march him out of the room?"

I studied the car's front dash. "Yeah, I did."

"That was probably the single biggest mistake," she said. "All of us normal and smaller-sized people know you're a big, strong man, but we trust you to use your strength appropriately. Reminding him of how small he is might have freaked him out some. C'mon," she said, opening the door. "Let's go."

In addition to the two large camera bags she carried, Eva had me bring two more big bags with sound equipment. When we got to the observation floor, she began setting up in the second from the last office.

I followed her in. "Why this one? I figured you'd choose the last one."

"I would have if you were setting up a honey trap and wanted me to record the evidence," she said. "But since I don't think much of the convo and photos we want will be taking place in the bedrooms, I thought this would be a more prudent shooting platform. Besides, if for some reason things move into the bedrooms, at least this one on the near side, I can shift down the hall to follow it. If they move to the far bedroom, it's likely gone, sorry."

"We can only do what we can do," I said, watching her unroll three long power strips and plug several chargers into them.

"These are the price of portability," she said, pointing to the strips. "This one is for cameras. That one is for sound equipment. The last one is for mobile phones and essential equipment."

"Which reminds me," I said, "Activate your phone's location ping and add me to the people who can see it," I said.

She looked at me hard. "Really?"

"Think of it as the spare carabiner you clip into, never expecting to need it. Whoever they turn out to be, these folks have acted dangerously in the past and put at least two people in the hospital. Which reminds me, text me when you're ready to leave. I can't stay the whole time, and Manny appears to be flaking out. Text me when you're ready to clear the joint," I said. "And here's a copy of the master key in case you need it. It will lock off the elevator after I go."

"Go already," she said, sitting down where she could see the parking lot and opening her tablet. "I'll be fine."

I headed out and down on the elevator, being careful to lock the front door.

❖

Eva was glad when Lyle finally left. Now she could start setting up the observation post the way she wanted it. Despite playing down her assignments with U.S. intelligence to Lyle and Manny, she had actually done significant work for her adopted country over the years and had a good deal more training and equipment than she let on.

After she rearranged things, she settled in. This was a chance to catch up on her recreational reading, and she had brought her Kindle along, operating it on a lower light setting to make sure it couldn't be seen from outside. She had finished her second chapter when she heard voices approaching from below. She quickly positioned the microphone and her headphones and got her cameras ready.

Two men walked across the parking area from the small alley that led to the street. Both wore jeans and T-shirts. Neither one had a hat, and they each carried something. The shorter, stockier one with the more extreme haircut hefted what appeared to be a case of beer in bottles. The taller and leaner one held a paper bag of groceries. They carried their burdens up the stairs onto the front deck and paused while the taller one hunted through a large key chain for the correct key.

"Damn! We forgot to buy a bulb for this porch light," the taller one said as he hunted through his key chain.

Eva felt a thrill of satisfaction at how clearly the microphone picked up the conversation. Even the jingling keys came through distinctly.

"I still don't know why you put that key on that big old chain of yours."

"Because while it takes me a moment to find it," the tall one said. "At least I know this is where it is. Aha!" He held up the key and fit it into the lock.

"'Bout time," the smaller man growled as he picked up the box.

The tall man held the door for Buzzcut, as Eva decided to call him, while he carried the box in and then followed him in with the grocery bag.

Eva stepped to the second window and turned on that microphone. She waited patiently as the men moved around the room. She could get clear shots of their faces while they were in the well-lit space. She silently gave thanks the men's carelessness about decor precluded their putting up curtains.

"Beer?" offered Buzzcut as he finished emptying the box into the refrigerator.

"Damn straight," replied the one she'd named Stretch.

"What all you got in there?" Buzzcut asked as he handed Stretch the open bottle.

"Essentials. Peanut butter, bread, canned stuff, a can opener, grape jelly, canned tuna, Spam, and some bacon."

"Spam and bacon? Did you find a frying pan in this place?"

"Nope, but I found an old cast-iron griddle that fits over two of the burners, so that should do the trick."

"What do we have to feed the captain?"

"Captain said he'll take pizza with us," Stretch replied. "He wants a veggie with extra cheese. I reckon I'll get a medium one for him and get us a large pepperoni or all meat."

The two men began setting paper plates and plastic utensils at three of the table's four seats. None of the places got a cup or glass.

"How much longer you think we got on this job?" Buzzcut asked.

"Not too much longer. I get the feeling things are wrapping up. Why?"

"I'll be glad to get back to sleeping in a real bed again."

"You've got a real bed with a bathroom right there if you weren't too crazy to take it," Stretch said.

"Like hell. I'd like to see you try to sleep back there with that god-awful fish smell and the humidity. That room might be the biggest, but it's also the clammiest and nastiest."

"Maybe so, but I reckon it's still better than anywhere we slept up in Walker State." Stretch gave a short laugh. "I'm getting showered. Stay out to let the captain in if he shows up."

"Okay." Buzzcut walked back into the living room, threw himself down on the couch, and turned on the television, changing channels until he found a football game.

"I've ordered the pizza," Stretch shouted from the back bedroom in a voice so loud it made Eva jump when it roared through her headphones. A few moments later, she heard the shower start in the hall bathroom.

Eva lowered the sound on the main mic and left it facing the rooms inside while she turned on one of her smaller, more portable, microphones that she trained on the parking area. Whoever the captain might be, he sounded like the leader, and she resolved not to leave without recording this voice and image.

When nobody appeared after fifteen minutes, Eva went back to listen to the rooms again. As soon as she turned up the volume, she heard Buzzcut's snore and Stretch's irritated shout.

"Dude!"

"What?" Buzzcut shifted and almost fell off the couch.

"Pizza's almost here. Go down to the gate and get it. It's already paid for."

"Okay." He got up, left the house, and headed across the parking area, returning in about five minutes with two pizza boxes. He had put them on the dining room table when Eva began to barely make out a staccato phut-phut-phut from the microphone trained on the parking area.

Is the captain arriving by scooter, she thought, because it sounded like a moto was approaching. She picked up the night camera and waited. Suddenly the noise ceased, but nothing in the parking area moved. Still, she stood by.

Then she saw a figure stepping out from the piers under the house. He was a strongly built man wearing a well-cut suit and shirt, the top white enough to show up in her viewfinder. She started shooting photos as he climbed the steps and entered the house without knocking.

How the fuck did he get here? Eva wondered. *Where did he park...* Then in a flash of insight she remembered Lyle and Manny's description of the property. By boat. She realized he arrived by vessel. The noise she'd heard wasn't a scooter, it was a small outboard motor. She hadn't seen the boat because it had approached from the part of the building she couldn't see.

"Captain's here," Buzzcut shouted to Stretch when he saw him and came near to shake hands. Stretch appeared from the bathroom hallway wearing jeans and a long T-shirt, his hair still looked wet.

"Captain," Stretch said.

The captain looked at the pizzas and nodded. "Good to see you both," he said.

"We still think your choice of pizza is whack, but we got what you wanted," Buzzcut said. "The medium pie is yours. We're gonna stick with the carnivore one."

The two of them sat down while Stretch went back to the kitchen and came out with three longneck beers he passed around before sitting down.

"Good to see you, Captain," Stretch said.

"The admiral called me last night and filled me in. We're gonna be closing this place up soon, so we need you two to be ready to clear out."

"Oh yeah?" Stretch said. "Where to?"

"You'll find out when it's time, but we want to have this place clean as a whistle as far as trace, right? That means wipe down every surface, every object. Nothing left in the trash. Nothing with names and no technology."

Eva stopped taking pictures momentarily to make sure the microphone picked up everything.

"What's going on, are the cops coming?" Buzzcut asked.

"Not now, but they might in the future, and we don't want to help them at all. And since you might only have a couple of hours before you need to go, I suggest you do most of the cleanup up work well in advance so it's done."

"We've already been doing a lot of that shit," Stretch said. "Dumping the house trash in different garbage cans in the neighborhood and using that little shredder on any documents."

"Good job," the captain said. "Now keep on doing that, but take it to the next level."

"Can't you give us a better idea of when all this is coming down?" Stretch asked.

"I really can't. It's likely to be in the next week to ten days, but it might come down in as little as one day."

The rest of the conversation dealt with movies, pop culture, and politics. Eva wasn't surprised the captain backed the current Republican governor, and that neither Buzzcut nor Stretch appeared to have any partisan opinions.

After about an hour, the captain said he needed to leave and got up from the table. Buzzcut and Stretch did so too, walking him to the front porch before he descended the stairs and disappeared again among the piers.

After a few minutes, Eva's mic picked up the clear sound of a lanyard being pulled and the rhythmic phut-phut-phut started again, gradually fading in the distance.

Eva packed up and left after the captain, adding the sound and image files to several flash drives and uploading them to her cloud account. Then she texted Lyle that she wouldn't need his escort to her car. She could hear the traffic on Breaker and Washington and felt reassured about her safety. She wanted to get the files home to her studio where she could clean and process them. She locked the elevator behind her as well as the door, then set out for her car.

The traffic back to Savannah was light, and she arrived in plenty of time to run the scrubbing and processing programs on the files. She uploaded them to her cloud and then copied them to flash drives. She was going to bring them with her when she next saw Lyle, but her training in tradecraft refused to be silenced.

"All right then," she finally blurted and pulled on her jacket. Kwanjo, her mixed bull terrier, whined and clearly wanted to come, but she refused.

"Only the drop box, Champ," she told him. "You wouldn't even have time to stick your head out the window."

She dropped the flash drives in a padded envelope, scrawled Lyle's address onto the form, and carefully sealed it. Then she headed out.

She swung the car up beside the drive-by drop box and carefully slid the envelope into the slot, feeling the familiar relief that the product was out of her hands and on its way. Then she dropped by Bangkok 54 and bought a take-out order of pad thai.

As soon as she stepped from her car in the driveway, she heard Kwanjo's agitated barking from the house and felt a pang or remorse for leaving him alone the last few days. Tomorrow morning, she resolved, she would take him for a nice long run.

She tapped the fob to lock the car and grabbed her bag of take-out food from the car roof.

She opened the garden gate, carefully latched it again, and walked the short distance to her door.

She had just shifted the bag to her left hand so she could open the door with her right when, from her right, she sensed more than saw a dark shape hurtling toward her. Tackled violently from that side, she fell hard into her flower beds, knocking the breath out of her.

At first it seemed an even match. She fought back like a leopard and landed at least one blow that drew a moan and a muttered curse. But a second assailant grabbed her hair, pulled back her head, and pressed a vile-smelling cloth to her face. No! She kicked and clawed, trying to hold her breath, but he hit her hard in the belly, so she gasped and fell deeply unconscious.

Chapter Twenty

White Russians

After Lyle's fourth call, I blocked his number on my phone. Let him get used to what it felt like not to control the agenda. I'm not usually a drinker, but right now I needed one, and I didn't know any bars downtown. I called Tommy. He picked up on the second ring.

"Culture desk." He sounded cheery.

"Hey, man, if you just wanted to grab a drink in the middle of the day, where would you go?"

"I never drink during the day."

"If. I said *if* you wanted to grab a drink."

"Uh-oh. What's happened?"

"Nothing. Except for finally seeing that Lyle James is really a huge, number one, prime asshole."

"Wow," he said. "What part of town are you in?"

"Right around the *Record*."

"Okay, about two blocks away on Standard Street you should find the Crowing Hen. It's a lesbian bar. They serve lunch, so I bet their bar would be open as well."

"Thanks, man," I said and hung up before he added anything else.

The Crowing Hen's whimsical sign portraying a chicken dressed in male drag and blowing a bugle was totally opposite the thoroughly establishment vibe. All the decor was dark woods and deep reds, from the bar with barstools in that color to booths and leather armchairs and library tables. Overall, it looked like an exclusive men's club, with the exception of the stage at one end with a piano.

I counted roughly a dozen other people seated at the bar or in various chairs when I arrived. I was the only male customer.

I took a seat at the bar closest to the windows and watched the barkeep as she arranged glassware and filled containers with supplies. She wore jeans, a white men's shirt, a leather bar apron with the straps gathered at her waist, and biceps almost as large as Lyle's. When she moved her bar wiping closer, I raised my eyebrows, and she stepped up.

"Name your poison," she said.

"Does it have to be poisonous?"

She glanced the clock over the bar. "At this hour, it's all poison."

"I'm not really a drinker," I said tentatively. "I just need a drink, and I don't like beer."

She paused for a moment, looking at me. "Do you like coffee?"

"Yeah, sure."

She walked down the bar, measured the contents of bottles into a shaker with some ice and milk and then returned to pour what looked like an iced latte in a short glass, leaving the balance in the shaker on the bar.

"What's this?"

"The recipe book calls it a White Russian. I call it a drink for those who don't like to drink."

I picked up the glass and cautiously took a sip. I could recognize the alcohol, but a rich coffee flavor made it seem like an adult iced java cocktail. And while it tasted a good deal sweeter than the joe I customarily drank, it wasn't too candied to enjoy.

I nodded to the barkeep to say thanks.

"My name's K.C.," she announced, extending her hand.

"Jose," I said, being sure to grip hers as strongly as she did mine.

"So, what brings a non-drinker into a bar in the middle of the day to buy a drink?"

I shrugged. "Man trouble. Not that I expect you know much about that," I said with a cheeky grin.

"Ha," she barked back. "I've had my share of that, plus woman trouble as well, so I can tell you they aren't that much different."

I sighed. "What makes people in a relationship with you think they can speak for you without even checking with you? I don't disagree with him about what he said or even the reasoning behind it, but his presumption ticked me off."

"Why do you think that is?"

I looked up and around. "I don't see a shrink shingle?"

"Ha!" The bark again. "I suspect I've been listening to people pour out their hearts longer than you've been alive, sweet pea."

I took a deeper gulp of the coffee cocktail. "Maybe because I feel shut out from him, from his life," I said. "And a little bit taken for granted. It's like he thinks 'Manny's always on board, so let's go' without even taking the trouble to check in with me."

She nodded and then moved off down the bar to serve a trio of women dressed like office workers who had taken three of her stools.

I drained the coffee drink and poured the extra from the shaker. Then I pushed it forward, indicating I wanted another. K.C. glanced down and caught my eye before coming back with a smirk.

"Be careful now, those go down like milkshakes but kick like mules," she said.

I thanked her for her concern but ordered another.

Then I started playing with my phone. A text from Tommy came across my screen.

Did you find it ok? Worried about you.

Yep, and it's very nice. Come join me when you leave work.

❖

After trying Manny about a dozen times since he stormed out of the bathroom at the *Record*, I gave in and called Tommy. If anyone might know, I thought he would.

"Culture desk," he answered.

"This is Lyle James calling for Tomas Kingsbury."

"Oh, hey, Lyle."

"Hey, Tomas. Would you happen to know where Manny is? I've called him like a dozen times since yesterday but he doesn't pick up."

"Sorry, can't help you. He might still be at home."

"Why? Is he sick?"

"You could say that. I wouldn't be surprised if the hangover fairy dropped by to see him."

"How come?"

"He called me about midday yesterday and wanted to know where he could get a drink, so I sent him to the Crowing Hen and picked him up there later."

"Why there?"

"I trusted K.C. to look after him. He was pretty upset with you."

"Oh. We had a misunderstanding. I didn't handle things well."

"According to him, that may be the biggest understatement of the year," Tommy said.

"What time did you get him home?"

"Not too late, but the damage had been done, if you know what I mean."

"Would you do me a favor and tell him I called?"

"Do I tell him you're sorry for whatever you said or did?"

"No. I am sorry. But that needs to come from me."

We hung up. We were supposed to meet Eva at Badda-Bean before she headed over to the Empire Cinema. I hoped Manny would show up for that, but I wasn't sure he would. I set about keeping myself busy with paperwork.

Parker came in. "Hey, boss."

"Morning, Parker."

"Staff wanted me to be sure to thank you for the dinner the other night. Everybody had a fun time and really felt appreciated."

"I had a good time as well," I said. "What we got in this morning?"

"Four thank you messages from the drivers of those municipal cars we worked on last week. Apparently, the one with the sticky window never had it work properly, and we fixed it. Another one, a parole officer, said just having such a nicely detailed car made him feel better about keeping appointments."

"Excellent. Anything else?"

"Naw, nothing urgent."

"Good. I'm going to take a midmorning workout," I said. "I'm feeling antsy."

"Sounds good, boss. We got the shop."

I retreated upstairs to stretch myself on the monkey bars and take out some frustration on the heavy bag. The shoulder still ached a little bit, but the dull pain that remained was a muted echo of the previous discomfort. I did three or four test pull-ups, letting the fibers tense and release, feeling the flow as I breathed in going up and released coming down.

Clearly manhandling Manny out of the office had been a mistake. But what would have been a better course? Would it have been worse to publicly contradict him in front of his father? I let my body sway slightly on the end and then set off down the line, moving with as much grace as I could muster.

Contradicting him in front of his father would have been the better choice, I decided. If he had found it embarrassing, he still would have appreciated the chance to defend his position, no matter that would not have helped in the long run.

I had just started working the heavy bag when the doorbell went. Out of breath a bit, I jogged over to the elevator and pressed the intercom button. "Speak," I said, gasping a little.

"Um, Lyle." Manny's voice came through the static. I punched the down button to send him the elevator, then went back to the bag.

I recognized the lift ding and yelled out "Gym!" before returning to punching, but I felt more than heard him arrive at the edge of my workout area.

"Hey," he said.

He looked embarrassed and a little unsteady on his feet from the hangover. I stopped punching, letting the bag swing.

"I'd give you a hug, but I'm a little wet and you're dressed pretty nicely," I said.

"That's okay."

"How about a lemonade? Parker brought some of his aunt's over this morning. Mostly lemons, not much sugar."

"Okay."

He sat at the kitchen counter while I pulled down two glasses and loaded them with ice before I poured.

"I can smell it from here," Manny said.

"Yeah. It's really sharp. Sip it first. I've got some more sugar if you need it."

Manny grinned at me and took a big mouthful, then swallowed it and pushed his seat back, making a face. "Oh my God, that's sour," he said.

"I warned you, you dolt. Why did you do that?"

"I guess I wanted to clear my palate."

"Well, that would have done it. This is meant to be sipped and savored," I said. "That's why I like it. Do you need some sugar?"

I got up and went to the cabinet.

"No, no," Manny protested. "If you drink it by sipping, I'll try it that way before I add more sugar." He tried it once more, a little sip this time. "I see what you mean."

"Yeaaah," I said and sat back down again.

"Lyle," he started, but I interrupted.

"No. Wait. Let me speak first, okay?"

Manny nodded.

"I owe you a tremendous apology," I said. "I don't know exactly why yet, but I reacted without thinking during that meeting. I didn't consider your thoughts or opinions, but just went with what was in my gut. I acted thoughtlessly. I apologize for it and regret how it might have made you feel."

"Thank you," Manny said. "And I accept your apology. For what it's worth, I think I understand why you might have acted as you did."

"Why?"

"Because that's the way you've always reacted as someone on his own. Your reaction in that room makes sense if you don't have anyone else to consider or think about. But you do now."

Manny reached out and took my hand. "For what it's worth, once I calmed down and stopped thinking you were the most arrogant jerk I had ever met…"

"Hey."

"No, I really did think some choice things about you!" he admitted with a smile. "But once I got over how I felt and really looked at what you said, I realized you were right. What I was trying to do had more to do with how I felt than with a thought-out position—which is not to say I agreed with what you did. But I understood the reasoning behind it."

"So, where do we go from here?"

"I guess bring me up to date."

I told him Eva sent me enthusiastic texts about her first night of surveillance work, implying she had hot material to share. We were supposed to meet her this afternoon at Badda-Bean before heading over to the Empire.

"Okay, I can be there. What time?"

"We said five, and Eva's usually punctual."

"I'll be there."

We got up from the table and I took the glasses to the sink, then came back and pulled him into a hug, burying my face in his neck and kissing his earlobe. Desire moved through me, tightening my crotch as I reached down to cup and grab his ass.

"Hmm. I really am sorry," I whispered to him. "Want to stay for lunch?"

But he pushed back.

"I would love to, but I can't. I really do have stories other than this one, and they have deadlines I need to meet, so I have to go to work."

"Are you sure?" I pulled his hand down to my crotch where he could feel my passion for him. "Make-up sex is supposed to be awesome."

He shuddered, but still pressed to break my embrace. "Yes. Sadly, I'm sure," he said.

"Then I hope you'll let me at least take you to work?"

"That would be great, thanks."

The trip from Bonne Chance to the *Record* building felt like it would take forever. Construction on Washington Street slowed traffic; then, when we finally did hit the freeway, an accident slowed our progress even more.

We remained mostly silent as I both exulted in what I saw as a breakthrough with Lyle and still nursed my slightly throbbing head. We pulled up in front of the paper, and he leaned over with a full-on kiss.

"I'm looking forward to having you over tonight," he said. "I hope you can make it."

"Me too," I said, sliding out of the car.

I went straight to Tommy's office, where I found him having an animated phone conversation with someone.

"Ms. Conveccio, I cannot fail to include service in a restaurant's overall rating," he said to a shrill voice. "Yes, the food at Mangiare is very good, but it should make it to your table before it gets cold." The other person came back more loudly. "Yes, certainly you can do that. Goodbye, Ms. Conveccio. Call me back when you're fully staffed."

He hung the phone up slowly and looked up at me. "The prodigal returns?"

"Just came from Lyle's."

"And are the lion and lamb back to sleeping together?"

"Yes."

"So, why aren't you radiating the peaceful satiety of the recently laid?"

"Because I'm not feeling entirely myself yet."

"Count yourself lucky," he said. "Being inclined to strong hangovers is a good disincentive to alcoholism."

I got up and shut the door, then sat down again. "Look, I want to apologize to you for yesterday."

"Why?"

"Because it couldn't have been fun to have come all the way down to the Crowing Hen to get me home," I said.

"And how many times have you gotten me home safely when I've been smashed," he asked. "Don't mention it. But I am going to text you the Crowing Hen's address later today. The owner there,

K.C. McAlister, deserves a thank you/apology note. It would be the gentlemanly thing to do."

The rest of the day passed in something of a daze, as I wrote and filed a couple of stories, then returned to Tommy's office. Danny had gone home to visit his folks for a few days, and I wondered if Tommy might want to hang with me and Lyle.

"Come on, what are you going to do, mope around the house?"

"I don't know. You know I'm not crazy about being the third wheel."

"You won't be! Lyle's amazing friend Eva is going to be there too. You'd like her. In fact, I think you really need to meet her. She could be a good source for you." Tommy's eyebrows rose at the last comment, but he agreed to come, so we set out.

I got to Badda-Bean about 4:45 and collected the key to their second small room. I reserved it for an hour. Eva could brief us on what she had before heading out. I ordered a café con leche and waited. The shop was filling up.

At 4:55, Manny and Tommy turned up. Tommy had come along to meet Eva. I hugged them both and we all sat down.

"What does Eva have?" Manny asked.

"Well, a few things," I said, "but I don't have many details yet. Where *is* she?"

"Are you sure she knows it's this place?" Tommy asked.

"She suggested it. She even suggested we get a room so we could talk in private."

The barista knocked on the door. "Thirty minutes, guys, then we have a party who needs the room."

I called her mobile and got voice mail again.

"Hey Eva, it's Lyle. Manny and Tommy are here with me, but you're not. Please give a call or text and let us know what's up."

"What should we do?" Manny asked.

"I don't know, but I'm really worried. This is so unlike her, especially without a phone call or message. If she isn't here by six, I'll head over to the Empire and see if she went there. Would you mind taking Tommy's car and checking out her place in Savannah? I can give you the address."

"If Tommy doesn't mind, I'm down to go," Manny said.

"Okay by me."

At five to six, we concurred she wasn't coming and split up. I headed to the surveillance post at the Empire, and they started up to her place.

Approaching the building I looked in vain among the parked cars, hoping to see hers. The usual door was locked, as it should have been, and the elevator too, though as soon as I put the key in, it opened, indicating the cab had been at the lobby level, waiting.

Upstairs all of her equipment stood ready and in place. All the cameras and recorders were charged, as well as the backup batteries. If Eva had returned since she left last night, she hadn't started up or used anything.

I checked the windows overlooking the bungalow, but our two jokers were out. I locked up the rooms and headed back downstairs, being careful to lock off the elevator and door again. Where could she be? Nothing in our friendship prepared me for this.

I called Manny on his hands-free mobile. "Any luck with you guys? I checked the surveillance post, but she hasn't been back there."

"We're just getting into Savannah now. Backup on 95. We'll call you as soon as we get there."

"If the house is shut, don't try to get in. Eva has a pretty protective dog that could be dangerous."

"Okay," Manny said. "Thanks for the heads-up about that." And hung up.

I went back to sit in my car, undecided about what to do. A big part of me wanted to report her missing to the police, but I realized we had nothing to show them to prove she'd actually disappeared. I had decided to head back home when my phone rang, showing her number.

"Eva. Are you okay? Where are you? I've been worried—"

"Lyle, it's me," said Manny. "We found her cell phone in the bushes along the walk from her gate to the door. There's no sign of her here. The house is locked up tight, no lights, and what sounds like a completely ferocious dog just inside the door."

"Meet me at Savannah's central precinct police station," I said. "We have to report her missing."

❖

We arrived back at Bonne Chance late. The new security lights Parker had installed after the rattlesnake morning arced night into day and woke Manny up as we pulled in to the driveway. He started for the elevator but I called him back to the front.

"Let's go in the front door," I said. "I want to check the mail."

A couple of bills awaited me on my desk, along with the envelopes from several checks Parker had deposited. There was also a package about the size of a shoebox and wrapped in butcher paper. The box's front had "Lyle James" written on it in neat block letters with the words "By Hand" in cursive underneath. I approached and tore off the wrapping to find a work boot box. I opened it to discover Eva's favorite camera and a sheet of common printer paper. Pasted onto it in letters from different publications, in the pattern of threats everywhere, were the words "If you want to ever see the bitch alive. BACK OFF!! Wait for our call."

"Holy shit," Manny said.

Chapter Twenty-one

On the Katie Ann

On a quiet afternoon, Eva rocks in the giant porch swing at her uncle's house somewhere in upstate New York. She's a little girl again, and this is the first time her mother has fled Beirut with her daughter in tow. The adults sit with drinks in the backyard talking. Their distant conversation sounds like insects buzzing. Eva remains silent and alone, happy to gently rock back and forth at the shaded end of the long porch. She's never had a swing set, never experienced the joy of making herself move through space without having her feet on the ground. She loves it.

Then she notices a fish flopping up the short steps from the front yard onto the porch. It can't breathe. Its gills expand and contract like bellows. Its eyes cast about wildly as it quakes and falls. She doesn't want to look, but she can't stop staring. Soon another. And one more. Now three. Then four. The entire porch teems with dying fish that are starting to smell. Soon, an adult from the house will come to rescue her from them, won't they? She pulls up her feet to keep the animals from touching her until one leaps up, lands in her lap, and she screams.

Eva started awake as she shouted. Where was she? It was cool, but with an awful stench. Her body was draped across pipes and boxes on a metal floor. She couldn't shake the impression of moving, though she was lying still. Her head hurt. In fact, a lot hurt. Cranium, neck, shoulders, torso. She took a deep inhalation and almost cried out at the pain. Shallow breaths.

Mustering her resources, she took an inventory, first of her body, then her equipment and her surroundings.

She started with fingers and toes. All moved. Hands free. Stretch the arms. Sore, but she could do it. Good. Legs. Movement was restricted. Clink. Clink. Clink. She was shackled, and the restraints appeared to be locked to a pipe of some sort. Could she stand? Tuck the knees and then push with the left arm. Roll? Yes, unsteadily, to her feet. God, she felt like crap.

She was still clothed. Good. Thank God for the sensible shoes she thought to wear. Pockets with phone, keys, extra drives, batteries. Empty, no camera. She was damp, but not soaking. And the air, while cool, was not freezing.

As her eyes adjusted to the gloom, she found she was in a medium-sized, mostly dark, empty space. There was a closed door on the far wall. The light filtered in from a partially covered opening in the roof about fifteen feet away. A tarp or some kind of cloth over the gap moved slightly in the wind, making strange shadows on the floor. The stench of dead fish and seaweed permeated everything.

Once she stood, she recognized waves or swells. She was on a boat. Specifically, some sort of fishing boat, based on the smell. She was the catch hold of an older trawler. Now, how to get out. She sat down again to study the shackles more closely.

❖

"Holy shit," I said, looking at Lyle.

He sat down. "What the fuck do we do now?"

From then on things moved rapidly. Lyle called someone he knew close to the Georgia Bureau of Investigation, and in the space of half an hour, a team of eight people from the agency and local law enforcement, some of whom Lyle knew, crowded Bonne Chance's small front office.

"Manny, this is Agent Anthony Blake, of the GBI," Lyle said, standing next to a tall, lean man with a serious expression. "Agent Blake, this is Jose Porter, a reporter with the *South Georgia Record* who is a friend of mine and Eva's and who is *not* wearing his reporter hat at the moment." He looked hard at me.

"Thanks for letting me know that," Agent Blake said. "I'm not at all opposed to having a reporter here, but I would ask that you consult with me about the timing of publication of anything you write. I would hate to inadvertently risk this lady's life with an ill-timed story."

"I completely agree," I said. "Though it's worth pointing out the note didn't say anything about not telling a reporter or even not calling the cops."

"We noticed that too," Blake said. "Right now, we're not expecting a ransom demand."

"Then why take her?" Lyle asked.

"We think you will be required to do something other than pay money," Blake said.

Then Detective Walker arrived on the scene, and I blushed flaming red, ducking into the hall bathroom before he caught sight of me. Of course, he would have to be here, I thought. I braced myself, splashed water on my face, and returned to the office where Lyle called me over.

"Detective Walker, this is Manny Porter, a reporter for the *South Georgia Record* and one of my closest friends," Lyle said. "He's here because he also knows Eva, but he won't report anything that happens with this case without first checking with Agent Blake."

"Pleased to meet you," I said, extending my hand to find him wearing a smirk on his face.

"Haven't we met before?" Walker said, finally extending his hand to shake mine with a firm grip. "I rarely forget a face."

I laughed brightly. "I imagine that kind of memory comes in handy," I said. "I suppose it's possible we've met. I've done a couple of stories off the police blotter. But I'm sure if we did, it was just in passing."

Lyle watched our interchange closely.

"Okay. Just in passing, then," he said. "I'm pleased to finally meet you more formally now."

"Yes." I agreed.

Agent Blake then called Walker over, and he excused himself.

"I didn't know you knew him," Lyle said.

"I didn't know I did either," I lied.

"When would you have met?"

"Last week I covered our crime reporter's beat for a couple of days, so I might have met him that way."

"I'm surprised he didn't make more of an impression on you. I think he's pretty hot myself," Lyle said, then lowered his voice. "Word is he's a big top, and he plays a bit in the leather community."

"Wow, I wouldn't have guessed. But for all we know that might mean he's had a drink in a leather bar from time to time."

"Yeah. Rumor mills aren't ever reliable," Lyle said.

Later in the evening my phone buzzed with a message from Walker.

In passing? I want the record to show I'm looking forward to a time when I get to form more than a short-lived acquaintance.

Hush, I texted back. *Aren't police supposed to be gentlemen? And I'll have you know that you caught me at a weak moment the other day.*

I am a gentleman. I would never let your hunky boyfriend know you looked like you could eat me up without salt the other afternoon. Your secret is safe with me.

The meeting broke up not long after I met Walker. It would take a while for the forensics team to get back with results from fingerprint searches and other tests, and we would need to be ready tomorrow for any communication from the kidnappers.

Lyle and I had planned on spending the night together. I longed for his touch. But we decided, in light of what had happened, that I would go back to my chauffeur's digs. I could get some fresh clothes and think about what our reply should be to the kidnappers' demands. I summoned a rideshare and went back to Tommy's Victorian. Little did I realize I wouldn't see Lyle again for days.

❖

I spent the night fitfully. The sleeping aids I had in my medicine cabinet weren't enough to slip me under. Instead, I passed the night in that weird stupor that mimics half-slumber, fighting through hallucinations where we rescued or failed to save Eva.

I called the staff together at about eight thirty and briefed them all generally on what had happened and asked each of them for their respect and confidentiality until we got word that we could talk about the situation.

"Officially, we're open for business, but as a practical matter, we won't be taking any new cars until next week," I told them.

After the meeting broke up, Carolyn Mondial called. "Good news, client," she almost sang out. "Old Judge Klinefeld has granted our petition to add all of the eminent domain cases into a single class."

She reminded me she'd been worried about this because there was no precedent for class action suits in eminent domain cases, and Klinefeld was not known for steering into unfamiliar waters.

"But he's also a stickler for procedure," she continued, "and I think the realization of how much work was going to be needed for 181 disputed eminent domain cases helped him see things our way. Now we just have to get ready because I think things are going to move pretty quickly from here."

But her attitude shifted after she heard my voice. "What's going on? I thought you would as happy or happier than I am."

I told her about what had happened with Eva and the uncertainty that hung over everything related to the case now. "We haven't heard from the kidnappers, so we don't really know what they're going to ask," I said. "But if they want me to drop the case, I think I may have to."

"But you *can't*," she said. "I've been taking depositions from people who are counting on this case to keep their lives from being overturned and destroyed. They know they might not win the case, so they're prepared to possibly lose. But I don't think they're ready to give up right out of the gate."

"I know that. But if they ask me to drop the case, and I don't and they kill Eva, what about that? Is keeping a bunch of people in their homes worth someone dying?"

She sighed. "Keep me posted. And please don't make any final decisions without talking to me first. Meanwhile, I'll start working on ways we might be able to salvage the case if worse comes to worst."

"Thank you," I said. "I know it's hard, but I really feel trapped."

"Have you called the police?"

"Yes, they're on it as well as the GBI."

"May I inform the court?"

"Of course, but please ask them to keep it confidential for now. Assuming we move forward with the case, what's our next step?"

"Well, because your case represents the whole class, you may have to show up in court on Monday for an important preliminary hearing. I'll let you know if it's definite or not."

"Okay."

She sighed again. "Nothing is ever easy," she said. "The key thing for you to understand is that while adding all these homeowners to this class means a major victory, it also means our flexibility in this particular case has shrunk a lot. When I argue now, I won't be arguing for just you but for everybody, and they will share our triumphs but also our mistakes. So, no pressure," she said.

"No, none at all."

"Keep me posted, ideally once a day at least. If nothing happens, call or text anyway."

"Right."

❖

The entire ride from Bonne Chance to Tommy's, I couldn't pull my mind away from Detective Walker. As annoying as I found him, he excited me in a way Lyle didn't and wouldn't.

I imagined Tommy's sarcasm. "Oh, poor boy, two hunky men interested in you at once, boo hoo." And he would be right, but merely knowing that didn't help.

My driver caught my eye in the rearview mirror. He looked to be in his early twenties, slim, cute. Definitely gay to boot.

"Can I ask you a question about that place I picked you up?"

"What? Bonne Chance? Sure."

"That's a garage, right? Are they good? Are they expensive?"

"I can't speak from personal experience, because I haven't used them. But I'm good friends with the owner, and I believe they're both good and honest. I expect if they say something is going to cost whatever amount to fix, that's what it will really cost. Why?"

"Because I just got this car from my older brother last week, and I don't have a garage."

"I would give them a try," I said.

"You're gay, aren't you?"

"Good to know your gaydar is functioning, even if that was a little forward," I said, shooting him a smile.

"Why not? You're cute. How about a drink sometime?"

"Now, that was *very* forward."

"I don't care. It's true, you are cute. And I need to build my network since I live here now."

"Sorry to disappoint, but I have a boyfriend," I said as we turned onto Tommy's street. Actually two, I thought.

He sighed. "The cute ones always do."

We stopped in front of the garden gate because the driveway was shut.

"Drive safely," I said as I got of the car. He thanked me, then drove off.

A new streetlamp Tommy had pushed for threw a pool of light in front of the gate. I was able to find my key and enter easily. Ahead I made out the dark upper floors of the house above the trees. Everyone looked to be in bed. I had passed the midpoint of the walk to the front door when I heard a branch crack behind me. I started to turn when someone covered my head with a dark bag, and I went down to the ground.

That was the last thing I remembered from that night.

❖

I woke up half seated on a cold metal floor in a dark room, but I had enough light to recognize Lyle's friend Eva Almisra gazing seriously at me.

"Ms. Almisra, you're alive. Thank God," I croaked through my dry mouth and throat. "What are you doing here? Where are we?"

"Shh," she said. "Don't talk. Let me try to give you some water."

She reached behind her, pulled up a gallon container of liquid, and shuffled closer, her small steps striking a metallic chime. I tried to lift my hands but found I couldn't. They had been cuffed together.

"We're going to have to coordinate this," she said with an attempt at a smile. "One mouthful at a time, okay?"

"Okay," I whispered.

She brought the container up to my lips and poured. My mouth started to fill, but she pulled it away. I swallowed. It tasted and felt good.

"One or two more, please," I said. "You can hold it up a little while longer."

She did it again, a second longer, and a third time brought me still more. She set the gallon down.

"Better?" she asked.

"Much."

We looked at each other.

"Your hands are free," I said.

"Yes, but not my feet." She lifted one and I could see the chain. I tried to move mine but found them held tightly together.

"What's on my feet?"

"Duct tape. It was over your mouth too, but I ripped it off."

"Is that why my face hurts?"

"Probably. I didn't have any solvent to loosen the adhesive, and I was afraid you couldn't breathe."

"How long have I been here?"

"I'm not entirely sure. Without my watch or cell phone, it's been hard to measure time." She stretched her arms. "But my body thinks it's been a long time. I tried waking you up a number of times, but whatever they used on you was more powerful than just chloroform."

"Who's they?"

"I don't know. So far I've only seen Caliban. He was the one that brought you here and probably me too, but I was unconscious. And I'm pretty sure he wasn't the one who captured me. He doesn't appear coordinated enough."

"Caliban?"

"Sorry for the Shakespeare reference, but it fits. About six-three, lots of muscle, shoulders like Hercules, really bad haircut, nose that's been broken several times, and needs a shave and a bath. Doesn't appear very smart."

"Where are we?"

"On a boat. An old fishing boat, I think, anchored somewhere probably not too far offshore."

"Yeah, I got the fish part," I said. "Oh my God, it stinks."

"You'll get used to it. Or at least I did."

I sized her up. "Any thoughts about getting off this tub?"

"Lots of them, but none terribly promising," she said. "First, let's assess your condition. How do you feel?"

"Like crap."

"More specific, please. Any sharp pains?"

I tried to move and everything hurt, but nothing sharply. "No, just aches."

"Great. Fingers and toes all move when you tell them to?"

"Yep."

"Great. Now stuff. Did they empty your pockets?"

"I can't be sure, but I don't think so."

"If they didn't, what does that give us?"

"Some loose change. My Swiss army pocketknife. My wallet with credit and debit cards and a ten dollar bill. My mobile phone."

"It would be amazing if we had the mobile phone," Eva said. "But that's probably too much to hope for. Still, the pocket knife would be great."

"Are we alone on board?"

"I think so. Caliban stayed on board last night after he brought you, but I heard the boat motor early this morning, and I haven't heard it again since."

"I think I can wriggle my way closer to you so you can reach me," I said. "We could find out if we have the knife or not."

"Let's try it," she said.

The day had gone well for the business so far, which meant it went terribly for finding out anything about where Eva was being held. Around noon, Agent Blake called the team, including me, back into Bonne Chance's small front office, transformed into a miniature command center.

"I wanted to brief you all on where we are," he began. "All of the clues have petered out short of giving us the information we need to locate her."

The bureau had gotten descriptions of a white contractor's van around Eva's house early on the day she disappeared, but when they had found the van, it yielded a paucity of clues.

"Essentially, we were able to firmly establish that she had been in the vehicle," he said, "but nothing about who was driving."

He had finished the briefing when Parker appeared at the door with a plain white business envelope he passed to me. "Mort brought this to me when he came with today's deliveries," he whispered. "I thought you should see it right off."

The envelope had my name written on it in cursive. I carefully slit it open end took out the one page. It was much like the other one, but longer. I read it and felt my heart sink further in my chest.

OK Fag, it said. *We have your fag hag and buttboy. If you ever want to see their disgusting skins in one piece again, you will join us on Buccaneer Pier at 11:30 p.m. tonight. Use the maintenance gate. Come alone. Any Cops or Others With YOU, the two of them GET it! You have been WARned.*

"They've made contact," I said, passing the paper to Agent Blake. "And they've kidnapped Manny!"

Agent Blake read the paper and shot me a furious glance. "How did you get this?"

"Parker said the package delivery guy brought it."

"Is he still here?"

I called Parker in. Mort had moved on to his next stop, but since that was only across the street, two representatives brought him back quickly. Soon he sat on a wooden chair in the office facing a stern Agent Blake.

"Name," Blake demanded.

"Uh. Mort. Morton Klondike, like the ice cream sandwich," Mort said, looking at us in bewilderment. "You guys know me. I've been delivering to you for like a decade."

Blake showed him the empty envelope. "Recognize this?"

"Yeah, I gave it to Parker to give to Mr. James today."

"How'd you get it?"

Mort described how he came out of the Southern Shores Mall, his third stop of the morning, and found a man standing next to his truck.

"What was the man like?" Blake said.

"Forties, early fifties. Fit. Snappy dresser. Not too tall, but strong. Hair cut short. Some kind of accent, but I couldn't place where it was from."

Mort said the man gave him the envelope and said it contained the location of a car his wife didn't know he owned but that he wanted Mr. James to work on.

"He said he didn't want to call or text Mr. James because those would show up on his cell phone where his wife might find it," Mort said. "I went ahead and did what he said because he gave me a twenty, and Mr. James has always been good to work with. I thought I was probably bringing him more business and maybe a valuable account if the guy's car turned out to be a fancy number."

"Again, two steps ahead of us," Blake growled. "I want to put these bastards away!"

"Maybe I can find out some more information when I meet them," I said.

"You're not going," Blake said.

"I don't see how I can't. Eva's a longtime friend and Manny is…a loved one. I can't just not go."

Blake stood up and turned his back to me before rounding again, this time his mobile phone in hand.

"Althea," he said. "We need a wire set up for Mr. James tonight, and I want a tracking device on him as well." He hung up. "We might not be able to go with you tonight, but I want to be as close as we can without actually being on the scene."

❖

Buccaneer Pier has been the most recognized of St. Michael's Harbor's entertainment venues since 1935, but all that felt long ago now as I stood in the shadow of the maintenance gate. Unlike the facility's main entrance that basked under rosy neon lights visible from the highway, the support gate remained forlorn and in shadow some two hundred yards away.

Inside the chain link, one of the park's visitor trolleys rested on blocks amid trash and boxes, cannibalized seats, tires, wiring, or anything else that could maintain the park's other tramcars. It didn't look like anyone had come through this entrance in a decade. But as the note had promised, when I pushed on the rusted metal, it swung open easily. Whatever lock usually kept the gate shut had gone.

I reached up and pushed a button on the device in my ear. Static and then Agent Blake's voice, loud enough I flinched. "This is a test. This is a test."

"Hear you way too loud and clear," I complained.

"Tap the power button to cycle through the volume," he said. Once the earpiece issue was resolved, the facility felt incredibly quiet. I heard waves hitting the beach not too far away, and the thud-whoosh they made as they energetically punched the pier's support pylons then, defeated, retreated as foam.

The note didn't specify where to go once inside. I set out walking with what I hoped was a firm and confident tread to the information gazebo at the center of the facility. I turned the corner into the square in front of the gazebo and jumped a little. A man in a gray raincoat and hat pulled low over his face sat in the space. When he saw me, he rose and motioned I should sit on one of the benches that made up the gazebo's outer circle while he sat on an inner ring seat behind me. Arranged thus, we could hear but not see each other.

"Thank you for coming," he said in a low, European-accented voice that made me think he might be German, Dutch, or Irish.

"I didn't have much choice. Where are my friends, you bastard!"

"Now, now. There is no call for insults. Your friends are fine, maybe a little bit damp, but we are caring for them nonetheless." He spoke with a kind of cultured weariness, as though this whole discussion wasted his time. It irritated me more than I had been.

"Prove it!"

With a rustle of clothing, a Polaroid photo brushed my right ear. When I reached up and got it, I saw it was of Manny and Eva, seated together in some industrial space, holding a newspaper.

"If you look closely at the headline, you will see it's today's paper," the gray-hatted man said smoothly.

I looked at the photo closely. It was Eva and Manny. They appeared angry and frightened, but alive.

"What do you want?"

"We both know that you are the principal defendant in a class action case against the condemnation of properties in St. Michael's Harbor," he said. "What we want is very simple. Drop your case."

"I can't do that."

"Can't or won't? We've looked into the financial life of your little garage with the clever name. You've done quite well, and we will be sure to recognize that in our offer for the property, as well as offering assistance in finding another, better location for you."

"What about everybody else?"

"Mr. James," he said, his voice becoming sharp. "We are prepared to make sure every owner of those Tinker Creek hovels is paid a fair amount for their property, but we are determined to buy that land."

"But they, like me, don't want to sell."

He made an exasperated, huffing sound.

"What you and these people want is immaterial. You don't understand. We want those properties, and we will buy them. We are a force of nature and time. We are like the hurricane in August. The forest fire in July. The deadly tornado on an April night. We are the river that keeps on rising, the wetlands that keep on sinking, the factory that closes its doors, and the Walmart that opens just outside of town. In short, Mr. James, we are the force of change, and we cannot be stopped. The sooner you and those others understand that, the better it will be for you all."

"And if I don't?"

"Then quite simply, you will never see your friends again," he said. "And you will live for the rest of your life in the knowledge that they did not meet an easy end, but a bloody, terrible, and tortured one."

"You're despicable. Throwing these people out of homes and business they have worked for years to establish and build. Threatening people who have never done anything to you."

"Now you're just being boring," the man sighed. "Is the tornado heartless or despicable when it kills a child in one household but skips entirely the one next door? Is the hurricane when it remains on course and plows at full strength into a town of antique homes and older people? No. Those are 'acts of God' that are left up to theologians to explain away as something other than acts of random cruelty from a largely indifferent, if not wicked, deity."

I heard the man stand up. I did as well.

"The fact is, Mr. James, that you are not giving yourself enough credit. I have studied your life and your accomplishments. You have never failed to seize upon opportunity, even when that chance has come dressed as a challenge, obstacle, or loss. Why you aren't doing so now, I am not entirely sure, but I do know you're not doing yourself any good."

I sized him up. Shorter than I, but likely more muscular as well. "What if I just vaulted this bench and captured you for the police?"

His voice grew steely. "You could try, but you would not find that an easy task," he said. "You aren't the only martial artist in our small space and, even more importantly, if you succeeded in detaining me past my appointed hour, you would only shorten your friends' lives even more."

"And if I do what you say?"

"Once the case files make it clear you have withdrawn your silly objections to the future, your friends will come back to you none the worse for wear and with a deeply stirring tale for future cocktail hours and dinner parties."

"You..."

"Tut tut. No more time for boring soliloquies. I would hate to run even a few minutes late to the next, all-important rendezvous. You can advise your police friends who are no doubt skulking nearby that they needn't try to follow me from the pier. I'm not headed to anywhere your friends are staying and, as I pointed out, they cannot capture me without condemning the innocents to a drawn-out and painful death. Au revoir, mon ami. If we had met under different circumstances, I believe we could have been productive colleagues, if not friends."

"I doubt it."

He gave a shrug of his shoulders and then retreated from the gazebo, walking at a steady, unhurried pace, taking pains to avoid pools of water on the ground.

"Stand by to move in," Blake said in my ear.

"No, don't. Didn't you hear him? If we take him down, we condemn Eva and Manny."

"One Baker Five." Another voice. "Subject is approaching dark sedan, license Georgia one, three, zero, Zulu, Charlie, Delta. What do we do, boss?"

"Stand down," Blake ordered.

I let out a sigh of relief.

"Alpha Charlie One?" Blake asked.

"Alpha Charlie One," came a tinny voice barely audible over the sound of helicopter blades.

"Have you got the car?"

"Affirmative."

"Follow it and let us know where he goes. I know he said he's not heading to where the hostages are, but in case he is."

"I'm heading back to my car," I said.

"Yeah, do that. Bring the photo for our folks to analyze. We'll debrief back at Bonne Chance."

I called Carolyn Mondial to bring up her up to date on what had happened so far. "Have you gotten an appointment yet for the next hearing?"

"Not yet, but I'm anticipating one being assigned first thing tomorrow," she told me.

"The kidnappers didn't give us a deadline. If the clerk's office schedules us, can you try to stall? Tell them I have a medical procedure or something. Anything to buy us some time."

"Well, I can truthfully say we still have two litigant statements to take and see if the judge goes for that."

"Thank you," I said. "We're working on this as hard as we can, and we're about to step up the pressure a notch."

❖

The next morning when we arrived at the *Record*, there were none of the security checks I had experienced before. Now the desk watchman stopped us to give us the badges that allowed the elevators to take us to the fifth floor.

Blake gave a cursory knock on Porter's office door, then opened it. Porter's secretary Rosa sat behind the desk, her eyes red as though she had been crying and her makeup had smudged. She waved us right through.

"He's waiting for you," she said.

We walked in and found Porter reading and signing papers. He had an air of compressed energy, like a man who had taken a week's worth of turbulent emotion, forced it deeply inside himself, and now struggled furiously to keep it contained. He nodded us into the chairs facing his desk. He spoke first.

"Agent Blake, I presume?"

Blake nodded.

"Could you please let me know of the latest progress the Georgia Bureau has made in discovering the whereabouts of my son," he asked in a strained voice.

"His kidnappers didn't take him outside of this immediate area. Right now, we're analyzing evidence to narrow his possible locations."

"And there still have been no monetary demands?"

"That is correct, sir."

"What sort of demands have there been?"

I cleared my throat.

"This is Mr. Lyle James, sir…"

"Mr. James and I have met."

"Well, he was the one who heard from the kidnappers directly about their demands, so he would be the best one to answer your question."

"Well?" he said, looking at me.

"Mr. Porter, I met with a man representing the kidnappers on Buccaneer Pier yesterday evening," I said. "He told me they would release Manny and my friend Eva Almisra if I dropped my case disputing the city's eminent domain claims against my home and business. I know it might sound absurd that anyone would go to such lengths of what sounds like a small amount of money, but mine is the representative case for a class action lawsuit involving 181 other owners."

"And if you don't?"

"He promised Manny and Eva will be killed. Actually, tortured to death." I saw him wince.

"These cases are the meat of the matter you and Manny have been working on with April Hewett, aren't they?"

"Yes sir."

"Well, you have the life of my son and your other friend in your hands, Mr. James. What are you going to do?"

"To tell you the truth, sir, that's why I came to see you. I will risk neither Eva nor Manny's life, but I shrink from the possibility of giving in to extortion. That's one reason I wanted to hear your thoughts on the matter."

"My thoughts?" Porter stood up suddenly from his chair and

paced from his desk to the right wall and back again. "My thoughts as a father? Bring him back, for God's sake. Pay what it takes, do what is needed, only don't let him disappear from our lives. His death would kill his mother and destroy me." He paced some more.

"But then my thoughts as the publisher of this paper? Yes, bring him back, but don't give in. Don't pay ransom. Don't do what they want. Don't do anything that will let anyone in the future believe they can force this newspaper's hand by endangering our reporters." Then he stopped and stared at us intensely.

"And then there are my thoughts as a citizen of this town. Don't give in. Fight harder. Get him back if you can, but don't stop fighting." He gulped slightly and removed his glasses. "So, you can see, gentlemen, my thoughts depend a lot on which Arthur Porter happens to be there when you ask."

Blake spoke up. "How is Mrs. Porter, sir?"

"She is as good as can be expected."

"Let me assure you, sir, we're doing everything in our power to get—"

"Of course you are! I know that. And my wife and I are grateful. But we all know luck plays a much larger role here than skill or even persistence."

I cleared my throat again.

"What?"

"We came here to ask you, sir, if the *South Georgia Record* would consider carrying a large story about all of this—the kidnapping certainly, but also the ransom demand and the issues underpinning it."

"How would that help?"

"Sir, these kidnappers believe they are all powerful. In my conversation with the man who we believe is behind all this, he compared himself to a natural disaster such as a hurricane or tornado, as an all-powerful agent of lasting change. I don't believe that. I believe if the facts of the situation are laid before the people of this community, they will rally to prevent the kidnappers from achieving their ends. Your paper can be the vehicle for telling the people what has gone on."

"How would that help get my son back?"

Agent Blake spoke up. "In two ways, sir. First, this community has knowledge about this crime they don't even realize they have. A story like this one will give them context for what they may already know and help them connect the dots and call us. Second, these kidnappings are the final acts of desperate men who know their cause is likely finished but don't want to leave the field without having tried everything. In short, they won't kill their hostages unless they feel they absolutely have to. A story like this will make it clear to them that killing the hostages would make their situation more difficult, not less."

"What supports your belief about their characterization?"

"Their progression of threats and actions," Blake said. "Even their most potentially deadly act, the car bomb, didn't wind up actually killing anyone, yet it still failed to move their cause forward. We want to prove that killing their hostages would only harm their cause with people, not help it."

"If Manny were here, I would agree with you and assign it to him," Porter said ruefully. "I'm not sure who would write it now."

"If I may make a suggestion," I said.

"Go ahead."

"Manny has a friend, Tomas Kingsolver, who reports for you, sir. I think if he were here, he would ask that Tommy be assigned the story."

"The cultural reporter? Do you think he's up to it?"

"I think Manny would say he is, sir."

"All right." He punched a button on his phone. "Rosa. If young Kingsolver is in the building, send him up here, right away."

"Yes, Mr. Porter."

"So, where do we go from here?" Porter asked.

"We continue our efforts to narrow the field and keep searching," Blake said. "We also intensify our investigations into the identities of some of the henchmen who we believe have been involved."

"We've been given an extension from the court, so that is at least one burden off our backs."

"What judge is hearing that case?"

"Judge Samuel Klinefeld."

"Good Lord, is he still on the bench?" Porter said. "I thought he retired. He was hearing cases when I was the crime reporter more than thirty years ago. Still, you could do worse. Klinefeld is fair and completely incorruptible."

Porter paused and took off his glasses again. Suddenly, he looked tired. "Gentlemen, I know you are working as hard as you can, but please find some way to work harder," he requested in a soft voice. "Bring our boy back to us."

We each stood up.

"We'll do our very best sir," Agent Blake said.

As we left Rosa's office, we met Kingsolver on his way to Porter's.

"Lyle, it's really good to see you," Tommy said. "How are you holding up?" He looked tired and worried, about like everyone else.

"I'm hanging in," I said. "Good luck with the new assignment. I know you're going to knock it out of the park."

"What new assignment?"

"You'll find out," I said and walked on.

CHAPTER TWENTY-TWO

Escaping Ship

After our fifth try at maneuvering into position across the filthy deck we had given up in exhaustion. But after a bit of fitful sleep, Eva was ready to try again.

"Can you get just a little bit closer?" she asked.

"Do you need me in your lap, Eva?"

"No, but this wretched chain has gotten twisted, so it's even shorter than before."

I lay still, catching my breath. A filthy coating of fish blood, metal oxides, and dead seaweed covered my front from chest to ankle. Now I truly stank. "This used to be one of my favorite suits."

"If this gets us out of here, I'll buy you another," she said. "C'mon, one more try and we'll probably get it."

Then we both heard the distant phut-phut of a small outdoor motor.

"Quick," she said, "we don't want Caliban to see you so close to me. Get back to where he put you down."

"I'll never make it in time."

"Just get closer, we'll think of something."

I started wriggling back as the boat drew near and cut the motor. Soon, Caliban's heavy tread sounded on the deck above us. I kept moving and had almost made it all the way back when the door opened at the end of the space and Caliban appeared, holding a sack and a newspaper.

"Oh good, something to read," I said.

"Naw," he said. "It's just for the picture." He walked over to me and bent down. "What the fuck," he said, pointing at my front.

"He woke up rough," she said. "Lots of thrashing around, crying out. Really wasn't pretty."

"Oh," he said. "I'm sorry. But that weren't me, though. You both was out like babies when I picked you up. Hah!"

He bent down, lifted me up by the belt and hefted me into place beside Eva with no sign of strain or effort, accomplishing in about three seconds what I had been trying to do for who knew how many hours.

"Here," he said suddenly, thrusting a copy of the *South Georgia Record* at me. "Hold it in front of both of you, but don't cover your faces. Yeah, like that."

He stepped back a few feet, brought an old Polaroid camera out of the bag and took a couple of photos. "How much water you two got?"

"A bit more than a gallon."

"I'll bring you some more. How much food?"

"You didn't leave any food."

He growled and stomped over to the water bag. Behind it was a second bag Eva hadn't seen, from which he drew a family size package of chocolate sandwich cookies.

"I knew I had," he said. "Here." He dropped them in my lap. "Them's the good ones with the extra creamy centers. I like those myself."

"Before you go, how long do we have to stay here?"

"For as long as the admiral says."

"Then what happens?"

"Depends on the admiral. If he says let you go, I'll probably put you ashore near a highway so you can hail a ride. But if he says something different, I'll do something different."

He returned to the door.

"Be good now," he said before leaving. "I'll be back soon."

Eventually, we heard his footsteps on deck again and the motorized cough as the outboard started, close at first but gradually getting farther away until we couldn't hear it anymore.

"Damn, if I had known that lunk was going to just put me right where I needed to be, I would have stayed clean and let him do it," I moaned.

She reached over and started patting my leg, looking for the identifying pocket knife bulge.

"Aren't you being just a wee bit forward?"

"This is not funny," she said. "And for your information, my tastes run to straight men about four years your junior."

"Really? Lyle never mentioned your robbing cradles."

"A good friend keeps your confidences. There, I'm sure that's it," she said triumphantly. She reached over with both hands and started opening my belt.

"Hey now, what's that about?"

"Oh, calm down, Mr. Tight Pants. If I get your belt open and your pants undone, I might be able to get my hand in the pocket to get the knife. May I also remind you that neither one of us has ever met this admiral, and we don't know if he'll let us go or cast us into the watery deep. Here, suck in your skinny gut. That's it."

With my gut clenched in, she got my belt and pants open and managed to fish out my admirable but old Swiss Army pocket knife.

"Quite nice," she said, envying it. "And very old school. Most men don't carry pocket knives anymore. Just one more thing to remove at the metal detector."

"My dad gave it to me the night he tried to explain why my mother is nuts," I said. "It was like a consolation prize since I couldn't follow his explanation. I use it to open mail sometimes."

"Your mother is nuts? So was mine. We need to share a few beers sometime." She opened the knife and tested the blade against her thumb. Sadly, it came nowhere near to cutting her. She shot me a look. "You know, a dull knife is like a dull mind, useless and taking up space. When was the last time you sharpened this?"

"I've never sharpened it. Who sharpens pocket knives? That would be like polishing a toy pistol."

She sighed. "Still, it's better than nothing. Time to wriggle again. I need you on your back with your feet near me."

"May I have some water first?" I said.

"Sure."

Since we had almost drained the first gallon, it was easier for her to give me water without drowning me. As she lowered the empty container, I eyed the package of cookies hungrily. "Maybe if this works, we can break those open."

"I didn't know you were a fan."

"Sister, at this point I would eat liver—and I really hate liver."

"On your back," she ordered.

This time, with a relatively small distance and feeling more optimistic, I soon presented her with my feet, bound firmly by layers of duct tape from my ankles to mid-shin. Unfortunately, the sun had already gone down, and it was too dark to do anything but attempt to sleep.

The next morning, after a makeshift meal of cookies and water,

Eva opened all the knife blades and determined they were equally dull. The corkscrew tool was still pretty sharp, so I suggested it could make a line of holes in the duct tape she could then connect with the dull knife. This she did, and with frequent breaks to rest her hands, she finally managed to saw through the fibrous tape to connect the holes.

"Have you given much thought to what we'll do after we get my feet free?"

"First thing is to keep him from noticing that we've done this," she said. "I'm being really careful to keep the appearance of the tape in place."

"And the second thing?"

"The second thing is to take him by surprise."

"I really wish I'd sharpened that knife now," I said. "Or that we had a pistol or sword or something. He's so huge."

"I've been looking closely at one of those short pipes over there. I think it's loose. We might be able to break it off and use it as a weapon. Aha!" she said as the dull knife cut its way through the last of the tape.

"You did it!" I said. "Thank God, it feels good to move them again."

"Can you stand?"

"Let me get my feet underneath me and see." I rolled to my belly and then pushed back to get to my knees. Once there, I used a nearby pole to support myself from there to my feet.

"God, I'm stiff," I groaned.

"Can you get to that short pole over there and see if it's as ready to break loose as it looks?"

I carefully picked my way across the uneven deck to the pole I indicated. I pressed against it and kicked it a couple of times. "Sorry to report, this thing is here to stay at least for another few years," I said.

"Damnit."

"However," I said with triumph, bending down and coming up with a length of pole in my handcuffed hands, "this one might do quite well."

"Bring it over here."

At around thirty inches long and slightly heavier at one end, she declared it a fine weapon.

"But what's the plan for using it?" I said. "I have my feet free and you have your hands free, but my hands are still bound and so are your feet."

"The key thing is to keep him from noticing that your feet are free," she said. "The next time he arrives, we get ourselves ready before he comes in. He's not very careful around us because he doesn't think we're dangerous."

"What will we do?"

"I'll do what I can to get him close to me, ideally bending over me for some reason. You just be ready to attack from behind. Remember, I'll have the pipe, so you just have to distract him long enough to let me get in a couple of good swings."

"Then what?"

"Then, hopefully, we've incapacitated him. We get the keys from him, unlock the damn locks, and get off this tub," she said.

"Do you think he has the keys on him?"

"I think so."

I considered this for a moment. "It's not much of a plan."

"If you have a better one, I'm all ears," she said.

"That's just it, I don't."

"The plan details aren't important," she said, sounding confident and optimistic. "What's important is that we have surprise. We're ready but he won't be."

"Yeah," I said. "Now how about we break into those cookies? I'm about ready to starve."

As evening approached and shadows began to cloak our space, Eva and I started to listen more closely for the telltale phut-phut that would signal Caliban's return. We had tried to place ourselves strategically in our space according to our plan. Eva was on her side, her body concealing the length of pipe we hoped to use as a weapon, while I sat nearby, propped up somewhat on a thick metal box.

"Where is he?" Eva said. "Previous days he's been like a clock, and today he's late."

I thought it ironic she would grumble about the absence of our guard, until I remembered we needed him, or at least his keys, to get out of this situation. What if something happened to him? Would anyone else know where we were?

Finally, just as the morning sunlight made its way into our space, we both heard the faint phut-phut that gradually grew louder and more distinct, heralding his approach.

"Showtime," Eva said. "Remember, once you're on his back, you have to get your hands and chain hard against his throat. We don't know how long we'll have. Try to get him turned around toward me so I can hit him cleanly."

We both made sure we were in position. As soon as I heard his heavy tread above, I started to shout.

"Help, help! Down here! We need help! Hurry!"

Above us the pace of the footsteps increased, then we heard a thumping and Caliban burst into the hold.

"What the fuck!"

"Quickly," I said, pointing to Eva's prone form. "I think she's having a diabetic seizure," I cried. "I told her not to eat those cookies, but she got so hungry. She had like ten or fifteen of them and she slumped over."

"Damn," he muttered, rushing over to her. He started talking to her and slapping her face. "C'mon, beautiful, come on back to us. You don't want to do this to old Peter now, do you? No sirree you don't. C'mon, darling."

His words were unexpectedly tender, and I forgot for a moment my role in the plan. Precious seconds passed where he stood bent over her body with his broad back as flat as a table before I carefully stood up, gathered up the strength in my legs, offered up a little prayer to St. Joseph, and launched myself with a bloodcurdling scream directly onto Caliban's back with my arms outstretched.

"Argh-oompf," he groaned as my full weight fell on him. Then he lost his footing on the slippery surface and toppled hard on his side with me hanging on like a limpet. I remembered to pull my hands backward, the handcuff chain cutting off the air to his windpipe.

"Bastard," he groaned. "I'll break your goddamned arms."

Meanwhile I had wrapped my legs around his torso. When I realized the proximity of my feet to his crotch, I started kicking hard in the hope of a lucky strike.

"Eva! Any moment now would be good." She had finally gotten to her feet. She took a couple of short steps in her chains, set a stern expression on her face, and swung the pipe like she stood on the first tee.

The tubing struck with a sickening thud-crunch you never want to hear in conjunction with a head injury. Blood gushed from his head, and he stopped moving.

"Holy crap, did you kill him?"

"I don't know," she said, putting a hand on his chest. "He's still breathing. Quick, the pockets. We need some keys."

We speedily emptied his cargo pants of a wallet with a five, a ten, and two ones but no ID. Other pockets yielded nothing, until finally, from the last pouch on his right leg, Eva triumphantly pulled out a key ring.

"Aha!" she yelled.

But this was at best a partial victory, because there were at least two hundred keys on this ring.

"Which one is it?" I said with a moan.

"I'll recognize it, but I still have to find it," she said, moving rapidly through them.

"Who has that many keys?"

"Maybe this is only one of the places he holds captives."

She stood, holding up a slim silver key. "Here, let me see your cuffs." I extended my hands. Eva maneuvered the key to fit while still on the ring. "Here goes nothing," she said. She inserted the key in the lock and turned. Mercifully, we heard a mild click, and the cuffs loosened.

"Thank God," I blurted, shaking out my hands get the blood flowing. "What now?"

"Now we have to get my legs free." She started going through the keys again, stopping every time she found one that looked about the right size. But we faced two locks when it came to her legs.

"You don't know what they look like?"

"No," she said. "These things look like they go back to 1910. Ahhh. This might do it." She held up a small key almost black with age and immediately bent down to start working it into the lock. I saw her get it in, but I couldn't tell if she was able to turn it.

She stood up panting, with her face red. "My kingdom for some graphite or lube. You give it a go."

I knelt and tried to jiggle the key. There was definitely no way it would turn to the right, but it felt easier to the left. I put my energy into it until we heard a quiet pop, and the lock dropped from the chain.

"Fantastic," she said. "Now, my ankles."

We had gone through about half the keys looking for a fit when we heard Caliban give a moan.

"Fuck, is he coming to?" she said.

"Maybe, do you want to hit him again?"

"No. Let's go before he wakes up."

"How do we get out of here?"

She pointed across the hold. "He always comes in through that door."

We started that way as fast as we could without falling, but Eva still could not take full steps and the shackles affected her balance. I watched her for a moment, then came back to her.

"What?"

"Pardon me," I said before bending down and hefting her across my shoulders in a fireman's carry.

"What are you doing? Put me down."

"I will once we're clear," I said. "We don't have the time to wait for you to pick your way out." It still took more time than I wanted. She wasn't heavy, but I felt doubly worried about slipping on the muck covering the floor.

"Well done getting him down here so fast," she said. "But you know, diabetic shock is caused by too little blood sugar, not too much," she said.

"Yes, but I made a bet he wouldn't know that."

Once we reached the door, I set her down as it was too narrow to pass through while carrying her. We found ourselves in a tapered passage heading farther into the boat with a spiral staircase to the right.

"This must lead to the deck," she said.

"Yes, but I want to see if I can find a cell phone or radio. He didn't have one on him."

As she waited by the stairs, I made a quick inspection down the passage. All I found was a tiny, filthy bathroom and some old sleeping quarters that looked like they hadn't been used in years. I returned down the passage to the stairs.

"Nothing," I said.

She shrugged.

"How weird is it that he didn't have a mobile?" I said. "Not even a flip-top. I would have thought they wanted him reachable at all times."

We heard a sound from the hold. I stepped up to the door and opened it a crack. In the shadowy light I saw him trying to get to his knees.

"Time to go," I said. She started up the stairs as I followed. At the top, we stepped into the boat's bridge and Caliban's living quarters as well, as evidenced by the unmade cot, scattered fast food containers, and other trash. The staircase had a hatch at the top that I lowered into position, but no lock.

"Here," Eva said, pointing to an office chair. I put it on top of the cover. By itself it was pretty light and wouldn't prove much of an obstacle, but with its legs wedged under the stairway railing, it would be difficult to move.

I glanced over the boat's helm. Still no mobile phone. *He doesn't use one?* But there was a new-looking radio. I reached for it, but Eva grabbed my hand.

"What are you doing?"

"Calling for help," I said. She shook her head vigorously.

"Marine radio is not like a cell phone or even a walkie-talkie. Anybody can hear what you say. People you want to hear, like the Coast Guard, or people you don't want to hear, like the people who put us here. And they might be a lot closer than the Coast Guard."

Then, as if to prove her point, the radio squawked alive.

"Admiral One to Katie Ann. Admiral One to Katie Ann. Do you read? Over." A pause for a few seconds. "Katie Ann, this is Admiral One. Do you copy? Over."

Eva grabbed my arm and pointed at one of the orange life rings mounted on a bulkhead. There, the name *Katie Ann* stood out in large white letters against the neon fabric.

"That's us," she said, her voice shaking a little. "And I think we can guess who Admiral One is."

"What do we do?"

"Katie Ann, this is Admiral One. Come in. Over." Admiral One had a little edge in his voice this time.

"We get off this boat. We have to find Caliban's outboard."

CHAPTER TWENTY-THREE

Eva's Photos Arrive

Another sleepless night that ended in a dream about a fire, complete with alarms, sirens, smoke, and death until I finally came to, finding my mobile ringing continuously. From the cracks around my window blinds, I could tell the sun was up. Parker was on the phone.

"Sorry to disturb you, boss, but it's seven thirty, and I'm here with the cops. Manny and Eva are on the *Record's* front page, and something came in FedEx yesterday the cops think you should see."

"Ugghh," I groaned. "Give them coffee. Make sure you pour some for me, and tell them I'll be right there."

I took a quick navy shower and headed down on the elevator. Agent Blake awaited me along with two others in suits, all sipping coffee.

"Agent Blake, so good to see you again after, um, five or six hours," I said sarcastically.

"Likewise, I'm sure," Blake said as I sat down behind my desk. "We would have given you more of a break if Parker here hadn't drawn our attention to this in the mail last night."

Parker passed me the paper first.

"Land Deal Thugs Kidnap Record Reporter, Freelance Photog," the headline screamed, adding "Seek Victory in Large Tinker Creek Case."

I scanned the article. Tommy had done a fine job of telling the story but withholding details the police didn't want us to mention. Though a few hours had passed since the issue had hit the newsstands, Parker said the answering machine was full of tips from people who thought they might have seen something in relation to the abductions or thought they knew where Tommy and Eva were now.

He passed me a padded envelope I hadn't noticed him holding. It originated in Savannah, and the writing on the front was clearly Eva's. My heart jumped a little.

"This is Eva's writing," I said.

"Parker thought it might be. That's why we figured you should open it sooner than later." He pointed to one of the other agents beside him. "Agent Brindle here is one of our bomb guys. He's already figured out it's not going to explode."

I grabbed the opening tab at the top of the envelope and gave it a sharp tug. It came away easily, revealing a piece of paper and two flash drives. I pulled out the note. It was written in Eva's familiar, upward-slanting cursive.

"Lyle," I read aloud. "These should make you happy. I wanted to send them safely because they're too hot for me to keep until I see you again. Please shoot me a text to let me know you got them. Your friend, Eva. P.S. I trust you remember our signal from the Blue Moon."

"Let's see what's on them," Blake said eagerly. I sat at my desk and fired up my computer.

"What do you think is there?" Blake asked.

"I haven't a clue, but I expect it could be something she discovered while doing surveillance for us at the Empire Cinema building."

Blake's eyebrows rose, and I remembered we hadn't completely filled him on what Eva had been doing in the surveillance nest. I proceeded to tell him about the observation of the suspicious characters occupying 217 Breaker Street, along with the links between that house and Alex Deutsch and his FairWinds Development company.

"You know, there are almost certainly laws against what you and Ms. Almisra were doing at the Empire," Blake said.

"Does that mean you can't use what we found, if we found anything?"

"I'm not sure, but maybe not. For now, we'll treat it as a tip and see if we can't take it from here to develop evidence we can use."

"Look, until we find out what's on the drives, it's all supposition, right?" said the ever-practical Parker. "Put the drives in and let's see what we got."

I inserted the drive into the port. The computer buzzed slightly and a window labeled "Magic Box 1" popped up on the screen. But when I tried to open it, all that appeared was a dialog box with the words "PASSWORD 1 of 5."

"Damn, it's password protected," I said.

"What's the password?" Blake asked.

"I don't know."

"How can you not know? She's your friend."

"Try her dog's name," Parker suggested. "She talks about him all the time."

I typed in "Kwanjo." The screen blinked but the dialog box reappeared, this time reading "PASSWORD 2 OF 5."

"Fuck. It's password protected, and we only have three more tries to get it right."

"Christ," Blake said. "Okay, what else? Mother's maiden name? Her middle name? Wait, doesn't she speak other languages? How do we know it's even in English?"

"She and her mom weren't close," Parker said.

"Wait, wait, wait," I cried. "Shut up for a second." The room fell silent. "Parker, please read the last line of Eva's note again."

Parker took the sheet out, cleared his throat, and read. "I trust you remember our signal from the Blue Moon."

The Blue Moon…The Blue Moon was a bar where we first developed our pickup routine and included a phrase we used to let each other know if we were okay.

"I have it," I shouted. "Or I think I have it. Parker, what horse won the Kentucky Derby this year?"

Parker's fingers fairly flew over his phone's keyboard. "A horse named Country House, boss."

I turned to the keyboard and carefully typed "Country House" into the password box. Then I held my breath, closed my eyes, and hit enter.

My machine whirred, and when I opened my eyes they beheld a pop-up screen with "Magic Box 1" at the top and showing two folders. One read "217 Breaker Street Files 1-5" and the other read "217 Breaker Street Files 6-10."

"We're in!"

Blake looked at me. "The Kentucky Derby winner?"

"It's a long story." I opened the first file and there was a series of photos, all clearly visible, of a man I knew walking through the parking area at 217 Breaker and up the stairs.

"Wait," I said. "I know him."

"Who?" Blake said.

"This guy. The one whose photo Eva took at the house." Emotions came back to me. Frustration. His smirk while he explained the Georgia Open Records Act to me without mentioning he was going to use it to keep me from getting the information I needed. "His name, at least when I met him, was James O'Hara, and he was the St. Michael's Harbor city clerk," I said.

At that point Blake asked to take the drives and I agreed. The GBI's advanced technical and photographic analysis could wring every bit of useful information from the mechanisms more quickly and thoroughly than we could. Meanwhile, Blake was on the phone about getting a warrant to search the 217 Breaker house.

❖

"Hold on, goddammit. I can't take full steps, Mr. Long Legs."

He looked at me as though I were simple, and I choked back my frustration for the fiftieth time since we left the hold.

"Eva, we need to get off this boat," Manny said, as though I required to be reminded. "We don't know how far away Admiral One is or when he might show up to find out why Caliban isn't answering the radio."

"I know that, you pup, but I can only go as fast as these metal anklets will let me!"

"Well, the deck's too treacherous for me to carry you again." He sniffed.

I breathed deeply. *Lord, I lift mine eyes unto the hills from whence cometh my strength*, I prayed.

"I know that. But if you'll just slow up enough for me to hold your shoulder for balance, I'll make much better time. We can only go as fast as our weakest link, right," I said, even though I hated to admit slowing down the Manny and Eva Escape Show.

"Right. Sorry." He came alongside me, and by my holding on to his shoulder, we made it to the stern where we found Caliban's dinghy, but also a five-foot climb down a ladder to reach it. Under normal circumstances such a ladder wouldn't make me pause a second, but without the use of my feet I wasn't sure what to do.

I turned to him. "Any ideas?"

"This might be a time to move past women and children first." He smirked.

"What?"

"I should go down first to pull the boat as close to the ladder as possible and to stabilize you as you come down. Then you can descend after me more easily. Thank God we have a calm sea."

I had to admit that made sense, and he dropped to the little craft in about thirty seconds. He used the rope tying the boat to the ladder to pull the skiff closer and then looped it once to discourage it from moving.

"Okay?" he asked.

"I suppose."

"Now, pay attention," he said. "You're going to back down the ladder, but from where I am it doesn't look like your chains are going to let you have a foot on two rungs at the same time. You'll have to come down one rung at a time."

"But I can't see the rungs!"

"Take the toe of your shoe and trace it down the ladder until it hits the next rung." I stretched out my right into a huge void but kept my toe touching the frame.

"Yeah, like that. Now start lowering your foot. Keep in contact with the frame. Yeah. Okay, now your right foot is over the rung, like one inch away. Start sliding your left foot off the deck slowly."

I did, and as my left foot left the deck, I felt my right come to rest on the rung. I quickly brought my left foot to match it there and paused, breathing hard.

"Excellent!" he crowed. "Now just do that six more times and we're home free." On the last three rungs he was able to reach the small of my back and my belt, and this helped stabilize me further, so in just a couple of minutes we were together in the dinghy's little space.

"I didn't know they even made boats this small," I complained, while trying to find a place for my legs that would be out of his way.

"Neither did I," he admitted. "I'm not even sure this qualifies as a rowboat, though I see it has oars." He pointed to paddles, one on either side of the craft.

"Since you're closer, can you get the painter untied and we can get out of here," he said. I looked at him blankly.

"Sorry, the rope. Please untie the rope from the ladder so we can go."

I quickly discovered the knot was easily mastered and we were free of the *Katie Ann*.

He got on his knees near the small but new-looking outboard

motor and grabbed the pull rope handle. I held my breath. "Here goes nothing."

He yanked the pull cord, and the motor made a whrrrr chop noise but didn't start. He tried it again, same result.

"I think you might have to pull that green button on the right," I speculated. "This looks like my lawnmower at home, and that's what I have to do to start that."

He pulled the button, which came out from the motor on a metal stem.

"Now try it." This time the engine coughed once and then roared to life.

"Woohoo," he said as he turned the engine and started propelling us away from the *Katie Ann*. I leaned close to him to make myself heard over its roar.

"One question," I shouted. "Where are we going?"

He slowed the throttle until we were creeping along and the motor was much quieter.

"That's a good question," he admitted. "Where should we go? I was going to aim us for the first private or public pier we saw, but we don't know where these bastards are. We could pull right up to their dock!"

"Exactly," I said. "I think we have to head for the public dock at St. Michael's Harbor. We know there's a Coast Guard office and dockmaster there."

"How far is that?"

"I have no idea."

We fell into a brief silence as we contemplated our options. And as we drifted about one hundred or a hundred and fifty yards from the *Katie Ann*, she startled us. A sort of whooshing noise came from her and then, as we watched in horror, she blew up. A loud crump filled the air as a tower of flame arose out from about where the engine must have been. We ducked our heads and yelled in fright as pieces of the doomed boat, some large, plunged from the sky to splash into the ocean around us. The *Katie Ann* became a floating platform of flame that, in a few minutes, began to sink beneath the surface.

"Oh my God," I said. "That could have been us!"

"Did we do that?"

"Of course not. How could we have done that? All we did was leave."

"Poor Caliban," Manny said.

"What do you mean, poor Caliban? If we hadn't left, it would have been poor us and poor Caliban."

"Do you think it was a bomb?" His voice was subdued.

"I don't know," I said. "But if it was a bomb, it was one that would kill us and their guy," I added.

"I know."

At that moment, as if in sympathy with the *Katie Ann*'s violent end, our own outboard motor gave two brief sputters and stopped.

"What the fuck," I swore again. We needed to catch at least a couple of breaks.

"I might have idled it too slowly," he said. "Let me get it started again." He knelt by the outboard, pulled the button to its full extension, and yanked the cord. The motor coughed, sputtered to life, then died again.

He growled and repeated the procedure. This time the motor coughed twice but never caught. He muttered under his breath. Then he reached down the machine and unscrewed a red cap on the side.

"Fuck! We're out of gas."

"No!"

"Yep. He must have been planning to refill it from the *Katie Ann* before he left."

"Shit. What do we do now?"

"Well, I still don't think it's a good idea for us to just sit here until the kidnappers come looking to see what happened to Caliban."

"Except maybe what happened to Caliban was supposed to happen to him—and us. They won't come back for that. But maybe somebody else will."

"Do you think we want to just sit here until that happens?" I asked. "We're drifting now and," I looked over my shoulder, "there's no sign the *Katie Ann* was ever here except for the debris."

"Okay, so we row. Have you ever rowed a boat before?"

"Nope. I'm great on the rowing machine at the gym, but I don't know if that translates into rowing a boat."

"It doesn't," he said. "My dad and I used to take out a boat when I was a kid, so I sort of know how to do it. First," he reached down and grabbed the closet oar, "we have to get these up and on these posts here."

Together we hefted the oars off the hull of the boat and got them into place. Then Manny turned around in his seat and faced the other way.

"I apologize for turning my back on you," he said over his shoulder, "but you really have to sit in this direction and on this seat to do it."

"Okay," I said. "Trust me, no offense taken."

"Which way?" he asked.

I looked around us. There were shorelines on three of our sides, indicating we were somewhere in the middle of Esperanza Bay with the largest and darkest mass of shore directly in front of us. "That way, I guess."

He started to row.

After Agent Blake left with the drives, I started fielding calls from other media outlets seeking comments and interviews about the story. All the large papers sought interviews along with national and even international broadcast outlets. By the time I'd finished the last, one o'clock had rolled around.

I headed upstairs to grab a sandwich when Agent Blake called. "So, what's up?" I asked.

"That guy O'Hara left a clear thumbprint on one of the bathroom mirrors at that Breaker Street house," he said, "and the guys on the video keep talking about an admiral. We're thinking that's most likely Deutsch. We also may have lucked out on Manny's abduction."

"How so?"

"A taxi driver called in that he was just down the street from Manny's on his way to pick up a fare when he was almost hit by a speeding white contractor's van with New York plates. He couldn't get the whole number, but he got the first three digits and the make, so we've reached out to New York state for a possible ID on the owner."

"Great!"

He paused. "There's some other news too."

"Okay."

"The Coast Guard has reported some kind of explosion at sea on Esperanza Bay, almost two miles out."

"So?"

"I'm just letting you know. It's probably not related at all, but I've learned to distrust coincidences."

"Wait. Are you telling me you think Manny and Eva were on a ship that blew up in Esperanza Bay?" I could feel as well as hear the stress in my voice as part of my heart fell into my abdomen.

"No, I'm not saying that. I'm just letting you know something that might turn out to be relevant later. It may be they'd been on the boat but were taken off before. It may be that the boat explosion was totally unrelated. We just don't know."

"God, do me a favor, please don't share this with Arthur Porter. That poor man's got enough to worry about now. Go ahead and pass on the news about the van, though."

We hung up.

Carolyn Mondial called. "Hello, Lyle. How you holding up?"

"Just getting through another hour."

"Well, this might help. The court clerk just left after coming to see little ole me."

"Really?"

"Yes. We'll be at the top of Judge Klinefeld's docket no matter when we manage to get back into his courtroom," she said. "His Honor apparently read the *Record* story this morning and totally understands. All we have to do is let the clerk know the day before, and they will schedule us."

"Phenomenal," I said.

"And here's what's weird about it, because judges are so tight-lipped about their opinions. The rumor is that Klinefeld called the state attorney's office this morning and asked if kidnapping to get a civil case dropped could be charged under the obstruction of justice statute."

"Wow."

"So, we haven't won yet, but this morning looks a lot better than yesterday morning did."

"Except Manny and Eva are still not here," I said. And, sadly, I hung up.

❖

Until I started trying to row that little boat with me and Eva on it, I'd thought I was in pretty good shape. I mean, of course, I didn't have Lyle James's level of fitness, but then who does? But I didn't have a bad physique for a gay boy who was never that much into sports and had a job where I sat down a lot of the time. Then came rowing that tiny boat with two people in it, and any thoughts I had about my fitness rocketed out the window.

Rowing that damn boat was the hardest physical thing I have ever done.

"Oh my God," I gasped, lifting the oars from the water to let their hand grips rest against my legs. "Whoever guessed that moving a little boat would be such hard work?" Sweat poured down my back and gathered like a string of soggy diamonds in my hair.

"Of course it's hard work," Eva snapped. "Why do you think the members of the crew have such muscular physiques? They row everywhere."

I ignored her and dipped the oars back in. My head pounded and I wished we'd brought some water, but I knew I had to keep rowing to get us home. After going a bit more, I heard the clear sound of fabric being torn. Eva had removed her blouse and was ripping it into strips, leaving her only in a sports bra.

"What are you doing?" I asked. "I don't think we need bandages."

"No, but we both need something to keep the sweat out of our faces. You more than me. So, I am making us something."

She tied two of the strips together and handed them to me. "Bring those oars in for a moment and fasten this around your head."

I did what she said, appreciating how quiet and peaceful the bay felt as soon as I stopped rowing. The current carried us along in the direction we wanted to go, But the sun beat down.

"You look like an actor in an apocalyptic movie," she said. "Like *Heart of Darkness* or *Apocalypse Now*."

"I read Conrad in school, but I don't remember a book called *Apocalypse Now*."

"It was a movie," she said. "Released before you were born. It's about the war in Vietnam and madness."

I put the oars back in the water and kept on rowing. Now that the current ran with us, it felt like we traveled wonderfully far with each stroke.

"Why do you think the boat blew up?" she asked. "Do you think it was a bomb?"

"I don't know. It could have been."

"We didn't see any bomb."

"We didn't exactly search either. I think it might have been an accident. It was an old boat. Who knows when and how they maintained it."

"Did you hear that?" she asked suddenly.

"What?"

"That sort of whiny buzz."

"No," I said, and then I did.

"Look there," she said, pointing. "It's a drone! We're here! We're here! Look at us!" she shouted.

For the first few moments, I couldn't see anything against a stubborn cloud, but soon I picked it out and joined Eva's shouting, lifting the oars to make us look bigger. The machine hovered above us for about two long minutes, then it zoomed away in the direction we were headed.

"Is that a good thing or not?" I said.

"I'm choosing to think it is."

"Why?"

"Because that was a photo drone. I recognized it from when I was looking to buy one last year. And I read where local emergency services have started using them to do things like find lost people."

"Let's hope," I said, resuming rowing. After another twenty minutes she pointed at the horizon behind us.

"Look," she said.

And there, against the edge of the sea, came a red and white tugboat after us. I pulled in the oars and set them down. Despite my arms feeling like jelly and my back sensing nothing but pain, never before had I been as happy.

Agent Blake called again. "I'm coming back down to Bonne Chance," he said. "I think we may be coming up on the end of this."

"Are you serious? That's great news."

"Not necessarily. Coming up on an end might not mean coming up on the end we want."

"What do you mean?"

The Bureau had found out the white contractor's van had been stolen two weeks prior. Tips had located it around some old warehouses near the Buccaneer Pier. When agents had followed up, they found the van, along with the bodies of the two men who had been occupying 217 Breaker Street in Eva's videos.

"They're dead?" I felt like the floor fell away underneath me. "I thought Deutsch wasn't violent."

"He's not, or he hasn't been. Forensic analysts and detectives are all over the warehouse now. I expect we'll know more in a few hours."

I shook but I made myself ask. "Was there any sign of Manny or Eva?"

"Not yet," he said, "but certainly nothing to indicate they had been killed."

I let my breath out slowly.

"I'll be back in your office in under an hour," he said, hanging up.

I longed to go upstairs again. My gym's cool steel called to me with its order, precision, balance, control, and strength. None of the things I felt like I had right now.

But Parker had his hands full with a difficult transmission job, and nobody else was free enough to watch the office. I sat at my desk and tried to focus on invoices and keeping my heart and my head on the same page.

I realized how much I had changed. Before I met Manny, I never let anyone get close enough for me to care for them. Eva, my bar-prowling compatriot and soulmate in everything non-romantic, didn't have that hold on me. But Manny did. And rather than be alarmed by that or resentful of it, I felt happy about it. Or I did until the notion of losing him made me feel sick inside.

Blake rang back.

"What's up? You got something?"

"Okay, this is a heads-up just for you," Blake said. "Both of them are safe."

"Oh, thank God."

"They're both on a St. Michael's Harbor fireboat due at municipal pier in about ten minutes. From there, they go to St. Clair's."

"Are they—"

"They're dehydrated and need to get checked out, but otherwise seem fine. If you leave now, you'll get to St. Clair's right before they do. I'll hold off calling the family or anyone else for fifteen minutes. That should be enough to let you two have a little time to yourselves before the world comes crashing in."

"Thank you," I said.

"Don't mention it. We're going to want to interview him later because the investigation's ongoing, but you guys deserve at least a few moments alone."

I made the distance to St. Clair's in about ten minutes and hurried into the emergency room reception area. Head ER Nurse Nancy

Benedict recognized me from my previous visits as she hurried along a hall.

"Well, Mr. James. This is a surprise. How can we help you?"

I lowered my voice. "An ambulance is bringing my two friends, Eva Almisra and Manny Porter, in right now," I said, and her eyes registered surprise. "I want to be allowed in the room when they're being seen."

"Yes, that's true, they are," she said. "How did you know that? And we don't let anyone into our exam rooms."

"Then how about just Manny? He's my fiancé, and he's just been through a terrible experience. Please."

She glanced up the hall. "Okay, go down to Exam Room Two and wait. I'll make sure he's taken there when he arrives. But you have to stay out of the nurse's way. And if the doctor comes in and kicks you out, you have to leave."

"Scout's honor," I said, giving her my best salute.

"Oh, get in there before someone sees you," she said, laughing.

I slipped down the hall into the room. It had a bed with a curtain rod around it, a bank of instruments, gauges, and hook-ups.

I didn't hear them arrive at first. The ambulance brought them up to the door without lights or sirens. A flurry of announcements over the hospital's public address system summoning medical staff to the ER and then scurrying feet alerted me before the door swung open and Nurse Benedict rolled Manny's wheelchair inside.

"I'll leave you two alone," she said, shooting me a look before she left.

I tried to hide my shock. Despite Blake's reassurance, he looked terrible. A significant sunburn covered his head, face, neck, and hands and had swollen his eyes to mere slits. He had a dirty band of cloth wrapped around his forehead, and his dried and chapped lips and mouth looked like a gash against his face. While I recognized the suit, I knew from the smell he would never wear it again.

"Manny, I'm here."

"Lyle! Oh God, Lyle! You're here?" He reached out. I took a step or two closer to let him find me.

"Oh Thank God. Thank God," he moaned as his hands got my waist. "I'm blind. I can't see anything but a little bit of light. Everything hurts. I can't really move my arms. I thought we might die, and I would never…never see you again."

"Shh, shh," I said, struggling to keep my own emotions in check. "That didn't happen. I'm here. You're safe. We're safe."

I tried to hug his shoulder but quit immediately as I saw him wince.

"And I'm pretty sure you're not blind. Your eyes are just too swollen to see, that's all. You're just all swollen, like you've just had one of those shocks that some people get from bee stings."

"Oh, great! I look like the Elephant Man?"

"Oh no! Of course not. Yes, you're all red and swollen and oh my God, you smell bad, but you're still Manny and oh thank God you're here."

"Is that why you're not hugging me? I'm ugly and I stink?"

"Not at all," I said as a few tears escaped my eyes. "You're looking better to me right now than you ever have. And if I'm not hugging you, it's only because I'm afraid of hurting you, that's all. Because, Manny, that is the last thing that I want to do. Ever."

I dropped to my knees in front of his wheelchair, allowing him to feel my face and head with his smelly, swollen hands.

"I love you," I said. "If you asked me how much right now, I wouldn't have the words to tell you. A few days ago you told me how you felt about me, but I wasn't ready to respond. But this experience has changed all that. All I've done since you got taken is work to bring you back safe and sound because, Manny Porter, I want you in my life, like Father Joe says sometimes, forever and ever amen."

"You're crying," he said tracing my wet cheeks with his fingers. "Oh my God, Lyle. I want to hug you so bad, but I can't."

"Shh. Shh. Don't worry! Soon. There's time. Doctors and nurses are coming soon and we're all gonna help you get better. I think I hear them now," I said, because I did. A rising kerfuffle of voices, feet, and wheels swept into the room.

As Nurse Benedict predicted, the doctors evicted me as well as Manny's parents, who had arrived at the room with them. I might have been annoyed at this if Manny's mother, a severely dressed older lady, hadn't taken one look at him and dropped in hysterics to the floor, needing two nurses to help her out of the room into someplace quiet.

I met Agent Blake in the ER reception area, and he suggested I head back to Bonne Chance, at least for a couple of hours, but I declined.

"Parker said to tell you the phone's been ringing off the hook from media and someone has to start making some decisions."

I called Carolyn Mondial from the hospital family room and asked if she could help by fielding the media calls, at least for a couple of days.

As soon as they put Manny in a room, I headed in to be with him. All they had done was sedate him, so his red, swollen face against a white pillow still hid those features I knew so well. But I didn't care. He was Manny and he was here. I settled into the chair next to the bed.

❖

I woke up like someone turned on a light switch in my brain. One second asleep, the next wide awake. I was in a darkened hospital room. An IV bag dripped clear fluid into a vein in my right hand, and when I turned my head a little, I saw Lyle slumped in a chair next to my bed, fast asleep.

"Hey, stud," I said in a low voice.

"Wha...what?" He jerked awake.

"What's a hunk like you doing in a place like this?" I tried to smile at my lame line but stopped when it hurt.

"Looking after my boyfriend," he said, stretching those amazing arms in either direction. "How you feeling? How much pain do you have?"

"Mostly I'm thirsty," I said. "And the pain's not too bad yet. How long have I been out?"

He glanced at the clock over the door. "Like six hours. Do you want me to call the nurse?"

"No. I like hanging out with just you for now."

He shot me one of those lovely crooked Lyle grins. "You would never believe how good you look right now," he said.

"Yeah right!" I crowed, touching my cheek. "I can tell my face is still swollen."

"Doesn't matter, all that's incidental," he said. "You're here right now. Twenty-four hours ago, I didn't know if you ever would be again. That's all that matters."

Lyle slid his hand over to mine. "Can I touch you?"

"Yeah, just don't grab me or anything."

He hooked one of his fingers into mine.

"I love you, Jose Immanuel Porter," he said. "I think part of me has loved you since the moment I saw you standing in that stupid L&F line. And I don't even care that you're a reporter. All the other reporters in the world can be terrible. I'm just lucky enough to love the one who isn't."

"And I love you, Lyle James," I said. "I loved you from the moment I watched you trying to heat up soup with one hand instead of asking for my help. And even though you frustrate the shit out of me sometimes, I haven't looked back since."

He brought my finger up to his mouth and kissed it. "I wish I could lie down with you," Lyle said.

"Um, do you have a medical kink I don't know about?" I tried to wink at him.

"No, not to fool around. Just to be close to you."

"I don't think the bed's wide enough for two," I said. "But we could see if they would let you put the aloe stuff on me. I feel like I'm due for another one of those soon."

"That's a great idea," he replied.

The next day, after Manny had improved enough to be allowed out of bed, I wheeled his chair down the hall to Eva's room. She was asleep with her feet elevated a bit when we arrived, so when she awoke about twenty minutes later, she found us sitting on either side of her bed.

"My two favorite men," she said with a smile.

"And our favorite photographer," Manny said. "We had to come see how you are."

"And to say thank you," I said.

"Nonsense. For what?"

"For conking Caliban hard enough that we had time to escape," Manny said. "For keeping your wits and coming up with a plan, and for helping get us to where we needed to be."

"And for being wise enough to tell me to stay the course when I didn't know what to do with this one here," I said.

"Thank you," she said, "but I view our escape as a joint effort in every way. And Lyle, I'm confident you would have figured it out eventually."

"I like to think I would have, but I hadn't up to that point," I said.

"Or you just hadn't met the right man yet," she said with a smile. "So, when are they going to spring you from here?" she asked Manny.

"I don't know. I hope tomorrow," he said. "He's been helping me apply the aloe lotion, but I think I'm still going to peel a lot," he added. "What about you?"

She grimaced and pointed down to her feet, which we could see now were bandaged.

"I'm fighting infections from those damn shackles," she said. "I had just started to contract septicemia when they picked us up, but we fought that off. Now we're just waiting for things to heal." She sighed. "It's so good to see you together. It probably did me more good than whatever it is they keep sticking in these IV bags."

She started to drift off to sleep again, so Manny and I bid her good night and headed back to the hall to his room. We had more aloe lotion to apply.

Chapter Twenty-four

Epilogue

In the end, Eva and Manny's rescue led the news cycle around the world for about a day. Nevertheless, the impromptu press conference we held when Manny walked out of St. Clair's drew the attention of a surprising number of outlets who sent crews.

If you remember anything at all about the Tinker Creek Kidnappings, it was probably our photo from that press conference. Manny, his face swathed in gauze and wearing dark glasses, and I in Bonne Chance coveralls, holding our hands up in victory, showing that he had survived, and that we did too.

I've got a copy of the photo hanging opposite the elevator, so no one can miss seeing it. It annoys Manny, who says it looks like I'm celebrating with the Invisible Man.

Searchers dove to try to find what was left of the *Katie Ann*. But though Esperanza Bay's depth is never much more than sixty feet, they didn't bring up anything. Manny and Eva weren't ever terribly sure of where the boat anchored, nor any clearer on where she sank, and even a body of water as small as a bay has a lot of area to cover.

Neither the identity nor the fate of the man Eva and Manny nicknamed Caliban have been determined.

The police had more luck identifying the two residents of 217 Breaker Street. A check of fingerprints taken from their corpses found matches in the United Kingdom and on Interpol's exhaustive database.

The man Eva christened Buzzcut was named Alan Torfay, a former racketeer and enforcer around Belfast, Northern Ireland. The man she called Stretch turned out to have been Gregor Nowak, a pimp and small-time thief in Warsaw, Poland.

Both of the men entered the U.S. on tourist visas that had long expired and wound up shot through the head and left, along with the van, in an unused warehouse north of St. Michael's Harbor.

Despite their lack of official papers, they both carried New York driver's licenses under false names.

Senior Agent Blake with the GBI doubts these two carried out the kidnappings but suggests they transported Manny and Eva after the abductions. He maintains the two men knew their executioners. Investigators found no signs of a fight or struggle at the warehouse, and an empty pizza box at the scene suggested their last meal was the same as the one Eva documented. Bullets retrieved from their bodies and the site did not match any on record for a gun used in any other crime.

That leaves James O'Hara and Alex Deutsch. An international warrant for O'Hara got him spotted at the airport in Istanbul, Turkey, where he ran when approached by police. According to witnesses, he was struck by a truck and killed as he tried to escape pursuers across a busy road.

Senior Agent Blake liked him for the murders of the two in the warehouse as well as for the death of Caliban, though the lack of a body or evidence suggests that killing will never be prosecuted.

"O'Hara was Deutsch's non-com," Blake said. "Deutsch gave the orders, but O'Hara made them happen. All the murder victims represented potential loose ends after the plan failed to gain the success they wanted."

Since O'Hara's death leaves the authorities without evidence, Alex Deutsch currently faces no warrants at all. I recently read online that he had joined the board of yet another international charity.

Police finally tracked down Hannah Mayo, the woman who had signed papers saying she owned the property at 217 Breaker Street when, effectively, FairWinds Development did. Canadian authorities found her living in Toronto, where she acknowledged inking the papers her uncle James asked she sign.

"I figured he was probably pulling the wool over somebody's eyes because that's Uncle James all over," she told investigators. "But I never guessed how serious it was or that it could get that serious. I didn't ask very many questions. I learned pretty early not to ask Uncle James too many questions."

Of course, the big news for Bonne Chance and the other Tinker Creek business and property owners is that we won the case. Critics pointed out it was by default and not on the merits, but we will take a win where we can get one.

The high-powered Atlanta law firm the city hired to litigate the dispute informed the court it was no longer representing St. Michael's Harbor in the afternoon after Tommy's story ran in the *Record*. The city's general counsel petitioned the judge to end the matter a week later.

Father Joe sent me and Manny a bottle of good champagne with a card that read "To the Champions over city hall." We stored it in the fridge for a few months, then split it with Tommy and Danny, sitting on the rooftop deck at Bonne Chance during one of the long summer twilights we get down here in on the South Georgia coast.

"To what do we toast?" Danny asked after carefully popping the bottle.

"Long life and success," said Tommy, holding up his glass. "And handsome men."

"Yes, to long life," I replied. Then, looking hard at Manny across the table, "and to loved ones."

Danny poured us each a healthy measure of the bubbling wine, then Manny stood up, so we all stood up with him. Glancing at all of us but looking hard at me, he said, "To the loved ones with whom we share our long lives. Salud!"

"Salud," we agreed.

PLEA FOR REVIEWS

Thank you for reading *A Champion for Tinker Creek*. I sincerely hope you enjoyed it. If you did, may I ask a small favor? If you purchased the book on Amazon or any other electronic book platforms, would you please return to the purchase page and leave a review? A discouraging percentage of books published each year languish on electronic shelves because too few of their readers leave a note for others thinking of purchasing the volume. Something as small as a three or four-sentence review about what you thought of the book will make a huge difference.

Thank you,
DC Robeline

About the Author

After a thirty-year career in journalism, D.C. Robeline began writing his first novel after his long-term partner challenged him to give it a try. Robeline never looked back. Now he writes suspenseful LGBTQ novels featuring strong characters fighting for justice, to reflect many of his readers' life stories and to inspire others.

Books Available From Bold Strokes Books

A Champion for Tinker Creek by D.C. Robeline. Lyle James has rescued his dad's auto repair business, but when city hall condemns his neighborhood, Lyle learns only trusting will save his life and help him find love. (978-1-63679-213-2)

Heckin' Lewd: Trans and Nonbinary Erotica, edited by Mx. Nillin Lore. If you want smutty, fearless, gender diverse erotica written by affirming own-voices folks who get it, then this is the book you've been looking for! (978-1-63679-240-8)

Inherit the Lightning by Bud Gundy. Darcy O'Brien and his sisters learn they are about to inherit an immense fortune, but a family mystery about to unravel after seventy years threatens to destroy everything. (978-1-63679-199-9)

Pursued: Lillian's Story by Felice Picano. Fleeing a disastrous marriage to the Lord Exchequer of England, Lillian of Ravenglass reveals an incident-filled, often bizarre, tale of great wealth and power, perfidy, and betrayal. (978-1-63679-197-5)

Murder on Monte Vista by David S. Pederson. Private Detective Mason Adler's angst at turning fifty is forgotten when his "birthday present," the handsome, young Henry Bowtrickle, turns up dead, and it's up to Mason to figure out who did it, and why. (978-1-63679-124-1)

Three Left Turns to Nowhere by Jeffrey Ricker, J. Marshall Freeman & 'Nathan Burgoine. Three strangers heading to a convention in Toronto are stranded in rural Ontario, where a small town with a subtle kind of magic leads each to discover what he's been searching for. (978-1-63679-050-3)

One Verse Multi by Sander Santiago. Life was good: promotion, friends, falling in love, discovering that the multi-verse is on a fast track to collision—wait, what? Good thing Martin King works for a company that can fix the problem, right...um...right? (978-1-63679-069-5)

Fresh Grave in Grand Canyon by Lee Patton. The age-old Grand Canyon becomes more and more ominous as a group of volunteers fight to survive alone in nature and uncover a murderer among them. (978-1-63679-047-3)

Loyalty, Love & Vermouth by Eric Peterson. A comic valentine to a gay man's family of choice, including the ones with cold noses and four paws. (978-1-63555-997-2)

Bury Me in Shadows by Greg Herren. College student Jake Chapman is forced to spend the summer at his dying grandmother's home and soon finds danger from long-buried family secrets. (978-1-63555-993-4)

A Different Man by Andrew L. Huerta. This diverse collection of stories chronicling the challenges of gay life at various ages shines a light on the progress made and the progress still to come. (978-1-63555-977-4)

Busy Ain't the Half of It by Frederick Smith and Chaz Lamar Cruz. Elijah and Justin seek happily-ever-afters in LA, but are they too busy to notice happiness when it's there? (978-1-63555-944-6)

Pursuit: A Victorian Entertainment by Felice Picano. An intelligent, handsome, ruthlessly ambitious young man who rose from the slums to become the right-hand man of the Lord Exchequer of England will stop at nothing as he pursues his Lord's vanished wife across Continental Europe. (978-1-63555-870-8)

Best of the Wrong Reasons by Sander Santiago. For Fin Ness and Orion Starr, it takes a funeral to remind them that love is worth living for. (978-1-63555-867-8)

Coming to Life on South High by Lee Patton. Twenty-one-year-old gay virgin Gabe Rafferty's first adult decade unfolds as an unpredictable journey into sex, love, and livelihood. (978-1-63555-906-4)

His Brother's Viscount by Stephanie Lake. Hector Somerville wants to rekindle his illicit love affair with Viscount Wentworth, but he must overcome one problem: Wentworth still loves Hector's brother. (978-1-63555-805-0)

BOLDSTROKESBOOKS.COM

Looking for your next great read?

Visit BOLDSTROKESBOOKS.COM
to browse our entire catalog of paperbacks, ebooks,
and audiobooks.

Want the first word on what's new?
Visit our website for event info,
author interviews, and blogs.

Subscribe to our free newsletter for sneak peeks,
new releases, plus first notice of promos
and daily bargains.

SIGN UP AT
BOLDSTROKESBOOKS.COM/signup

Bold Strokes Books
Quality and Diversity in LGBTQ Literature

*Bold Strokes Books is an award-winning publisher
committed to quality and diversity in LGBTQ fiction.*